A GAZ

Best Wishes
John Boverley

A GAZE INTO HOLIDAZE

by

JOHN BEVERLEY

Casa Publications Ltd

This novel, although based around true stories, is a work of fiction.
The names, characters and some incidents portrayed in it are
the work of the author's imagination. Any resemblance to actual
persons, living or dead, events or localities is entirely coincidental.

Casa Publications Ltd
PO Box 35
Ammanford
SA18 3WA

casaguide@vodafone.net

First published in Great Britain by
Casa Publications Ltd. 2005

Copyright © Casa Publications Ltd

The Author asserts the moral right to be
identified as the author of this work.

ISBN 0-9549577-0-9

Cover Illustration: James 'Aki' Naimi-Akbar
WESTON COLLEGE Post 'A' Level Foundation Art & Design, Graphic Student.

All rights reserved. No part of this publication may be reproduced, stored in a
retrieval system, or transmitted, in any form or by any means, electronic,
mechanical, photocopying, recording or otherwise, without the
prior permission of the author and publishers.

This book is sold subject to the condition that it shall not, by way of trade
or otherwise, be lent, re-sold, hired out or otherwise circulated without the
publisher's prior consent in any form of binding or cover other than
that in which it is published and without a similar condition
including this condition being imposed on the subsequent purchaser.

To my patient and ever-loving wife,
a genuine pour-oil-on-troubled-water and
see-the-best-in-everybody Jayne character,
if ever there was one.

INTRODUCTION

Camping is a wonderful way of spending a holiday whether you are seven years old or seventy years old. Let me hasten to add that there will be many who will challenge this statement. 'Loudly and clearly,' I can hear the shouting from some of you. 'What a load of rubbish!' 'You must be mad!' But have these profound challengers really tried the wonders of living under a thin piece of canvas called a tent, or thriving in a shiny strip of sheet-aluminium called a caravan and/or camper-van?

Camping embraces a wide variety of habitats from a weatherproof sleeping-bag and very little else, to the highly sophisticated, lordly and extremely expensive camper-vans of which the American variety is the most desired and dreamed of – by some people, that is.

In between the humble all-weather sleeping-bag and the American dream-home on wheels, lie your small ridge one-man tents; your two to five-man ridge-tents; your small and large frame-tents; your bubble-tents which come in a vast variety of clever (or is it ridiculous) shapes and sizes; your trailer-tents; and your various-berth caravans, some of which remain in one lump and some that extend both upwards and horizontally. Phew!! Makes one tired just thinking about them all, let alone putting some of them up. And then there is the sorting of the multitude of kit that each contains – especially in heavy rain or driving wind, or both. Sounds like fabulous fun, doesn't it?

However, what is the common factor with all of this camping paraphernalia? They are all mobile to meet modern man's primitive urges to escape from his daily toil and travel to meet the challenges of the natural elements. In other words, they meet man's needs to simply 'rough it' in the country or seaside. Perhaps it meets man's urges for the 'call of the wild' like in the wagon trains of the Western movies, moving across the prairie in the setting sun, with the distant prairie dogs, together with the injuns, 'howlin' and howlin' in them thar mount'ns'. Perhaps it's the desire of man to make love under the stars or just plain exhibitionism to have sex in a canvas cocoon surrounded by hundreds of people who are capable of hearing every moan and sound that he, or she, makes. Mm! Mm! Now I think that I am getting a little carried away so let me get back to the point.

No matter what the reasons are that make the millions of people of Europe pursue camping every year, they all seem to thoroughly enjoy themselves and obtain considerable blooming of their cheeks both facial and otherwise in the healthy life-style that camping appears to provide. Whether these campers believe it to offer freedom, fitness, good health, cheapness, variety, travel, comradeship, friendship (it's amazing how friendly you can become when you share a washbasin, shower, toilet – and even toilet paper in extreme emergencies), who knows? But no matter what their reasons, they all claim it to be a lot of fun and wouldn't holiday any other way.

I agree with them. Camping is marvellous fun and provides barrels of laughs from the people you meet and the events in which you sometimes find yourself trapped, through no fault of your own. You can even giggle at the snobbishness, both real and invented, where the camper-van owners look down their noses at the caravan owners, who look down their noses at the trailer-tent owners, who look down their noses at the tent owners (frame or bubble, doesn't matter), who look down their noses at the ridge-tent owners. Poor old ridge-tent owners have nobody at which to look down unless it's the odd individual who lies in the grass completely covered by a very soggy all-weather sleeping-bag. Makes you chuckle, doesn't it? Unfortunately, there is more than an element of truth in the comedy above, but fortunately it is not too prevalent and is only practiced by a relatively few individuals of the millions of happy campers. Regrettably, from my experience, this minority seem to be British. However, I am delighted to say that when on the Continent, after these Brits have crossed the Channel, snobbery disappears and doesn't seem to exist on the campsite. Either that or it's conveniently laid to rest whilst amongst our foreign friends. Everyone intermingles where Joe Bloggs with his super-duper, top-of-the-range caravan pulled by his spotlessly gleaming 4x4 is neighboured unceremoniously by an even bigger brand-new Mercedes out of which jumps a German family of four who hastily and expertly set up their tiny ridge-tent. Good grief!! Caravans and tents mixing in the same field!! Whatever next. But no, they all live together happily ever after – or at least for a week or so anyway!!

So, what is this book all about? Well, in a few words – laughter in campsites. Sounds a bit like the old British film 'Laughter in Paradise', doesn't it? However, please believe it when I say that not even the wonderful and great Alistair Sim could make you laugh more than some of the characters outlined in the forthcoming pages. The book is about humorous camping experiences gained by myself, alone in the early days, and then later, gained by my wife and myself as a couple. Experiences that made us laugh, and laugh, and laugh. The stories are mainly about people and characters that we met, and sometimes became very much involved with, through our travels in tents and caravans both in Britain and on the Continent. All the stories are true but written with perhaps a wee amount of poetic licence. They are not written in any particular order other than maybe timescale where I have tried to go through the experiences in some form of chronological order. Certainly names and sometimes places have been changed so as not to cause embarrassment to anyone – including myself.

A Gaze into Holidaze

I apologise for some of the rather fruity language that is contained in a few of the stories, but I hasten to add that this distasteful language is only used to illustrate what actually happened at the time and is intended to bring out the mood and drama of the situation in question. Certainly it is not intended to be offensive in any way. (Sounds like the way some modern filmmakers get out of their responsibilities by claiming realism, doesn't it?)

I also apologise for the apparent obsession of the author regarding natural bodily functions, particularly concerning the use of the bowels. Not so. As any camper knows, the natural pleasures of going to the toilet on some campsites presents a major problem, especially on small campsites in mainland Europe. The owners of modern caravans and camper-vans are, of course, not included in the above statement because they have their own built-in loos. Let's just say that they are not aware of the fun that they are missing when visiting the loo after the quiet and spotlessly clean campsite that they have chosen, has been invaded for a night or two by some of the French fraternity. Yuk, yuk and even more yuk!!!

The stories are narrated, and hopefully brought to life, through a fictitious couple called John and Jayne. They are in their early fifties and love travelling, playing the guitar and singing together as a pretty lousy duet, drinking wine or anything remotely alcoholic that can be poured into a glass.

JOHN BEVERLEY

They have no children, which means they are relatively free of commitments and have, above all, the huge 'must' for happy campers – a great sense of humour. Please read on and hopefully enjoy vast amounts of giggles and titters as John and Jayne did, when they lived through the events. Perhaps you will even identify yourselves with some of the experiences and situations in which John and Jayne found themselves and are able to say, **'been there, got the tee-shirt'**.

****

CHAPTER ONE

THE EARLY YEARS – LEARNING, OFTEN THE HARD WAY

The biking years . . .
John sped down the French motorway on his way to Spain as happy as the proverbial pig in clover. It was 1968 and he was eighteen years old and riding his first powerful motorcycle – all 125 cc's of it. John considered himself an adventurous young man because how many of his mates would have had the courage to do what he was going to do over the next three weeks of his long awaited holiday? Having never been on the outside of Great Britain before, John's plan was to tour into Spain, France, Switzerland, Italy, Austria and Germany before returning back to the UK. What an adventure!

Behind him on his bike he had a top-box, which contained his plastic wet gear (plastic because that's all that he could afford) and his visored crash-helmet. He had been clever enough to buy a cheap open-faced helmet in a second-hand shop in his local town because with the expected stifling July weather of mainland Europe, there was no way that he was going to stop getting his face nicely tanned by wearing an enclosed helmet. He smiled to himself knowingly after crossing from

Portsmouth to Le Havre where he changed to his open-faced helmet, looking forward to the thrill he was going to have when he felt the force of the hot wind in his face combined with the smell of the cornfields of mid-France in his nostrils. Yes, he was a very adventurous young man!

He leaned back comfortably against the large green canvas bag that lay between himself and the top-box. 'Fabulous,' he said aloud. 'Like sitting in the armchair of a Rolls Royce.' This certainly was the life for him. Speedily travelling on his dream-machine through lands of colour and mystery to meet the excitement and daring of life.

In the green canvas bag behind him, which he had on long-loan from his Dad, were his worldly possessions for the trip. These were a borrowed one-man plastic tent with no flysheet (apparently the flysheet had been lost but John didn't care because he was off to hotter and sunnier parts, wasn't he?), tent pegs, toiletries, a sleeping-bag, a wooden mallet, a torch, a Swiss army knife, a tiny portable gas-cooker, a couple of spare gas cylinders for the cooker, tea bags and about a dozen packets of Beanfeasts. (The Beanfeasts were Mum's addition because apparently you only had to add a pint of boiling water, stir for five minutes and bob's-your-uncle, a nutritious and delicious hot meal!)

John could remember the conversation now. 'What about clean underwear and socks, John?'

'Don't need them, Mum. I'll wash the ones I'm wearing as I go along.'

A Gaze into Holidaze

'No son of mine is going off gallivanting around Europe without a change of pants and socks, so there. What if you have to go into hospital?'

John smiled to himself again. Mum had won the day and five pairs of clean underpants, three pairs of clean socks, four clean tee-shirts and a woolly sweater – 'in case it gets cold in the night you see, John!'– were sitting neatly folded in the bottom of the green bag.

John checked his wristwatch to find that he had been travelling for some ten hours. Admittedly, he had stopped for a fantastic lunch of tomatoes, cheese and French-bread supplemented with a nice cup of tea, sweetened with condensed milk from a tube like toothpaste, but that had been nearly six hours before. It was nearly 6 p.m. and there was no doubt that he was tired. It was time to think about a campsite. It had been a great day of motorway and N-road biking and the weather had been superb, even a little too hot, causing him to perspire freely to say the least. In fact, the only minor problem, which had occurred throughout the entire journey, had been the damned flies hitting him in the face. At anything over 50 mph it was like being hit in the face by machine gun bullets and these tiny collisions stung like the blazes, especially when being hit directly in the eye. 'Sod it,' thought John, masterfully decisive. 'To blazes with the open-faced helmet and the suntan. The enclosed job is going on tomorrow.'

A short time later John found himself a large,

commercial campsite near Montpellier in the South of France. He was a bit disappointed that he hadn't been able to find one of the smaller municipal sites which he had been told by all and sundry before the trip, were in great abundance throughout France. Yes, in great abundance until you really wanted one, that is. Anyway, he was utterly shattered and really needed to shower, eat and get his head down.

John roared into the campsite with much eighteen-year-old Steve McQueen-type gusto and a lot of dust spurting from his rear wheels. 'Let's show 'em whose British, eh?' He roared up to the building marked 'Reception' and braked to a skidding halt, which probably took six months of fair wear-and-tear off his tyres. Just like his heroes in 'Easy Rider' he swung off his bike, pulled it on to its stand (with a strength that nearly tipped the bike over because it was so top heavy with the green bag and top box) and swaggered Marlon Brando-like into the office.

'Was that you on the motorcycle, monsieur?' came the harsh, booming challenge from the huge, bearded man behind the desk.

'Yes,' said John, his gusto diminishing at a rate of knots when he saw the size of this Frankenstein's monster.

'Well, monsieur, there is a speed limit on this campsite of 5 kph. It is there to protect the visitors and their children. On this campsite at this time, there are Belgian, Dutch, Swiss and German persons and if you do not respect their lives by persistently riding your machine in a dangerous manner then you will not be allowed to stay here. Do you wish to stay here, monsieur?'

'Yes, please,' whispered our hero. 'I-I-I'm t-t-terribly s-sorry.'

'Very well, monsieur, this is your first and final warning. Now for how many nights do you wish to stay and may I have your passport?'

'What a welcome to France,' thought John, but decided to keep that comment to himself when considering the size of the bloke in question. After the administrative bit which included paying, John was about to leave when the Beard turned to the pretty young female, who appeared from nowhere behind the desk, and said something to her in French. John, not speaking the language, could not understand but couldn't help but notice that whatever had been said had resulted in both Beard and the girl laughing hysterically.

'What's so funny,' said John politely, not seeing the reason for the amusement which he felt had been aimed at himself. 'Can I share the joke?'

'Forgive me, monsieur, but it is a private joke and we mean no harm.'

John snorted defiantly in a manner that he thought looked sufficiently tough enough to recover his damaged dignity, but not tough enough to arouse any anger in Frankenstein's monster. He then spun on his heel and promptly left the office to seek his allotted camping space, which apparently was some way off in the surrounding forest.

JOHN BEVERLEY

On the way, John found it necessary to stop to ask directions from several people. All of them were more than helpful and, apart from the obvious language difficulties, did their best to guide him. However, John noticed that invariably the brief meetings ended with an embarrassed giggle at the very least. More often than not, a hand-to-the-mouth snigger from his helpers appeared to be the norm. In fact, on the second enquiry, two small children burst out crying and ran hand-in-hand for the protection of their mother's bosom, as if the Devil himself were chasing them.

Finally, a very tired John arrived at his pitch and thankfully parked the bike on its stand. 'Time for a shower,' he thought. Taking his towel with him, he once again was forced to ask some other people for directions to the toilet-block. Again, John observed the stifled giggles. 'Bugger 'em,' was John's defiant response. 'Bloody foreigners. Must have a warped sense of humour.'

Our hero, with a firm, determined pose and a James Bond swaggering gait, eventually found the toilet-block to which he had been directed. Glad to be inside away from the sniggering that had followed him all the way from his pitch to the toilet-block, John decided to have a shave before showering. He walked to the counter of washbasins and mirrors. When he looked at the face that was staring back at him, his determined jaw dropped and his mouth gaped in horror. No wonder the bastards had been laughing at him!! John's face did not have a square centimetre that was not covered with sweat-drenched, squashed, splattered, blood-smeared, dead flies. His boyish complexion was completely covered in a reddish, yellowish, brownish, bluish, blackish goo.

'Oh, balls!' John, although exhausted, turned and hurtled from the toilet-block back to his camping pitch, where he grabbed his yellow open-faced helmet and went straight to the nearest rubbish bin. 'Bollocks,' was his last farewell to the bloody thing as he slammed the lid of the bin tightly closed in disgust.

However, after a shave and a cracking hot shower, John's embarrassment over his 'measles spots only a hundred times worse' diminished, and he was soon back to himself again. He towelled himself down vigorously and looked at the boyish, unblemished good-looks of his reflection. 'Time for a pee,' John said aloud to the mirror. He looked around to find that there were no urinals that he could see in the washroom. No problem. There were lots of the usual stalls around and anyway, perhaps they did not have urinal bowls in France. 'Who knows?' shrugged John.

John opened the stall door and went inside. His face became immediately adorned with a frowning look of bewilderment and confusion. There, in the absence of the toilet bowl, was a ceramic pan with slightly raised footprints in the centre. Slightly behind these footprints was a round and rather badly stained black hole.

'Oh, shit!' declared John, not fully realizing the profoundness of his statement. However, being an intelligent lad, John soon twigged where his feet were supposed to fit and what part of his anatomy was supposed to be aimed and pointed at where.

'Bloody ridiculous,' thought John as he squatted at an angle of about forty-five degrees. 'How do elderly people manage in this situation?'

Having successfully completed his business and feeling proud to have aimed straight into the hole – what a bomb-aimer he would have made – John reached for the toilet paper. None. 'Bloody hell,' he squeaked, annoyance and frustration in his voice. 'What am I supposed to do now?'

With that, the main door of the block opened and John heard footsteps walking into the stall next-door. 'Thank goodness for that,' John whispered, still crouched at forty-five degrees to the horizontal. Then louder, 'Excuse me, mate. Do you think you could pass me some bumf 'cos there's none in here?'

There was a stifled scream of horror before John heard the rustle of hastily retrieved clothing. This was immediately followed by the sound of the door to the next stall opening, footsteps rapidly retreating and the main door banging closed.

'Thanks a lot, mate. What the hell is wrong with these people!'

Without going into the gory details here, John used his initiative in cleansing himself after his natural bodily functions. He then re-showered, dressed and walked casually back to his camping-pitch. As he turned the last corner, there, waiting for him and leaning with a hand casually placed on John's motorbike was, you've guessed it, Beard! On his face he wore his best impression of Frankenstein's monster to date.

'I want you to leave this campsite immediately, you are not welcome here.' The deep resonant tone suggested in no uncertain terms that Beard meant business.

'Come on, mate, it's 8 o'clock in the night and . . .'

'I do not care,' interrupted Beard. 'We cannot tolerate your indecent behaviour so you must leave at once. I wish to discuss the matter no longer.'

'Look, just because I rode into the site a little fast and probably frightened some kids with my spotty face, there is no need to get tough about it. They were only dead flies anyway and it wasn't really my fault. I just wore the wrong crash helmet, didn't I?'

'It has nothing to do with your face, monsieur. It is to do with your behaviour in the toilet.' Beard was getting angry now, and a little red in the face.

'What behaviour in the damned toilet? I ran out of toilet paper, which was your fault really, and I asked this guy in the next stall to pass me some. He panicked and left. I managed to help myself eventually and came back here. So what's the problem?' John's anger was starting to match Beard's.

'The fact is that if you had a proper sit-down loo, and you fed it with toilet-paper regularly, this wouldn't have happened. What's the matter with that idiot in the next stall anyway? Is he some queer or something? Why did he run to complain to you? Doesn't he wipe his arse like everybody else?' John had steam up by now and the injustice of it all was getting through to him.

'Monsieur, this is France and even in France, contrary to belief, we do not allow men in the Ladies Toilet, especially not trouble-making sex-maniacs like you.'

'But . . .' started John in shock.

'You will be given your money back and you will leave immediately. Leave or I will call the police.'

And, at 8.30 p.m. that night, as whacked as he was, John left the campsite at Montpellier. Although absolutely starving, John rode for about twenty or thirty miles before finding a quiet road off the N9 near Pizenas. Without erecting the tent or even undressing, he burrowed under a hedge on the side of the road and went fast asleep in spite of the indignity that he felt.

Welcome to camping!!!

****

The following morning, John awakened to a clear, hot, sunny day. What a great feeling and already the mishaps of the previous day and night were gone. Let's face it, at eighteen years of age you can face anything and you can take on the world with a smile and a spring in your step. With a roaring

A Gaze into Holidaze

blip of his throttle he sped away to his southernmost destination, Salou, on the Costa Dorada.

An uneventful but enjoyable ride brought him to the busy seaside resort where he found a great campsite, right on the beach at Cambrils, a small fishing-village south-west of Salou. 'Just what the doctor ordered,' thought John as he savoured the blue, twinkling sea of the Mediterranean. But first a constitutional and a shave before wandering through the delights of the town.

The toilet-blocks were very few and far between it seemed, but after a long walk around the site he eventually found one which was little more than a single cubicle made of wood. After his experiences of yesterday he made sure that he did not make the same mistake twice.

'Is this the men's toilet, señor?' John asked the man who seemed to be tending the grounds nearby.

'Si, señor, para hombres,' came the friendly reply. John went to the only door in the cubicle and when he tried the handle found that it was engaged. No problem. A short wait on the sand outside in the now very-hot sun would be enjoyable to say the least.

John sprawled on the sand outside the toilet, and listened contentedly to the swish of the waves breaking on the nearby beach, followed by the rustling of the shingle as the broken wave returned to the deep blue, velvet lushness of the Mediterranean beyond. Suddenly, the moment was broken by a loud report of flatulence from within the single cubicle, which was immediately followed by a constant splattering sound of a heavy liquid against ceramics. The sound seemed to be endless, as it went on and on with hardly an interruption. A noisy sigh of satisfaction, or was it a grunt, illustrated the obvious pleasure of the occupant who promptly opened the small window, set high in the wall of the cubicle, a little wider.

John soon realised why. The stench rolling from the window was disgusting. Great Scot! What had this man eaten last night? Or was it the vast quantity of wine that he had probably guzzled, the way that some blokes do. John had heard about the garlic that Spaniards enjoyed in their food but this was ridiculous. The smell was overpowering and clung to everything around including John.

Louder flatulence with more grunts, more splatterings and more sighs prevailed. The entire performance was repeated time after time, as the man inside enjoyed the very fluent process of nature, a process which seemed to shake the very walls and foundations of the cubicle repeatedly. Surely the building would collapse with all that blasting of the bowels?

'I really don't fancy going in there after all this,' thought John, as he remembered the two footprints and the hole of the previous day. 'Where on earth do I put my feet after this bastard?' John knew the type of man that was in there – fat, gross, oafishly overfed, who drank wine until it

A Gaze into Holidaze

came out of his ears or, judging by the sounds, some other part of his anatomy. What should he do? Try to get a hosepipe to wash the place down before going in with a more than adequate supply of toilet-paper stuffed up his nose against that revolting nose-wrinkling stench?

With that, the sound of a flush operating could be heard from within. There was a short pause before the door opened and out glided this absolute vision of female, raven-haired loveliness with a body that anyone would die for. The deeply-tanned, long and slender limbs that led into the slimmest and tiniest of waists topped by the perfectly-rounded and firm breasts, were clad in the skimpiest of bikinis which, although tautly stretched across a flatly-tight stomach, barely left anything to the imagination – not to John's imagination anyway.

'God, she's bloody gorgeous,' drooled John to himself.

The dark eyes fixed upon John, who had by now leapt to his feet as if he had been stung. Her full mouth smiled warmly to reveal dazzlingly white, perfect teeth as she huskily whispered, 'Bonjour, monsieur,' as only the French ladies can say it. John's mouth gaped. He could not believe what he was seeing.

'G-g-g-g-ood-d m-m-o-rning,' stammered John shyly as the nymphette slid sensuously past him. Each of John's eyes attempted to move in opposite directions in time to the swaying motion of the young girl's thong-clad buttocks as she sensuously glided down the beach to finally disappear with a perfect dive into the sea.

Needless to say, the cubicle upon John's entry was absolutely spotless and only smelled of roses. John had had his first introduction to the mixed toilets of Europe. (Now long gone in most countries, as are the footprints and hole-in-the-ground toilets. Thank goodness!!!!)

****

Another lunch of French-bread (or Spanish really which is just as good), cheese and those wonderfully ugly tomatoes that you can only seem to get in Spain and France, fortified John. (Or could it have been the bottle of red wine that he greedily consumed with the meal?) Now to his next task – putting up the one-man ridge-tent. Easy peasy!!

Now John had never ever put up any sort of tent before. However, he was not remotely worried at this prospect because he had been given the confident assurance of the friend who had loaned him the tent, that putting up the said tent was simplicity itself. All the instructions were inside and all he had to do was follow them.

John took the folded tent-case from the green bag and emptied all of its contents on to the sand. He picked up the folded instructions and carefully read through them, paying particular attention to the diagram therein:

A Gaze into Holidaze

(1) Select a pitch which is flat, grassy and firm, ensuring that any stones are removed.

John glanced around at his allotted pitch. Flat – yes. Grassy – no, sandy. Firm – no. Not too great a start but at least there were no stones.

(2) Check contents of pack which is as follows: tent (one); flysheet (one); pegs (fourteen); guy-ropes (four); plastic water-caps (two); poles (four).

John laid everything out carefully on the sand and began his checks loudly to himself:

'Tent (one) – Check.'
'Flysheet (one) – None. It's been lost but who cares, it's not raining.'
'Pegs (fourteen) – Sod it, only twelve. Never mind, I can manage with twelve.'
'Guy-ropes (four) – Check.'
'Plastic water-caps (two) – Nil. Damn and blast!!' John looked again at the clear sky. 'No problem, and if it does rain only a drop can get into the tent down the poles.'
'Poles (four) – Damn and double blast – only three! Let's count them again. One . . . two . . . three.' No matter how John counted them, from the front or from the back of his line of poles, the answer came out the same. 'Only three bloody poles!!'

JOHN BEVERLEY

The air became blue with a regular mixture of Queen's English and Anglo-Saxon interjections. The most common of these were 'fuck' and 'idiot bastard' which, in both cases, referred to the friend who had loaned John the tent.

John sat on the sand looking really sorry for himself. It was now early evening so what on earth was he going to do now? The three-week holiday had only just begun and here he was with a pole missing which meant, loudly and clearly, that the tent could not be erected. What a state of affairs!! Why hadn't he checked the tent before he had left the UK? Bloody, bugger, damn!!

Like a breath of spring, Nymphette appeared, floating down the path towards John's pitch, dressed sexily in tight-fitting jeans and blouse. 'Maybe she's been farting in the loo again,' thought John blackly. He was in a foul mood by this time.

Nymphette's smile was magic. 'Are you not 'appy, monsieur? Is there something wrong? Per'aps I can 'elp.' The soft French accent combined with her little caring-frown, melted John's heart.

'Yes, I've come without my pole,' said John. He then flushed at what he had said when he realised the innuendo of his statement. Nymphette appeared not to notice.

'Do not worry. My Papa will know 'ow to 'elp you.' She turned to lead the way. 'Come, it is not far.'

And it wasn't and Papa did.

Papa gave John a piece of quality round wood

A Gaze into Holidaze

which would do the job of replacing the missing pole with the 'leetle 'elp of a knife', as Papa explained.

Two hours of carving, with the help of his Swiss army knife, solved the problem. But John was not amused. This had been the second night of disaster regarding his camping holiday and John certainly had a sense-of-humour failure. However, there were two positives that had come out of the disaster as far as John was concerned. One, he had met Nymphette – or Denise as she was really called – and the next few days, unbeknown to John at this time, were to be heaven. (But that's not for this book.) Two, the tent went up easily, and this inspired John's confidence. It was a clear, moonlit sky and a warm night. He was a bit worried about the lack of flysheet but was equally satisfied that everything would be fine, including the weather.

Time for bed and John slipped, for the first time, into the snugness of his new home. On hands and knees he pushed between the guy-ropes to take up his place, on top of his sleeping-bag, inside the tent. This movement in such a small tent caused the pegs to pull out of the sand. Result – the tent fell down!

'So that's why you want firm ground then,' sighed John. 'Never mind. I'll be more careful next time.' Tent up again, John cleverly and successfully negotiated the guy-ropes on his re-entry to find himself lying flat on his back on top of his sleeping-bag. Again the pegs pulled partially out of the sand to allow sufficient slack in the tent for the sides and ceiling to hang in John's face.

'Sod it! This is like sleeping in a plastic condom,' John said. 'In fact it smells a bit like a condom!!' John laughed heartily at his own joke, his sense-of-humour not completely deserting him. Well, that was until he attempted to get into his sleeping-bag. Result – the tent fell down!

Finally, after several more practices, John lay awake in his sleeping-bag, his head against the top of the tent, his feet against the bottom of the tent, his shoulders against the sides of the tent, the top hanging in his face. He was cosy, warm and happy. Yes, he had had his problems but he had handled them well, and it really was proving to be an adventure. John fell asleep a contented man, knowing that this was the holiday life for him. He couldn't wait for the morning and whatever promises the lovely Denise might bring. 'Oh my! Boys will be boys!!'

And the holiday was great in every respect, except for Denise. Although she was any man's dream on two gorgeous legs, she was devoted to her German boyfriend who had been unable to make the holiday. In spite of John's James Bond-type tactics he failed continuously time and time again, and Denise continued to be an unspoiled picture of charm and beauty.

****

A Gaze into Holidaze

John's plan of the tour worked out one hundred percent. He left Spain and travelled through the French Riviera into Italy to Genoa. Several nights later he went to the Italian Lakes – which were fantastically beautiful and teeming with fish – to pass into Austria at St Anton. On through Liechtenstein and Switzerland, into Germany, he continued northwest through Luxemburg and Belgium into France and finally to the port of Calais.

The ferry crossing back to dear old Blighty was a proud moment for John. As he stood with legs braced apart, firmly gripping the stern-rail of the upper deck against the gusting wind and the drunken roll of the ship in the heavy sea, he smiled with self-satisfaction at the coast of France as it grew smaller and smaller in the frothing wake below him. What a fantastic adventure it had been!! He had been master of his own destiny for three whole weeks and had achieved such a lot for a very young man.

Everything had gone wonderfully well and even the three-week-old stick of wood that John had laboriously transferred into a tent-pole with his Swiss army knife, had lasted the entire journey. Yes, it is true that he continued to make mistakes but he found, or so he convinced himself anyway, that it was good character-building stuff. For example, and guess what, the weather didn't last! Especially in breathtaking Switzerland where the rain never seemed to stop from morning until night. What man wouldn't enjoy at 3 a.m. every morning for three days in a row, waking-up in a damp sleeping-bag to find the freezing, water-saturated top of the tent hanging in his face?

John concluded that cheap tents with no fly-sheets did not work and therefore were definitely not the answer. Furthermore, the one-man ridge-tent was too small because you couldn't swing a cat in them and storage of your gear was definitely a non-starter. Thank goodness John did not meet a willing member of the opposite sex, eh, because he certainly could not have done her justice in a one-man tent!

Also worth mentioning was the performance of his 125cc machine. It was okay on the flat bits of his trip but useless in the mountains of the Alps. On one occasion he had to get off the bike and, selecting first gear, walk alongside the bike controlling the clutch and throttle all the way up what seemed like Mount Everest. This was the only way he could get himself, the machine, and his gear up the steeply winding mountain-roads that often climbed to well above the snow line. Not exactly 007 stuff, eh?

Perhaps an incident, or near-disaster, that happened to John which is worth mentioning, is the occasion during the early part of his journey, that he decided to accept his Mum's recommendations and try one of the Beanfeasts that he had in his green bag. He had been travelling all day from Spain into France to finally arrive at a campsite on the French Riviera at St Tropez.

A Gaze into Holidaze

The evening was sunny and very hot and upon arrival at the site he found that the place was jam-packed with happy campers. You couldn't swing a proverbial cat. In fact, the only pitch that John was offered was one that no one else wanted – in the sun with absolutely no shade whatsoever.

John was starving by now but nevertheless proceeded to erect the tent which would give him shade to eat his meal after he had cooked it. With tent standing proudly it was then out with the small stove, on with the gas, contents of Beanfeast packet (a curry would you believe) tipped into his metal mess-tin, a pint of water added, brought to the boil, simmered and stirred for five minutes. Yum! Yum! Well not quite yum, yum because although smelling quite appetising it looked a right stodgy mess. 'Never mind,' John considered reservedly. 'With a little bread and a lot of wine it will be like the Feast of the Passover.'

Unfortunately, bread and wine meant a short trip to the camp shop which was only fifty yards away. John estimated that he could do this and return in two minutes flat. So, shutting off the gas but leaving his mess-tin on top of the primus, off John galloped.

Lo and behold, John, true to his plans was back in next to no time armed with a nice fresh baguette and a litre of red wine. As he approached his tent he saw a small animal, probably a cat which had been sniffing around his small home, scuttle away smartly in fright. As it did so it brushed against the small primus stove, top-heavy with the mess-tin full of Beanfeast goodies, sending the whole lot literally flying across the hard, sandy terrain, a good deal of the curried goo ending up over the side of the tent whilst the remainder splashed itself generously over the built-in ground sheet inside.

'Oh knickers!' John exclaimed, despair in his voice. When he saw the mess on and in the tent he could have wept with frustration. It looked as if someone had thrown-up all over the place. 'What the fuck am I going to eat now?' he sighed. John had no intention of having another go at Mr Beanfeast but he was still starving for food and didn't have anything to eat but the baguette. So, baguette it was. Accompanied by the litre or so of red wine, which had an appropriate numbing effect to the disaster, John got stuck into the bread.

This lifted John's morale sufficiently for him to clean up the mess as best he could from inside the tent, resolving to finish the rest of the cleaning of the side of the tent and groundsheet in the morning. He carefully washed the dishes and feeling slightly tipsy, hit the sack early to face the long trip into Italy on the following day.

John slept soundly until about midnight when he felt something which caused itching on his cheek. Still half asleep he put his hand up to scratch the itch, which had moved over to his nose. Now he was fully awake because he sensed rather than felt movement on his hand – in fact all over his arm. He tore away his sleeping-bag and scrambled from the tent, knocking down the poles in the process, making the tent collapse yet again like a pancake behind him. He ran to an electric-light which marked a footpath through the campsite to Reception, and carefully studied his hand. It was not only itching like mad but appeared puffy and swollen. 'Bollocks!' John yelled in horror. 'Bloody ants and big bastards at that. Good God, they're eating me alive!'

Well, this might have been a slight exaggeration on John's part but the ants were certainly biting him and his hand and arms were covered with them. Unfortunately, John soon realised that it was not just his hand that was being attacked but most of his body. The blasted things were swarming all over it: arms, torso, legs, all were covered with the blighters. The least of John's problems was the fact that his hasty departure from the now collapsed tent had rendered him completely naked on the main footpath to Reception in the glare of the very-bright night-light.

'Oh, shit from a rocking horse,' bellowed John loudly, his hand shooting down to his genitals in an automatic reaction of protection as he realised his rather awkward predicament. He dashed for the tent, flicking off ants as he ran. 'I'll get my towel and flick 'em off,' thought John desperately as he lifted the front opening of his flattened tent. Grabbing the torch, which, for a change, was in its proper place, he switched it on. With his head and shoulders inside the tent and his ant-covered buttocks gleaming in the moonlight outside, John screamed in exasperation. The entire inside of the tent, together with all of its contents, seemed to be moving with ants. His sleeping-bag was black with the little bastards and John shuddered as he thought of himself lying in it only minutes before.

'Can't sleep in here; must grab my towel; must get to the showers; must cover up; will get slung off this campsite if I run around starkers.' All of these thoughts rushed instantly and simultaneously through John's tormented mind whilst the ants, running all over him, were driving him out of his head. Grabbing his towel and shaking it madly like a man swatting a thousand wasps, he hurtled like a contender for the four-minute-mile, for the showers some two hundred metres distant. Did he cover himself with his ant-infested towel during his Olympic dash – no chance! Weighing up the vast number of tents between him and the showers against the time of night and his rate of travel over the ground whilst scratching like a man possessed in his frantic efforts to get rid of the little bleeders (or not so little because these ants were big buggers), all John could muster in the name of decency was a single hand clamped defensively around the matrimonials. 'A man's gotta do what a man's gotta do!!'

John showered for at least half-an-hour before he became satisfied that he was free from the monsters that had claimed his body. The ants had probably disappeared down the plughole in the first thirty seconds but John continued to spray himself long after this time because the nightmare remained imprinted in his brain. He could still feel the tramping of thousands of little black feet as they rushed all over him. 'Buggers are having their annual football match on my testicles,' he muttered, shivering at the thought.

John knew that he couldn't sleep in the tent that night because he would be unable to get rid of the thousands of ants that had invaded it. He was annoyed with himself because he realised that he had innocently caused the problem by not properly ridding the tent, inside and out together with the surrounding ground, of spilled Beanfeast. He had certainly paid the price for the bread and red wine that he had consumed during the evening when he should have spent that time cleaning up the mess. There was now nothing for it but to sleep on the floor of the shower block. Thank goodness the ants had given-up on his towel and had craftily disappeared into the night. Now the towel would serve both as his pillow and only covering throughout the very uncomfortable and long night that lay ahead. 'When the going gets tough, then the tough get going,' he muttered as he settled down in a tight ball for the forthcoming ordeal. 'Thank God it's warm.'

Early the following morning, John, now with towel around him, sneaked his way back to his flat, pancake-shaped tent. En route he fully expected to have the urine taken from him regarding his frantic, birthday-suit dash to the showers, but was relieved to find that no one had seemed to notice him. Although there was much activity in the tents around, not one soul said a word. What a relief!

Another relief was that when John got back and gingerly opened-up the tent, to his amazement there was not a single ant to be seen. His clothes, sleeping-bag and everything else were lying unmolested where he had left them. Yet another simple lesson had been learned – when camping, especially in a tent, if you spill something, clean it up carefully, thoroughly and immediately – or suffer the consequences!!

****

John, after the wonderful, and some not-so-wonderful, experiences of his European bike-trip, became completely converted to this exciting way of holidaying. He learned by his early mistakes and strove to overcome them. He bought a brand-new three-man ridge-tent and a much larger motorbike in the form of a powerful 650cc machine, which came with side panniers for extra storage. He even made a check-list so that all of his camping and personal gear could be neatly ticked off as it was packed into the panniers, top-box and Dad's good 'old-fashioned' green bag. He treated himself to proper biking leathers for decent protection in the event of an accident and got rid of all of his old, cheap, plastic gear which would have proved to be utterly useless in the circumstances of a bump. A knee-cap travelling over tarmac at even just 30mph doesn't bear thinking about, does it?

He travelled all over the UK on his dream-machine and ventured as far as Sicily, Yugoslavia and Greece on the mainland of Europe. Over the years that followed John learned that he loved his own company during these trips, and this enabled him to enjoy his holidays in the most inaccessible of places.

For example, he spent nearly one month entirely on his own in the Pyrenean Mountains of northern Spain. He found what was little more than a dirt track off the main mountain-road and followed it for mile after mile until he came to a remote Spanish village of no more than a church, shop and two dozen or so small cottages. A few miles along the dirt track after this village, he encountered a steep climb to the very top of the Pyrenees ending in a small, pined valley with a waterfall cascading into a deep pool. John set up camp alongside the pool and, other than meeting a few people in the village shop when he went to top-up provisions once a week, John never spoke to a soul for the entire three or four weeks of his stay.

However, he still made mistakes, but in all fairness to him, he did learn by them. Just like the time that he had been camping in the wilds of the

JOHN BEVERLEY

Yorkshire moors and was returning to do a night-stop with relatives in Ipswich before proceeding home. Whilst roaring through a remote part of Norfolk, John became aware of a rather desperate rumbling tummy which implied that an urgent call of nature was required – pronto!

(Let me stress that John, although it may seem so, was not obsessed with his bodily functions. It is just that when camping, hiking and motor-cycling, such natural bodily functions always seem to happen at the most awkward and difficult times. If you are a city-slicker in a hotel where a flush-toilet is only a short stretch of the legs away – no problem. Not so with the fresh air, wide-open-spaces type of people like John.)

John went along the trunk road for another ten minutes. Not a garage or anywhere where there was likely to be a toilet in sight. His need now making his eyes water, he turned off the main A-road to take a B-road for a few miles into the countryside. Not a cottage or even a barn in sight – just the job. A few hundred yards later he came across a track, which he readily and with buttocks tightly clenched, took. The track led deeply into the surrounding pine forests. Parking the bike, he rushed through the bushes to be met by a broken fence above which was mounted a large wooden notice, 'MOD Property – Keep Out.' With no time to argue the toss, and anyway there wasn't anyone within ten miles John reasoned, he pushed through a gap in the broken fence and ran about fifty metres

A Gaze into Holidaze

until he was in terrain of clumpy grass adorned with a few young trees which offered him adequate concealment for his forthcoming desperate, but natural functions. With much haste after scrabbling with the belts, buckles and zips of his leathers, John dropped his kecks and squatted for the final, much-awaited assault. With an enormously loud sigh of relief and expected contentment, John commenced his business.

'Bloody bikers piss me off,' said voice number one.

'Aye, and me,' voice number two this time, of Scottish persuasion. 'What right has he got to do his shitting here then?'

'No bloody right, mate,' declared voice number three.

John froze, his buttocks clamped tightly in shock. He quickly glanced around surveying the area within the limited vision allowed by his lowly-squatted position. No-one about that he could see. Slowly he straightened his back and stretched his neck almost swan-like, being careful not to lose his balance whilst still holding his severely-crouched posture. Still there was nothing to be seen in any direction. 'They must be further away than they sound so can't really see me,' concluded John as he hastily shrank himself into almost a ball behind the low bushes.

'Holy Mary!' exclaimed a much closer voice, this time with a broad Irish accent. 'Must have been on the curry last night by the smell of him.'

'Hope he isn't going to use my hat for toilet paper 'cos it took me ages to do my hat, see.' This time the accent was Welsh.

'Nice arse though,' came voice number one again accompanied by sniggers from all directions around John.

'All right lads, that will be enough,' came a very authoritative, cultured voice for the first time. 'I think he's learned his lesson so let's leave him alone, shall we? You men follow me – now!'

With that a young tree a few metres in front of the gaping-mouthed, squatting John, became uprooted. This was immediately followed by all of the surrounding young trees, low bushes and even clumpy-grass. All vegetation stood around six feet tall and carried rifles and sub-machine guns. The first 'young tree' to stand up said in a calm, unhurried voice, 'Do not enter MOD property again, young man, because you could easily get yourself accidentally shot. In your current position I shudder to think in which part of your anatomy the bullet might strike.' With a snigger he turned to the other assortment of foliage and shouted, 'Right men, let's do it.'

John flushed as the heavily and cleverly camouflaged, loudly laughing soldiers walked slowly down the slope away from him. He frantically adjusted his attire to beat a hasty retreat from the humiliating situation in which he had found himself. He sheepishly recovered his bike and rode off from the scene like a 'bat out of hell' in a weak attempt to regain some of his dignity. Make no bones about it, John's tail was well and truly situated somewhere between his legs.

****

And along came Jayne ...
The years went by and John's expertise in camping grew and grew. He gained the 'know-how' as they say in that mobile world and his mistakes became less and less. This was because John had learned how to plan for his trips rather than just stuff randomly selected gear into the various storage containers that adorned his bike. His bike, incidentally, had grown into a massive 1300cc machine which allowed him to travel any terrain in Europe with the greatest of ease.

He prided himself that he could almost fly down the roads of the Continent as free as a bird with the minimum of camping kit. In fact, short of a tent, with a flysheet I hasten to add, sleeping-bag, small gas-cooker, a few personal items and a small container full of kit to meet the emergencies of opening tins and such like, John could face the world.

Then, along came Jayne some six years later and that was the end of 'as free as a bird' and 'travelling light.' But there you are, love is love and what can you do about it, eh? Well, to tell you the truth, what John did about it was to marry the girl and, up to date, lived happily ever after.

Jayne loved the outdoor life. She liked walks in the country, walks along coastal paths, walks up mountains and so on but had never ever been camping in her life. Furthermore, she hated motorcycles and was more than honest when she told John that there was no possibility that she would ever go on one. So, the bike had to go. A degree of sadness for John but he considered that he had had a fair run for his money and he had to grow up at some time.

So his brand-new 1300cc dream-machine became a second-hand, six-year-old Renault 5 hatchback, which Jayne duly named the 'Red Bug', after insisting to John that it was an ideal vehicle for camping.

From that moment onwards John's camping life – you remember the one? – the carefree, travel-light, devil-may-care one – changed forever. The three-man ridge-tent became a five-man complete with small porch 'in case it rained'; the small sleeping-bag of John's became a large, double sleeping-bag so that 'we can cuddle-up if it's cold'; four huge frilly pillows materialised from nowhere to match the cover for the sleeping-bag; colour-matching carpets for the floor area of the porch emerged as if by magic; a folding-table with two folding-chairs; a four-burner cooker appeared complete with its accompanying gas bottle and mobile kitchen unit. Almost finally, a picnic-hamper for four people loomed, looking just a wee bit smaller than the Red Bug itself, but 'just perfect,' Jayne insisted, 'because it will be ideal for dinner-parties when we

A Gaze into Holidaze

have guests.' Accompanying all of this were pots and pans for every occasion together with a storage cupboard to hold them.

When John saw all of this gear assembled he was not amused. They were off for a trial camp in West Wales and this could well have been the cause of their first tiff.

'Look, Jayne, this amount of kit is ridiculous. We've got to leave some of it at home.'

'I disagree with you, John. As I've already explained to you on several occasions, everything here is essential.'

'Jayne!' The voice was a little firmer now. 'No one goes camping with carpets for the floor. We all manage with the grass inside the tent and . . .'

'Not me! I am not walking around barefooted on damp grass,' Jayne interrupted. 'There could be all sorts in the grass – snakes, spiders! All sorts of things – ugh! Horrible!'

'Don't be so silly and childish,' John said flatly. 'There is nothing to fear in West Wales.'

'Don't you dare call me childish. If anyone is a child, it's you, and don't you dare patronise me either.'

John was starting to rise to the bait a little now and he could not keep sarcasm from his voice. 'And what about this stupid four-person picnic-hamper in case we have guests? What are we running from the tent – a bloody B&B? Tell you what, let's go all the way and go for a guest-house on half-board terms 'cos we've got a fitted kitchen with all the appropriate pots and pans. We could make a fortune. Why not cook a little curry on the side and then we could have a Balti house and run it from the back of the Red Bug. I can see the sign now – the Red Bug Balti Takeaway!'

A slight smile tugged at Jayne's mouth and John knew that the point had been taken. 'I'm only trying to make sure that we are comfortable so that we can enjoy West Wales,' Jayne whispered.

'I know you are, darling,' John softened. 'But how are we going to get all of this stuff in the car?'

'I'll pack,' Jayne offered immediately. 'You know women are better packers than men.'

'Okay,' replied John with a sigh, knowing that without a doubt Jayne had no chance of getting all of that gear in that ever-so-little Renault 5.

But she did. True to her word and with very little effort, and absolutely no struggle whatsoever, Jayne loaded all the gear into the Red Bug. She even managed a few extras in the form of a couple of blow-up airbeds so that 'we can lie in the sun and get nicely tanned.' 'Clearly she's never been to Pembrokeshire in the rain before,' thought John. Yes, the little car was full to the brim with about a foot or so of headspace above all the kit. But, all of the gear was in and safely stowed away. Well done Jayne!

The journey to West Wales was uneventful apart from the puncture, which occurred between Carmarthen and Haverfordwest. No problem other than the fact that all the gear had to be unpacked to get at the spare-wheel. Jayne took this mishap in her stride and remained calm and collected throughout the entire operation. John on the other hand, being of an entirely different nature – they say that opposites attract, don't they – blew his top on three occasions. One, when unloading the car; two, when changing the wheel; three, when repacking the car, an operation that Jayne did yet again. Oh yes, there was a four for John. He lost his cool when it started to rain quite heavily just after they recommenced their journey.

They had about an hour or so to get to the campsite and John certainly did not cherish the thought of putting up the tent in the rain. It was true that over the years he had done it many times before but never a tent of this size. Could he rely on the help of Jayne, an absolute novice to camping? Well at least she would be able to hold things and pass things to him when he needed them, anyone could do that! Anyway, he had absolutely no choice and he would have to manage the erection one way or another, rain or no rain.

No matter, the rain stopped before they arrived at John's favourite campsite. Unfortunately, the rain had been replaced by a force-10 gale.

'No matter,' John said to Jayne as they pulled into their pitch. 'It's only two o'clock in the afternoon so we can sit in the car for a bit and wait for the wind to die down.' He smiled at her reassuringly although he wasn't feeling quite as confident as he sounded. They were on the top of a cliff and out to sea John could see nothing but wild, thrashing whitecaps and what looked like angry, black rain-clouds.

Meanwhile, Jayne looked around the campsite to find that it was not quite what she expected. The way John had described it she thought that it was going to be the next best thing to heaven on earth. It looked to her like a cow-field complete with cowpats every few metres. No, it was worse than that because the more she looked the more manure she saw. Ugh! However, she was determined not to complain under any circumstances, but she felt that perhaps she could gently advise John when the occasion arose.

'John, how are we going to put up the tent?' she shouted as a gust of wind rocked the car violently.

'Oh, the wind will be gone soon,' John replied.

'No, I don't mean the wind,' Jayne said as she pointed out of the window, 'I mean the cowpats. There must be two every square metre and that's not including the sheep manure in between.'

'Oh, we'll clear that away in a jiffy,' John declared. 'We'll make room just enough for the tent.'

'But what about room for the table and chairs? Did you bring a shovel with you?'

John fell silent for a moment. Damn and blast, he hadn't given the cleaning up of the pitch a thought and he certainly wasn't going to do it with his bare hands.

'Don't worry, Jayne, I'll sort it,' was all that he could muster in reply.

A Gaze into Holidaze

And sort it he did. After about another two hours the wind dropped to a workable, tent-erecting level, enabling John to walk the one-and-a-half-miles each way to the farmer who owned the land upon which the camp was sited. He returned an hour later armed with a spade whereby he proceeded to shovel manure at a rate of knots. Almost twenty minutes of this soul-destroying, nose-wrinkling shovelling rendered the pitch fit for habitation – almost anyway!

'What about that?' Jayne asked, pointing to the neat pile of manure that John had built up from his exertions.

'That will be fine,' replied John. 'Just be careful when you walk around in the dark. Anyway, I've got to take the spade back now. Don't worry, I'll be back in two ticks.'

Another hour later, a very lonely hour for Jayne sitting by herself in the car, John returned. It was now nearly six o'clock and the wind was still a little strong for putting a tent up. Nevertheless, it had to be done.

'Come on, Jayne, let's get stuck into getting the tent up. We've got a great pitch now that the cow and sheep manure has gone.'

In all honesty, considering the high wind, the two of them did very well. They emptied out the tent-bag and laid out the contents on the lee-side of the car. John briefed Jayne on what he wanted her to do and the teamwork commenced.

The first operation was laying the groundsheet,

which, being rather large for the five-man tent, became quite volatile in the wind and flapped around like a demented, over-sized sheet of paper.

'Keep it low!' John shouted against the noise of the wind. 'Keep it low!'

Both of them crouched as low as they could and John fumbled for a peg to secure his side of the sheet.

'E-e-e-e-k!' was all that John heard of the loud scream that Jayne gave – the rest was carried away by the wind. He looked up to find Jayne looking a little shocked as she sat on the ground on the other side of the groundsheet, her legs outstretched in front of her, her arms held out to John in a helpless gesture as if she wanted to embrace him.

'Oh no! What have I done now?' she said, her face contorted in disgust.

'What's happened?' shouted John.

'I must have lost my balance when I was crouched trying to keep the groundsheet as low as I could, like you asked me to.' Jayne's tears were not far away.

'Well, I've secured my end of the sheet so you can release yours now and stand up.'

'No I can't, John,' shot back the answer.

'Why not?' shouted John, perhaps a little curtly.

'Because I'm sitting in the pile of cow-manure that you neatly piled up close to our pitch!'

John's mouth sagged open. He didn't know whether to laugh at or sympathise with Jayne's predicament. He rushed to her side and helped her to her feet ignoring the loud sucking, squelching sound as her bottom left the huge pile of dung. He also ignored the flysheet when, being only inadequately secured by two pegs at one end, it got lifted by the wind to go sailing away and finally disappear over the cliff-tops.

'What am I going to do, John?' Jayne asked as she stood bowlegged like John Wayne after a hard ride across the prairie. 'Where's the showers? I'll go and have a shower. Perhaps I can wash my clothes at the same time.'

John swallowed hard before replying, 'There aren't any love. There's only a single toilet here. Never mind, I can always hose you down in the farmyard. Ha! Ha!' John's attempt at a feeble joke to lighten the situation merely received a freezing look of contempt from Jayne.

Suddenly, she laughed. 'Oh no! Get a whiff of me,' snorted Jayne, her sense of humour returning.

John slowly looked around the field trying not to notice the overpowering stench that radiated from Jayne. The only other campers on the site were in a single caravan at the far side of the field.

'Come on, we'll get help for you over there,' stated John confidently. Putting his arm around Jayne's shoulders he helped her to walk the uncomfortable four-hundred yards to the caravan. God, what were the caravanners going to think of this terrible smell!!

The caravanners couldn't have been more helpful. On realising what had happened the wife, a motherly woman of about fifty, took complete charge of the situation. Ordering her husband to boil a large kettle of water whilst hustling John down the other end of the caravan with, 'Keep out of the way and stay down there with my husband, George,' she drew a curtain which separated the lounge from the kitchen area.

After husband George had passed in the boiling water, Jayne's dirty, cowpat-stained clothes appeared with orders of 'sling 'em outside.' Finally, Jayne appeared all rosy-cheeked and just-washed shiny, in clean clothes which had obviously come from the wife whose name was Freda.

'She'll have to stay with us for the night because this young thing has had enough for one day I'm thinkin'!' Freda spoke quietly now, a soft Devonshire lilt to her voice. 'I'm afraid there's no room for you so you'll have to sleep in your car. You should know better than try to put a tent up in all this wind anyhow. George will help you in the mornin'. Won't you George?'

George grunted his agreement.

'There that's settled then. Now, have a bite to eat with us and a nice cup of tea. Then off you go and we'll be seein' you in the mornin'.'

'Thank God for caravanners,' thought John.

The meal was excellent, and Freda seemed to have produced it with no effort at all. This was followed with not just hot, sweet tea but several pints of scrumpy cider, which George seemed to have in abundance up his sleeve.

A Gaze into Holidaze

After leaving George and Freda at about ten o'clock, John found that the wind had dropped totally. He repacked the gear from the grass into the rear of the Renault before climbing into the front passenger seat. In spite of the lack of space, John, with head on one of the soft frilly-pillows which supported his head against the side-window, slept soundly right through the night.

True to his word, at eight o'clock the following morning, George appeared. Armed with a stack of bacon sandwiches and a flask of tea for breakfast, he then proceeded to help John erect the tent. George had even recovered the ground-sheet which had blown over the cliff in the howling gale of the previous night.

After the tent was up, a job which took only about twenty minutes, Freda and Jayne joined them. Freda held out a black plastic bag.

'I think you know what's in 'ere,' she smiled. 'There's a launderette in the village so you'll soon get these clothes sorted out. Now you look after this lovely girl and don't you be getting into any more bother now, you hear me? Come on, George, let's be leavin' these young 'uns in peace.'

John never even had time to thank them for their generosity and help. By the time that he and Jayne had returned from the launderette in the nearby village, George, Freda and their caravan had gone.

'What are we going to do with this lot?' murmured a disappointed Jayne as she looked at the carrier bags of groceries and beer that they had bought for George and Freda in an effort to return their hospitality and kindness.

'We'll have to keep them ourselves now,' whispered John. Then turning to Jayne he added with humour, 'So let's eat, drink and be merry!'

They were now alone on the campsite in West Wales on a sunny, calm day, overlooking a beautiful, sandy bay with a wonderfully blue-green sea which was alive with sparkling twinkles from the morning sun.

'I'm sorry for what happened to you,' John said as he took Jayne in his arms.

'Nothing to be sorry about John, because it wasn't your fault. Come on, give us a kiss.

'Darling, will you ever go camping again after this? Will you ever actually like camping?'

Jayne looked up at John, a mischievous twinkle in her eye. 'Like camping John? I am going to absolutely love it.'

And love it she did, and love it she does. John and Jayne have not only been husband and wife for twenty-five years but have been camping-mates and partners for twenty-five years. With tremendous energy, a bubbly and fun-loving, full-of-life Jayne has learned and accepted the camping way of life, a way of life that demands that you love and enjoy the good bits, accept and get-on-with-it during the bad bits. What better chum than Jayne could John possibly have had, to continue the adventures of the outdoor life and face the trials and tribulations yet to come?

****

CHAPTER TWO

AREN'T PEOPLE FUNNY

A breakfast yolk . . .
It's quite amazing when you consider the number of accents that people have throughout the British Isles. Some of these accents are very favourable to the ear whereas perhaps some are not too kind to listen to. The experience that John and Jayne are about to relate took place on a campsite, which was once again in West Wales, and involves the dialect of North Wales.

Now let me make it clear that no offence to the Welsh is intended in this narrative because although the accent of North Wales played its part in the story, the real humour comes from the situation and the circumstances prevailing at the time. (So you Welsh readers, I hope that this will enable you to enjoy what follows, particularly when you understand that both John and Jayne are Welsh so are really taking the Michael out of themselves.)

First, a word or two regarding interpretation of the Welsh regional pronunciation of the word 'runny'. In South Wales it is pronounced 'runnie'. In West and Mid-Wales the word is pronounced as 'rrunnie', whilst in North Wales we have 'rrrruunneee'.

JOHN BEVERLEY

Second, sound travels very easily through a canvas tent, or even a thin caravan wall, particularly from the outside inwards. You can literally hear a person break-wind in a tent which may be ten paces away from your tent. Any sound is very acute to the ear of the person inside a tent if the sound originates from outside.

John and Jayne were enjoying a lovely week on the Llŷn Peninsular in North West Wales. They were in a deserted field on a cliff-top overlooking the sea, the peace of which they both relished to the extreme.

However, after a few days of residence, their solitude was broken by a young couple who joined them and set up their bubble-tent some thirty yards away.

'With all this bloody field in which to camp, they have to put their damned tent next to us,' was John's comment. 'It's amazing how after being on one's own in a field for a few days, one resents the intrusion of a fellow camper.' Although thirty yards away, John felt that the new arrivals were virtually camped in his lap.

'Come on, John,' was Jayne's calming reply. 'They are at least twenty-five yards or more away and anyway, you don't own this field, you know?'

John grunted but remained silent. And the couple, for the next couple of days, were no trouble at all when they kept themselves entirely to themselves. In fact, John and Jayne hardly ever saw the

A Gaze into Holidaze

two fellow-campers who were more than happy to go off hiking each and every day.

It had been a peaceful night when something of a rattle disturbed John from a deep sleep. He glanced at his wristwatch to find that it was 5.15 a.m. and was surprised to see that outside the tent it was well into the dawn.

'What's the matter?' Jayne asked sleepily. 'Your restlessness has woken me up.'

'Sorry,' John replied, listening carefully. 'Thought I heard something outside.'

After a few minutes more noises occurred but these were familiar to John and Jayne. It was obvious that the couple thirty yards away were packing up ready for moving on somewhere. John and Jayne, now fully awake, lay listening to the little noises satisfied that there was no fault on the part of the departing couple who were doing their best to be as quiet as possible. Soon there was the noise of a gas primus-stove being lit after which John and Jayne heard the following dialogue.

'Hugh! 'ow do ewe like your eggs, rrrruunnneee or rrrruunnneee, rrrruunnneee?'

'No! Not rrrruunnneee, rrrruunnneee, just rrrruunnneee.'

'Oh! Not rrrruunnneee, rrrruunnneee then, just rrrruunnneee.'

'That's right, Blodwyn, not rrrruunnneee, rrrruunnneee, just rrrruunnneee.'

'Oh! Not . . . etc. etc. etc.' The two lines of conversation seemed endless and endless, as the two departing campers appeared not to know when to give it a rest at 5.15 in the morning.

John and Jayne were rolling around the inside of their tent, eyes running with tears, socks stuffed into their mouths in an attempt to prevent the belly-laughter which threatened to burst out and which they knew would travel only too well!!!

****

Bags – sleeping for the use . . .

Another story regarding how sound travelled from tent-to-outside and vice-versa again took place in West Wales, this time at a busier campsite in St David's.

John and Jayne loved to relax on sunny afternoons, preferably with a glass of wine or a gin-and-tonic, and watch the people go by. A particular fascination of theirs was to watch people putting up their variety of tents – big ones, small ones, bubble ones, it didn't matter. In fact John had learned a lot over the years by watching these tenters, some of whom were skilled at their task whilst some left a bit to be desired in their abilities to say the very least.

In all fairness, if John had seen someone having great difficulty in erecting their tent, then he had often offered his help. Usually the recipients were more than glad to receive his offer but on more than one occasion John had been told politely to 'mind his own business.'

A Gaze into Holidaze

On this particular hot and sunny June afternoon, John and Jayne were indeed in their cups in sampling an odd bottle or two of red wine whilst watching the new arrivals on the campsite.

About 2 p.m. along came an old Ford Granada estate pulling a trailer piled high with camping paraphernalia. After a brief pause, the driver of the Granada selected a pitch about fifty yards from John's and Jayne's tent and drove to it accordingly. Out of the car got a couple in their mid-thirties and three children aged between three and six years old.

'Off you go my darlings,' said the lady of the car with a very okay-ya, pseudo Henley-regatta accent. 'Mummy and Daddy will put up our new home while you children play over there on the rocks.' Turning to Daddy she asked, 'Is that alright, Damien?'

'You be careful there, children,' Daddy boomed, his okay-ya being even more okay-ya than Mummy's. 'Mummy and Daddy won't be long with the tent and then we will all have some tea.' Turning to Mummy he added, 'Come, come, Christina, let's make a start.'

Hearing this conversation very clearly over the fifty yards or so of separation, John and Jayne decided to discreetly watch and listen. A number of other campers being attracted by the very loud pseudo, upper-class accents of the new arrivals also decided to enjoy the entertainment from a distance.

The tent erection commenced. However, it soon became very apparent to John and Jayne and the surrounding but hidden audience, that Damien and Christina would have a great deal of trouble putting up one of the largest tents that John had ever seen.

'I'm going to give a hand,' John said to Jayne.

'Me too,' Jayne replied eagerly. 'It's no joke putting up a tent when you're tired. We've been there and got the tee-shirt.'

Together they walked to the 'tip-like' pitch, camping gear covering every square metre of the available ground.

'We'll give you a hand, mate,' John offered. 'These big frame-tents can be a bit tricky to put up sometimes.'

'No thank you very much,' replied the booming voice of Damien. 'I'm an ex-Army officer and I know all about these things.' He turned to his wife. 'Correct, darling?'

'Correct, dearest,' came the confidently smug reply from Christina.

'Suit yourself,' said John and with a get-on-with-it shrug took Jayne's hand and returned to their tent. Retrieving their unfinished wine they sat and watched the proceedings.

It was getting dark when the tent was finally in a fit state for habitation. Although Damien and Christina had had only one interruption from the children, when they declared their hunger and received a few packets of crisps and some fizzy

A Gaze into Holidaze

lemonade, it had taken them over five hours to erect the tent. 'Darling this' and 'darling that,' just hadn't seemed to have worked. Both Damien and Christina had worked hard and continuously apart from a few cups of tea which had been supplied in sympathy from the hidden audience. Damien and Christina had certainly not eaten a thing since they had arrived. This combined with the time that they must have been travelling on the road that morning to get to the campsite must have rendered them pretty knackered.

They were now putting things inside the tent. Damien passed the bedrooms for hanging to Christina who proceeded to hang them.

'Can I have the sleeping-bags now, darling?' Christina asked, loud enough to inform the rest of the campsite. Obviously, she was oblivious to the way that sound travelled.

'Where are they, old girl?'

Christina's tiredness, and a touch of impatience could be heard in her voice when she said, 'In the back of the car where you packed them, darling.'

'I didn't pack them,' replied Damien sharply.

'Well I didn't pack the bloody things,' Christina stated firmly. She was losing her rag and her okay-ya mask was beginning to slip.

'Are you telling me then that we have no fucking sleeping-bags?' Damien's okay-ya had disappeared without trace, possibly never to return.

'Well, if you didn't pack 'em then you are dead right. We have no fucking sleeping-bags! You told me, you fucking idiot, that you fucking well packed the bastard things.'

John and Jayne couldn't believe the Anglo-Saxon language that was floating on the still night air from the tent fifty yards away – and the language got worse and worse! What a complete change of character Damien and Christina suffered as the result of the lack of a few sleeping-bags. Even the children, who were obviously frightened by the noisy behaviour of their parents, were told unceremoniously to 'bugger off' when they approached the tent.

By about 9 p.m. all had quietened down and the tent in question was in complete darkness. Presumably all the occupants were asleep because not a sound was heard for the remainder of the night. How on earth come the morning, were Damien and Christina going to face their neighbours who had heard every single word?

John and Jayne were determined to find out. Early the next morning they got up and took their places around the breakfast table, awaiting the second round of the 'battle of the sleeping-bags.' At around 8.30 a.m. Damien and Christina appeared with a hearty display of love and affection to all and sundry.

'Good morning, darling,' said Damien, with a gushing smile, his okay-ya confidence beaming. 'Did you sleep well?'

'Yes, my love,' replied Christina, with an even bigger smile.

A Gaze into Holidaze

Then looking around at the gathered neighbours who had suddenly and mysteriously appeared from nowhere, 'Good morning, good morning,' okay-ya in charming abundance.

Full marks for courage, eh?

****

Sleep, perchance to dream...
John decided that it was time that Jayne and he made their first journey together across the English Channel into France and on to Switzerland, a trip that he had done twice before on his 1300cc dream-machine.

'You'll love it, Jayne,' John declared enthusiastically. 'It's a different world over there and wait until you see the mountains of Switzerland. They're out of this world.'

'It seems a long way to go to me, John. But, if that's what you want, let's do it.'

John outlined the plan and route to Jayne with boyish eagerness. 'You can navigate, Jayne, 'cos it will be good experience and practice for you when we travel further afield in later years.'

'Are you sure that we can afford this trip, John? They say that the motorway tolls are very expensive in France and Switzerland and you know that things are a bit tight with us financially at the moment.'

That was an understatement. John and Jayne

had been married for a year and what with the usual expenses of living and paying a mortgage, there was very little money left in the pot for things like holidays.

'Don't worry about a thing, darling,' John told her. 'We will travel on the N-roads, that's the red ones on the map, because they don't cost anything.' John showed her the map of France and Switzerland. 'We'll cross the Channel from Portsmouth to Le Havre, getting off the ferry at 10 a.m. We'll fly through Paris, on to Dijon and then Pontarlier and Lausanne. Along the lake, gorgeous that, to Montreux and then finally down the valley to our destination, Zermatt. Bob's-your-uncle, eh? Great stuff!!'

'It seems a long way to me,' Jayne said, shaking her head. 'How long will it take us?'

'No problem! I reckon it will take us about seven hours with a stop or two for lunch and a stretch of the legs. We'll arrive in a little campsite I know in Zermatt at about 5 p.m., tent up and be settled in by 5.30., first bottle of red and a cracking meal consumed by 6.30. How does that sound?'

'As long as you're sure, John.'

'Trust me, Jayne, I've done this thing a few times before,' John said proudly.

'Yes, but that was on your bike not in the Red Bug.'

'Have a little faith, sweetheart,' John said, hugging Jayne to him. 'You can rely on my judgement.'

So, off they went, Bug packed to the gills with the usual nine inches of head-space above the gear

A Gaze into Holidaze

in the back. It was a glorious July-day when they left the UK and the weather held not only for the ferry crossing, but for all the way to Paris. The only hiccup in John's plan that occurred was that he forgot to allow for the extra hour that French-time was ahead of the UK. This meant that instead of getting off the ferry at the planned 10 a.m., their arrival in France was one hour later at 11 a.m., French-time.

'Will that be OK, John?' asked a worried Jayne.

'Of course, Jayne. Just means we arrive at the campsite a bit later. Trust me.'

Jayne's first attempt at navigation was excellent and she found little difficulty in guiding John along the red N-roads to the wonderful capital of France. Soon they were on the Périphérique, the ring road that ran all around the outskirts of Paris.

'Soon be saying goodbye to good old Paree,' said John, smiling all over his face as he drove the Red Bug along the wide trunk road.

And that's where the problem began. Ten minutes later they hit the bumper-to-bumper traffic of the jam that was to take them two hours to clear. It was a miserable two hours of barely moving with the windows wound fully-down in an effort to keep the interior of the car cool in a sweltering 27 degrees Celsius of heat. Finally, they were on their way.

'We've lost three hours now, John, what with that traffic-jam and the hour difference that you forgot about.' Jayne was starting to get concerned because they still had a very long way to go.

'There's no need to rub it in, you know,' John replied sharply. 'Anyone can make a mistake.'

'But won't we be arriving too late because we won't be there until at least 8 p.m. now? Won't the campsite be closed? Shouldn't we look for a campsite in France soon and then cross into Switzerland in the morning?'

'Definitely not!' John was adamant. 'So we arrive at 8 p.m., so what? I know this campsite very well and it doesn't matter what time we arrive 'cos they don't close their gates. All we have to do is go in, put the tent up and book-in in the morning. No problem, trust me.'

And trust John Jayne did, even though the traffic got worse and worse and their progress through France became pathetic. They only had a brief stop for a simple meal but even so, it was still 8 p.m. when they crossed into Switzerland. Also it was getting dark and Jayne, who had heard about driving through the Swiss mountains, was getting very worried.

'There's no need to be worried, Jayne,' John reassured. 'We'll be at the campsite in Zermatt by 10 o'clock, I promise you. Trust me, it will be fine.'

Well, after another hazardous four hours, some were spent driving about forty miles through the typically heavy summer-evening mists of the area, they arrived at Visp, a small town about fifteen miles from Zermatt. It was now past midnight and both John and Jayne were very, very tired.

A Gaze into Holidaze

'Tell you what, love,' John whispered, a wee bit embarrassed at the events so far. 'We won't be at the campsite until about 1 a.m. and it will be too late to put our tent up.'

'Why not?' Jayne asked, shock together with exhaustion in her voice.

'Well, we'll disturb all the other campers and it's much too late for that. What we'll do is this. It's a gorgeous night and all the stars are out as bright as can be. We'll park the car on the campsite, climb into our sleeping-bag and sleep under the stars like the cowboys do. You'll love it, trust me.'

True to John's word, they arrived at the campsite near Zermatt at 1 a.m. It was as silent as a tomb. Also true was the fact that the campsite was still open and they had no trouble finding a decent pitch alongside a fast-flowing mountain-stream. What wasn't true was John's summation of the gorgeous starlit night. Yes, the stars were bright and beautiful but they shone down on a pitch that was some thousands of feet above sea level. You've guessed it – the outside temperature was 5 degrees Celsius, just a wee bit above freezing.

'I'm not sleeping out there,' declared Jayne firmly. 'I can take a joke but pneumonia I can't take. We'll have to sleep in the car, that's all there is to it.'

John knew that Jayne was absolutely right because in the short time that they had stopped, the cold was more than just apparent. Equally he knew that there was no room for two people to sleep in the front of a Renault 5 Campus. He thought hard through his befuddled, tired mind for a solution to their problem. Then a possibility hit him!

'Jayne, down the road is a small hostel which I partied-in with some Aussies a few years back. It's cheap and we can afford it for one night. I know it's late but it's worth a try. You stay here and I'll do a recce and come back for you. Are you game?'

'Anything you say, John, anything you say.' Jayne had had enough. She would do almost anything for a quiet life and a decent sleep.

Off John went. He found the hostel and it was exactly as he remembered it. The door was open but, as he had expected, there was no-one at the small reception at that time of the morning. Should he take a chance and see if he could find an empty room? No, he concluded. Too dodgy because he might wake someone and cause a disturbance. However, what he did find was that the building was centrally-heated and hence wonderfully warm compared with the air outside. 'That's it then,' John said triumphantly to himself.

On returning to the car, John outlined his newly-planned sleeping arrangements for the night to a very sleepy Jayne.

'I'm not happy about sleeping in the corridor of that hostel but providing that it's warm, and we'll be away before anyone is about, I'll give it a go. What will happen if we're caught?'

'Nothing love, trust me,' said John as he started the car.

A Gaze into Holidaze

They crept into the silent hostel and found a wide hallway on the second floor which was more than suitable to kip for the night. However, once they settled down in the well-lit hallway on the carpeted floor, lying fully clothed on top of their double sleeping-bag, all Jayne did was toss and turn. Clearly, there was to be no sleep here. 'I'm scared that someone will catch us,' was all that John heard from Jayne at regular five-minute intervals.

John was knackered and he knew that Jayne was too. It had been a hell of a long day. He looked at his watch. The dial showed 2.15 a.m.

'Right! I've got it!' John exclaimed. 'Come on, woman, we're going back down the valley to Visp. There is a railway station there which will be warm and we are going to spend the rest of the night there. It's not negotiable so let's go.'

And without a murmur from Jayne, they rolled up the sleeping-bag and left. Driving down the valley with the heater of the car fully-on, the car became very warm and Jayne dropped off to sleep. Although an effort to keep awake, John made the fifteen mile-or-so journey to Visp in record time. Finally, and virtually on his knees through lack of sleep, he hurtled into the car-park of the railway station.

To his horror he soon realised that the place was in total darkness. He opened the door of the Bug and attempted to get out without disturbing Jayne.

'Where are you going? Are we at the railway

station?' she sighed as she stretched her cramped limbs.

'Just going to do a recce. Be back in a jiffy.'

John knew the answer before he read 'Open at 7 a.m.' on the locked main door of the railway station. Wearily he returned to the car.

'It's closed until 7 a.m.,' was all that he could say to Jayne as he slid behind the steering-wheel. He was well and truly beaten.

'Come here,' she said. 'Let me suggest something. Let's see if we can sleep by leaning against each other.'

Well, the car was warm, they were exhausted and it was 3 a.m. Whatever the reason, they leaned against each other with heads together in the front seats of the Renault 5, and went fast asleep. They slept the sleep of the dead and did not move an inch all night. In fact, the first awareness came to John at about 8.30 a.m. when he awoke to find several faces peering at him through the windscreen – all had a combination of bewilderment and amusement upon them.

****

Sleep, perchance to dream – homeward bound . . .

And the holiday in Switzerland, in spite of the little mishaps during the sleeping arrangements that first night, proved to be absolutely champion. The wonders and beauty of the Swiss mountains were thoroughly explored in that the Matterhorn, Eiger and Schilthorn were all conquered on foot both going up and coming down – as far as the safe-walking paths would allow anyway.

Alas, all good things come to an end and it was all too soon time to return to the UK. 'Don't worry,' John told Jayne, 'I'm not going to make the same mistake as I did coming to Switzerland. On the way back we'll stop for the night around Nancy in France. Then we'll continue to the north coast of France and spend a few days just outside Le Havre which will be handy for the ferry home.'

'Will there be plenty of campsites for our night stop?' quizzed Jayne, not wanting to spend another night in the car after her introduction-to-Switzerland experience.

'There are plenty of campsites, sweetheart. Loads and loads of 'em. Trust me, you'll have campsites coming out of your ears in France. They'll be on our route begging us to come in.'

And there were plenty of campsites travelling back through France. Unfortunately, all of them seemed to be the big expensive ones which on their very limited remaining budget, John and Jayne chose not to use. This was certainly the case at 4.30 p.m when they found themselves at a particlar campsite that wanted an arm-and-a-leg to stay the night. Anyway, in John's opinion it was far too early to stop and he felt that they should press on.

'We'll give it another hour or so and then we'll

slot in for the night. No problem, just trust me, Jayne. Just make sure that your navigation keeps us off the motorway 'cos we only have a 100 franc note to last us for the few days that we have left.'

Well, to be honest, John's statement about lots of campsites in France is generally true, but what he forgot in his casual planning of the return journey was the old adage: 'you can never find one when you want one!' It was now 9.30 and very dark as they drove along the N-roads heading north. Since the 4.30 p.m. campsite they had not sighted a single one. Well, not quite true, they had stumbled upon another large, commercial site but yet again it was ridiculously expensive and way, way above their budget.

Jayne was getting a little despondent and certainly very tired. They had been travelling since 10 a.m. that morning and had had only a brief stop for lunch. Also in the time that they had been on the road she had been concentrating very hard on her navigation and her patience was getting a wee bit thin. They were now skirting the town of Abbeville in northern France and Jayne's concentration was at its lowest ebb.

'Bloody hell!' John yelled. 'We're on a sodding motorway!'

'We can't be,' replied Jayne shakily, totally at a loss.

'I know a bloody motorway when I see one,' barked John. 'I told you to keep off 'em, didn't I? We'll have to pay the bloody toll now and break

A Gaze into Holidaze

into that 100-franc note. It's all we've got left and I wanted to keep that for a few days' campsite fees.'

'Sorry, John,' mumbled Jayne. 'I must have missed a signpost somewhere or other. Can't you come off the motorway at the next exit?'

'That's what I'm going to do, but we'll still have to pay the toll,' John snapped. 'Hell's bells and buckets of blood, that's what I say!'

The moment that he had said it, John regretted it. He knew that Jayne had made a great job of navigating throughout the entire journey and she certainly didn't deserve his short temper. He was tired so he knew that Jayne also was tired. It had been a long, long day.

'Sorry, Jayne,' he apologised humbly. 'Anyone can make a mistake and after the boo-boos I've made on this trip, I'm a clever one to talk. It'll only be a couple of francs at the most so it won't make a lot of difference to our budget. Don't worry.'

With that, the well-illuminated toll plaza appeared out of the darkness about a half-mile ahead.

'You've got the 100 franc note in your purse, Jayne. I'll drive into the booth where there will be a man to take the money, just like our tolls over the Severn Bridge. Because the chap will be on your side of the car give him the note and he will give you the change. There are no barriers to worry about and all that will happen is that he will change a red light at the booth to green, and away we go.'

'Okay,' replied Jayne, clutching the 100-franc note tightly.

John slowed the Red Bug to approach the three toll-booths of the plaza with extreme caution. Carefully he scanned each booth looking for the head and shoulders of the man who would control his selected booth.

'Oh my God!' John exclaimed, his eyes wide with horror. 'There are no manual controls. All three booths are throw-your-money-into-a-basket jobs.'

He pulled up at the red-light of the nearest booth and saw the toll price illuminated in front of him. 'Two and a half bloody francs. Jayne, have you got any change whatsoever?' he asked desperately.

'I don't think so,' Jayne gasped as she fumbled frantically in the dark looking for her purse. 'I gave the last of my change to you.'

They had only been stopped at the toll for a matter of fifteen seconds before the inevitable carhorns started blasting behind them.

John glanced into his mirror and panicked when he saw the stream of stationary headlights behind him. 'Bloody hell! Half of France must be stuck behind us. Oh shit!'

'What are we going to do, John?' Jayne was really frightened with the noise of all the horns blasting away. 'Why are they being so beastly to us? It's not our fault is it, John?'

John was not listening. With a look of sheer determination he growled, 'I'm not throwing our last 100-franc note into that soddin' basket! Hang

A Gaze into Holidaze

on, love, there is no barrier so we are going through. To blazes with the buggers!' As if at a Le Mans start, John, ignoring the red light, tore through the narrow gap of the booth, front wheels of the Bug spinning.

All hell broke loose. A flash of light temporarily blinded John as soon as he passed the red light, to be followed by the turmoil and utter bedlam of sirens screeching and lights flashing. It was as if World War Three had broken out.

'Bloody hell! Anyone would think I've robbed a bank not fiddled the toll for two-and-a-half French bleedin' francs,' John shouted, the Red Bug flat-out as he raced away from the uproar of noise and flashing lights. 'I reckon we are for it now. The gendarmes will be after us and will catch us in a matter of minutes. They even took our picture as we went through the toll.'

'Aren't you scared, John? What will they do to us?'

'Me scared? Not at all,' John replied, a twinkle in his eye and a wicked grin on his lips. Then he turned to look at Jayne in the darkness, 'I'm bloody terrified. It's the Bastille prison for me. Hope you'll come and visit me on visiting days.'

That's all it took to ease the tension of the long day on the road coupled with their recent frightening trauma at the tollbooth. They both laughed and laughed and laughed.

The gendarmes did not catch them and probably didn't even try. They left the motorway at the next exit and picked up their N-road for the north coast, some forty miles away. They were once again exhausted and still had not solved the problem of finding a campsite for the night.

It was now 11.30 p.m. and having reached the coast of the English Channel, they were wandering westwards along the French coast towards Le Havre. John knew that there was little chance of finding a campsite and, even if they did, at that time of night it was doubtful if it would be open. What he didn't know was how he could break this news to Jayne, who appeared to be asleep in the passenger-seat beside him. He felt awful about the way he had cocked everything up again, so thought it better to keep driving for as long as he could and keep the peace.

'Stop the car!' Jayne's voice broke the silence like a pistol shot. 'I've had enough and I cannot take any more. I suggest we sleep in the car – again.'

Still trying to retain some dignity and authority, John stepped in. 'Come on Jayne, we don't have to sleep in the car. I'll find us a place where we can stretch-out and sleep properly. Let's keep going for a little while longer – say until midnight. If we don't find anything then I'll give in and we'll kip in the car.'

They drove on but it was not to be their night. Ten minutes later they did find a campsite and, as John predicted, it was closed.

'Never mind,' John insisted. 'Closed or not there will be somewhere here to sleep. Trust me, I'll find a place to sleep. Stay here, I'll do a recce and I'll be back in two ticks.'

Returning to the car some fifteen minutes later he whispered to the zombie-like Jayne, 'Got a place for us. Just the job and there's no-one about so we'll be fine. We'll kip the night in the sleeping-bag and leave in the morning before anyone sees us. Trust me.'

'If you say trust me again, John, I'll kick you where I think your brains appear to be –in your arse! Now where have you found for us to sleep?'

'In the Ladies' Toilet,' John declared smugly. 'It's a cubicle really with a washbasin and a sit-down loo. We can stretch out and . . .'

That's as far as he got. 'In the Ladies' Loo!' Jayne screamed. 'Both of us! I can't believe it, I just simply cannot believe it. Get back in the car – now! Drive me to a quiet spot down the road and I will sleep in the back of the car. Is that absolutely clear?'

And she did. Upon arrival at a dark and secluded spot just off the coast-road she climbed into the nine-inch headspace between the camping-gear and the roof of the car and immediately went to sleep. John, on the other hand, feeling very sorry for himself remained in the front of the Renault 5 and fitfully dozed on and off for the remainder of the very, very long and chilly night.

****

A Frenchman's charm...

The following morning John expected yet again to face the music from Jayne. Through a fairly sleepless night John had come to realise that his route planning did leave quite a bit to be desired. Certainly he knew that Jayne was upset, because he had never heard her use words like 'arse' before. Still, he concluded, he certainly deserved it!

Jayne, at 8 a.m. sharp, climbed out of her headspace at the back of the car. With a yawn, a stretch of the limbs and a very cheery, 'Hello, my love, what are we going to do now?' she opened John's door and gave him a kiss.

John couldn't believe his luck. 'Well, if it's okay with you, we'll still have a couple of days here and then drive the twenty miles or so to Le Havre for the crossing home.'

'Sounds good to me. Let's find us a campsite then if we can,' Jayne suggested enthusiastically. 'Anything can happen on a lovely day like this.'

Once again there was a distinct shortage of campsites. John, after his biking experience all over Europe, just could not believe it. However, the location was beautiful and the drive in the Red Bug along the French coast towards Le Havre was wonderful. As they approached a small coastal village called Yport near Fécamp, John spotted a small hand-painted sign marked 'Camping' on the side of the road.

'This will do nicely,' declared John, as he swung off the road and proceeded slowly down a narrow, dusty and very bumpy track. The winding track led through a small wood and into a large clearing about one hundred and fifty yards long by a hundred yards wide. There, at the far-side of the clearing, stood a very old and very battered caravan which appeared to be empty and unused.

John parked up on the opposite side of the clearing as far away as possible from the unknown caravan. Within a half-an-hour the tent was up and food was being eaten. John looked around the clearing and liked what he saw. It was surrounded by a dense conifer forest which gave the clearing both beauty and absolute privacy.

'Jayne, this will be great for a few days and if the weather remains as gorgeous as it is now we'll have a great suntan to go home with. These trees will be a natural windbreak for any breeze which might come in off the sea.'

'Seems good to me,' replied Jayne lazily, sighing as she snuggled deeper into the picnic blanket upon which she and John both lay. 'A couple of days to unwind in the sun sounds pretty good to me. But first, before we settle down, let's find the loos, shall we?'

Off they went into the surrounding woods looking for the campsite toilet. After about fifteen minutes of searching they found it.

'Good grief!' exclaimed John, looking at the pathetic tired-looking, open-fronted, wooden structure which was leaning like a relic from some old shantytown. The structure was open-fronted because the one and only door was completely missing but could be seen leaning drunkenly against the outer side-wall. The cubicle itself consisted of three walls and a roof, which had more holes in it than there was solid covering. Speaking of holes, the round business-hole of the toilet was extremely large and cut into planking which stretched from the two side-walls. The whole thing was moving, with ants and flies buzzing everywhere, particularly around the deep, dark hole of mystery.

'Where's the flush?' Jayne asked, her nostrils pinched tightly between finger and thumb.

'There isn't one,' replied John as he walked forward and craned his neck to look down the hole into the dark depths below. 'They just put some chemical down there and the whole lot just rots into the bare earth. Ugh! What a stench! Come on, let's go. There is no way that we are going to use this thunder-box 'cos the flies will probably eat us alive during the process.'

'So what do we do for a toilet if we stay here?' asked Jayne.

John, by way of reply, gestured with his hand in the general direction of the surrounding trees and, holding Jayne's eye steadily with his, broadly smiled.

'That's what I thought,' Jayne said flatly. 'Back to nature, I suppose.'

Exploring the clearing further John and Jayne found that the only other thing there of any interest whatsoever was a tap in the ground. From the tap ran a long length of hosepipe.

A Gaze into Holidaze

'And this, I assume, is our water supply,' muttered John as he turned on the tap. Water flowed freely from the end of the hosepipe before he turned it off once more. 'Never mind, sweetheart, we'll manage for a few days, won't we? Just think of all the peace, that's the thing. We'll be the only ones here.'

But that was not to be. At about 3 p.m. a Citroen, battered to match the state of the old caravan on the other side of the field, arrived and parked next to it. Out of the car got a man of about thirty, a woman of indeterminate age and three small children between the ages of two and five. Immediately, the children started running around, yelling and screaming. The man who, upon closer inspection looked like Mr. Pickwick from the point of view of his huge paunch, unlocked the caravan and went inside. The woman, after staring blankly at John and Jayne for some minutes, joined the man inside the caravan. Instantly there was a loud booming, which reverberated throughout the clearing from some sort of stereo system within the caravan.

'I can't believe it,' declared John. 'I am not going to put up with that racket. He must have it on full-blast because we are at least a hundred yards away and it sounds like a bloody disco.'

With that the man emerged from the caravan. He was dressed in the baggiest shorts that can be imagined, whilst his hairy body was covered with the dirtiest and oldest string-vest that John had ever seen. His paunch made him look as if he were carrying twins, but this obviously didn't bother him as he slowly scratched his huge belly and glowered challengingly across the clearing at John and Jayne. He was soon joined by the woman who, clad in a skimpy bikini, appeared much younger than him. She put a dirty blanket on the ground in front of the caravan and lay out in the sun.

Jayne looked at John and placed a restraining hand on his arm. 'Now I know what you are thinking, John. Don't do it because we'll only have trouble.'

'Trouble? Never! I'll just go and ask him to turn his ghetto-blaster down. It's not fair to us, that bloody racket.'

'Leave it be, John.' This time Jayne faced John and put both hands on his shoulders. With feet apart in her favourite calming stance she looked directly into John's eyes. 'Now, the man is not causing any harm and all he wants is time with his family. Anyway, after last night at the toll plaza do you really want the police involved?'

That did it. John sat down on the grass and was as quiet as a mouse. Quiet for about half-an-hour that is. He then suddenly got up, and walked the hundred yards or so over to the caravan. With arms folded over his massive belly, Fatso watched John all the way but the woman did not move.

'Excuse me, monsieur, but would you mind turning the volume of your stereo down a bit, it's deafening over the other side of the clearing.'

A Gaze into Holidaze

Fatso held the palms of his hand outwards and shrugged as only the French can do. He either could not speak English or he pretended not to speak English. In any event he made no effort whatsoever to reduce the decibels. Still the woman remained quietly and horizontally in the sun.

John did the only thing he could do to try to get the Frenchman to understand him. He pointed inside the caravan at the stereo and did an unwinding motion with his hand before covering his ears with both hands. 'Too loud!' John shouted. 'Too loud!'

With that, the woman got up, stared blankly at John and going inside the caravan lowered the volume to a lower and calmer level. Returning, with a now beautiful smile revealing perfect white teeth she said in almost perfect English. 'Is that satisfactory, monsieur?'

'Fine thank you, madam,' John replied pleasantly. Turning, he walked back across the field to the tent. Before he had covered half the distance the man had turned the volume up once more.

'Bastard!' John said flatly to Jayne. 'She's okay, but he's a right bastard.'

This went on for the remainder of the evening and John went over at least four times to ask Fatso to turn the volume down. Each time Fatso gestured his lack of understanding of English, each time the woman apologised and lowered the noise. Each time John walked back to the tent, the volume was back to its pounding level by the time he reached it.

JOHN BEVERLEY

'Looks as if this could mean fisticuffs,' John laughed after the last attempt. Although John was trying to laugh it off for Jayne's sake, he was approaching his boiling point and the steam was starting to rise.

Suddenly, the noise stopped. John looked at his watch. Ten p.m. and peace reigned. 'I'll have a word with this guy in the morning,' John thought quietly to himself. 'I'll just advise him of his bad manners.'

'No you won't, John,' Jayne said loudly, reading the thoughts of her husband. 'I know you, you'll land yourself in trouble. Remember you are in another person's country and therefore you are just a guest. We will leave first thing in the morning because I simply have had enough. If this is camping, then you can have it.'

The night passed peacefully and John and Jayne slept well. In fact, so well that it was late into the morning before they were woken by someone tapping loudly on the canvas door of the tent.

'Monsieur, monsieur, please come at once. Come quickly, I need your 'elp.'

John dressed quickly, triggered by the urgency in the voice. He unzipped the front of the tent to find Fatso on his knees.

'Monsieur, please 'elp me. There has been an accident with my three-year-old son and I need your 'elp. Please follow me.' The man was desperate. He got up and ran towards the toilet as fast as his wobbling paunch would allow. John did not hesitate to follow, but now became fully aware that

A Gaze into Holidaze

Fatso could certainly speak English, and only too well.

On arrival at the thunder-box, as John and Jayne had nicknamed the pathetic excuse for a toilet, John could see no sign of the boy.

'What's happened?' John shouted to Fatso. 'Where is the boy?' By now Jayne had arrived panting heavily from her exertions by running frantically across the field.

'Down there, monsieur,' Fatso pointed. 'He has fallen down the hole and my belly is too big for me to reach him and pull him out.'

'Now you're in the shit, mate, if you forgive the pun,' John sniggered. 'Well at least your lad is.'

John doubled up with laughter, closely followed by Jayne. Talk about justice being carried out! John looked down and saw the small child sitting in the abundance of excrement, seemingly enjoying himself as he splashed away contentedly. John reached down and grabbed the boy's arms, easily lifting him through the grossly oversized hole in the planks. Holding the boy by the arms at armslength, John carried him to the tap in the clearing. There he set the lad down on the grass and proceeded to literally hose the boy, much to both John's and the child's enjoyment, until the mess had been washed away.

'Thank you, monsieur,' wheezed Fatso as he finally wobbled to the tap.

'The pleasure was all mine,' stated John coolly. 'Now, about your stereo . . .'

'Please, monsieur, let me apologise. It was very silly of me and it will not 'appen again.'

And it didn't. John and Jayne spent another two enjoyable days on the site before leaving for Le Havre. Oh yes, another bonus was that the campsite was absolutely free which rendered John and Jayne extra spending money for the end of their holiday.

All's well that ends well. The only other thing of an adverse nature that happened to them after the thunder-box incident was when they went through French customs a couple of days later. The car was stopped and thoroughly searched by not only the customs officers but the French police. John, in a very nervous and twitchy state, was convinced that they were going to put him into prison because he had broken through the toll a few nights previously. Jayne reassured him that it was purely coincidence. As luck would have it, it was.

In spite of John's cock-ups and in summing-up the holiday, Jayne said to John as they looked back at France from the upper-deck of the Le Havre/Portsmouth ferry, 'Bloody fabulous, let's do it again next year.' And they did.

****

That'll larn ya...

John and Jayne had been driving most of the day and were well down into the heart of France. The July sun was hot and the inside of the Red Bug was stifling as they trickled along a particular D-road that led them through the most spectacular countryside imaginable. One moment they were passing through deep valleys in the tree-covered mountains only to be forced to climb to the tops of these mountains, to drop down yet again into vast plains of trees bearing fruit of all descriptions.

'Gosh, this is lovely,' whispered Jayne in appreciation of such beauty, the passenger-window fully-down beside her and the hot wind blowing her hair into playful disarray. 'I've never seen such a variety of fruit; apples, plums, nectarines – you name it and it's all here. Utterly fantastic!'

'Yes,' agreed John. 'They say that Kent is the Garden of England and to be honest, it is quite pleasant. However, the plains of central France will knock spots off Kent if you want my opinion.' He glanced around him to see miles and miles of nothing but fruit trees.

'What time do we make Moulins, John?' questioned Jayne. 'I'm more than ready for a break and a nice cup of coffee. There aren't many cafés along this road, are there?'

'No, that's the problem with D-roads. They're lovely and quiet regarding traffic but there aren't too many facilities on them. Never mind, I reckon we'll be in Moulins in another hour or so 'cos we've already crossed the Loire river. We can have a bite to eat there as well as a couple of coffees. I'm starving.'

Once again John's estimate of distance, speed and time proved to be a little inaccurate. Two hours later there was still a long way to go to Moulins.

'John, my stomach feels as if my throat is cut. If I don't eat something soon I'll pass out. We haven't had a bite since breakfast and it's nearly a quarter-to-six now.'

'Told you to get some bread and things in that town we passed through at lunchtime.'

'No you didn't. I was the one that asked you to stop at that supermarket, John, and you said to wait for a while before stopping because you wanted to get further south. That's what you said, come on, admit it.'

'Cor!' John retaliated sheepishly but with a smile tugging at the corners of his mouth. 'You always have to be right, don't you?'

'Come on,' Jayne picked up the humour. 'Admit it. Who's trying to weasel out of this?'

'OK. You're right and I'm wrong. We should have stopped to get some goodies and if it's any consolation I'm hungrier than you are.'

'So what are we going to do, John?'

John looked out of the open window of the Bug. 'I don't know whether you've noticed, darling, but we are in the heart of fruit country. At this particular moment there are trees, trees and even more trees as far as the eye can see. Guess what's on these trees that are slipping past us, sweetheart?'

'Plums,' said Jayne nervously as she tuned-in to the message that John was sending her. 'You are not going to steal some plums, are you?'

A Gaze into Holidaze

'No, darling, I'm not going to steal some plums.'

'That's a relief because I thought that . . .'

John interrupted with a gleam in his eye and a grin on his face from ear to ear. 'I'm not going to steal any plums because I'm going to nick some nectarines. That's what they are out there and have been for the last ten miles or so.'

'But if you get caught, you'll be in a heap of trouble.' Then Jayne added as an afterthought, 'Furthermore, it's sunny and as clear as a bell for miles so anyone can see you.'

'No-one is going to see me because we are way out in the sticks. We haven't passed a car or seen a farmhouse for at least twenty minutes, so trust me, sweetheart, everything will be fine. I'll pull in at the next opportunity and I guarantee that it will be a piece-of-cake. The trees are right alongside the road and there is no fence to climb. It will be a piece of old doddle!'

'I don't want anything to do with this, John, I'd rather go hungry.'

'Well I'm not going hungry,' said John mischievously. 'And you can't beat a few nectarines for the bowels. Keeps you regular, you know?'

In next to no time, a small, rough clearing appeared on the side of the road into which John eagerly drove. Grabbing a plastic carrier bag from the back of the Bug he turned to Jayne. 'No-one's going to come but if they do tell them . . .'

'I want nothing to do with it, and anyway I can't speak French.'

John carried on emphatically, ignoring Jayne's objections. 'Tell them I'm having a pee. If you can't tell them, get out of the car and show them with a mime. You know, squat down a bit.'

'I'll do no such thing,' replied Jayne, flabbergasted.

John knew that there was absolutely no chance of anyone catching them. What, at six o'clock in the evening in the wilds of the countryside? No chance! Off he went into the orchard and within a few yards of the roadside was surrounded by trees laden with nectarines. Like a child in a sweetshop he started picking the fruit for all he was worth.

The carrier bag was about a quarter-full when John heard the sound of a car engine in the distance being very much over-revved. Seconds later a car raced along the road, to literally screech to a halt in the small clearing where he had left the Bug, stones and dust spitting everywhere from its tyres.

John could only hear this, because although only a matter of yards from the clearing, the orchard was too dense to see anything. Next he heard the sound of a car-door slamming, boots crunching on stony dirt as someone briskly walked in the direction of where John had left the Red Bug with Jayne inside.

Immediately, a man's voice was heard yelling in anger. By the tone of the voice John felt that the French was quite expletive, but unfortunately John couldn't understand a word of it. The man went on and on with little pause as only the French can do. However, even the French have to draw breath at some time which, although a mini-pause, gave the chance for Jayne to weakly squeak, 'But my husband has only gone for a pee.'

John felt an absolute prat because he knew that he had been caught in the act, hook, line and sinker. However, all was not lost. He only had about a dozen nectarines in the bag but Jayne needed them with certainty because she was hungry. Therefore, he was going to brave it out with this Froggie farmer. After all, he was British, wasn't he?

Pulling himself up to his full six-feet height, or just under in his flip-flops, he stuffed the bag of nectarines under the front of his tee-shirt and positively stormed out of the orchard into the clearing. There standing next to the Bug, was a bull of a man, six-feet in any direction and burned almost black by long days in the sun. His muscles were like melons under his coarse farmer's shirt, and he carried a shotgun in the crook of his arm. A man anyone would call, 'Sir'.

'Is there a problem, Sir?' bluffed John as to meet Jayne's lie, he pretended to do up the flies of his shorts. John was a little surprised that the tone of his voice was much higher than he had intended it. It was a mere croak really.

Off roared the big farmer again, the effort of his anger making him very red in the face. He stormed over to John, who seemed to shrink as the man dwarfed him, and yelled in French at the top of his voice whilst gesticulating wildly with his arms, again as only the French can do.

'There's no need to be like that,' John said to Big Frenchie with more confidence than he felt, his right-hand leaving his flies to accompany the other hand which was desperately trying to control the hidden bag of nectarines which were determined to slip down from inside his tee-shirt.

John's movement was enough. Big Frenchie dropped his gaze and stared at John's stomach in a way that made John want to relieve his bladder and bowels simultaneously.

'Sacré bleu!' boomed Big Frenchie (or words to that effect anyway). He raised a hand as big as the hind quarter of a very large cow, and struck downwards at John's tee-shirt almost tearing it from his body.

Nectarines spilled everywhere. There seemed to be dozens of them rolling around their feet. Suddenly, there was absolute silence in the clearing and the only sound of which John became aware was the birds chirping away merrily in the trees around them.

'Sorry about that, mate,' John fumbled. He just didn't know what else to say.

Big Frenchie was lost for words. With mouth wide open he followed John with his blazing eyes as John returned to the Bug, got behind the wheel and slammed the door. Starting the car he looked sheepishly at the farmer.

A Gaze into Holidaze

'Okay if I go now, Sir?'

Big Frenchie did not change his expression of utter disbelief and still wordless, he just raised his shotgun and pointed with it down the road.

John was out of the clearing like a racing driver. 'Bloody hell!' he snapped as he drove down the road as if possessed. 'What's the matter with him?'

'Well, you were stealing his nectarines, darling,' replied Jayne smugly, not trying to hide the sarcasm in her voice. 'How would you like it?'

John felt ashamed. What was initially devilment on his part had badly backfired on him and he felt like a schoolboy caught doing something he shouldn't have been doing by his schoolmaster. He glanced in the mirror.

'Oh shit!' yelled John, eyes wide-open with fright. 'The bastard's following me!'

And follow John Big Frenchie did. For nearly twenty miles.

'That's it,' John declared resolutely when he could see that Frenchie did not intend to give up the chase. 'Next village he's going to turn me in to the police. Look out Bastille, here I come.' John tried to laugh but he couldn't hide from Jayne that he was a very worried man.

'Do you think he will?' Jayne's voice betrayed that she was even more worried than John.

'Well, he's still stuck to me like glue and about ten feet from my boot so I think he is very serious about this whole damn thing. Will the bugger never turn off?'

But Frenchie did. After almost forty-five minutes and twenty miles John looked into his mirror and sighed to himself with relief. The Frenchman had gone.

'Thank the good Lord for that, eh?' said John with a broad grin, quite cocky now that the chase had ended and he had won.

'Perhaps,' replied Jayne quietly, but not being fooled by John's feigned bravado for a moment. 'Perhaps you should really thank that kind-hearted Frenchman instead of the good Lord. He could have got you into deep trouble, you know? In any event, John, there is one thing that is certain.'

'What's that, pet?' John glanced sideways at Jayne.

'That'll larn ya!'

And it did. John hasn't scrumped fruit of any description from anywhere since this occasion, and that was over twenty years ago.

****

Good old tent sales . . .

John and Jayne were spending a couple of weeks in Northern Spain near an unusual little man-made, Venice-like place called Empuriabrava. What a cracking little spot! Talk about money – or at least German money – that's the place where it is. Man-made canals are interwoven with villas worth millions of pounds with sea-going boats moored to them, worth close on the same amount.

A Gaze into Holidaze

All this set in the very picturesque Bay of Roses on the good old Mediterranean Sea.

The actual site was a wonderful campsite on the main Roses – Figueres road, just outside the small and very old and traditional Spanish town of Castelló d'Empuries. It was wonderful. Wonderful anyway for the campers but perhaps not so wonderful for the owners of the place because it was situated on the wrong side of the very, very busy Roses – Figueres main road. People who wanted to stay the night but were travelling towards Roses from Figueres could simply not cross the traffic-laden road to get into the site. After a few minutes of people honking their horns at them they just simply gave up the effort and carried on towards Roses.

John and Jayne, being a little more determined, persevered in crossing the road and found a Utopia that lasted them for a number of years. It was a good site with plenty of grass and considerable shade – the shade against the hot sun being a 'must' as experienced campers will know. It also had an Olympic-sized swimming-pool and bar which was hardly ever used. In fact, John and Jayne have since been there on a number of occasions in July and August to find that they, more often than not, have had the entire pool to themselves. Fantastic! (Sorry readers, the place has now closed, or to be more precise, has now been converted into a zoo.)

Anyway, John and Jayne had had a great day out at Empuriabrava where they had sat on the end of the pier at the harbour-entrance, consuming cheap champagne and a gorgeous spit-roast chicken – as only the Spanish can do it – watching the sleek and magnificent high-powered cruisers opening-up to full throttle as they left the confines of the harbour to seek their natural environment of the sea. Very exciting indeed and wonderful to watch the amateur captains complete with suitable Humphrey Bogart-type hats, posing on the high bridges of their vessels in their moment of glory as the engines roared throatily and the razor-like bows bit into the deep blue waves of the Mediterranean. Absolutely magic!

After lunch at Empuriabrava, our pair returned to the campsite to find that an Englishwoman, who later became known to them as Pat, with an old, heavily-laden Granada-estate and six children between the ages of 3 and 10 years, was having great difficulty in putting up a massive marquee-like frame-tent. The poor lady didn't have a clue, and judging by the amount of perspiration that poured from her body in the hot July afternoon sun, she had had enough.

John and Jayne, after introducing themselves, immediately offered to help her.

'You just sit in the shade and amuse the kids, Pat. Jayne and I will sort this out,' John sympathised. 'You look just about done-in.'

A very relieved Pat only too readily did as she was bid and in no time at all was fast asleep under a tree, her kids playing by themselves quietly.

A Gaze into Holidaze

John and Jayne worked non-stop for an hour-and-a-half before the tent was up and capable of habitation. John crossed to the sleeping Pat and gently shook her awake. 'Come on, sleepyhead, wake up.' Slowly the woman returned to the land of the living before John continued.

'There you go, Pat, at least all you have to do now is put your bits and pieces inside. We've even put up the three bedrooms and the larder for you. It'll be a home-from-home for you,' Jayne encouraged. 'Where did you stay last night?'

'Nowhere last night, we've been travelling all through the night. The night before we stayed in Paris on a small campsite in the middle of the city. We've been on the road for such a long time that the kids and I are shattered.'

'In the middle of Paris?' John questioned, horrified. 'That must have been very difficult for you. How on earth did you manage?'

'I didn't, quite honestly. I got in a bit of a pickle and fortunately some lads on motorcycles helped me.' Pat's face was worried. 'I think that the tent is too much for me to handle on my own but the salesperson who sold the tent said it would be easy to put up.'

'That's what they always say,' muttered John to himself in disgust.

Pat continued. 'You see, I lost my husband last year to cancer and I wanted ever so much to bring the kids away on holiday abroad to help them get over their father. Bert, my husband that is, and I had never been abroad and we'd promised the kids that we would go this year. Unfortunately, Bert died but I couldn't let them down, could I?'

'No, of course not,' whispered Jayne tenderly, her arm gently holding Pat's shoulder. 'You couldn't disappoint them after losing their Dad.'

'Come on,' said John cheerfully. 'Let's go over to our little tent and have a cuppa and relax a bit.' Turning to the six kids John shouted, 'Come on, kids, it's tea-and-biscuits-time so follow me.'

So, all nine of them sat on the grass outside John and Jayne's five-man tent and enjoyed cups of tea and several packets of biscuits in the shade of the large, leafy trees that surrounded them. The kids were as good as gold and just sat there quietly, and readily drank the cool lemonade that Jayne provided for them.

Pat looked pitifully but longingly at the five-man ridge-tent belonging to John and Jayne. 'Is it easy to put up . . . your tent?'

'Yes it is,' said John. 'A lot easier than yours, to be honest. There is no way that one person can put up your tent, Pat. It's much too heavy for one strong man let alone a woman on her own. Frankly, it's much too large for you to handle.'

'But there are seven of us you see, John. That's why Betty, the salesperson, sold me this big one.'

John had to be careful because he knew that Pat had made a big mistake. He knew that all the salesperson had been interested in doing was to sell a very large and expensive tent to result in the

A Gaze into Holidaze

fattest possible commission for her. John was inwardly angry because it was only too obvious that Pat had been totally conned by the so-called Betty.

John said as gently as he could, 'If you take it back to the dealer when you get back to the UK and explain your difficulties he may be able to help you.' He didn't really believe a word of what he had just said but felt that he had to suggest something useful. 'Perhaps he will buy the tent back from you at a good price because you will have only used the tent for one holiday.'

'Do you think so, John?' Pat asked, a pleading look in her eyes. 'You see it was very expensive and I would hate to think that I had wasted money that I could hardly afford.'

'Yes, I think so,' John assured her. 'Then you can buy two five-man ridge-tents like ours and you'll be able to put those up in a jiffy. Even your ten-year-old lad could put one up while you put the other one up. Half-an-hour between you lot and you'll be laughing.'

Pat seemed to brighten up in spite of her fatigue from the long journey. 'Thank you both for your kind help and advice. I feel better about the whole thing already. I'm going to get myself and the kids in the swimming-pool now and then we'll all feel much better.'

'Good idea,' said Jayne. 'John and I are going to the local supermarket now for some bits and pieces for dinner. Do you want anything?'

'No thanks,' replied Pat. 'I've got plenty of things in the car and the kids and I are looking forward to a home-cooked paella. I've always wanted to try one.'

'OK. See you in about two hours then,' said Jayne. 'At six o'clock it will be much cooler, I think.'

John and Jayne left Pat and the kids rushing towards the pool as they drove the Red Bug towards Figueres, some ten miles away.

'That poor woman,' whispered Jayne as they drove on and she blankly looked out at the passing traffic. 'What fool would sell her such a tent. You can see she has little money and now she's spent it on the wrong tent. And after losing her husband last year. What a terrible tragedy.'

John also felt tremendous sympathy for the woman – he just had to do something to help her. He remained silent for a few minutes before suddenly declaring, his jaw firm in determination, 'I am going to take this problem on-board on behalf of Pat. When we get back to the UK I will speak to the dealer concerned and explain the situation very clearly to him. Maybe a man-to-man talk will help.'

'And I will join you so we'll both have a go. Someone's got to help Pat.' Jayne held her hand out to John. 'Is it a deal?'

'It's a deal,' agreed John with a big smile as he shook Jayne's hand heartily.

True to their word, John and Jayne arrived back at the campsite almost at the stroke of six o'clock.

A Gaze into Holidaze

Running to meet them was Pat, her face on the point of tears. Behind her, almost in military order, ran the children.

'What's the matter?' Jayne demanded urgently.

'Please come quickly, I'm frightened and I don't know what to do.' Pat spun around and ran towards the big tent, John, Jayne and the kids closely at her heels.

There, upon the cooker in the kitchen-area of the massive tent was a huge paella-dish full of rice and other delicacies to complete the tasty, traditional Spanish dish. Unfortunately, John and Jayne could not see the goodies, because the entire thirty-inches diameter dish, together with all of its contents, was completely covered in very large, very buzzing, black flies. The dish appeared to be moving with them as they got stuck into the cooking paella which was obviously to their delight and taste.

'What can I do,' murmured Pat. 'Nothing is going right for me.'

'It's not your fault, Pat,' soothed Jayne. 'It's partly my fault because I should have told you not to start thinking of cooking in this part of Spain until at least eight o'clock at night. Nine o'clock would be better because all of those beastly flies will have disappeared by then. Maybe they go back to bed or something, who knows?'

Pat, now cradled in Jayne's arms, looked tearfully up at her. 'Will they go away Jayne? All the paella is ruined now and the kids are starving.'

'No problem. John will get rid of this mess together with the confounded flies.' She looked over at John as she hugged the woman closer to her. 'Right, John?'

'Right, Jayne.'

Jayne was now fully in charge. 'Then we are all going to a little inexpensive restaurant that John and I use in Castelló d'Empuries. It's not far and we can walk it.' Jayne pointed. 'Over that little bridge and a short walk along the road and we are there.' Turning to Pat she continued. 'Put your glad rags on and we'll have some fun.'

'But Jayne . . .' Pat broke off, embarrassment on her face.

Jayne sensed what was coming. 'Pat, it's our treat and our pleasure.'

'How can I ever repay you?' Pat whispered. 'I really don't . . .'

Jayne put her hand gently over Pat's mouth as she interrupted her. 'With a smile, Pat, with a smile.'

And they had a lovely, simple, inexpensive Spanish meal of paella and wine together with a great night. Pat and the kids loved it. John even brought hope to Pat when he enlightened her that he would consider it a privilege if she would let him do all that he could to get a good deal for her on the trade-in of her huge frame-tent against the two smaller five-man ridge-tents.

On their return to the UK, John and Jayne took up their promised 'fight' with the dealer who happened to be in Cambridge. Only it turned out not to be a fight because the dealer couldn't have been more apologetic and helpful – without any prompting from either John or Jayne. His only comment was simply, 'We shouldn't have sold her the tent in the first place. You just can't get the staff these days, can you?'

****

Whiskers galore . . .
The following year, John and Jayne returned to the same campsite at Castelló d'Empuries near Roses in Northern Spain. As usual, even though it was the hot month of July, the campsite was virtually empty and they could erect their five-manner in the usual spot which had sufficient shade to meet the heat of the day whilst remaining not too far from the toilets in one direction and the Olympic-sized swimming-pool in the other. Absolutely first class, and there was certainly going to be nothing to spoil this holiday. John and Jayne had even brought two pedal-bikes on the back of the Red Bug to cycle and explore the wonderfully-flat surrounding countryside between Roses and L'Escala to the south.

Our heroes had been on the campsite for about a week and on this particular late afternoon were settling down for a bite to eat. The barbecue was sizzling nicely as John looked around at the few people that were on the site. They were well dispersed and other than greeting a 'good morning' in their native languages of French, Dutch, Spanish and German, seemed more than happy to keep themselves to themselves.

'Absolute peace, Jayne, eh?' John commented contentedly as he turned over a sausage on the barbie.

'Fantastic,' Jayne replied. 'It's great that the other campers spread themselves out. It gives you such a feeling of space, doesn't it?'

Even as she said the words, around the bend of the single track in the campsite came this apparition on a pedal cycle. The apparition consisted of a man of indeterminate age, but probably in his late fifties to early sixties, with long and flowing grey hair at the sides of his head whilst lacking most of it on top. Making up for this was a greying beard that went almost to his navel. His clothes, namely denim jeans and a long-sleeved shirt, although whole appeared to be shabby and dirty. In fact, all of him seemed shabby and dirty and a good scrub of him and his clothes would have been completely in order.

The man stopped his bike, leaned back and looked around. One flip-flop-covered foot remained on the ground to support the machine whilst, his body twisted in a half-turn, one arm rested on the small bag that was tied with thick rope to a carrier-frame behind the saddle.

'God, I hope he isn't going to stay near us,' Jayne whispered, panicking. 'He's filthy. I don't want him near us.'

A Gaze into Holidaze

'Yes, I bet he's a bit smelly too,' returned John. 'Don't look at him, Jayne. If he catches your eye he might interpret it as a sign of friendship and come over to us. I don't want that bloody tramp near me.' John attempted to lighten the situation a bit. 'Think of all the flies he will draw with that pong. I bet he doesn't know what a bath or shower is. With bloody whiskers like that he's probably got six-months of old dribbled food in 'em.'

'Shut up, John, he might hear you,' scolded Jayne. 'Poor chap has probably had some bad luck to be so down and out. Have some pity.'

'Too bloody lazy more than likely,' John replied. 'And anyway, I don't want Whiskers near us, okay?'

John and Jayne busied themselves with the barbeque and pretended to ignore the progress of the tramp. By now, Whiskers had dismounted from his bike and proceeded to untie the small bag at the back.

'Well, at least he's far enough away from us,' John volunteered angrily. 'But with all the damned campsite nearly empty he's still only about thirty yards away. And what's more, he's going to set-up right between us and the toilets. Sod's law, isn't it?'

And that is exactly what Whiskers did. He laid the bicycle on the ground and proceeded to lay out a ground sheet right bang in the middle of the route that John and Jayne would normally have taken to go to the toilet-block.

'Shall we ask him to move a bit?' Jayne asked sheepishly.

'We can't do that,' John replied firmly. 'The man has the right to park himself wherever he wants to on the entire campsite. Anyway, I'm not going near him 'cos you don't know what I might catch. He's probably riddled with lice and things.'

'Oh John, do you think so?'

'Don't be daft,' John returned quickly to reassure Jayne. 'I'm only teasing, Jayne, because I don't think any form of lice could stand the smell!'

Jayne slapped John on the shoulder as hard as she could. 'Are you ever going to stop taking the mickey out of me?'

'No,' stated John flatly but with a twinkle in his eye. 'You are very teasable, you know. Don't worry about Whiskers. He'll do you no harm and anyway, I'll protect you!'

Out of the corner of their eyes, John and Jayne watched Whiskers put up a small one-man tent. He then removed a full litre-bottle of red wine from his bag, took a long swig from it and then lay on the ground flat on his back. In minutes he was asleep and soundly snoring.

'I'll pretend to go to the loo and do a recce,' murmured John. 'I'll make sure that there is no problem with this chap.'

'Be careful,' whispered Jayne, afraid that the sound of her voice would wake the sleeping tramp some thirty yards away.

John walked quietly over and, as he slowly and deliberately passed the sleeping man, carefully studied him taking in every detail of the man's very-tanned face. John's assumption of the man's age proved to be about right by placing him at around sixty. The man lay on his back snoring loudly with his mouth wide open. In the dark cavern of his mouth, the lips of which vibrated jelly-like every time the man exhaled, were only a few surprisingly white teeth. The remainder of the set had been removed at some time or other leaving large black gaps in between the few remaining fangs. The man's wild beard and thick unruly moustache were stained a dark-yellow around the mouth as if something had been dribbled into the hair time and time again.

'Probably can't find his mouth when he's drunk,' thought John as he turned around and walked back to the waiting Jayne.

'What's he like?' questioned Jayne as John sat next to her.

'Bloody scruffy to say the least,' John replied. 'Look Jayne, there is no problem so don't panic. But when you want to go to the loo, I'm coming with you.'

'Is that necessary?' Jayne asked quietly. 'I'm sure I'll be alright. The man is harmless and just a bit dirty.'

'I'm sure you're right,' stated John firmly. 'But let's not take a chance, eh? I don't want you walking past Whiskers on your own at any time. This is not a request, it's an order, okay?'

'Do you think he's Spanish, John?'

'Must be I suppose. He can't have come far on a push-bike, can he?'

A week passed and John and Jayne noticed that Whiskers got into a set routine. He would go off on his bike around ten o'clock each morning and return each evening at about six. Religiously he would then eat almost a complete baguette with cheese, accompanied with a full litre of red wine. Cradling the bottle under his arm he would then lie on his groundsheet, flat on his back, go to sleep, snoring, whistling and mouth vibrating profusely. This would continue until about eight or nine o'clock when he would wake up, go to the toilet-block armed with a small towel and plastic carrier-bag only to return a half-an-hour later to disappear inside his tent for the night. After a minute or so of fumbling inside the tent, all would be still.

'Funny bloke, eh Jayne?'

'Certainly is, John, but at least he does no harm. What do you think he fumbles with when he goes to bed?' asked Jayne.

'No, he doesn't do any harm is the answer to your first statement. Ladies shouldn't ask questions like that is the answer to your second bit,' declared John. 'You know, I fancy that he looks a bit cleaner now. Do you think so?'

'I don't look at him. He looks the same to me as the day he arrived. I wonder where he goes each day?'

'I don't know. Still, he's no trouble, that's the main thing. All he seems to want to do on the campsite is eat and sleep,' John said. 'Let's not forget his daily rations of a litre of vino-tinto,' he added quickly.

A Gaze into Holidaze

Now, John and Jayne enjoyed making their own light-entertainment on the campsite in the evenings, by playing the guitar and singing together. Although John only strummed chords on the guitar it sounded pretty good during the songs when Jayne's soprano voice harmonised with John's bass tones. In fact, it was not unusual for quite a crowd to congregate around the pair on an evening and listen to their rendering of various folk-songs and ballads.

On this particular warm night it was about nine o'clock and Whiskers had gone to bed in his one-man tent after his usual litre of red wine. John and Jayne, for the first time since they had arrived, started playing the guitar and singing their versions of particular John Denver numbers, fortified by a bottle or two of red wine. They were in the middle of *Country Roads* when the one-man tent started shaking vigorously as the man inside obviously tried to turn-over, not an easy feat in a one-man tent of this minute size. Next thing the balding, shaggy head of Whiskers thrust out through the flap and turned towards the singing duo. A brief pause and the pyjama-clad body of Whiskers followed the head until he was standing beside the one-man tent openly listening to John's and Jayne's performance.

'Didn't know Whiskers wore pyjamas,' thought John as he caught Jayne's eye and nodded to her as a signal to keep on singing.

All through the song Whiskers stood and watched,

listening intently, not moving a muscle. Then as the last notes died he clapped heartily and immediately started walking smartly towards John and Jayne who were sitting outside their tent on a couple of folding chairs.

'Don't say a word,' muttered John, his words muffled behind his hand. 'I'll deal with this, don't you worry.'

'But what if . . .' started Jayne.

'Leave it entirely to me. I'll sort it.' John's flashing eyes told Jayne that it was time to shut up.

Whiskers stopped in front of John. John looked coldly up at the bearded man but could not help but notice that Whiskers' pyjamas were spotlessly clean.

'Did I kinda hear you play a John Denver number there guy?' The voice was deep, cultured and educated.

'Good grief!' exclaimed John, shocked. 'You're an American.'

'Well I guess you could say that,' the soft drawl was quite captivating.

'Please sit down and join us,' offered Jayne, somehow hypnotised by the accent from the deep-south of the United States.

'Yes,' John added, annoyed at Jayne's invitation after all that he had said to her about Whiskers. 'Do join us and have a glass of wine.'

And sit down Whiskers did. Sitting cross-legged on the grass he introduced himself as Tom Jefferson. He was delighted to share the bottle, or later bottles, of red wine and even joined in some of the songs. John could not help but see that, although perhaps a little unkempt in appearance, Tom was actually spotless in every way. The staining of his moustache and beard around his mouth area was due to an automobile accident that resulted in severe scar-tissue in that region. Tom had simply grown the whiskers in an attempt to hide these scars. What is more, the accident which occurred in Death Valley, California, had actually medically 'killed' Tom and he had been pronounced dead. Fortunately, the medical team concerned with the incident brought him back to life, to allow him to write a book about his out-of-body 'death' experience, which he had had published. (Later, Tom sent a signed copy to John and Jayne from the United States.) Obviously, a fascinating debate took place well into the night about Tom's experience, and Tom proved to be a very interesting and worldly character.

John teased Tom about the first impressions that they had had of him when he first arrived on the campsite, to which Tom unhesitatingly replied, 'And so would you look dirty if you had spent as long as I have in these duds.'

'Where have you come from then, Tom?' John asked innocently.

'Paris, John, Paris,' Tom replied. 'And believe me, it's a heck of a long way, especially when you don't have a change of clothes.'

'Great Scot! Paris. That's got to be six hundred miles?' John questioned in amazement.

'Yup,' agreed Tom. 'And it's going to be six hundred hard and long miles back.'

'But on the train, surely?' questioned Jayne.

'Nope. On the bicycle. I am going to meet my son who's flying in from the US of A and I'm riding all the way back to meet him. It's something I've always wanted to do and I am determined to do it.'

'Well, good luck on that, mate,' chuckled John. 'By the way, what do you do for a living back in the States, if you don't mind me asking?'

'Not at all,' answered Tom. 'I'm a Professor at Harvard University. Have you heard of it?'

Tom left a few days later with fondest wishes for his future from John and Jayne. Tom made it back to Paris on the bike and met his son on time. He kept in touch with John and Jayne for a good number of years until, regrettably, Tom died in the mid-nineties.

****

Then there was Martine and Igor . . .

During the same holiday that John and Jayne had met Tom Jefferson of the USA, they also met a Belgian couple called Martine and Igor. Martine and Igor were camped on the far side of the campsite at Castelló d'Empuries, and the two couples had very little contact until the last few days of the holiday and well after Tom had returned to Paris.

Igor was a six-feet four-inch giant of a man who rarely spoke at all, whereas Martine, who was

A Gaze into Holidaze

apparently his second wife, was a petite little blonde who made up for Igor's 'man-of-few-words' character in no uncertain manner. Both had a good command of the English language and Igor actually taught English in a school in Belgium. However, both of them, particularly Igor, were very under-confident about speaking English in conversation, which again surprised John and Jayne because the Belgian couple's English was really good. Not that this mattered one iota to John and Jayne who, on the only occasion that they spent with Martine and Igor, found the evening to be pleasant although a little boring to say the least.

'Thank God that's over,' commented John at the end of the particularly long and laborious evening after Martine and Igor had returned to their trailer-tent.

'Why do you say that, John?' replied Jayne. 'I thought that it was a very nice evening and Martine was very pleasant company in her own way.'

'Yes, Martine may have been chatty but Igor was bloody hard work with his 'yes' and 'no' answers to my questions when I tried my best to get a conversation going with him. It was like trying to wade through treacle. No! Wading through treacle would have been a bloody lot easier.'

'Well I thought Igor was a very pleasant man and he chatted to me fine. It must have been you, John, you probably frightened him to death.'

'Frightened him!' exclaimed John with a laugh. 'It's me that should have been frightened. The bloke reminded me of Lurch in the Adams Family on tele. Six-feet-four if he's an inch and with the personality of a pall bearer carrying a coffin.'

The conversation paused for a full minute before Jayne blurted out, 'I think Martine is a very nice person.'

'How do you mean?'

'I mean what I say. I think Martine is a very nice person,' repeated Jayne. 'She's chatty and good company. She's told me all about her family. Did you hear that she's one of six children and her Mum, who is a widow, has held the entire family together during their growing up?'

'Yes, I picked that up,' agreed John. 'She's streets ahead of Igor regarding conversational ability. I repeat that Igor is bloody hard work.'

Jayne changed the subject. 'Martine's got a good figure for her age, hasn't she? She keeps herself very trim by exercising a lot.'

'Yes,' John nodded. 'She's got a good figure. Very petite and trim. Unfortunately she hasn't got much of a bust though.'

John failed to avoid Jayne's swift slap which landed behind his ear.

'Ouch! That hurt,' John shouted, rubbing the side of his head. 'Anyway, it's true. She is very non-busted.'

'Trust you to notice,' replied Jayne, not hiding the sarcasm in her voice. 'Is that all you can think of?'

'Well, most of the time, I suppose. Certainly most of the time when I'm awake anyway.' John paused before continuing. 'Come to think of it, most of the time when I'm asleep too.'

This time, John was ready and easily avoided the swishing hand that was aimed at his head. A few minutes passed before Jayne spoke again.

'Anyway, the girl can't help it.'

'Help what?'

'Having no bust, as you put it,' sighed Jayne. 'Or as I would prefer to put it, she can't help being flat-chested.'

'Flat-chested isn't the word for it,' John added. 'She's got no chest at all and I reckon she's actually going in where she should be poking out.'

'I agree,' Jayne continued stubbornly. 'But again she can't help it so you shouldn't comment on it. In fact, you are being downright rude.'

'Okay! Point taken, if you'll forgive the pun,' said John resignedly. 'But I still must say that with hubby being like Lurch with about as much conversational ability as a lavatory seat, perhaps we should not get too involved with them again.'

Jayne thought for a while before continuing. 'Anyway, they're going home tomorrow so that's the end of that.' Jayne looked at John as he suddenly beamed and started to chuckle. 'Why are you laughing, John?'

'I'm laughing at the injustice I have just created when I compared Igor's conversational ability with a lavatory seat!'

'What injustice?' questioned Jayne, being totally puzzled by John's humour at times.

'Well, I did the lavatory seat an injustice because it makes more noise than Igor.'

'How?'

'It speaks to me when I press the bit on the top to make it flush. And that's more noise than I've had out of Lurch all night!'

They both laughed and finally agreed that Martine and Igor were not their cup of tea. Therefore, short of saying goodbye to them on the following day, that would be the end of the relationship and they would never set eyes on the couple again.

Or so they thought!

The following year, again in July, John and Jayne returned to the campsite at Castelló d'Empuries. It was again wonderfully quiet and had lost none of its charm. The few tents that were there on their arrival were well spread throughout the entire site, and the couple managed to erect the tent with no one within fifty yards of them. Peace, perfect peace!!

It was late afternoon and they were just settling down to a splendid cup of tea after all the work had been done. Jayne casually looked across the field at nothing in particular when she saw, boldly striding towards them, Lurch. He was not carrying a coffin, but judging by the deadpan look on his face he certainly should have been.

At the same time, John spotted him. 'Oh no! I can't believe it!' Drawing his lips back over his teeth in his impersonation of Humphrey Bogart, John continued in the modified classical lines of

A Gaze into Holidaze

Casablanca. 'Of all the campsites, in all the world, he has to walk into mine . . . and he still hasn't bloody-well learned how to smile!'

'Shut up, John, behave yourself. He'll hear you.'

By now Igor had arrived. He kissed Jayne on both cheeks in greeting and holding out his hand to John he said, 'John, we are pleased to see you. Martine and I have been waiting and hoping that you would come to this campsite again this year.'

'Hello, Igor,' was all that John could muster in reply as he shook Igor's hand, even though his inner feelings were, 'Bloody-hell, not again!'

'Come,' Igor invited, still with no warmth in his drawn features. 'We have champagne waiting for you. Martine has a bottle of your favourite Du Bois chilling as we speak.'

'Well, we've just arrived, Igor,' John stated firmly. 'We've had a long drive and we are pretty shattered. But thanks for the kind thought.'

'Nonsense,' insisted Igor. 'Du Bois is just what you need to brighten you up and I would like you to meet my son, Boris. We have told Boris all about you and he very much wants to meet you.'

John caught Jayne's nod of agreement. 'We would love to come over and meet him, Igor, wouldn't we, John?'

'Er . . . well, perhaps for a moment then,' John stammered. 'But we won't stay too long, Igor. We are very tired.'

Across the site they went, John with a face like a child's smacked bottom, until they finally arrived at Igor's trailer-tent. John and Jayne stopped in their tracks. Jayne's mouth gaped open in amazement. John's eyes stuck out like organ-stops.

There, standing with feet astride in the skimpiest of bikini bottoms imaginable, a glass of bubbling champagne in each hand, was a totally-topless Martine. She was as petite as ever but possessed an enormous pair of breasts which stood out from her tiny body like a pair of very-rounded watermelons.

'Hello Jayne,' she said, a broad smile on her face. 'We have been waiting a long time to see you again.' She gave Jayne her drink and kissed her on both cheeks in warm greeting. 'And one for you, John,' she said huskily. Putting the drink into John's hand she reached up to kiss John on his cheeks.

John was still suffering from shock as he felt the glass of champagne placed in his hand. His shock intensified incredibly as he felt two severely hard points of the 36C bosoms pressing into his chest. 36C at least if John was any sort of judge. As Martine pulled away, a broad smile on her face, John just did not know where to put his eyes. He only hoped that Martine was not aware of his embarrassment because he knew that he was blushing deeply.

'Hello, Martine,' he gasped. 'Gosh, you've changed.' What else could he say?

'Do you like them?' she beamed, thrusting out her chest proudly.

A Gaze into Holidaze

'Well, er . . . y . . . y . . . yesss,' stammered John as he glanced sideways at Jayne, his eyes pleading for help.

'They, I mean, you look lovely Martine,' Jayne came to the rescue. 'When did you have the operation for bigger . . . I mean . . . to change your appearance?' Jayne was desperate to be tactful.

'Igor bought them for me for Christmas,' replied Martine innocently. 'He is ever so pleased with them, aren't you, Igor?'

'Would you like to touch them, John?' Igor offered, obviously not realising the way that the British felt about things of this nature. 'They are very firm, firmer than usual in fact. Please feel them, they are a lovely texture.'

'Well, not just now, Igor, if you don't mind,' John hastened, feeling an absolute prat. 'I am sure that they feel fine and they certainly look lovely, but I'd rather not just now.'

'Thank you, John,' Martine said beaming like a Cheshire cat at the cream. The Belgian woman was obviously and genuinely delighted by the compliments she had received, her new assets still pointing proudly upwards at an angle more than sufficient to defeat the pull of gravity.

'Meet Boris, my son,' Igor said, pushing a tall, gangly twelve year-old boy forward into the group.

John and Jayne, more than embarrassed at meeting Martine and her new additions, gladly turned their attention to the young lad and shook his hand over-zealously in greeting. John in particular was beetroot-red from the top of his head to the part of his neck that disappeared into his tee-shirt.

And that is how the remainder of the holiday proceeded. John and Jayne could not move without Igor and Martine, and sometimes Boris, at all times being there in their faces as it were. From first thing in the morning as soon as John opened the flap of their five-man tent, Igor was there offering a beer. God, a beer at eight o'clock in the morning. Yuk!! Every time John was in range of Igor's tent, Igor would demand that John enter and have a beer or a glass of Du Bois. Igor seemed overawed or even infatuated with John.

'Bloody man fancies me!' John complained to Jayne after a week of being followed around by Igor who was still behaving like Lurch, the pallbearer. 'He still doesn't say a bloody word to me in conversation unless it's about his wife's bloody boob-job or trying to get me to drink at all hours of the day.'

'Don't be silly,' Jayne replied in her best peacekeeping tone. 'He just likes you.'

'Well, like me or not, I feel like punching him on the nose and I don't care how big he is. Do you know what happened this morning when I got up early to go to the loo?'

'No darling, what?'

'I crept from bush to bush like bloody 007. As you know, we have to pass Igor's tent to get to the loo because there is no other way. When I got close

A Gaze into Holidaze

to his tent I almost crawled on my stomach sniper-style to get past without being seen. Fortunately, there was no-one around to see me or they would have thought that I was off my chump sneaking around at eight o'clock in the morning like the bloody SAS.'

'I can't believe it,' laughed Jayne, unable to keep a straight face any longer. 'Did you make it to the loo without being seen by Igor?'

'Yes,' confirmed John coldly, not amused by Jayne's outburst of laughter. 'Yes, I made it and had just settled down on the throne to relax for a morning constitutional when guess what?'

'What?' croaked Jayne, her hand pressed into her mouth in an attempt to suppress further giggles.

'There was a knock on the door of the loo accompanied by Igor's deep voice, "John, are you in there? We have San Miguel's waiting for you in our tent." The bastard must have been laying in wait for me.'

Jayne laughed uncontrollably, the tears running down her cheeks. 'You mean he actually followed you into the toilet?' John nodded, but a smile had started to tug at the corner of his mouth as he started to see the funny side of the situation. 'What did you say to him then, John?'

'I mustered up my best Scottish accent and said "Bollocks! Can a wee man no' have a shit in peace on this bloody campsite!"'

'That's not very nice, John, after the man had

just offered you a San Miguel beer. Especially when it's one of your favourite beers. Was he angry at what you said?'

'No,' stated John. 'In fact, for the first time since I have known him, Igor actually laughed. At least I assume that the deep throaty roar that I heard through the toilet door was a laugh, although I suppose it could have been wind!'

'Did you go back with Igor for a drink afterwards and was everything okay?' questioned Jayne anxiously. Jayne was always worried about offending anyone.

'Yes, I did go back for a quick one with Igor, Boris, Martine and her two beauties which were bare and poking my eyes out even at eight-thirty in the morning. But only after I had finished my morning ablutions. I made him wait until then.'

'You mean that Martine's breasts were uncovered in front of you even at that time of the morning?'

'Yes,' stated John flatly. 'Even young Boris had them thrust down his throat – er, if you'll forgive the pun – and he's only about twelve or thirteen. She thinks that he's too young to realise what's going on with his step-mum's boobs. Well, she couldn't be more wrong because Boris is a healthy young lad whose hormones appear to be functioning normally judging by the way he couldn't take his eyes off Martine's latest bits.' Jayne's eyes widened.

'I said bits not . . .'

'John!' Jayne stopped him.

A Gaze into Holidaze

Another week of the holiday went by but nothing changed regarding Martine and Igor who insisted on being constantly in John and Jayne's faces. Especially Martine's boobs which were flaunted at any and every opportunity that arose. Everywhere that John and Jayne went, Martine's mammaries seemed to get there before them. She was totally obsessed with them and if it were possible for Martine to go topless, a thing that Jayne never did, then Martine would go topless. Martine didn't bother to talk any more, all she did was pose as provocatively as she was able and thrust out her magnificent silicon-jobs. Pose and thrust, pose and thrust, pose and thrust. Even Jayne got hacked-off with Martine's endless showing-off of her new toys.

Finally, the holiday came to an end and both couples said their goodbyes, John and Jayne vowing never to see Martine and Igor again.

And they didn't. As John said to Jayne on the long drive home to the United Kingdom after a disappointing holiday, 'You cannot win them all.'

John did compose and sing a little song to Jayne on the way home in an attempt to lighten the gloom which seemed to have descended on the spirits of the pair, particularly Jayne, who always got the most from her holiday and was usually on a high when returning from them to face the drudgery of everyday life in the months ahead.

Sung to the tune of 'Old MacDonald had a Farm,' John began:

'Martine's flat-chest was not good
Yes that's very true.
Igor said to eat more food,
But alas it didn't do.
With a tweek tweek here
And a tweek tweek there
Here a tweek, there a tweek
Everywhere a tweek tweek,
Martine's flat-chest started to grow
Like two twin peaks of dough.
Martine's pleased, she starts to pose
Giving new breasts a thrust
John did blush from head to toe.
She said, 'John, you like my bust?'
With a tweek tweek here
And a tweek tweek there
Here a tweek, there a tweek
Everywhere a tweek tweek.
With a pose – thrust here
And a pose – thrust there.
Here a pose, there a thrust.
Everywhere a new thrust.
Martine's pleased with her brand new toys
They're for men not boys.'

This was all it took to make Jayne burst out laughing when she started to see the funny-side of the previous couple of weeks. 'Well, the holiday with the three of them did have some bright moments I suppose.'

'Oh yes!' exclaimed John with a smile. 'When was that then? And don't you mean the holiday with the five of them? You forgot to mention Martine's new boobs – er, I mean Martine's new playmates!'

'And when Boris popped the champagne corks and ran to catch them before they hit the ground,' Jayne volunteered with a smile.

'Yes, I suppose so,' John agreed sarcastically. 'That gave a pleasant ten minutes in the whole two weeks I guess. Tell you what, let's make a pact never to bother with people on holiday whom we don't like – no matter how offended they may get. Deal?' He held out his hand. 'Let's shake on it.'

Taking his hand and shaking it energetically, Jayne declared very emphatically, 'It's a deal.'

And they both meant it at the time of their declaration, but who were they trying to kid? John and Jayne were both lovely people who made up an even nicer couple, who could not offend anyone to save their lives.

****

A bigger one . . . ?

It was April and just at the start of a new camping season, probably about three or four years since the commencement of John's and Jayne's camping adventures in their five-man ridge-tent. John and Jayne found themselves camping on their favourite campsite in West Wales on a miserably cold and windy day, with the rain coming off the Irish Sea in torrents. It was two in the afternoon and it was obvious that there would be no let-up in the weather for the remainder of the day. John was getting very restless.

Putting aside the book that he was reading, he gazed out of the rain-smeared Perspex window of the tent at the sea, two hundred cliff-faced feet below them. He gave a deep sigh and thought quietly for a few moments.

'I want a bigger one.'

'That's what every man I have ever known says,' replied Jayne, not even looking up from her book. 'I keep telling you that size doesn't matter. It's love, not length, that a girl looks for in a man.'

'Oh! Be serious can't you?' snapped John impatiently as he jumped to his feet from his folding-chair only to hit his head on the sodden canvas-roof of the tent above him. This caused a stream of cold water to pour down his neck uncomfortably.

'Hell's bells and buckets of blood!' shouted John in anger as he abruptly sat back in his chair. 'I'm damned-well soaked now and I haven't even been outside in the bloody rain. You can't even stand up straight in this blasted tent.'

'There is no need to swear, John,' Jayne sighed as she marked her page and closed her book. 'You wanted to come camping this weekend in spite of me telling you it was too early in the year. And,' she enforced the word, 'in spite of the weather forecast which was absolutely ridiculous. Who did you think you were – Noah, because you certainly need an ark to get about in this weather?'

A Gaze into Holidaze

'Look Jayne,' John continued, ignoring Jayne's sarcasm. 'Look at us. We both love camping, that's why we're here in April and . . .'

'I said not to come, so . . .' interrupted Jayne.

John held up his hand in protest and said, patiently but firmly, 'Jayne, let me finish please.' Seeing Jayne frowning in frustration but saying nothing, he continued. 'We love camping and here we are, stuck in this so-called five-man tent. God knows why they call it a five-man tent because you can only get two people in the bedroom area where they told us we could sleep three. That's the area where we planned to store our gear if you remember, Jayne, only to find that it was impossible. Now we have to store it out here in the porch. And in this porch you can't swing a cat let alone if you had to sleep another two persons in here. Look at it,' he pointed around the tiny porch. 'There's room for you and me to sit on small folding-chairs to huddle around a table which is quite laughable when you consider that two cups and a plate and the damned thing's full.'

Jayne opened her mouth to speak but, after a pause, thought better of it and allowed John to continue.

John went on with confidence to vent his pent up frustration. 'Furthermore, you can't stand up in the bloody tent and even when sitting down you can't lean back in your chair because your head and shoulders hit the sides of the thing. And, when it's raining like this the whole thing is bloody uncomfortable. Five men in a floor area of nine feet by four-feet-six inches, what a bloody farce! After a day inside this tent I feel like the Hunchback of Notre Dame, just call me Quasimodo from now on if you don't mind.'

'Finished?' Jayne asked quietly, looking at the rain as it lashed against the Perspex windows of the tent which shook violently in the coastal winds that plagued the entire region of the campsite.

'Yes,' sighed John. 'I'm finished.'

'Do you feel better now?'

'Yes! Much better, thank you.'

'Well, I suggest that we go and buy a bigger tent.'

John's eyes lit up. 'Do you mean it, do you honestly mean it? Can we afford it? Do we have enough money in the bank? 'Cos you are Old Money-Bags looking after our account.'

'Yes we have, John, more than enough. And there is enough there to do the other little thing that seems to have slipped your mind.'

'What's that?' puzzled John.

'I think we are going to need a bigger car to carry the bigger tent, don't you?' Jayne smiled and continued. 'Not just that, we will need a bigger car to have my extra kit around. Kit like sun beds, decent table and chairs, a gas cooker . . . Gosh! Imagine having a couple of gas rings instead of that little primus-type cooker you used when you went off on your motorbike all those years ago. Think of eating proper food instead of tins of soup. Yum! Yum!'

A Gaze into Holidaze

They hugged and kissed each other happily and a couple of hours later and in spite of the near-gale blowing at the time, they took down the five-man ridge-tent that, notwithstanding John's complaints, had served them well. However, John and Jayne were now experienced campers and it was time to move on.

And move on they did. The following morning they visited various tent-dealers in the area around them and by the end of the day returned to their home with a brand-new Cabanon frame-tent with floor dimensions of about ten feet long by ten feet wide. In addition to this they had purchased all of the 'extras' that Jayne thought would make the tent-on-location a home-from-home.

All of this kit was carried in a brand-new two-wheeled trailer, which was towed by a second-hand Volvo estate car.

'I didn't think that you would need the trailer to carry the gear, John,' said Jayne when they arrived back at their bungalow. 'I know it's a bit bulky but surely it would have gone in the back of the Volvo?'

'I think you're right, sweetheart,' chuckled John mischievously. 'But I had a flash of brilliance when I thought of all the wine that we can bring back with us from France, Spain and Italy. Gosh! The money we'll save will more than cover the cost of the holiday. It will certainly cover the cost of fuel and ferries and we'll be able to drink the wine all the year round.'

'Good thinking, my love, good thinking.'

JOHN BEVERLEY

The following weekend, John and Jayne excitedly returned to West Wales to try out the new tent. When they arrived, being so early in the season, they again had the campsite to themselves and even the weather was kind to them, being absolutely beautiful with almost clear blue skies containing bags of bright sunshine.

Immediately on their arrival at the campsite they started to erect the new tent. They found that it was remarkably easy to put up and, in fact, John found that it went up as easily, if not more easily, than the old five-man tent. The added bonus of course, was that the new tent had five or six times the floor area of the old tent and it had a head-height of six feet-six inches.

'Look, Jayne,' John shouted excitedly. 'I can now stand up straight at long last.'

They had just about finished the erection when a Dutch car drove up and parked about ten metres away from them. Out of the car appeared a middle-aged couple who bid John and Jayne a cheerful good-day and then went about the business of erecting their own tent.

For the remainder of the day John and Jayne wallowed on their new sun-loungers, and feasted well on their new, large table with its corresponding new and comfortable chairs. The feast, of course, was cooked by Jayne on her handsomely-new Gaz-cooker with its three large burners!!

Drifting around the campsite on the daytime and evening breezes until quite late into the night

A Gaze into Holidaze

were the constant and numerous not-so-hushed whispers of, 'I love the new tent,' 'Gosh, it's so big, isn't it?' 'It's a lovely tent,' 'Isn't the new cooker fabulous?' 'I think the new table and chairs are wonderful,' 'I could lie on the sun-loungers all day, couldn't you?' 'I think the new tent is fabulous,' 'Cor! I can stand up in our new tent, it's absolutely fantastic,' and so on and so on and so on.

The following morning, which again was beautiful, John and Jayne were outside the tent having breakfast. The Dutch couple emerged from their tent and walked hand-in-hand across the field to stop immediately in front of John and Jayne's breakfast-table.

'Good morning,' said the Dutchman pleasantly.

'Good morning,' replied John and Jayne in unison.

The man looked at his wife and gave her a sly wink before returning to John. 'We just wanted to say that we also like your new tent and yes, it is fabulous. Also, we like very much your new cooker and table and chairs.'

They all burst out laughing very, very loudly.

Yes, noise does travel when under canvas, doesn't it?

****

I like museums, I do...

Yes, John and Jayne were thrilled to bits with their new Cabanon. Compared to the old five-man ridge-tent it was like a bungalow in which, as John insisted on saying time and time again, he could stand-up bolt-upright. 'No more aches and back-pains for me, Quasimodo is now as straight as a die.' Many people learn the hard way because so many people buy small ridge and bubble-tents. It's only when you are confined inside them for long periods of time due to bad weather, that you realise the strain and pain of being in a constant crouch whenever you have to do something.

The following July, John and Jayne set-off in the Volvo and set sail for France. More specifically for the Loire Valley and the delightful location of Saumur, an old fortress-town which stood on the very banks of the River Loire.

'I know a great little campsite, right alongside the river, about a mile up the road,' boasted John as they arrived at Saumur, proud of his knowledge of the area from his motorcycle days.

'Hope it's not too expensive,' replied Jayne who, looking after the funds for their journeys, was always counting the pennies.

'Not at all,' declared John. 'It's a municipal site run from the local council or something so it shouldn't be more than a few pounds or so. You'll love it. We can even go swimming in the Loire because they have a small beach there and it's really quite safe.'

'Sounds marvellous,' agreed Jayne, her enthusiasm showing clearly in her voice. 'It's beautiful countryside here and reasonably flat. It would be great to hire a couple of bikes and cycle around, don't you think?'

A Gaze into Holidaze

'Definitely,' nodded John. 'Let's get the tent up and have some lunch, then we'll walk back into town. It's only a mile or so and it's a gorgeous day. Then we'll see if we can hire a couple of bikes for a week. How does that sound?'

'Great,' replied Jayne. 'I've always fancied cycling around parts of France on a hot day in a pair of shorts. Well, we've certainly got the weather so let's see if we can get the bikes.'

The plan worked out splendidly. The walk into Saumur was pleasant, even if sometimes a little alarming because they were forced to walk along the unpavemented long and straight main-road. The traffic moved at great speed along it even though it was speed controlled, but there, that's French driving!

The hiring of bicycles proved to be effortless and surprisingly cheap. So cheap in fact that they hired the 'top-of-the-range' tourers, which came with a multitude of gears – not that you really needed them because the surrounding countryside was so flat. 'It's worth paying the extra couple of quid to get a broad, comfortably-sprung saddle,' insisted John when questioned by Jayne about the extra-hiring charge.

'What's the matter with the other seats then?' insisted Jayne.

'They are longer, narrower and harder,' replied John.

'So what about that?' Jayne persisted.

'You would have such a sore bum after riding for

an hour that you wouldn't sit down without a grimace for the rest of the holiday,' John laughed. 'Let's just say that you would certainly develop rosy cheeks and you would have blisters where you've never had blisters before.'

Jayne blushed but gave up the argument. She mounted the bicycle, and off she pedalled. John soon caught up with her and stayed just behind her as they cycled back to the campsite.

'Cute little ass,' teased John as he admired Jayne's shorts-clad bottom as it wiggled back and forth in rhythm to her pedalling.

'Cut that out, John,' shouted Jayne with a giggle. 'If you keep passing comments like that I'll take my shorts off!"

'Yes please,' pleaded John. 'Now you're talking. Is that a promise?'

They both laughed heartily. This was a great start to their holiday, a holiday that would be vastly improved over the previous year's capers with Martine and Igor. Capers which were now long, long forgotten.

And the holiday proved to be wonderful in every way. The sun shone in clear skies for most of the time, which kept the temperature up to a delightful level. The cycling was fabulous and almost effortless because the countryside was so flat around the river Loire. The few modest hills that John and Jayne did meet were easily overcome with the many gears of the bicycles.

One small incident which caused a slight stir of

conscience, occurred when John and Jayne decided to go to the tank-museum in Saumur. This was a museum which had a considerable display of WWI and WW2 tanks of all shapes and sizes and was quite renowned in the tourist guides of the area.

'I must go to the supermarket first,' declared Jayne.

'No problem,' stated John. 'You know where the museum is because, if you remember, we passed it yesterday when we were riding around town. It's not far from the supermarket.'

'Yes, I remember,' said Jayne. 'Look John, rather than drag you around the supermarket, why don't you go straight to the museum and I'll follow you in about a half an hour or so. I'm sure that that would suit you far better 'cos you love your tanks and aeroplanes of the wars, don't you?'

'Are you sure you'll be alright if I go on, love?' said John, a wee bit concerned about the splitting-up. John and Jayne were like book-ends and went everywhere together.

'Yes, of course,' Jayne said emphatically. 'I'll be fine so off you go.'

So off John went. Easily finding the museum, he parked, locked his bike and entered the establishment through an open door on the side of the compound.

The tank content was fantastic, particularly the tanks of WW2 vintage. John would have loved to have clambered around the British, American, French and German tanks on display but, unfortunately, this was not allowed. However, the sight of these monolithic giants in their prime war-paint and markings was very exciting and conjured up a thousand battles in John's mind as he strolled around the compound.

As agreed, in less than half-an-hour, Jayne joined John inside the compound of the museum.

'Get what you wanted at the supermarket, love?' John asked casually as he read the display board about a German Tiger tank.

'Yes thanks,' replied Jayne.

'No problems then?'

'None, other than getting in here,' Jayne stated. 'Gosh, it's expensive to get in, isn't it?'

'Pardon?' said John, a puzzled expression on his face. 'What do you mean expensive?'

'Well I thought a hundred francs was a bit steep. I never expected to pay that much and had I known, I doubt whether I would have come in. In fact, if it wasn't for the fact that I had arranged to meet you inside the museum, I definitely wouldn't have come in.'

'I didn't pay a thing to come in,' whispered John, trying not to attract the attention of a passer-by. 'I just walked through the door and that was that. I'm not sure myself if I would have paid as much as a hundred francs. How much is that in English money?'

'About fourteen or fifteen pounds, I think,' Jayne returned John's whisper, now realising what had probably happened. 'By which door did you come in, John?'

A Gaze into Holidaze

'The one on the side of the compound, over there,' John pointed. 'It was wide open so I walked in.' John now realised the gravity of the situation of his getting in without paying, and he was starting to get a bit concerned.

'Well, you had better go back out that way quickly and quietly because the main-door by which you should have come in, is over there.' Jayne turned and pointed to the building at the other end of the compound. 'On second thoughts, there's a man in a ticket-box on the way-in and there's a man on the exit-turnstile on the way out. Why don't you buy a ticket right now and say that you made a mistake on getting in? I'm sure they will understand.'

'No bloody chance! I'm not paying a hundred francs to anyone, especially now that I've seen all that I want to see in here. I'll sneak out in true SAS-style the way I came in and I shall pass through those doors like an invisible man. Au revoir, and I'll see you outside by the main entrance.'

John left Jayne with her mouth hanging open in bewilderment. He casually walked through the lines of tanks towards the side-door by which he had entered. Finally he reached the last right-hand turn around a British Matilda tank. There it was, in front of him, the door to freedom – firmly closed and multi-locked. Well it must have been locked judging by the three huge padlocks hanging from the three thick chains which clamped the slatted-steel door firmly to the strong iron fence.

JOHN BEVERLEY

'Shit!' was all that John could manage when he saw the end of his escape-plan.

John's imagination immediately went into overdrive. He could see it all now in his mind. He would retrace his steps through the rows of heavy armour, each tank sneering gloomily at him as he passed, to reach the dreaded ticket-box at the main entrance. There he would climb the hundred or more steps to the highly-illuminated-by-searchlight-box that stood alone to sell tickets. Alone that is except for the heavy machine-guns that totally covered the lone ticket-box. Here, he would be confronted by a huge, heavily-moustached Frenchman, in a smart brightly-coloured uniform with gold epaulettes, who would be surrounded by a band of uniformed and armed soldiers.

'So, you 'ave no ticket, monsieur, and you 'ave got in 'ere without the permission. Oui?' This would be the knowing accusation from the brightly uniformed official as the band of armed soldiers would close-in tightly to completely surround John. There would be no escape.

'Yes,' would squeak John. 'I am guilty. The sidegate was open and I walked in.'

'I will call the gendarmes to attend to you. You know the penalty for such a terrible crime, monsieur?' The voice is a snarl.

'No,' John would mutter hoarsely, hardly able to speak with fear, 'Probably a fine.'

'No, monsieur, far worse. You could well go to prison for a very long time.'

A Gaze into Holidaze

'Prison! No!' John would scream, his world coming to an end.

John was suddenly wakened from his trance-like day-dream by a small bald-headed man in shirt-sleeves and dungarees who was shaking him firmly.

'Why are you here at this gate, monsieur?' asked Shiny Top with a smile. 'Are you lost?'

'No, I am trying to find my way out,' whispered John nervously.

'The way is over there, monsieur, in that building. Come, follow me and I will show you.'

Sheepishly John followed Shiny Top through the rows of tanks, which surprisingly enough were now not sneering at him in any way, to the exit at the main entrance. 'Thank you,' said John to Shiny Top as the little man smiled and left John in front of another shirt-sleeved man. Once again this man was dressed in dungarees like Shiny Top, but lolled casually against the wall beside the exit-turnstile.

'Your ticket, monsieur,' came the demand in a low, gruff voice.

'I'm afraid I haven't got one,' said John with more confidence as he thought that you might as well be hung for a sheep as a lamb. 'I made a mistake when I came in by coming in through a side-gate in the fence over there. The gate was wide open and I thought that that was the way-in and the museum was free.' John held the unblinking gaze of the other man's eyes for what seemed an eternity before mumbling a humble, 'Sorry'.

Shirt-Sleeves stood up from his lolling position to tower over John. With the usual, typical French-like shrug and arm gestures, he said, 'No problem, monsieur. It 'appens all the time.' With that he gestured to the exit-turnstile. 'Au revoir, monsieur and enjoy your 'oliday. Tell your friends about us so that they will come and see the tanks, eh?'

John went through the turnstile like the proverbial bat-out-of-hell, vowing never to try to get away without paying again. When he told the story to Jayne, who was waiting outside, her only comment was, 'That'll larn yer – again!'

****

Grapes of wrath and aid to a fellow traveller . . .

After the incident at the Tank Museum in Saumur life settled down again and the weather remained absolutely glorious. John and Jayne cycled every day along the river Loire sticking, where possible, to the abundance of narrow country-roads and cycle tracks.

The gently-rolling hills of the surrounding countryside were very beautiful and serene, being regularly broken by the many woods and country estates with their inevitable army of chateaux. The plain bordering the River Loire in the immediate region of Saumur, was ideal for cycling, and John's and Jayne's hot summer-days consisted of wandering and rambling throughout this wonderful region.

A Gaze into Holidaze

When the day became too hot then a quick swim in the Loire at the campsite more than solved the problem.

The warm, leisurely evenings were spent barbequing, playing the guitar, singing and teasing with lots of laughter and even more red wine.

'You know, I can't believe that I only used to drink white wine,' stated Jayne as she comfortably sat around the barbeque enjoying the hot August night. 'Now I just adore red. You've introduced me to that, John.'

'Well, I really started drinking red when I used to go off on my motor-bike trips,' replied John. 'You see, the beer that you could get in Europe was great when it was chilled. Unfortunately, in the hotter countries of Europe it soon got very warm in the top box and I didn't really like it then. Also, there was no means of keeping beer or white wine cold in the tent and white wine in particular is rubbish unless it is chilled. So I started drinking what most of the locals drank throughout Europe – red wine.'

'Good for you,' Jayne added as she smiled and held her glass up to John in a toast. 'Here's to your discovery of red wine.'

John laughed. 'Here's to the Frenchmen that showed me how to enjoy the cheapest and the dustiest bottles of red wine on the bottom shelves of the shops. It tastes gorgeous even if it does melt your teeth and gets you running to the loo in the middle of the night.'

'Yes,' agreed Jayne with an embarrassed smile. 'It is a damn good laxative at that.'

John looked up at the sky which a short time before had been as clear-as-a-bell with thousands of stars sparkling as brightly as diamonds. 'Don't like the look of those clouds. I think we might have a change in the weather tomorrow.'

'You could be right, John,' Jayne nodded as she hunched her shoulders. 'I fancy its got a bit cold all of a sudden. Do you think it will rain?'

'Well, we haven't had a drop of rain in the week that we've been here, so my vote says, no rain. Trust me, it will not rain, you have my personal guarantee.'

'I seem to have heard that one before somewhere,' muttered Jayne under her breath. 'Anyway, I know it's only eight o'clock in the evening but I'm going inside. I find it a bit chilly now.'

'Okay,' said John, and then added with playful sarcasm. 'But note, it is not going to rain.'

Ten minutes later the heavens just burst. It rained as if it had never rained before and the campsite outside soon became a virtual quagmire even though the ground had been very hard due to the lack of water over the previous weeks, or even months.

John and Jayne didn't give a damn. They were safely inside their brand-new Cabanon frame-tent with all of that internal space. They laughed at the rain as it drummed on the roof of the tent and they drank red wine contentedly. They sat around their

A Gaze into Holidaze

large table and drank red wine, sat in their nice comfortable chairs and drank red wine, played cards and drank red wine, played backgammon and drank red wine, played the guitar and drank red wine, sang songs and drank red wine, did stupid things and drank red wine, got very drunk and drank even more red wine.

'Yoush got a shlovely tan, Jayne,' cooed John to Jayne, both parties being well the worse for alcoholic wear.

'Shank you, John. Yoush got a shlovely tan, too,' slurred Jayne in return. 'Yoush alsho got ash nish mooooostash. How shlong have yoush 'ad it?'

'I wash born with it,' John giggled, totally out of his box by now.

Jayne stretched out her right arm to the full and stuck her forefinger horizontally over John's mouth as if to cover his moustache. Squinting along her arm with one eye open, she said, 'Ish bet yoush look good weshout it though.'

'Well, itsh not goin' to shappen,' murmured John, trying desperately to remain dignified. He was fully aware of his heavy slurring but couldn't do anything whatsoever about it.

They drank more red wine and laughed and giggled like two small children. They played silly games and teased constantly until both of them simply fell into bed and passed into a deep sleep.

The following morning, John awoke early to find it still raining torrentially. The rain hammered on the roof of the tent giving a sound which matched the hangover which John well deserved from the night before. He groaned as he turned over to try to put his head in a place where it would stop pounding.

'What's the matter?" asked Jayne who had been disturbed by John's movement. In spite of her efforts, she could not open her eyes.

'I've got a steam-hammer in my head which is doing its best to shatter my skull. How do you feel?'

'Tired,' said Jayne aggressively. 'Now if you keep quiet and stop jumping about I'll get back off to sleep. What time is it anyway?'

John studied his wristwatch for a full half-minute trying to force his eyes to focus on the small dial. It was almost impossible with the hammering in his head but finally he managed a weak, 'Six-thirty, I think.'

'Well, go back to sleep. If you can't drink – don't drink. That's what you taught me.'

'I'm thirsty.'

'Well, there's no water here,' declared Jayne impatiently, pulling the duvet over her. 'We drank it all yesterday and you didn't replace it when I asked you to because you were too drunk.'

John thought it over as carefully as his throbbing head would allow. 'I'll have to go and get some drinking water right now, and if I'm going to do that in all this bloody rain then I might as well get shaved and showered at the same time.'

Hearing no reply from Jayne, he climbed over

A Gaze into Holidaze

her to emerge into the living-room part of the tent. Here he found his clothes heaped on a chair and went to put them on.

'God, these clothes are soaking wet,' he said aloud to himself. 'How can that be?' He looked up through red-rimmed eyes and strained to focus on the canvas roof above him. 'It's as dry as a cork up there,' he mused, puzzled by his wet clothes.

After walking the short distance to the toilet-block through the driving rain, he felt much better. His head cleared even more when he took a long draught of cool water from the drinking-tap, accompanied by deep gulps of the chilled, morning air. His eyes, however, were still reluctant in agreeing to focus on any object no matter what the range.

Finally, he took himself to a suitable washbasin, hung up his wet anorak, removed his tee-shirt and carefully laid out his shaving gear. Squirting shaving-cream on his brush he looked for the first time into the mirror above his washbasin. He froze in horror!

'Jesus Christ!' John shouted, his voice choked with shock and disbelief. Quickly he snatched his head to look away from the mirror, unable to stand the sight of his heavily-tanned face. Very slowly his head turned back to the mirror as if being forced by an unseen hand. There, staring back at him was a face that he did not remotely recognise. A face that he did not like one little bit, with its red-rimmed and bloodshot eyes peering out of a tanned yet sallow skin. Yes, the nose was the same, the cheeks although drawn were the same, the full mouth was the same, even if it was just a straight line of worry at this moment of time. So what was so frighteningly different?

In his hung-over condition, John once again subconsciously started to check the inventory of his face – eyebrows, two, one on each side of the head; eyes, two – brown, each one under an eyebrow; nose, one; mouth, one; then what's missing?

'My fucking moustache, that's what's missing!' exclaimed John in utter despair. There, where once his thick black-moustache had been was an awesome expanse of skin, which, in comparison to the remainder of his tanned face, was as white as the driven snow. In fact, John could see no other feature on his face other than this huge plateau of white skin just below his nose and above his mouth.

Leaving everything scattered around him and in great panic, John ran. Stripped to the waist and through the cold downpour of rain, he regained the tent like an arrow shot from a bow.

'Jayne, Jayne!' he shouted as he unzipped the bedroom-door in the tent, his dishevelled figure streaming water in all directions.

'What's the matter?' Jayne screamed, frightened at having been disturbed from sleep so abruptly. 'You'll wake the entire campsite the way you are shouting your head off.'

'My moustache has gone,' pleaded John in desperation.

'Where has it gone to?' replied Jayne, con-

A Gaze into Holidaze

descendingly. Then she saw the state that John was in and got quickly out of bed to join the trembling figure standing in front of her. She looked into his face and at once saw the huge white, almost luminous strip of flesh that stretched across the middle of it. She then looked deeply into John's frightened eyes and – doubled-up with laughter.

'So that's where you disappeared to last night,' stammered Jayne, hardly able to control herself. 'You left the tent after our drunken teasing and must have gone and shaved it off. By the time you came back from wherever, I had gone to bed. Anyway, you only look as if you've got a strip of white Elastoplast beneath your nose so what's the problem?'

'Very funny,' snarled John, the straight line of his angry lips only emphasising the white gap between nose and mouth. 'Stop laughing at me for God's sake. Tell me what we were teasing about.'

'Well, we were both a bit tipsy and I said that I thought you'd look even better without your moustache. So I dared you to shave it off. I was only teasing but you must have gone and done it, I suppose.'

'There's no supposing about it,' shouted John, getting angrier by the second. 'I can't remember a thing, not a single bloody thing about last night. All I know is – here is my moustache – gone! And you never tried to stop me! I've had the bloody thing since Pontius was a Pilot!' John looked dazed. All he could manage as a very weak defence was to repeat over and over again that he couldn't remember anything whatsoever of the previous night.

'Don't you blame me,' Jayne said calmly. 'I was drunk myself and anyway I never thought that you would do it. If I had been sober I would have stopped you.' Jayne could see that John was indeed upset so, placing her fingers gently on his upper-lip, she said tenderly, 'Anyway, I like it and it suits you. You look years younger.'

'Do I really?' John quietened considerably. 'Say honestly that it suits me.'

'Honest, John. Your moustache suits you . . . er, I mean . . .' Jayne struggled to correct her mistake. 'I mean you look much better without your moustache. Just you wait until the white skin has tanned like the rest of your face. You'll be so handsome.'

'Mmmm,' John snorted, trying his best to believe Jayne. Without another word he stormed out of the tent and went back to his ablutions.

John pouted for the rest of the morning and well into the afternoon. In spite of Jayne's frequent efforts at comforting support, he was still not amused. In fact, he became paranoid. Every time he caught Jayne looking at him he was convinced that she was staring at his upper lip. Whenever she spoke to him in conversation he felt that she no longer looked him in the eyes, but stared as if mesmerised by the ghastly white expanse just below his nose. She just couldn't take her eyes off it.

This, coupled with his hangover which, although clearing, was still a source of pain in the form of a more-than-thick head, made John feel miserable to the nth degree. He was still topped to the brim with alcohol and was probably still a wee bit intoxicated.

John looked gloomily through the plastic window at the driving rain. 'Is it ever going to stop?' he muttered, feeling totally sorry for himself.

'Oh, for goodness sake, John, cheer up,' Jayne retorted, now getting really fed-up with John's mood. 'It's only been raining for about a day. If you were at home in Wales it would rain for a month without stopping at this time of year.'

'I suppose you're right,' John agreed reluctantly, still peering out through the rain-streaked plastic window. 'Anyway, it could be worse. Look at that poor Brit out there. He has just arrived in a beaten-up old Skoda and now he's trying to put up his tent in all of this rain.'

Jayne joined John at the window and looked out at their newly-arrived neighbour. 'Oh, the poor chap, he's going to get soaked. Go and help him, John.'

'Not bloody likely, it's absolutely persisting down out there,' John replied spitefully. 'If he had any sense he wouldn't attempt to put up his tent in this stupid weather. He should stay in his Skoda until the rain has passed over.'

'He has probably considered and dismissed that,' said Jayne. 'By the look of the sky it's never going to stop raining.'

'Well, he could always sleep in his mighty Skoda if that is the case. Anyway, I'm staying put here, and that is that,' John finished stubbornly, his hangover still a negatively paramount feature in his well-being. 'What's more, if he couldn't take a joke then he shouldn't have joined the tenting club.'

'That's not like you at all, John,' Jayne continued. 'You are always helping people out of trouble. I think your kindness has gone out with your black moustache.'

'You leave my moustache out of this,' commanded John, getting a trifle closer to boiling point.

'Well, I never thought my thoughtful-to-other-people husband would change because of a stupid bit of hair,' insisted Jayne. 'I'm going to help that poor man.'

'No you're not and that's final!' yelled John. 'You are not going out in this rain.'

Jayne knew when it was time to stop. She shrugged her shoulders and snorted in defiance but decided to let the matter go. Anyway, deep down, she knew that John was right because it had been stupid of the man to attempt to erect his tent in such foul weather.

Moodily, for the next half-hour, they sat at the window and watched the man painfully slowly complete the task of erecting his one-man ridge-tent. The man then walked casually to his car as if the heavens were not pouring their hearts out, and removed several items before disappearing inside his tent and finally zipping up.

'That's it,' stated Jayne resolutely. 'I'm taking him over a nice cup of tea. I bet the poor bloke is dripping-wet and freezing.'

Five minutes later, heavily anoraked with hood up and armed with a plate of ham sandwiches and a flask of sweet tea, Jayne crossed the fifteen-metre, very muddy distance to Stranger's tent.

John watched through the plastic window and saw Jayne knock on the tent flap. The flap opened and a pale thin face appeared. John saw the goodies being handed over and a very short conversation taking place. Jayne then turned, and waded back across the saturated ground to their tent.

Jayne came through the door-flap to remove and shake her dripping anorak. 'I think it's raining for Great Britain out there,' she said, sniffing at the rain globules that hung from her nose.

'Is he okay?' asked John lightly.

'Oh!' exclaimed Jayne, a note of irony in her voice. 'You're interested now, are you?'

'Well, yes,' replied John cockily. 'I suppose I am. After all he is a fellow traveller, isn't he?'

'Well, you've certainly changed your tune,' Jayne stated flatly. 'He's a fellow traveller who happens to be very cold and very wet.' She paused and looked over at John. Then taking a deep breath she blurted out, 'Because of this I have invited him over for dinner tonight at six o'clock. It's five o'clock now so you had better get cleaned-up and changed.'

'You've what?' shouted John despairingly. 'I am shattered, hung-over, and probably still semi-drunk and you have invited over a ragged waif for dinner? I was going to have an early night tonight because I am desperate to sleep-off the effects of last night.'

'Well tough luck, matie,' answered Jayne firmly. 'This boy needs a hot meal and we are going to give it to him. Regarding your hangover, I'll say to you as you have said many times to me in the past – if you can't drink, don't drink! Now get ready and get rid of your mood because you haven't got much time and neither have I!' She paused and looked John straight in the eye. 'I suggest that you don't drink tonight for obvious reasons.'

'I will drink what I feel like drinking,' said John indignantly. With that he reached for some bottles of red wine and opened them. 'For dinner I suggest, and we had better let them breathe in plenty of time.'

They both went about their chores in silence for the next hour before sitting at the table to await their honoured guest, or not-so-honoured a guest in John's mind.

At precisely six o'clock there was a knock on the door-flap of the tent, barely audible through the rain hammering on the tent's roof.

A Gaze into Holidaze

'Come in!' shouted Jayne.

In walked a young man in his early thirties. He wore a loosely-fitting raincoat which hung open to reveal baggy jeans and a sloppy sweater. On his feet were green Wellington boots, well-splattered with mud. Seeing John's frown as he looked down at the dripping goo brought into the tent by the boots, he said quietly, 'Sorry about the Wellies, Mister...er...Mister...?'

'Just call me John,' John said coolly.

'My name's Gerald,' added the young man, politely holding out his right-hand in greeting. Smilingly, he looked into John's eyes before suddenly dropping his gaze to John's upper-lip.

John shook the offered hand, but catching Gerald's line of sight immediately reacted by shooting his left-hand to cover the yawning gap between nose and mouth. 'This is my wife, Jayne,' he mumbled with embarrassment from behind his hand.

'Pleased to meet you, Jayne,' Gerald smiled, again offering his hand. 'Sorry about the Wellies, but it's an absolute mud-bath out there.'

'Not at all,' assured Jayne, noting that Gerald was extremely well-spoken. 'Take them off if you'll feel more comfortable and let me have your raincoat.'

'May I?' asked Gerald, removing and handing Jayne his dripping coat. 'That's very kind of you. I would prefer to sit around in my socks for a bit. I've been driving for about seven hours or so from

Calais, and it would be great to get rid of my footwear for a while and stretch my toes.'

'Take your socks off if you like, we don't mind what you do,' stated John, his hand still held in the regions of his missing facial fur. 'Come and sit down over here in the comfy chair. By the look of your camping-gear out there, you won't be having a lot of comfort during your holiday so perhaps you should make the most of it. Glass of red wine?'

'Yes, I'd love one, thank you,' replied Gerald, who, having removed his raincoat and rubber boots, sat next to John at the table. 'Oh, I almost forgot,' he added as he went to his coat and returned with a litre bottle of Martell brandy. 'Thought that this would be useful on a night like this, especially after your kind invitation to dinner. I hope I'm no trouble.'

'We're very pleased to see you, Gerald,' said John, glancing over at Jayne who was by the cooker doing dinner. 'I was only saying to Jayne earlier that we really must have you over after you getting soaking wet when you put up your tent.'

Jayne slowly shook her head in amazement, but said nothing.

Dinner was a splendid, if simple, affair which came mainly out of cans – canned soup for starters, canned potatoes, peas and carrots accompanied by canned stewed-steak for the main course and canned peaches with canned cream for dessert. All this was followed by cheese and biscuits which did not come from a can, and coffee which also did not come from a can – it was a jar! In the short notice that Jayne, who incidentally was a wonderful cook under normal circumstances, had had, she had produced a lovely meal. Red wine flowed freely throughout the canned feast and both bottles that John had previously opened were now empty. Accordingly, by now all parties were in a happy and contented mood, to say the least.

John raised and looked at the last empty bottle of red wine. 'Another dead soldier,' he said, fully aware that the alcohol that he had just consumed, had started to happily top-up the alcohol that was already gurgling through his bloodstream. 'Another bottle, Gerald?' John looked up and caught Gerald staring at his upper lip – or so it seemed to John.

'Oh, no thanks. Why don't you have a brandy from the bottle of Martell that I brought?' questioned Gerald happily.

'Only if you'll join me, Gerald. I do enjoy a brandy after dinner.' John looked at Gerald carefully as he spoke. Was he staring at that enormous expanse of raw flesh left by his missing moustache?

'Certainly I'll join you,' said Gerald eagerly with good humour. 'What about you, Jayne? Are you going to have a nightcap?'

'Not for me thanks,' replied Jayne as she rustled up two glasses. 'I've had a couple or three glasses of wine and I don't think I want anymore alcohol tonight.' She sat at the table.

'Never mind, Jayne,' said John as he poured two large cognacs, the slight slur in his voice now quite apparent. Offering Gerald a full glass of brandy he raised his own glass in a toast, 'Here's to camping, here's to the weather and to both you and your tent drying out for your forthcoming travels.'

'Hear, hear!' smiled Gerald as he touched John's glass.

The evening continued into night and the conversation was light and entertaining, as was the brandy. Gerald proved to be good company, in that he was a fluent conversationalist and told quite a few stories. John warmed towards him immensely. As the brandy flowed, so the two men got louder and louder and the stories bolder and bolder. Never dirty, because both men respected the presence of Jayne, but certainly bordering on perhaps smutty adult entertainment. John found that he no longer cared about his missing hairy pride-and-joy. Gerald wasn't staring any longer because in John's view, he was a great bloke!

'Have you heard the one about the flat-chested lady,' volunteered Gerald. His voice clear, in spite of the glasses of brandy that he had consumed.

'No, I don't shink sho,' replied John, starting to lose his conversational capabilities.

'Well, this flat-chested lady suffered so much from an inferiority complex that she wouldn't even go outside her front door. Her nerves were in a terrible state. She suffered so much that a friend of hers forced her to go to the doctor's surgery. The doctor was a Dr .Smith, as a matter of fact. "Doctor Smith. Can you help me?" said the woman. "My

A Gaze into Holidaze

nerves are in such a state because of my flat-chest that I am afraid to go outside the house. I only leave the house for work and I feel that I am going to have a nervous breakdown." "Of course I can help," Dr Smith said. "All you have to do is a few simple exercises each morning. Take each breast in turn and, lightly massaging it, say out loud, and out loud is most important:

> Doobie, doobie, doobie,
> Give me a bigger boobie.
> Doobie, doobie, doobie,
> Give me a bigger boobie.

You will be amazed at the results." So the flat-chested woman went away and every morning did her exercises saying out loud, "Doobie, doobie, doobie" . . . etcetera, etcetera. After a week of this, there was no doubt that the lady's breasts were beginning to grow. She was ecstatic! However, one morning the woman slept late for work and didn't have time to do her exercises. She dashed off to work and ended up on the top-deck of a double-decker bus. Looking around, she saw only one man a few seats behind her, so she thought that she would do her exercises where no-one could see or hear her. So she started, "Doobie, doobie, doobie, give me a bigger . . . " Suddenly, she was interrupted by the man behind who grabbed her by the shoulder. "You've been to see Dr Smith," he said, "haven't you?" "How do you know?" she replied in embarrassment. The man smiled and said, "Hickory, dickory dock . . .!"'

John and Jayne doubled up with laughter.

'Yoush quite a sharacter, Gerald,' slurred John, wiping the tears from his eyes, his alcoholic blood-flow now having fully caught up with his brain. 'What do yoush do for a living?'

'Well, I used to be a policeman,' replied Gerald.

'Are there shoo are,' struggled John. 'I knew there wash shomeshing I didn't like about shoo when I first met shoo.'

All three of them laughed, including Gerald who was remarkably sober considering what he had drunk.

'What do you do now, Gerald?' This time it was Jayne who asked the question.

Slowly, Gerald looked from one to the other of them. First he looked at John, whose eyes were half-closed and heavy for sleep, then he slowly turned to look at Jayne. Gerald whispered quietly, his voice barely audible above the pounding rain as it lashed the sides of the tent in the newly-arisen wind, 'I am a priest.'

'Good Lord,' declared Jayne, her mouth gaping in shock. 'I mean, good God . . . er, I mean great . . .!'

Gerald put up his hand to stop Jayne's ranting. 'I know what you mean,' he said, a broad smile on his handsome face. 'My being a priest always gets that reaction.'

'Well, it is a bit of a party stopper, isn't it?' said Jayne quietly, feeling embarrassed. 'Well, it's certainly quietened John down a bit anyway.'

A Gaze into Holidaze

John was speechless and just didn't know what to say. Even through his intoxication the questions hurtled through his mind. Did I swear? No, I don't think so, other than bloody, bugger and damn . . . well, maybe the odd sod or two. Did I do my usual striptease, as I seem to always want to do when I get oiled? No, I don't think so. Did I talk about sex? No, I don't think so – I'll have to ask Jayne in the morning!

Well, other than politeness, it was the end of the party. The conversation continued for almost another half-an-hour, but it was a bit strained. It seems that Gerald had been a priest for five years after leaving the police-force. He had just left his wife in Kent where his parish was, to single-handedly follow a trail which apparently was taken thousands of years before by St Paul. The journey Gerald was taking had commenced in Brittany, Northern France and would end, for Gerald, in about three weeks time somewhere in mid-Italy.

Gerald left the tent at midnight. The wind had dropped and the rain was far gone. In fact, the night was cool and clear, showing an abundance of stars twinkling in the heavens above.

'Stars shine on the righteous,' were the only words that John could mumble before he literally hit the sack minutes after Gerald's departure.

Jayne looked down at his sprawled, senseless figure and smiled lovingly. 'Well, that's certainly you, John. The fact that Gerald was a priest more than took the wind out of your sails.'

JOHN BEVERLEY

John was understandably a little late in rising the following morning. At nine thirty, with no sign of Jayne, John poked his head out of the tent intending to see Gerald, to apologise for anything offensive that he may have said on the previous night. He didn't think that he had, but he was far from being certain. His mind was blank and he just couldn't remember much about the events of the evening.

But Gerald, his tent and beaten up old Skoda had gone.

Returning from the toilet-block, Jayne greeted John cheerily. 'Good morning, darling, and how do you feel today?'

'Pretty good actually considering I've had two heavy nights on the booze. You know that two nights on the trot is just not me.'

'Well, the weather is back to normal. Look at it, sunshine at last. It's amazing how you miss the sun and we've only been without it for a day or so.'

'Yes, that's true,' said John sheepishly. 'Jayne, about that priest . . . er, Gerald, last night. Was my behaviour a bit much? You know, considering he was a priest.'

Jayne smiled impishly. 'I got up to see Gerald off this morning. He was fine and in very good spirits but was more than concerned about you. Actually, he gave me this note. It's to the both of us really. Do you want to read it?'

John took the note from Jayne's hand and studied it carefully.

A Gaze into Holidaze

"Dear Jayne and John,

Thank you for a lovely meal and an even more lovely evening. I thoroughly enjoyed your company and particularly the sense of humour and fun that we exchanged.

Believe me, I don't get too much laughter in my chosen vocation. Ha! Ha!

Once again, I thank you, and may God go with you.

Your friend,
Gerald.

P.S. No, John, you didn't swear or say anything untoward so don't worry about anything as I know you will when you wake up in the morning.

Cheers and good health, Gerald.

P.P.S. Also, don't worry about the white gap above your upper-lip. I know you are embarrassed about it right now but in a week it will either be tanned like the rest of your face or your moustache will have grown back. No problem. Either way you will be a handsome devil – ha! ha! ha!

Keep laughing. Gerald.

John gently folded the note and gave it back to Jane. 'Now that's what I call a nice man and a real gentleman.'

A week later, John's hairy pride-and-joy had eighty percent returned. John was happy. This made Jayne happy. So both being happy, they lived happily ever after.

****

One man and his dog . . .

The following year John, Jayne, Volvo and trailer ventured to the South of France. The area of Provence was superb, as was the climate of long, hot days with barely a cloud in the deepest of blue skies.

Everything was going well until they reached the coastal road slightly to the east of Toulon. They had hoped to reach this location by about 10 a.m. and then drive along the coast-road until they found a good campsite for the four weeks of the August-holiday that they had planned. Unfortunately, they were over an hour behind schedule and found the N98 at this later time absolutely choked with traffic. Traffic which insisted on moving at a snail's pace.

'This is going to be bad news,' declared John after trailing the car ahead of him in bumper-to-bumper fashion for what seemed an eternity.

'Yes,' agreed Jayne. 'And it's so hot. How long have we been crawling along now, John?'

John looked at his wristwatch. 'About three hours and I bet we haven't travelled twenty miles. This is ridiculous.'

A Gaze into Holidaze

'Do you think we will find a campsite okay?' Jayne asked.

'Well, in theory, yes. In practice, I don't know.' John eased the car forward in the traffic for another ten yards or so before coming to a halt for the thousandth time. 'The trouble is that we've passed loads of campsites on the route as we expected, but they're all absolutely chocka. God! They cram them in so tightly that the guy-ropes of each tent all overlap. Yuk! It's dreadful and not what we're used to. And what's more, they are damned expensive. Far more expensive than we were led to believe.'

'They can charge what they like at this time of year, John. It's so popular here that people will pay anything to camp on the Côte d'Azur.' Jayne looked at her watch. 'Well, it's half-past-two now, John. I think that it's decision time. Do we stay in this awful traffic or try somewhere else?'

'You're right,' stated John flatly. 'My vote is to get out of this mess pronto and head north. If we go about forty or fifty miles inland I reckon the campsites will be much quieter.'

'Let's do it,' echoed Jayne enthusiastically. 'I've had enough of this.'

So they did just that, and by half-past-four they were driving through a village called Barjols, the heavy traffic of the southern coastal-roads left far behind.

Seeing a directional sign for a campsite as they entered the village, John said, 'We'll try here. We'll go to this campsite and if we don't like it, we'll move on.'

'No matter what it's like, John, I think that we should spend a night here. We've been on the road all day and I am hot, tired, sweaty and hungry.'

'Fair enough,' agreed John. 'I've had enough too. We'll kip here for the night and check the map as to where to go in the morning. So, let's find the campsite.'

The village proved to be delightful with its stone, whitewashed houses with their picturesque, red-tiled roofs. After passing through a large central square, they picked up the directional sign once more which took them a short distance out of the village, alongside a football pitch, to finally point them at the entrance to the campsite.

'Hey, this looks nice,' said John as he drove through the gate. 'There is no reception here as far as I can see. That's a bit unusual.' They carried on into the site.

'It's very peaceful, isn't it?' whispered Jayne, as she looked around. 'There's the toilet-block and it looks nice and clean.'

'Bet they're hole-in-the-floor jobs,' chuckled John. 'I'll stop before we go any further into the site, and you can check 'em out. If you are happy, I'm happy.'

Jayne left the car and ran to the building. A minute later she was back. 'Fantastic! They are very Christian sit-down loos just like back home,' she sighed. 'I'm looking forward to giving myself the pleasure of sitting on one.'

A Gaze into Holidaze

'All in good time. Did you see any showers in there?'

'Yes, and they are all spotless. It's just the job here, John.'

'Great! This should do us for tonight then,' John concluded. Looking ahead he saw a car with a Dutch number-plate parked a short distance away. Near it were a man and woman sitting outside their tent drinking wine. 'We'll have a chat to these people and get the gen.'

John eased the car forward to stop beside the couple. 'Good afternoon,' greeted John brightly. 'Do you speak English?'

'Good afternoon,' came the friendly reply. 'I speak English a little.'

'Oh, good,' said John with a smile, knowing from past experience that when a Dutchman said he spoke a 'little English' then his English would be perfect and usually far better than the average Brit. 'I could not find a reception building at the entrance to the site so I could not enquire as to whether there are any vacancies for tonight. Do you know if there are? Perhaps you could tell us the camping-rate for the night?'

The Dutchman looked at his female companion and smiled before returning his gaze back to John. 'There is no reception here and, as you can see, there are many vacant spaces.' He gestured around the site. 'You can pick any vacant pitch you like, they are yours to choose.'

'Then I assume that someone will call around in the morning to collect the fee.'

'No, my friend, no-one will come to collect the fee,' smiled the Dutchman.

'Then how do you pay?' asked John, his eyebrows raised in confusion.

'You don't pay,' said the Dutchman quietly, the smile never leaving his lips. 'You don't pay because, my friend, it is gratis to stay here.' Seeing John's puzzled look deepen, his smile became even broader. 'Free. It's absolutely free to stay here.'

'How can that be?' questioned John, amazed.

'Well, it seems that the mayor of Barjols is a communist and he believed that the town should supply a free campsite for travellers.' He paused. 'And this is it.'

'Well, that's absolutely fantastic,' declared John. 'I can't believe it.'

'It is true, my friend. There is even a full-size swimming-pool right next door but I am afraid that you must pay for that, a few francs only because it is a municipal pool run by the local council.'

John turned to Jayne. 'Did you hear that Jayne? The campsite's free and there is a swimming-pool.'

'Sound's like heaven to me,' sighed Jayne in contentment. 'A visit to a sit-down loo, a nice hot shower followed by a cooked meal and a swim. What more could a girl ask for?'

After thanking the Dutchman for his help, but gently refusing the offer of a glass of wine, John and Jayne continued into the campsite to find a pitch as close as possible to the toilets and swimming-pool respectively. By six o'clock the tent was up, and the pair were well and truly settled-in to their new home.

'This is the life, isn't it, Jayne?' John questioned, stretching his limbs luxuriously as he sprawled on the sun-lounger next to the equally-sprawled Jayne. It was now well past eleven o'clock and sufficient alcoholic beverages in the form of brandy-sours had been consumed by way of a nightcap or two.

'Yes, it's gorgeous, John. Look at the stars, they are so clear and appear huge in the sky.'

They both looked up at the truly wonderful sight of the star-studded sky with its myriads of twinkling lights.

'A shame to go to bed really,' claimed John, basking in the warmth of the south-of-France night.

'Yes, but we must. Come on, we've had a hard and long day and we have to be up first thing in the morning to get an early start.'

'No we don't have to, Jayne. Look, this is a free campsite and it's got a lot going for it. First, its spotlessly clean with great toilets and showers. Second, I looked at the map after supper and it's well placed for a lot of interesting places within an hour or so's drive. Namely, St Tropez, Cannes, Nice and Monte Carlo along the coast, whilst inland we will have a large lake area and the Great Canyon du Verdon to the north-east. There will be plenty to see from here so I think that we should have a nice lie-in in the morning and spend the next three or four days driving around sightseeing.'

'Yes, okay, John. Seems like a good idea to me. However, I really am ready for sleep and your idea for a longer stay in bed in the morning suits me fine. I'm absolutely whacked!'

So, both being exhausted, they went to bed and were fast asleep almost as soon as their heads hit their respective pillows.

They were rudely awakened at about 4.30 a.m. just as dawn was breaking. This rude awakening came from the roar of diesel engines which sounded as if some heavy-goods vehicles were attempting to get into the tent alongside them.

'What the hell is that?' snapped John, his anger immediately rising at the disturbance to themselves and the campsite at that ridiculously-early hour of the morning.

After a loud squeal of brakes, the engines stopped, only to be followed by the banging of vehicle doors being slammed and loud, jabbering French voices from a gang of excited people who had obviously dismounted from the vehicles.

'Selfish bastards!' shouted John, hopefully loud enough for the offending culprits to hear.

'Shhhh,' shushed Jayne, her finger held to her mouth. 'They'll hear you if you're not careful.'

'I bloody-well hope they do,' John snapped back.

And then the dogs started barking. Barking which sounded as if it could have been coming from the lounge-part of John and Jayne's tent for what good effect the walls of the tent had on deadening the sound. First one deep and throaty bark commenced, to be joined by yet another, and another, and another. All the time the French people babbled on and on and on.

'Good God !' exclaimed John, his existing boil gradually rising to furnace heat. 'I'm not putting up with this. It's like the bloody Hounds of the Baskervilles out there and I'm going to put a stop to it. This bloody noise at this time of the morning is bloody ridiculous.'

'Stop swearing, John, please.'

'I'll bloody swear with non-caring buggers like that around,' John managed as he struggled to get out of the bedroom of the tent only to trip over the canvas lip of the bedroom-door and sprawl flat-out and naked on the floor of the lounge.

'You'd better put something on, John, or they'll have you arrested for indecent exposure,' Jayne said casually after the disappearing figure of John. 'My, what a cute little bum you've got first thing in the morning,' she added in attempt to lighten John's mood.

Ignoring Jayne's remark, John reached the tent-flap and unzipped it. On hands and knees he stuck his head outside and, being unaware of the spectacle that his backside presented to the worried Jayne about four feet behind him, he surveyed what was going on. From outside the tent, John looked like a man in the stocks from days gone by, waiting to be pelted with rotten vegetables.

Two 4x4 vehicles, complete with caravans in tow, had stopped at the vacant pitches opposite John and Jayne's tent. The obvious occupants of the vehicles numbering three men, three women and one small boy of about six-years, were gathered outside one of the caravans talking loudly at the tops of their voices as if it were the middle of the day. As John watched the events, head only protruding from the front of the tent, four huge dogs emerged from behind the second caravan.

'Good God, Jayne, there's four Alsatian dogs here. No there's not, there's five . . . six . . . seven, oh shit, eight of them,' John hissed.

However, John's hissing, inaudible to any human, was enough to attract the attention of the dogs. Two of them, one white German shepherd and one large, black German shepherd, left the pack and trotted over to where John's head stuck out from the tent. The white German shepherd stopped about two feet in front of John and looked at him eyeball-to-eyeball for a full minute. Then, without warning, it gave John a hot, sticky lick right across the face.

'Bugger off!' shouted John, struggling to get the hand that was holding the tent-flap together to hide his nakedness, from inside the tent and through the hole made by his head, in a desperate attempt to wipe his face. 'Bloody hound,' was all he could say as the dog's saliva ran down his face.

The white dog, startled by John's outburst, jumped back from the front of the tent. This movement was sufficient to allow John to sight the second dog squatting down on its haunches with a look of absolute bliss on its face as it carried out its natural functions on the foot-rug that Jayne had placed outside the door of the tent. The French people, having not seen any of this, just continued their babbling.

'What the hell is the meaning of this?' John shouted at the top of his voice.

The babbling stopped instantly and one of the men, a big man, turned around. 'Monsieur,' he gestured, his arms outstretched in bewilderment.

'Can't you keep your bloody dogs under control? Or is it customary in France to allow your dogs to shit on your neighbours' doorsteps?' John was now red in the face as he totally let out at the French men and women. 'Furthermore, do you know what bloody time it is? It's half-past-bloody-four in the morning, that's what time it is, and people like me are trying to sleep. So shut-up and clean-up this soddin' dog-shit from our front door.' With that he pulled his head and arm back into the tent and madly zipped the tent-flap up in a final show of defiance and disgust. Unfortunately, he caught his pubic-hairs in the zip as he did so. 'Jesus Christ!' he hissed as he bit his lip in agony. 'This is just not my night.'

Finally, he got back into bed to lie alongside a very worried Jayne. 'That dog's shit on your carpet.'

'Yes, I heard,' replied Jayne patiently. 'Never mind, I'll clean it up in the morning.'

'Like hell you will. I've just told those Frenchies to clear it up, so don't you dare do it. It's all their fault. Four-thirty in the morning and dogs as big as bleeding elephants are shitting all over the place. It's not right! Do you know that one of them licked me on my face.'

'It was only giving you a nice big kiss, John,' Jayne said softly as she cuddled up to her husband. 'He was obviously very fond of you. Was it a he or were you having an affair with a she-dog?'

'Very funny,' mumbled John, his ears straining for further disturbance in the early morning.

But there was no further noise. Other than an odd clunk here and there the French settled in very quickly and the site returned to utter peace and tranquillity.

The following morning, at around nine o'clock, John awoke to find Jayne already up and moving around in the kitchen-area of the outside tent. The smell of frying bacon drifted into the bedroom making John drool. So with a yawn he got up and joined Jayne as she fussed about breakfast.

'Good morning, sweetheart,' greeted Jayne playfully. 'I hope you are in a better mood now because there's a lovely breakfast waiting for you.'

'Yes, I am fine, thank you. Just a bit annoyed about the din last night, that's all.'

Jayne placed John's breakfast in front of him. 'Well, as you used to tell me time and time again whenever I wasn't a happy bunny, if you couldn't take a joke you shouldn't have come camping. Come on, mate, it's over so let's enjoy breakfast.'

John glanced across at the two French caravans

and saw that the group of last night was also gathered around their table eating breakfast. 'Did they clean-up the dog's mess, Jayne?' John asked, suddenly remembering the pile of treasure that the German shepherd had deposited on Jayne's carpet.

'Look, John, they probably didn't even know that their dog had made a mess over here so don't make such a fuss. Anyway, it was no problem because I have cleared up after dogs before, you know?'

'Did they?' John insisted.

'No, I cleared it up.'

'Where is it now?' John's anger of the previous night was returning at a rate of knots.

'In the small plastic-bag over there,' Jayne pointed.

Without another word, John crossed to the single bag which was neatly tied and lying next to the tent. 'I'll get rid of this.' He walked past the anxious Jayne and strode boldly across the short distance to the group of breakfasting dog-owners with eight dogs lying at their feet.

'I think that this belongs to you,' stated John without emotion as he emptied the contents of the bag on the ground, almost at the big Frenchman's feet. 'I shall be reporting the behaviour at four o'clock this morning of your group and your dogs. I don't think that the local council set up this lovely campsite for the likes of you, do you? In Britain we have responsible dog-owners who control their animals and clean-up their dogs' mess after them. I suggest you learn to do the same.'

Deliberately staring each of the group in the eye in turn and correspondingly receiving no reply or argument, John turned and went back to the flabbergasted Jayne.

'What did you say?' enquired Jayne anxiously.

'Don't worry your pretty little head about it, Jayne,' said John, a satisfied tone in his voice. 'Justice has been done.' After a pause he added, cheerfully, 'Come on, let's go and have a great day. Where do you want to go?'

And a great day they had exploring the Great Canyon du Verdon. It was superb in every way with the 'Little Grand Canyon' being a spectacular sight, when viewed from the road around its rim, with its steeply-cliffed sides dropping into the deep ravine, where the river appeared as a silvery sliver at its bottom. The canoeists on the River Verdon far below looked like tiny water-beetles as they busied themselves, scurrying up and down the river in the heat of the day.

From the Canyon du Verdon they went to a large lake bounded by beautifully wooded hills and dales. They even hired a rowboat and proceeded to explore the several little wooded islands that appeared a few hundred yards offshore. The weather was absolutely gorgeous with clear skies and a hot sun which forced the couple to swim off the boat in the cool waters of the lake. They had a great time and returned to the campsite at around five o'clock.

As they got out of the car, John noticed that the group of dog-owners was sitting casually around a long table made up of three individual tables. All

A Gaze into Holidaze

tables were covered with a brightly-coloured tablecloth. Once again, the inevitable eight dogs were lying at their masters' feet. The conversation was buzzing and the women were busy making a huge bowl of salad in preparation of a forthcoming meal. On sighting John and Jayne, the conversations abruptly ended as if switched off. All, including the dogs, looked over and studied John and Jayne but remained silent.

John pretended not to notice the group as he joined Jayne on the loungers outside their tent.

'I feel awfully embarrassed,' Jayne said quietly and very coyly. 'I wish you hadn't approached them this morning.'

'Cut that out, Jayne,' John hissed firmly between clenched teeth.

'Well, we've had such a lovely day and now we've come home to this. I feel terrible.'

'Well, you shouldn't,' declared John positively. 'We have done nothing and what's more ...'

'Are you really going to report them for their behaviour, John?' interrupted Jayne in a whisper.

'Of course not,' whispered John in reply. 'What do you think I am, and—' defiantly he raised his voice, '—why are we whispering? Come on, let's have a bottle of red and a little sing-song.' With that, he went into the tent to get a bottle of wine together with his guitar.

Jayne sheepishly glanced at the French group out of the corner of her eye. Seeing that they were still staring in silence, she quickly looked away.

JOHN BEVERLEY

John soon returned, poured two glasses of red wine, sat down and started strumming his guitar.

'They're still looking over, John,' said Jayne, again in a nervous whisper.

'Let 'em look,' replied John at the top of his voice. 'Come on, Jayne, let's sing.' With that he broke into a boisterous, 'Land of Hope and Glory.'

As if John's singing was a signal, one of the French women got up, looked around the table at her comrades as if looking for approval, then with a nod, walked across the camp-track that separated the group from John and Jayne.

'Excuse me, monsieur and madame. May I speak with you?'

John stopped singing and put the guitar down on the grass. 'Yes, mademoiselle,' John said authoritatively, seeing that the attractive woman in front of him was probably only about eighteen to twenty years old. 'What can I do for you?'

'Please, I am madame and my 'usband ees there,' she pointed at the big Frenchman that John instantly recognised from the early morning. 'But my name ees Mona, and I would like if you call me thees.'

'Okay, Mona,' repeated John, softening to the young woman's incredible smile. 'What can we do for you?' Jayne noticed the subtle 'we' from the more authoritative 'I' of John's last question.

'My 'usband and friends speak no Engleesh so they 'ave asked me to come 'ere and talk with you about thees morning,' Mona said nervously, obviously struggling with her English vocabulary. 'I 'ope that you will forgive us for being, how you say, so nosey. We did not realise eet was so late in the morning.'

John loved her French accent. 'The word is noisy and I think you mean early, not late, in the morning.'

Mona flushed. 'I am sorry, monsieur, my Engleesh ees so bad. I only teached – er, I mean learned eet at school.'

'Your English is wonderful,' Jayne said reassuringly to the young woman. 'Please come and sit down. John, get a chair for Mona.'

Duly seated, Mona went on. 'We feel 'orrible about what 'appened with the noise and the dogs. Please, if you give me your carpet I will clean eet and return eet to you this day.'

'There is no need,' said Jayne, her tone friendly. 'I have already cleaned up the rug so please don't worry yourself about it anymore.'

The young woman looked into Jayne's eyes. 'I am so sorry.' Then she turned to John. 'My friends and I—' she clasped her hand to her breast to stress the word 'I', '—would like you to come to us for supper now.'

John looked at Jayne who nodded her approval.

'We would really love to,' said John, now glad to pour oil-on-troubled-water now that he had met Mona and seen her obvious sincerity. 'However, I don't think that we should because, you see, it would be very difficult for us because we cannot speak French.'

177

'Please, monsieur, wait a moment.' Mona ran across to her companions.

Soon, Big Frenchman, Mona's husband, stood up and crossed over to where John sat. Smilingly, he lifted John to his feet and taking him by the arm led him to where Jayne also stood. Forcibly but in a gentle and friendly manner, he marched them across to the French-table and sat them next to Mona.

'Marcel said that eet does not matter if you cannot speak French,' Mona smiled, showing her perfect teeth. 'The important thing ees to eat, drink and have much laughter.'

And that's what John and Jayne had. The food was wonderful, being of many courses of salad, cold lamb and cold beef accompanied with mounds of slices of French bread. The drink with the meal was red wine followed by bottle after bottle of Pernod, the aniseed-tasting French liqueur. The laughter proved to be endless with John and Jayne enjoying the company and conversation, but only through Mona's efforts of acting as interpreter. Without Mona, the situation of noisy conversation and even-noisier joke-telling would have been impossible. Apologies for the early morning disturbance, particularly the dogs, never ceased, as did John and Jayne's acceptance of these apologies. Throughout all of the noise and boisterous fun, the eight dogs just lay around under the long table and never moved a muscle.

'What are you and your lovely dogs doing here,'

asked Jayne. 'Are you on holiday? How long are you here?'

'No,' replied Mona. 'We are not on 'oliday and we are only 'ere for the weekend. You see, Marcel and I, we are a dog-training company from Marseille. Every year at thees time, the mayor of Barjols invites us to his town to give a demonstration of our obedient dogs. Today ees Friday, yes?'

Jayne nodded and looked at John who sat listening, his mouth gaping in surprise.

'Well, tomorrow, Saturday, the six of us will be involved een giving all kinds of demonstrations with the dogs to show how clever they are. There will be hundreds of people there to see us een the town square. Would you like to come also?'

'We would love to,' John said eagerly.

'Who is looking after the young lad, was it André you called him?' asked Jayne.

'André ees Denise's child,' she pointed to one of the other ladies. ' 'e usually just sits een one of the cars. We are afraid that if 'e ees with us een the square 'e might wander off when we are all busy and cannot look after 'im.'

'No problem. Tell you what, if Denise and her husband approve, we will look after him for you. What time do you start in the morning?'

'We will be een the square for nine o'clock een the morning to arrange our equipment. The show starts at twelve o'clock and finishes at two o'clock een the afternoon.'

'Then we will have André all day and get him back to Denise by, shall we say, six o'clock?'

'Are you sure?' questioned Mona.

'After the hospitality that you have shown us tonight, it's the least we could do. Do you agree, John?'

'Absolutely!' John agreed willingly. 'Better get permission first though, eh Mona? Oh, and ask if he can bring his swimming trunks.'

And that was that. Denise readily agreed and André was met by John the following morning. With a big smile, André held John's hand in one tiny hand and his roll of towel-and-bathers in the other as he walked over to Jayne. They all waved goodbye to the French group as they, with their ever-faithful dogs, left for the town square a mile or so away.

The three hours or so before the dog-demonstration commenced had John, Jayne and young André having a ball. First they took André to the swimming-pool which was virtually right next to their tent. It was a bit crowded and noisy with the weekend school-children and it was this that probably accounted for André's nervousness at the poolside. He was so timid that he would only stand on the steps of the shallow-end with the water lapping around his ankles. There was no way that the little fellow was going in any deeper no matter how hard Jayne tried to coax him – a coaxing that wasn't easy with the language, or lack of language, barrier that existed between them.

'I know what we'll do, Jayne,' suggested John. 'You go and hold his hand at the side of the pool.

A Gaze into Holidaze

I'll stand in the water below you in the shallow end and hold out my arms to catch him, smiling and laughing all the time. You then jump in with him and I'll catch him and make sure that he doesn't go under.'

So they tried it. In they went and André was caught in John's arms. André absolutely loved it. Catching Jayne's hand, he dragged her back to the steps to climb out and do it all over again. This they did, not once, not twice, not three times but . . . at least thirty times.

However, by now John had gradually allowed André to settle deeper and deeper in the water when he caught him. In fact, the last few times John allowed André to briefly go completely under for a second or two before John lifted him back up and clear of the water. This made André laugh even more.

'Right then, Mister André,' John laughed, as he lifted André right out of the water and stood him at the poolside on his own. Taking a pace backwards, John held out his arms encouragingly and commanded, 'Come on, André, jump!'

With no hesitation young André jumped. John caught him after allowing him to completely submerge for the usual second or two before he spluttered to the surface. André, water pouring down his face, screamed with delight and shouted what John assumed was the French equivalent of 'more.'

About another forty of these and John breathlessly turned to Jayne, who was sitting on the side of the pool with legs dangling in the water. 'Jayne, I'm knackered. Come on, it's your turn. You catch him for a bit.'

'No! It's ten-thirty and it's time to go to the square. I reckon the wee lad has earned an ice-cream though, don't you?'

So they went to the Barjols town-square, which was heaving with people. There weren't hundreds of people, there were thousands. All bustling around the roped-off area, which was where the dog-demonstration was obviously going to take place, creating a wonderful atmosphere of excitement.

André got his well-deserved ice-cream. In fact, he got four well-deserved ice-creams and a well-deserved hot-dog before the demonstration started. It was also before John and Jayne lost him in the crowd.

'Oh God !' exclaimed John, panic sounding in his voice. 'Where the hell has he gone? I only let his hand go for a second. We'll never find him in this crowd.'

'Well, let's not panic, eh?' Jayne said, restoring calm to the situation. 'He can't have gone far. I'll stay put right here while you go around the crowd and look for him. Don't worry, you'll find him.'

'Right,' said John, not feeling the least bit confident as he set off through the crowd. 'Why did I let go of the little sod's hand? Well, I was only getting him some sweets off that stall, wasn't I? No excuse, I shouldn't have let go of his hand. Do you think he's been abducted by someone in the crowd?

A Gaze into Holidaze

Shit! Surely not. What are we going to tell André's parents? A fine minder I turned out to be. Thanks for your lovely meal, now I've lost your little boy. Oh shit!'

All of these thoughts rushed through John's head as he pushed his way through the multitude of people. He had probably gone no more than twenty yards when the throng thinned out momentarily and – there he was! There was André holding yet another ice-cream with one hand and the hand of his father with the other.

His father, after getting some change from the ice-cream salesman, turned and saw John. His face lit up in a huge grin as he spoke for quite some time to John.

John couldn't understand a word of it but didn't care. Young André was safe and that was all that mattered. John could feel his body sag with the comforting relief that coursed through his mind. It was obvious that André's father must have seen his son in the crowd and came to take the boy away to treat him to an ice-cream. With a smile John patted the Frenchman on the shoulder. 'I can't understand a bloody word you're saying but please don't do that again, there's a good chap. You nearly gave Jayne and me heart-attacks.'

The Frenchman, still smiling happily, merely shrugged innocently. John might as well have been speaking Chinese for all the understanding that he had of the threatened calamity.

The three of them returned to the anxious Jayne

who, true to her word, had not moved one iota from her last position. She sighed, the worry on her face disappearing when John told her what must have happened. 'I was so frightened,' was all she could manage.

'Me too,' John agreed then laughed as he looked at his wristwatch. 'You know I thought we'd lost the boy for hours and it's only been about six minutes.'

Without another word, André's father took John's arm quite forcefully to guide John, who now held André's hand tightly, and Jayne through the crowd. Soon they passed under the ropes of the enclosed demonstration area to the place where Mona and the rest of them were busy grooming the eight dogs.

'We 'ave a seat 'ere away from the crowd for you, André and Jayne,' she said, her face beaming. 'We are about to start the show so, please, I 'ope you enjoy eet.'

And enjoy it they did. It was a fantastic demonstration of skill and leadership on the part of the handling team, and obedience, co-ordination and intelligence on the part of the dogs. The dogs were made to obey simple, one-word commands which made them run, halt, round-up simulated sheep, climb and run across narrow beams set fifteen-feet off the ground, and even leap through flaming hoops. The dogs even jumped into a three-feet-deep tank of water from a high diving-platform, again some fifteen-feet off the ground. They were fantastic!

A Gaze into Holidaze

To much applause and adoration the interval came around and the team and dogs joined our three spectators.

'Did you enjoy that?' Mona asked as she handed John and Jayne a coffee which had miraculously appeared from nowhere.

'It was wonderful,' replied John, his eyes filled with respect. 'It's truly amazing what you have done with those dogs. They obey your commands with more intelligence than I would credit to a lot of people I know. You must have spent a lot of time working with the dogs to build up the confidence that you have between handler and dog.'

'Yes, we 'ave,' agreed Mona. 'Eet takes a lot of time. Would you like to take part een the show, John?'

'Yes please,' John replied without hesitation. 'What do I have to do?'

Mona and Marcel dressed John in a thickly-padded suit and fitted him with chain-mail gloves and a face-barred helmet. In the heat of the early afternoon it was stiflingly hot inside the Martian-like outfit. Into his hand they thrust a blank-firing pistol.

Mona instructed quietly. 'When you 'ear me shout, John, all you 'ave to do ees run for about thirty metres een that direction.' She pointed. 'Then you fire the pistol once before you turn around and run as fast as you can een the direction of that mattress on the ground there.' Again she pointed to a red mattress which lay on the grass about fifty metres away.

'And what then?' John asked enthusiastically.

'You will see' Mona smiled. 'Do not worry, you will be quite safe. Eet ees merely a demonstration to show 'ow obedient the dogs are even under fire.'

Five sweltering minutes later, after announcements in French had been made to the crowd, Mona turned to John and shouted in a loud voice. 'Go!'

Away John went, pistol in hand, as fast as his heavy suit would allow. Thirty metres later, he turned and fired the pistol which went off with an extremely loud bang before setting off again, legs going like pistons, towards the red mattress which only looked a few metres away.

That was as far as John got. Seconds later he was hit in the back by an express train. At least that is what it felt like. One moment he was running in his heavy suit, reasonably happy with his efforts, the next he was lying helplessly on his stomach in the grass with something clamped vice-like around the wrist of the hand holding the pistol. All the while his hand was being shaken like a rag-doll and there was a continuous and vicious snarling.

Slowly, he managed to turn himself over to find one black German shepherd clamped to his wrist, whilst another white German shepherd leaned heavily on his chest to place its snarling mouth inches away from his face. 'Thank God for the barred face-mask' thought John, breathless, and buttocks clenched in terror. 'This looks like the same dog that gave me a kiss yesterday morning!'

A Gaze into Holidaze

At the sound of a shrill whistle, both dogs obediently moved away from John and sat on their haunches, much to the delight and rapturous applause of the crowd.

John and Jayne didn't see the remainder of the dog-handling demonstration because they spent the rest of the afternoon in the local doctor's medical centre. John had a suspected fracture of the wrist.

'Do you think those French buggers did this on purpose, Jayne?' asked John painfully as he looked down at his swollen wrist. 'You know, to get back at me for returning their dog-shit.'

'No, of course not,' returned Jayne. 'They were only trying to make you feel part of the show and it was very kind of them to involve you in their special day.'

'Involve me!' exclaimed John. 'It's like involving someone by inviting them to take part in an arm-wrestling match with a gorilla. I'm aching all over and . . .'

'Oh, stop grizzling, it's only a sprained wrist which will be fine in a day or two. Anyway, you could have declined taking part when they offered you the chance.'

And it proved to be only a sprained wrist with not a fracture in sight. It was bandaged tightly and left to heal over the next few days.

On arrival back at the campsite later that evening, the French could not do enough to apologise for the accident. Time and time again, Mona would come over to John and Jayne and enquire about

John's wrist. 'Are you alright, John? We are so sorry for what 'appened. You must 'ave landed awkwardly on your, 'ow you say eet, whist, when Sheba 'eet you from behind?'

'Wrist,' said John, a smile tugging at the corners of his mouth. 'We say wrist. And it's no problem, it was just an accident.'

The following morning, the French dog-handlers left for their homes in Marseilles, but not before each and every one of them came over to the tent to say their goodbyes. Unfortunately, John had to shake hands with his left hand.

The positive side to John's performance in the dog-handling demonstration was that he became a minor star. For the next week or so, whenever he went on the campsite, or into Barjols if it comes to that, John was recognised as the 'gunman-who-was-knocked-over-and-injured-by-the-dogs.' Everyone seemed to want to greet him warmly with a shake of the hand – left hand of course!

****

CHAPTER THREE

CARAVANS (THE LEARNING CURVE) – OR AREN'T PEOPLE EVEN MORE FUNNY?

An excitingly new and luxurious adventure which is great fun . . .!
'How long have we been camping, John?' asked Jayne on a particularly wet April-day on their favourite campsite in West Wales.

John turned up his collar from the damp, cold air and leaned forward in his chair to look out through the plastic window of the tent at the dark cliffs and crashing waves as they broke over the rocks far below them. 'I don't really know to be honest with you. What with time in the ridge-tent and the frame-tent, I suppose about twelve years give or take a year.' He turned from the window to look at Jayne who, before she had just spoken, had been deep in thought for the past half-an-hour or so. 'Why do you ask?'

'We both love our camping, don't we?' Jayne said. John nodded agreement so Jayne continued. 'Other than the weeks we spend abroad, most of the time we camp in this country where it's perpetually cold or damp or both.'

John again nodded but added, 'You mean bloody cold or bloody wet and both, don't you?'

'Right,' said Jayne emphatically. 'Let's get a caravan, or to be more precise, let's get ourselves a mobile-home.'

'Can we afford it?' came John's usual financial pessimism.

Jayne laughed. 'John, you have been a company senior-manager for the last two years, and, don't forget that we are DINKIES. Of course we can afford it.' It was true. John had worked his way up the professional ladder within his company and was now earning a good salary.

'What's DINKIES?' enquired John, a puzzled frown on his face.

'Dual income, no kids,' came Jayne's reply.

John thought for the briefest of moments. 'Done,' said John decisively. 'Let's get ourselves a mobile-home.'

So they did. The following day, they excitedly started their tour of the showrooms to find out what type of touring-caravan they wanted. They did not know anything about tourers but they were confident that the guidance of the caravan-dealers in general, and the caravan salespeople in particular, would be of great assistance to them.

Well, it didn't quite work out like that. In the case of simple questions like, 'What size caravan do we want because there are only the two of us?' or 'Should we have a single-axle or a double-axle?' the average 'helpful' reply from the respective salesperson seemed to be, 'Well, it depends on what you want really. It's up to you. Why don't you wander around the showroom and pick out what you want?' How John and Jayne were supposed to pick out what they wanted when they didn't have a clue as to what they wanted, John and Jayne did not know. By the end of the day, and perhaps a half-dozen dealers in South Wales later, John and Jayne were none the wiser.

'Who do we know who has been touring in caravans for years?' asked the frustrated John. 'Who do we know who knows quite a lot about caravans and is down-to-earth when explaining about them? A person who will not give you a lot of sales bull.'

Spontaneously and simultaneously, when outside a particular caravan-dealership in West-Wales in the pouring rain, they looked at each other and loudly declared, 'Derek.'

And so a visit to Derek's was planned.

Derek was an old friend and neighbour who had had touring-caravans, or tourers/mobile-homes as they are known in the camping world, for years and years. In fact, Derek had been hinting to John and Jayne for many a year that it was time to put their tent away because a tourer was the answer to John's and Jayne's holiday frolics.

In one visit Derek passed on to the couple what were, in his opinion, the do's and don'ts of buying a caravan. Like, if you can afford to buy a new one rather than a second-hand one, the three year warranty was worth its weight in gold; don't buy a two-berth, a four-berth was more acceptable when it came to a re-sell or trade-in; a single-axle was probably better over a double-axle because it was easier to manoeuvre on small campsites, and it was cheaper on some of the continental motorways where the authorities cost their tolls on the number of axles using the motorway; ideally the laden weight of the tourer should be about eighty percent of the un-laden weight of the towing-vehicle. Derek passed on a wealth of information which John and Jayne absorbed like sponges.

The couple was thrilled to bits when, armed with all the information and advice gained from Derek, they tackled the dealerships in the 'world of touring-caravans'. However, the task of selection still did not come easily, what with the multitude of options that existed in caravans. For example, front bedroom or back bedroom; permanently made-up double-bed or nightly made-up double-bed; single-beds in front, middle or rear; bunk-beds or proper single-beds; front kitchen, side kitchen or middle kitchen; back bathroom or side bathroom; included shower in bathroom or shower separate from bathroom; included toilet in bathroom or toilet separate from bathroom; standard upholstery or deluxe, super-duper, hard-wearing, last-forever upholstery. The alternatives were endless!

'God! It wasn't like this when we chose our new tent, was it?' John grumbled to Jayne after visiting about ten touring-caravan dealerships. 'All we cared about was size and whether the damn thing was fully waterproof.'

A Gaze into Holidaze

'Yes,' Jayne agreed, equally as disappointed as John. 'Well, we've got to decide, and we've got to decide today or we'll keep going around in ever-decreasing circles.'

And decide they did that very day. They settled on a brand-new Castillo caravan and of all the various models that the manufacturer provided, they chose a Bueno. The tourer offered them everything in-house that camping had never done. Four beds, not that they needed the extra two bunks; a kitchen with a four-hob gas-cooker and a fridge; a bathroom in the rear of the caravan with a separate shower. Oh yes, and cupboards galore. There was even a decently-sized wardrobe in it!

'And it's got an external water supply instead of in-board water-tanks,' boasted John, remembering the advice that he had obtained from Derek. 'In-board water-tanks can leak all over the floor, and, if you forget to drain 'em in winter they can freeze on you and split the tank.'

'Will the Volvo be okay to pull it, John?'

'No problem, sweetheart. I've done the sums and we are well within the eighty-percent bit.'

Jayne looked at the shiny and magnificent caravan. It seemed to be gleaming just for her in the bright lights of the showroom. She studied the name for the hundredth time. 'Castillo Bueno,' she muttered to herself. Then, turning to John, who seemed much happier now that a decision on the caravan had been made, she asked, 'John, with a name like Castillo Bueno, are you sure it's one of our caravans? You know, a British-made one.'

'Yes, yes,' assured John smugly. 'I've already checked on that. It is British and it's got a three-year warranty, not that I expect we will need it.'

Because John and Jayne had no caravan to trade-in, they tried to arrange a discount on the price. The salesman, whose name was Percy, would not remotely budge on this point. What Percy said that he would do, was instead of a discount, and providing that they would take delivery immediately, he would throw-in a considerable amount of extras.

'Like what?' asked John, a little bit suspicious of the offer. John, whose experience of wheeler-dealing lay mostly in car-buying, wanted a firm cash-discount.

'We'll give you all of these things,' beamed Percy, his painted smile allowing his bleached white teeth with the gold front-replacement to almost sparkle in the bright lights of the showroom. He reached below the counter and placed a typed sheet of paper in front of John. 'I'm sure you'll be pleased with this, sir.'

'You've obviously prepared yourself for discount-hunters,' John said sarcastically as he looked down at the list in front of him. He read out loud, 'Full-size awning, 40-litre water-container, waste-water disposal unit with connecting pipes, chromium caravan steps, stabiliser and three-piece wheel clamp.' John looked up at Percy of the painted smile. 'What's a stabiliser?'

'It's a device that is fitted onto the towing-hitch

of the caravan, sir, to stop the tourer from snaking on the road whilst at speed.' Although Gold Tooth was still smiling, John could not help but feel that there was sneering behind the fixed mask of the salesman's face. 'You'll certainly find it invaluable when being overtaken by a heavy vehicle on the motorway, sir.'

'How much does this lot cost?' John said flatly as he looked Gold Tooth directly in the eye.

'I'll work it out now for you, sir.' Gold Tooth busied himself on his calculator for a minute or so.

'Bullshit,' said John impatiently, his face reflecting his annoyance. He glanced at Jayne, who stood with her mouth open.

'Pardon?' said the puzzled Gold Tooth.

'If you've got a typed and printed list of the gear that you are prepared to give away on the Castillo Bueno, don't tell me that you haven't got the value of that gear sorted out well in advance. Don't give me any more bullshit.'

Gold Tooth flushed. 'I was only trying to . . .'

'Give me bullshit,' interrupted John sharply. 'How much do the extras cost, please?'

'Eight hundred and thirty-two pounds,' stammered Gold Tooth, his confidence completely gone to the dogs.

'Make it a nice round thousand pounds and you've got yourself a deal.'

Gold Tooth seemed out of his depth. 'I'll have to see my boss because I cannot make a decision like this.'

'Do that,' replied John firmly as he turned and winked at Jayne who had stood quietly throughout the negotiations with mouth agape.

The salesman shuffled off and disappeared into a small office at the side of the showroom. Within literally two minutes he was back accompanied by a tall man in a black pin-stripe suit, blue shirt and the gaudiest tie that John and Jayne had ever seen.

Bright Tie beamed with exactly the same painted smile of Gold Tooth. 'Providing you take the tourer immediately, sir, you've bought yourself a caravan.'

'I don't really want it until July,' said John, thinking that Gold Tooth and Bright Tie looked like a right pair of book-ends.

'I'm sorry, sir, but we need the space for more caravans so that is the only condition that enables me to meet your demands. Incidentally, you will need a special ball for your tow-bar ... er, I assume that you have a tow-bar with double-electrics fitted to your car.'

'Yes, to the tow-bar, no, to the double-electrics,' John replied. 'I have only single-electrics.'

'Then let's say that we will give you time – let's say a week, shall we – to get the special ball fitted together with the double-electrics? We will supply the special ball. Does that suit you?'

'That's fine,' nodded John.

'Good,' Bright Tie said gushingly. Holding out his hand he shook hands with John. 'I will leave you with Percy to do the final arrangements with the paperwork and I will arrange for a hand-over of

A Gaze into Holidaze

the caravan from us to you for one week from today. Oh yes, the number plates will also be fitted for you. Nice to have met you, sir.' Then he was gone.

Driving home from the showrooms, Jayne sat quietly in the car, not saying a word.

'What's the matter, Jayne?' John asked cheerfully. 'Why so gloomy? We've got a cracking caravan, a great deal, bags of kit, three-year guarantee, and it's paid for. We can even tow it with the Volvo. What more could a girl ask for?'

'Where are we going to keep it, John?'

'Out in the drive, of course. That's the beauty of owning a detached bungalow, isn't it?'

'But we share the drive with our neighbours and perhaps they won't like it.'

'Jayne, you always worry about other people far too much,' John assured gently. 'Look, there is no reason why they should object. The drive down from the road to our garage is ours, so don't worry yourself and leave the neighbours to me. There will be no problem, trust me.'

A week later, at 9 a.m. in the morning, special towing-ball and double-electrics fitted to the Volvo, John and Jayne arrived at the showroom full of the joys of spring. Gold Tooth greeted them with the inevitable painted smile, and held out his hand. 'Good morning, John.'

Taking the other man's hand, John noted that now that the tourer had been paid for, the 'sir' had disappeared in conversation only to be replaced by the informal 'John'.

'Some bad news I'm afraid,' Gold Tooth continued. 'Bit of delay on our part really. The caravan won't be ready until about three o'clock this afternoon. Short of staff you see.'

'I don't believe it,' John said angrily. 'Look, mate, I rang up yesterday to make sure that 9 a.m. this morning was suitable as we agreed – and now this! I'm bloody annoyed!'

But nothing could be done about it no matter how much complaining was done by John. The caravan was not ready and that was that! All that John and Jayne could do was run into the nearest town, which was Cardiff, and pass away the time. Their excitement had certainly waned to say the least.

At 3 p.m. promptly the couple returned to the dealership to find the ever-smiling Gold Tooth standing proudly outside their gleaming Castillo Bueno, a young man in dirty overalls at his side.

'Here we are at last,' Gold Tooth glittered. 'All's well that end's well, eh?'

John snorted in reply.

'All the promised kit is in the van and Dai here, our service engineer, will run you around inside to show you the bits and pieces. If you have any questions, Dai is your man, he's our expert.' With that, Gold Tooth disappeared as if by magic.

So there they were, one bitterly-cold, wet and windy April afternoon, about to take-over their expensively new tourer from Dai, a young man in dirty overalls, who seemed barely out of school.

A Gaze into Holidaze

'Have you done this before?' enquired John of Dai, a bit concerned at the youthfulness of the young, dirty engineer.

'Aye, mun. Many times,' came the barely discernible reply from Dai. 'I am the chief engineer yer and I see to the despatch of all the new vans.'

Although John could hardly understand the heavy Welsh dialect, the three of them entered John and Jayne's prize possession. It was like the inside of a freezer!

'Sorry about the cold, innit?' Dai said. 'But it's always like this about this time of year, see?'

'Well, aren't you going to plug the caravan into the electric mains or something. It will warm us all up and we can ensure that everything is working?' John eyed Dai with suspicion.

'No need, see? I've done the inspection and everything is fine, see?'

John looked at Jayne who shrugged in reply. She then asked, 'Is that the way you always do handovers, Dai?'

'Aye, missus. That's right, see? No need to worry, see? It's all in the handbook that comes with the van anyway.'

Jayne looked blankly at John and this time it was John's turn to shrug helplessly.

Fifteen very cold minutes later, Dai looked at them and said, 'There you are, handover complete. Nothin' to it, was there?'

John and Jayne's heads were buzzing where they had tried to absorb so much in such a short time. 'Look Dai, we know very little about touring-caravans. This is our first. Is there anything else that we should know? I think that I understand everything that you've told us, but it's all so confusing.'

'Oh, don't worry, mun,' Dai soothed. 'It's all in the handbook anyway, see? Come on. I'll show you how to connect up to get you on your way.'

John reversed the Volvo through the pouring rain to the front of the caravan, stopping expertly with the ball of the tow-bar directly beneath the socket of the caravan's tow-hitch.

'There you are, mun,' laughed Dai. 'Done like a professional, you.' He then proceeded to show John how to connect up the new stabilised hitching-mechanism. 'There you are, see? Easy, innit?' Dai added triumphantly when the mechanism locked into position. 'Off you go and enjoy yourselves. Think of us poor workers back here while you sun yourself on the Gower.' He laughed profusely at what he thought was a great joke.

Gingerly, John and Jayne climbed into the Volvo and even more gingerly edged out into the traffic to drive the thirty miles or so home.

'Are you alright to tow this caravan, John?' Jayne asked nervously, after they had travelled about a mile.

'Piece of cake,' declared John confidently. 'With the power of the Volvo you can't remotely feel that there is a caravan being towed behind you.'

'Wasn't much of a handover, was it?' Jayne continued.

A Gaze into Holidaze

'Bloody disgusting to be honest,' replied John. 'Still, I suppose it's normal. I just couldn't help but feel that everything was done in a rush despite the time we had to wait.' He paused as he steered the car and caravan between double-parked cars before continuing. 'Anyway, as Dai said – if you could understand what Dai said – it's all in the handbook.'

An hour later, as the rain stopped, they arrived home. The towing of the caravan had proved no problem and, other than the loss of the car's centre rear-view mirror, John didn't even know that the caravan was behind him.

'We've now got the advantage of living at the bottom of a cul-de-sac,' said John as they turned into their road. 'The square gives us bags of room to pull-in outside the bungalow. We can then unhitch and push the caravan backwards into the drive. It's nice and flat so it will be easy.'

Well, it was a great idea until it came to the unhitching. They did everything opposite to what they had been shown by Dai during the hitching-up process, but all that happened when they tried to raise the 'socket' of the caravan clear of the 'ball' of the car, was to raise the entire rear of the car skywards. No way did the ball want to disengage from the socket. On top of that, the dark clouds overhead decided to empty themselves in a torrential downpour, drenching the struggling couple in the process.

'Oh, bollocks!' hissed John through clenched

teeth, his patience after six attempts to unhitch, at an end.

'There's no need for that,' Jayne retorted frostily, water dripping from her nose. 'Let's go inside and have a nice cup of tea and we'll figure out what we're doing wrong in the process.'

'We can't leave the bloody thing here,' snarled John, his temper bubbling below the surface. 'We're blocking everyone's driveways and I can already see curtains twitching where the bloody nosey-parkers are peeping out. Don't give a hand and help though, do they?'

Jayne looked around the small cul-de-sac with its six bungalows. Yes, there were neighbours peeping from behind curtains. 'You should have asked Dai to show you how to unhitch,' Jayne said, shaking her head so that rainwater sprayed from her hair in all directions.

'Now you tell me,' shouted John helplessly. 'Bloody marvellous! Do you think I don't wish I had asked him. It's supposing too much to think that that silly bugger, Dai, could have shown us how to unhitch if there was a magic way of doing it. Bloody idiot!'

'Come on, John, calm down,' hushed Jayne, putting her hand reassuringly on John's arm. 'Let's try one more time together.'

John nodded. 'I'll call out what I'm doing and you follow me through, okay?' He looked over at Jayne who smiled, dripped, and gave him the thumbs-up. 'Right, jockey wheel is solid, handbrake on, electrics are disconnected, brake connector is disconnected, friction screw is released, both levers are up.' John laughed as he saw Jayne's thumbs-up signal once more. 'It's like a bloody cockpit-check in an aeroplane, isn't it?' he said as he once again turned the handle of the jockey-wheel to raise the socket of the caravan. Yet again, the back of the car went skywards, but the caravan's socket refused to drop the ball of the car.

'Shit! Bugger! Damn!' said John quietly. 'What are we going to do now?'

'Well, you can stop swearing for a start,' replied Jayne sharply. 'Let's see. Can you reverse the caravan in the drive, John? At least we won't be in anyone's way.'

'You must be joking!' John exclaimed. 'I haven't tried reversing the bloody thing yet. I think it's too difficult until I have practiced it. You know, reverse lock on the car and all that sort of thing. Anyway, there is not enough room to manoeuvre the car in this small space.'

'Right,' said Jayne with an air of finality. 'Ring Dai and get him up here.'

John was on the telephone in a flash. 'Hello, is that the caravan service department?' A muffled unintelligible response was heard on the end of the line. 'Dai, is that you?'

'Aye, that's me, mun,' the thickly accented voice replied.

'Dai, this is John. You know, the caravan idiot to whom you handed over a Castillo Bueno about two hours ago? Well, I can't unhitch the bloody thing. I'm in the street and I'm bloody-well stuck. Can you come and help me?'

'No, I don't do that, see?' Dai mumbled, John barely being able to decipher his words on the telephone line. 'The boss wouldn't let me do that, innit?'

'Put your boss on the line right now,' shouted John aggressively, desperately trying to control his temper.

'Well, he's not yer, see?' said Dai calmly, as if he had all the time in the world. 'In fact, there's no-one yer now because we are closing and they've all gone home. There's only me yer, innit?'

'Well, you've got to do something Dai,' John said pleadingly. Realising that Dai was his only hope he forced himself to calm down. 'It's raining torrents and we are stuck in the street.'

'Have you done what I showed you?' Dai asked.

'You didn't show me anything regarding unhitching,' whispered John, thinking that Dai sounded like the runnnneeee egg gentleman of days gone by.

'Oh, didn't I, that's silly of me, innit? Must 'ave forgot or something I suppose. Tell me what you've tried.'

John patiently went through the unhitching process that he had tried so many times in the pouring rain outside of his bungalow.

'Well, you've done everything right, see?' Dai came back. 'It's probably a bit new and is stickin' a bit. Tell you what, is the handbrake on your car on or off?'

'On.'

'Well, release the handbrake on your car and push the car back and fore a bit. I bet that'll do it.'

'Okay, I'll try it, but don't hang up.'

John rushed out into the rain once more and released the handbrake of the car. Instead of pushing his car back and fore as Dai had suggested, he started the car. The vibration of the engine starting was all that was needed, the socket and ball parted smoothly.

'Yes!' shouted John triumphantly. He got out of the car and dashed to the phone in the bungalow to tell Dai of his success. The line was dead.

'So much for after-sales, eh?' John said to Jayne as they easily pushed the caravan back into their drive. 'Now I'll enjoy a nice cup of tea and we'll both settle down for the night.'

'I could certainly do with that,' Jayne replied, soaked to the skin but still grinning like a Cheshire cat. 'Well, at least we've learned how to unhitch.'

'Yes, the hard way, as usual. Some start to a new and excitingly luxurious adventure – what?'

****

One good deed deserves . . .

Over the next couple of days, two to be precise, John and Jayne could not help but keep sneaking out of the bungalow to see their shiny and gleamingly new fun-machine. Even in the rain it looked proudly magnificent as it stood there with its legs down on the drive.

'Can't wait to go off in it, can you?' Jayne asked eagerly.

'Cor! We've only had it two days and you are itching to give it a whirl, aren't you?' replied John. 'Tell you what, I've got to go to Weston-Super-Mare on business the Thursday of next week. Let's take the caravan and I can go to work from it and turn the business-trip into a long weekend. How does that sound?'

'Terrific!' replied Jayne. 'I'm dying to try everything out.'

That evening, after the fiftieth time they had gone into the drive to admire and walk around Clarence, as they had nicknamed the caravan, they had just settled down in front of the television when there was a knock at the front door.

'Unusual,' said John as he went and opened the door. 'We don't get many visitors.' His jaw dropped. There, standing in all his glory complete with tall, black helmet, was a police constable.

'Good evening, sir,' greeted the tall policeman. 'May I come in?'

'Of c-c-course,' stammered John uncertainly. He stepped back to allow the policeman to enter. 'Let me have your hat, I mean helmet, constable.'

'No thank you, sir,' said the policemen, his face expressionless as he removed his helmet and held it to his chest. 'I won't keep you long.'

A Gaze into Holidaze

'Please, come into the lounge,' said John, and led the way into the lounge where Jayne was sitting. 'Put the kettle on, Jayne, we have a visitor. Sit down there constable.'

'I've had a complaint about your caravan,' the policeman went on. 'It seems it's causing an obstruction.'

'An obstruction!' exclaimed John. 'Absolute rubbish! Hell, we've only had it two days and it's only been in my drive during that time. We haven't taken it out yet.'

'You mean you haven't even moved it yet?' queried the police officer, a questioning frown on his face but still unsmiling.

'No, constable, not an inch since we brought it from the dealers two days ago.' It was Jayne's turn to speak up. 'Admittedly we did block our neighbours drive when we first arrived because we had trouble unhitching the caravan – you see it's our first one – but that was only for about a half-an-hour or so.'

'Now that I've come to see the situation and details of the complaint for myself, I must say that I don't understand what it's all about.' The policeman paused. 'Admittedly, you share a drive with your next-door neighbours, but there is bags of access for them to get their car into their garage.'

'Who made the complaint?' Jayne asked gingerly.

'Sorry, madam, but I am not at liberty to tell you that,' replied the visitor. 'However, what I am at liberty to tell you is that you are not in any way obstructing anything and I am annoyed that I have been forced to bother you.'

'It's these bloody silly-bugger neighbours of ours,' John reacted. 'They are bloody jealous of everything we've ever done. First my promotion in work, then our Volvo and now our new caravan. What the hell is the matter with them?'

'Relax John,' Jayne sighed. 'It's no good getting het-up about it.' Turning to the police-officer she said, 'Are we in any sort of trouble, constable?'

'No, definitely not,' the man said with authority. Then, his tone softening with a degree of sympathy, he spoke quietly. 'Off the record, madam, I think I know what the trouble is. You see, the complainants, when I paid them a visit before coming to see you, couldn't show me the deeds to their house quick enough.'

'Why the deeds to their house?' John asked, a puzzled frown on his face.

'Well you see, sir,' the law enforcement officer continued. 'It appears that the deeds refer to all of this cul-de-sac and you are not permitted, according to the deeds, to park a caravan here overnight.'

'Not even in your own driveway?' Jayne asked.

'Apparently not,' the constable replied.

'Then are you telling me that we are committing an offence?' John's annoyance was once again showing through.

'Not at all,' the constable answered quickly. 'This is nothing to do with the police and that's final. This is a civil matter and is between you and your neighbours.'

A Gaze into Holidaze

'Then it was the neighbours who complained,' John stated flatly.

The police constable did not reply. There was a silence.

'Will you have a cup of tea, constable?' Jayne offered, desperate to break the atmosphere of despondency that had descended on the room.

'No thank you,' the policeman answered politely. 'I'd better be off. My job is done now and I must report back to the Station.' He stood to leave.

'What can we do, constable?' It was Jayne who asked.

'Well, if you want my unofficial advice, I'd certainly move the caravan as quickly as possible.'

'Or what?' John's aggressiveness lingered.

The police constable sighed deeply. 'They could take you to a civil court, sir, for breaching the terms of your contract – namely your deeds.'

John remained silent.

'Why don't you park your caravan in a storage area?' the policeman suggested helpfully. 'There's one I know about fifteen miles from here.'

'Fifteen miles,' John said in disgust.

'Better that, sir, than possible civil court action. I will leave you now. I'm very sorry to have disturbed you so I bid you both goodnight.'

John closed the front door behind the policeman. 'Nice chap really. He was only doing his job and he didn't have to tell us about those deeds.'

'Or our charming neighbours,' remarked Jayne. 'Why are people so petty John? What harm are we doing parking Clarence in our own drive?'

'Beats me,' sighed John. 'Bloody neighbours can't mind their own business. I knew about those deeds but I didn't think anyone would care. Anyway, no problem, I'll find a caravan-storage tomorrow and hopefully it will be a bit closer than fifteen miles away.'

And he did. The following day he found a suitable storage only about eight miles away from home. John didn't like the owner of the storage place very much because he made John feel as if he were doing him a big favour. Nevertheless, John bit his lip, swallowed his pride and booked an annual storage-pitch at the site.

The following day he took Clarence to storage. When he returned to the bungalow he was just getting out of his car when a neighbour from the cul-de-sac stopped him.

'See you've moved your caravan, then,' she smirked, a superior look on her face.

John grunted in reply and walked into the bungalow. He thought silently to himself, 'You really can't win them all but it would be nice to win just one occasionally!'

****

Setting up is a piece of old doddle . . .

John and Jayne left for Weston-Super-Mare the following Thursday, the incident involving the neighbours completely forgotten.

After retrieving Clarence from storage, John

called in to a caravan-accessories shop to pick up an 'easy-to-fit' security hitch-lock which was specially designed to fit the ball-type stabiliser that was fitted to the caravan.

'No-one will steal your caravan with this fitted to your towing-hitch,' the salesman guaranteed.

'I should think not for fifty-quid,' remarked John as he paid for the lock. 'For that kind of money it should be fitted for me, and in gold.'

'You'll fit it in ten minutes, sir. Just screw on the two brackets that are in the box to your tow-hitch, the holes are already there, and bob's-your-uncle. Anyway, there are simple instructions inside together with the keys to the lock.'

It was now the end of April and the weather had not let up. It was the usual torrential rain when they arrived in the early afternoon at their very first certified-site which was on a farm about three miles outside Weston-Super-Mare.

'This looks nice,' said Jayne. 'I'm glad we joined the Caravan and Camping Club if this is a sample of their quiet sites. You can only have up to five caravans on these certified sites, you know?'

John looked around the site. The site was empty except for one caravan which was tucked away behind a barn but near the toilet-block. 'The ground is too soggy with all of this rain,' John stated. 'We'll park next to the white caravan over there. Behind that barn is a hard-standing which is best at this time of year. Can you see any electric hook-ups?'

'Yes,' replied Jayne. 'There is one next to the other caravan. I think that you'll have to reverse into the hard-standing though, John. Do you think that you can manage it?'

'No problem. You just watch me back and tell me when to stop.'

John, although it was his first time, reversed the caravan like a true professional. Yes, he found the use of the reverse-lock on the car a bit strange, but it was relatively easy in spite of the pounding rain which added a little more difficulty. The only slight mishap was when Jayne ran breathlessly to the open window of the car and screamed at the top of her voice, 'Stop!' John immediately stopped.

'Couldn't you hear me shouting "stop"?' panted Jayne, soaking wet for the umpteenth time since they had taken charge of the caravan.

'No,' said John calmly. 'I couldn't hear you with all of this rain tamping on the roof.'

'Well, I shouted at least three times as loudly as I could. You nearly reversed into a tree.'

John shot out of the car and rushed to the back of the caravan. As sure as God made little apples, there was a thin lath-like tree about one foot from the back of Clarence. Lesson – never underestimate the length of the combination of car and caravan because there is the best part of forty-feet to push backwards or forwards!!

'Well, we're safely parked now,' said John. 'I'll stay outside and do the outside jobs like putting on the security-locks, connecting up the electricity and sorting out the water and things, you do the bits and pieces inside the caravan. There's no point in us both getting wet.'

So Jayne disappeared inside Clarence while John unhitched, which proved to be easy this time with the car-engine running, put the supporting-legs down to give the caravan a solid base and connected up the electric cable from caravan to site-mains. This done he set about the hitch-lock. No-one was going to steal their brand-new Clarence, that was a certainty.

In the pelting rain, John struggled with the usual nuisance and seemingly yards of Sellotape that ensured that one could not easily open the red cardboard box that contained the brand-new, fifty-pounds sterling, should-have-been-gold hitch-lock. 'Bloody packers,' muttered John to himself. 'I reckon they do this quite deliberately to make sure that you can't open the blasted box.'

After a severe burst of silent swearing John finally succeeded in opening the box. 'Right!' John said triumphantly to no-one in particular. 'Beat you, you bastard. Now to fix the two small brackets and the security-lock on and bob's-your-uncle.' He peered into the rain-sodden box. No brackets! He frantically took out the hitch-lock which was present and correct. He then removed the 'Instructions to Fit' leaflet which was virtually a soggy piece of paper that started to fall apart in his hands. Quickly he read the instructions before looking up at the black, rain-filled sky, seemingly oblivious to the rain that drenched his face.

JOHN BEVERLEY

John was almost in prayer. 'It says quite clearly in step four to fit the two enclosed side-brackets using the existing holes in the tow-hitch. And there are no fucking brackets in the box! Oh, shit!' Then he became aware of the cold rain which insisted on running down inside the front of his sweater in spite of the hooded anorak that he was wearing. 'Oh, fuck! Does it ever stop pissing with rain in this God-forsaken country?' As soon as the words uncontrollably left his mouth, he sheepishly looked around in case Jayne had heard him. No sign of her – thank God for that!

Deciding that he wasn't happy about not hitch-locking Clarence, John went and knocked on the only caravan on site, right next-door to them. The door was opened by a nice man who introduced himself as Alex. John explained his predicament regarding the hitch-lock and, being new to caravanning, would be grateful for any advice. Better than giving advice, Alex put on his coat and went with John to have a look at the situation.

'Yes, I know this type of lock,' said Alex confidently. 'It's a good one but you do have to have the two side-brackets. It's no good without them. Do you have any other kind of lock – a wheel clamp for instance?'

'Yes,' replied John. 'I've got one of those but I haven't even taken it out of the box yet.'

'Oh, that's alright then. As long as you've got some form of lock, because there is a travellers' camp not far away and allegedly they'll steal anything that's not nailed down. Personally, I don't believe it but you never know, do you?' With a laugh, Alex returned to his caravan.

John did manage to successfully get the three-piece wheel clamp out of the box and read the corresponding fitting instructions which might as well have been written in Chinese for what good they were. 'Undoubtedly, they must have been written by a half-wit who liked to have his head up his arse as he wrote them,' was John's only comment as he struggled with the three-piece metallic jigsaw-puzzle.

Finally, after another rain-soaked half-an-hour, the wheel-clamp was on. 'God knows how the hell I'm going to get it off!' John exclaimed loudly to himself through the rain. 'Need a bloody degree to fit this thing! I'm bloody freezing so I think a cup of coffee is in order.'

Although he hadn't noticed before, being busy with the problems of the hitch-lock and wheel-clamp, the caravan was in complete darkness even though the daylight was fading outside. 'What's up Jayne? Why no lights?'

'No anything I'm afraid, John,' Jayne said timidly. 'I've done as much unpacking as I can but when I went to put on the lights I had nothing. I didn't want to tell you because I knew that you would be upset what with your struggling with the locks in the rain.'

'Hells bells and buckets of blood!' John said in despair as he flopped on to the back seat of the caravan, not caring about the water that dripped from him on to the carpeted floor. 'If we have no power it means that we have no water, no lights, no fridge and what's more important – no heat!'

'We still have gas, John,' Jayne hastened to help. 'I can always boil a kettle on the cooker for a hot drink and the heater will work on gas.'

'That's if we can get the damn thing to work. I asked for the dealer to connect-up the gas-bottles for us because we weren't sure how to do it. When I went in the bottle-compartment at the front of the caravan to get the leg-brace out, I see that the bastards haven't done it.'

'Have a coffee, John, before you do anything. I made a flask of it before we left. You'll feel better after a cup because you must be cold after all that rain.'

'No thanks, love, not just now. It'll be dark soon and I want to get these electrics sorted.' John was determined. 'I reckon that there must be a mains-switch here somewhere. Come on, let's have a look.'

They hunted the inside of the caravan high and low. No mains-switch. In fact, there was no sign of any electric switches anywhere other than light switches. 'There's no cable in sight anywhere, Jayne, or I could trace the wires back to the mains. There must be a mains and fuse-box somewhere!' But they couldn't find it.

Back out into the rain John went, again in search of their neighbour, Alex.

'Come in,' invited Alex pleasantly. 'What's the problem now?'

A Gaze into Holidaze

John told him.

'Oh yes, there is a mains and a fuse-box in there somewhere because there must be by law,' declared Alex. 'All manufacturers must provide them or they will be breaking the law. Have you looked underneath the bench-seats?'

'The bench-seats?' John raised his eyebrows in surprise. 'Didn't think of looking there to be honest.'

Alex laughed. 'You said you were new to caravanning, how long have you had one?'

'About a week and this is the first time for us to use it.'

'Didn't the dealer give you a proper handover brief?' asked Alex.

'Yes,' replied John. 'We had a quarter-of-an-hour's chat with a bloke – er, a caravan service-engineer called Dai.'

'A quarter-of-an-hour's chat!' Alex was shocked. 'That's disgusting. That only gives them time to show you how to connect up.'

'They didn't show me,' stated John. 'Dai just rushed around for a quarter-of-an-hour and . . .'

Alex interrupted. 'Are you telling me that you didn't have the electrics, gas and water connected so that you could be shown how to run everything?' John nodded, confirming Alex's suspicions. 'Well, I can't believe it. If you buy a caravan here in Weston-Super-Mare, they actually site it for you in a nearby field and connect all the services for you to try them out. They leave you overnight to play with all the switches and things and then return the following day to see if you have any problems that you don't understand. What you had was a dealer that wanted your money and, having had it, wanted to get rid of you as fast as he could.'

'I couldn't agree more,' came a voice from the bathroom of the caravan. For the first time Alex's wife, Sally, appeared. They shook hands. 'Better go and help them, Alex.'

'Just about to, dear,' replied Alex reaching for his coat to go out into the foul weather yet again.

Under the bench-seat of Clarence, Alex found the carefully concealed mains and fuse-box. 'Couldn't have hidden it better if they tried, could they?' he declared. 'Yes, as I thought, the mains has not been switched on.'

With a click of the mains isolator the caravan was suddenly filled with light. Alex immediately set the heating thermostat and switched on the heater. 'There you are, you'll be like toast in about ten minutes. Come on, John, I'll show you the water system. It's an external water container, isn't it?' John nodded. 'Okay, bring the pump with you.'

'What pump?' John asked despondently.

'There'll be one here somewhere,' replied Alex. A couple of minutes of lifting seats and Alex found the pump underneath one of the cushions in the breakfast area. 'I think that they are trying to hide things to confuse you, John,' Alex laughed.

'Well, they've succeeded,' John said without humour.

'Come on, mate,' Alex offered, good-heartedly.

A Gaze into Holidaze

'We've all been there and had to start at the beginning. Don't worry, I'll show you everything in the light of day tomorrow because it's a bit dark now. We'll get the water-barrel filled up and set the water system. Do you know how to switch on the hot water?'

'No,' admitted John sheepishly.

'Then I'll show you. Let's go.'

Five minutes later, with still no let-up in the rain, the water-container was full and attached to the caravan by means of an electric water-pump.

'Okay, Jayne, you can switch on the water-pump now,' shouted Alex to Jayne who was inside the now-lovely-and-warm caravan. 'It's the one I showed you earlier on.'

Nothing happened.

'Jayne, have you switched it on?' Alex questioned. Hearing Jayne's reply to the affirmative, Alex turned to the cold and tired John. 'Pop in and see if she's operated the right switch, John, will you? You know the one?'

John obediently entered the caravan to find that Jayne had put the pump-operating switch in the correct position.

'It's on alright, Alex,' John shouted. Then to Jayne he whispered. 'I've had enough now. I'm tired, cold and bloody starving. You just wait until I get home, I'll have a thing or two to say to good old Percy and his boss.'

After another half-hour of poring over the electrical diagram of the caravan, Alex, who seemed to be enjoying himself, said confidently, 'I reckon it's a faulty pump.'

'How do you know?' quizzed John. 'Are you genned up on this sort of thing?'

'Well, funnily enough, I am. I'm an electrician by trade – or was before I retired.' Seeing the look of relief on John's face, he smiled and continued. 'Anyway, I can easily check it. Come with me and I'll show you.'

Back into the heavy rain went John and Alex where they disconnected the pump and took it over to Alex's 4x4. By means of a simple check of running some wire from the battery terminals of the 4x4 to the plates of the pump, it was quickly proved that the brand-new-with-the-caravan waterpump was well and truly useless.

Disappointed, John informed Jayne of the fault as they all sat in the internal warmth of Clarence.

'What are we going to do now?' asked Jayne. 'We can't ...'

'Your caravan is fine now for sleeping in,' interrupted the endlessly smiling Alex. 'You've got electricity and warmth, but no water. So, come over to our place. We'll all chip in and get a fish-and-chip supper from the village and you can have bags of hot tea from us. How do you feel about that?'

'Wonderful,' John and Jayne chirped simultaneously.

So, that's what they did.

****

A Gaze into Holidaze

A short trip . . .

First thing the following morning, John rang Gold Tooth back at the dealership in South Wales where the caravan was purchased.

'Good morning, sir. How are you?' came the bright and cheery greeting. 'What can I do for you?'

'Firstly, I would like you to know what a bloody awful handover I had when I bought this caravan,' John said firmly. He then outlined in detail what had happened with Dai and stated how virtually useless it had been in preparing John for the normal operation of the caravan.

'Really, sir. Well that's what we always do and we haven't had any complaints up to now,' chirped Gold Tooth.

John could almost feel the sickly smile on Percy's face. 'Well, you've got one now,' snapped John who then told Gold Tooth, in no uncertain terms, how other dealers carried out their handovers having the best interests of their customers at heart. When John finished talking, silence prevailed over the telephone line for long moments. 'Are you still there, Percy, or are you at a complete loss for words – for once?' John added sarcastically.

'No . . . er . . . Mr . . . er . . . Barcrosse,' stuttered Gold Tooth. 'I'm still here.'

'Good!' exclaimed John. 'Then here is my second point. I am ringing you from Weston-Super-Mare, where we are having our first tryout of the caravan. Last night, after setting up in the torrents of rain, we thought it would be nice to have a hot cup of tea. Reasonable, Percy?'

'Of course, sir,' came Percy's reply, anxious to please and say the right thing.

'Well, to have a cup of tea you need water. Do you agree, Percy?' There was no answer. John went on, not trying to hide the cutting sarcasm in his voice. 'Well, we couldn't get our water to the taps in the caravan, Percy dearest. Do you want to know why, Percy, old chum?' Still no reply. 'Well, let me tell you why. The bloody soddin' water-pump didn't work. A bloody-well new caravan and the bastard water-pump didn't work. Don't you think that this should have been found during the handover if we had done it properly?'

This time, Percy was more than eager to reply. 'Oh! That is terrible for you Mr Barcrosse. This has never happened before with any of our customers.'

'Well, it has . . .' was as far as John got before he was interrupted by a now anxiously-chatterbox Percy.

'But I can certainly help you now,' Gold Tooth rushed in, almost tripping over his words in his gushing eagerness to help. 'All you have to do is bring the faulty water-pump back to us and we will not hesitate to provide you with a new one. That's the least we can do, sir.'

'And meanwhile, what do I do for the remainder of the weekend regarding the facilities in the caravan that require water? You know, Percy, facilities like water for washing the dishes, water for washing one's body parts like in the shower, making tea, etcetera, etcetera. Just what do we do?' John could feel his anger burning inside him.

A Gaze into Holidaze

'I could possibly send you a pump, but I would have to get my boss to authorise it.'

'That won't work because we will not receive the pump in the timescale that we have available,' replied John. 'Why can't I go to a dealer in Weston-Super-Mare and buy one? Then you can refund me the money when I get back.'

'Oh!' exclaimed Percy, his voice rising a pitch in his confusion. 'I would have to get authorisation from my boss for that.'

'Then put your bloody boss on the line then,' John shouted. 'Or, I'll authorise you a good kick in the arse.'

'There's no need to be angry, sir. Anyway, my boss isn't here at the moment so . . .'

'Bollocks!' snarled John into the mouthpiece as he finally snapped and slammed the telephone down. 'Bloody idiot,' he hissed through clenched teeth. 'I won't buy a bloody tent-peg from them in the future.'

After a few minutes John had calmed himself down and regained his composure sufficiently to ring the Castillo caravan manufacturer, which happened to be in Bristol some twenty miles or so from Weston-Super-Mare.

In no time John was talking to a Mr Biggs, who was manager of the warranty section of the company. After listening patiently to John's dilemma and the saga of the disastrous handover and failed water-pump, Mr Biggs spoke confidently and encouragingly to John.

'Well, Mr Barcrosse, on behalf of Castillo Caravans Limited, I can only apologise for the treatment and inconvenience that you have received from your dealership. I'm afraid, as you probably know, that not all dealerships are as we would like. There are good ones and there are bad ones. Let me assure you that the matter will be thoroughly investigated and appropriate remedial action taken. Regarding your immediate problem of the failed water-pump, please take it along to the Castillo dealership in Weston-Super-Mare and tell them that you have spoken with me. I will ensure that by the time you arrive at the dealership, they will be fully informed on the matter and a replacement pump will be waiting for you. Is that okay, Mr Barcrosse?'

And it was. With no fuss at all John picked up the replacement water-pump from Weston-Super-Mare and returned to the caravan. The new pump worked perfectly and all was well with our happy caravanners – until the evening anyway!

It was about 9 p.m. and totally dark on the campsite. The rain had now stopped but had been replaced by a cold, northerly wind.

'Oh, it's lovely to be nice and snug in the caravan on a night like this,' said Jayne happily as she dished up the steak-dinner that she had just cooked on the newly-purchased electric multi-cooker.

'Yes,' replied John, smiling in his contentment now that he had resolved and forgotten the problems of the morning. 'We have never had such

A Gaze into Holidaze

luxury, not even in the new frame-tent that we loved. We thought that we were the bees-knees when we bought that. Now look at us.' He beamed as he saw the wonderful plate of steak and vegetables that Jayne placed before him. 'Just what the doctor ordered! Look at us – TV on, electrical heating on, as much hot-water as we like – absolute heaven! Even the electric kettle is boiling away merrily. Home from home, isn't it?'

'Yes,' whispered Jayne as she sat at the table. 'All the comforts of home and more, we have absolute freedom.' She raised the glass of red wine that John had previously poured. 'Good health, darling.'

'Good health to you too, my sweet.'

There was a loud 'click', and then – total darkness!!

'Bloody hell, what's happened now?' yelled John. 'We've lost all the electrical power. It's pitch dark and I can't see a bloody thing.'

'Switch on the lights, John. We must have some light to finish our meal.'

'You're not listening, Jayne,' John said impatiently. 'We have no electrical power so the lights won't work.'

'Some of them will because they work off the battery 12-volt supply and are independent of the mains,' Jayne retorted.

'Oh yes, I forgot. Bloody right little know-all, aren't you?' John said as he fumbled down the length of the caravan, struggling in his search for the light-switch.

Suddenly there was a loud crash and the pitch-dark caravan rocked on its legs. 'Ouch! I've tripped over the waste-bin and fallen flat on my face,' screamed John. 'I think I've fractured my skull or something – oh hell, I'm bleeding like a pig.'

Jayne jumped up without hesitation and ran for the light-switch that John had failed to find. In so doing she tripped over John's sprawled form on the floor. Down she went with another crash which shook the mobile-home on its very foundations – its legs.'

'Oh shit!' yelled John, then suddenly seeing the funny side of their situation, started laughing loudly. 'If our neighbours, Alex and Sally, can hear us now they'll think we are having a sexual orgy.' He grabbed at Jayne's body in the total darkness. 'Yum, yum.'

'Shut up!' snapped Jayne, a sudden flush of modesty overcoming her. 'Someone will hear you.'

With that there was a knock on the door.

'John! Jayne! What have you done? You've fused the electrical circuit.' The near hysterical voice belonged to Alex. 'We have no electricity anywhere. You've blown the main fuses for the campsite.'

Jayne found the light-switch and immediately the battery-powered overhead lights dimly illuminated the interior of the caravan. Jayne opened the caravan door and allowed Alex to enter.

'How do you know we have blown the main fuses, Alex?' enquired Jayne innocently, trying unsuccessfully to hide their guilt.

A Gaze into Holidaze

Alex spotted Jayne's blushing even in the dull glow of the overhead lights. 'No need to feel guilty, Jayne, we've all done it before so you've got to learn like everyone else. You've obviously had too many electrical things going on at the same time. Let's have a look at your mains-trip. Have you got your torch? We'll need more than the 12-volt lights to see the trip-switches under the seat.'

'Haven't got one, or at least I can't bloody-well find mine,' croaked John as he pulled himself off the floor.

'In caravanning, there's a place for everything and everything in its place,' said Alex calmly as he scraped his fingers lightly across John's forehead. 'What's this?'

'I knocked my head when I fell in the dark,' said John, embarrassed. 'It's blood I'm afraid.'

'Mmm. There's a delicious taste to your blood, John,' said Alex as he licked his fingers and smacked his mouth. 'I reckon it's strawberry blood.'

Jayne looked at John and then at the overturned pot of strawberry jam that must have dripped over him when he was lying on the floor of the caravan. 'Fractured skull, eh? Maybe it would have knocked some sense into you if you had.' John said nothing, Jayne continued. 'Alex, you were saying that it's us who tripped the mains?'

'Yes, our electricity went totally off too. When we checked, we found that our mains had tripped inside the caravan, and when we reset it the power did not come back on. I reckon yours will be the same.'

And it was. Clarence's electrical overload-trip had operated and when Alex reset it the power did not come back on.

'There you are,' said Alex with a long sigh. 'Told you. That's the end of our electricity until eight o'clock tomorrow night.'

'Why until then?' asked the baffled John. 'Why don't we just switch it back on?'

'Well, the main campsite fuse-box is in the barn under lock and key, and . . .' Alex paused, '. . . the owners have gone to a family wedding and they won't be back until . . .'

'Eight o'clock tomorrow night,' John repeated quietly. Turning to Alex he said, his voice washed out, 'I feel an absolute plonker, Alex.'

'Forget it, mate!' laughed Alex. 'We've all done it at some time or another. It's all part of the learning curve.' He turned to Jayne. 'Have you eaten?'

'Just about to literally put food in our mouths when we lost the electric.'

'Well, it's gone cold now,' declared Alex. 'Shove it in a dish or something and cover it up and you can have it tomorrow. Come over to us again and we'll have a candlelit fish-and-chip supper – again!' His face beamed with a wicked grin. 'Because you tripped the mains, you bugger, you can pay. It's your treat tonight, that'll larn yer!'

'The least I could do,' said John and they all burst out laughing. 'I'll bring the wine and we'll get . . .'

'. . . pissed,' interrupted Alex.

'Pissed,' confirmed John with a meaningful nod. 'I think I need it. Come back tent, all is forgiven.'

A Gaze into Holidaze

Things seemed a lot better the following morning. In spite of the lack of heating, as the gas still wasn't connected-up to supplement the electricity supply, the night had been mild and hence kind to them. They had had a good night of teasing and banter with Alex and Sally, who had proved to be little treasures and excellent camping neighbours.

After breakfast, Alex went over the electrical system with John and even listed the likely consumption of each individual appliance.

'There you are, you see. If you have everything electrical in the caravan operating at the same time, you will be using well over 20 amps,' instructed Alex. 'Your system is only designed to take 16 amps so you will trip your main circuit-breaker.' And so the most-welcome instructions went on and John learned a tremendous amount regarding caravan operations.

John did trip the odd circuit-breaker on occasions but soon learned that, providing he learned to switch-off one appliance or two when using another to balance the electrical load, there was no problem.

'Remember, John, it's all part of the learning curve,' shouted Alex as he and Sally waved the couple goodbye at the end of John and Jayne's first weekend in their caravan.

'Thanks, Alex,' called John in reply. He then turned to Jayne. 'Thank God for the Alexes and Sallys of this world. Where on earth would we have been without them?'

****

Drip ... drip ... drip ... drip ... drip, bloody drip

John and Jayne had had Clarence for a couple of months or so. A couple of months that had strengthened their knowledge of and confidence in the caravan. A couple of months in which the caravan had proved to be an absolutely wonderful and semi-luxurious home-from-home in every way. Absolutely wonderful that is, until they were in Truro in June of that year, when Clarence was merely a caravan in its infancy – but fortunately, still under the manufacturer's warranty.

The campsite at Truro was absolutely marvellous and offered wonderfully flat individual pitches together with very modern facilities such as luxuriously-heated bathrooms and toilets. Although Clarence provided the comfort of a shower and lavatory, they were a bit cramped and so did not compare with the spacious offerings of the campsite.

'They've even got one of those triangular double-baths, Jayne,' smiled John wickedly and craftily as he snuggled up to Jayne on their first night. 'You know, the ones that allow us both to get in at the same time. Cor! That'll be a treat, eh Jayne? You and I in the bath with a bottle of red wine. What do you think about that, sweetheart? Is that a great idea or what?'

'You mean when the other people on the campsite who want to use the facility for bathing their kids are knocking on the door? Seems a bit on the silly side to me, John. Got any other bright ideas?'

A Gaze into Holidaze

Unfortunately, although it offered some great things, what the campsite could not offer was decent weather. For the first two days and nights, the only climatic conditions that John and Jayne were allowed to experience, were the usual English torrential rain, whereby it rained, and it rained, and it rained.

It was just after breakfast on the third day, and John was sitting quietly reading on one of the bench seats in the front of Clarence. Sitting opposite him, also enjoying a good book, was Jayne.

'It's great being able to sit like this, isn't it, Jayne?' John said as he stretched and yawned. 'The weather is terrible outside and here we are, as snug as two bugs in a rug, quietly reading. The peace of it makes it all worthwhile. What do you think?'

'It's fantastic, John. Yes, I do want the weather to clear up but to be honest, it doesn't really matter that much, does it?'

'No, darling, we are warm and dry in here and that's all that really matters,' replied John as he gazed through lazy eyes at the rivulets of rain as they ran down the generously-sized window-panes. 'This is the life for me, not a care in the world.'

Then . . . drip, drip, drip. A flow of raindrops landed right in the centre of John's head.

'God, what's that!' John exclaimed, his knowing, dread-filled eyes suddenly looking upwards at the large, modern Perspex-skylight immediately above his head. 'I hope we haven't got ourselves a bloody . . .' He was interrupted on his last word and winced as a series of raindrops dripped from the plastic base of the skylight straight into his upturned right eye, '. . . leak,' he finished. Soon he felt a longer flow of water from the skylight which covered most of his head and shoulders.

Jumping up in immediate frustration and shock, he shouted. 'Quick, Jayne, we've got a bloody leak! Quick, get a bowl or a towel or something.'

Jayne returned in a flash armed with a plastic-bowl from the kitchen area of the caravan. 'Is it much, John?' she asked as she handed John the bowl, horrified to see that the few drips had increased to a regular, thin stream of water. John collected the water into the bowl that he now held at head height.

'It's a bloody waterfall and I'm damn well soaked,' snapped John angrily. Then, realising that Jayne did not deserve such treatment, he looked down at her as she returned to sit on the bench-seat opposite him, concern and worry in her eyes. 'I'm sorry, Jayne. I shouldn't have barked at you like that. It's not your fault, so please forgive me.'

'That's okay,' Jayne assured him as she stood and placed her hand on his arm. 'I know that you are worried. It's the one thing that we've been dreading, a leak in the roof of the caravan.'

'Yes, we've been dreading it,' John nodded. 'I just can't believe that the modern caravan can leak after all the assurances that we've had from dealers and friends alike regarding the new sealants that are used today. What do we get – a leaking bloody caravan! And a leak in the roof of all places.'

'What are we going to do, John?'

'Well first, see if you can borrow a bigger bowl to catch the water. This bowl isn't big enough for me to put down on the bench-seat in a position where it will catch the water without the bowl tipping into the aisle. I can't risk that because, as you know, the bench-seats are our beds and if water gets on those we've had it.'

Jayne put on her coat and went out into the driving rain, leaving John kneeling on the bench-seat holding the small bowl to the flow of water. Ten minutes later she returned. Her hair was stuck to her head as it dripped rainwater on to her saturated raincoat which in turn, dripped water over the carpeted floor of the caravan.

'No-one's got a bigger bowl or even a bucket,' panted Jayne, breathless from her running from caravan to caravan in her fruitless attempt to keep as dry as possible. 'Shall I try the offices of the campsite to see if they've got one?'

'No, Jayne,' stated John decisively, surprisingly calm under the circumstances. 'Don't waste any more time with neighbouring caravans or the office. Drive into the village and buy the largest plastic-bowl that you can get. You know, like the one you've got at home for holding your washing. That'll do the trick nicely.'

Without another word, Jayne had gone. She realised that the situation was serious and that there was no way that she wanted John and herself to sleep in a wet bed that night. Furthermore, once clothes and bedding got wet it would be almost impossible to dry them out. And, the leak was getting worse.

After fifteen minutes John found that the bowl was over three-quarters full and was getting very heavy. 'If Jayne isn't back in another few minutes or less I will be forced to empty the bowl and then . . .' He shrugged as he saw the helplessness of their situation.

But Jayne was back inside two minutes. Although soaked to the skin, she proudly struggled through the narrow door of the caravan with the biggest bowl that John had ever seen. 'Is this okay?' she panted yet again. 'It's the biggest one I could get.'

'That's not a bowl, pet,' John laughed, a lump in his throat as he felt love tugging at his heartstrings when he looked at the dripping Jayne as she pushed and pulled in her frantic attempts to get the bowl through the narrow doorway and into the caravan. 'That's more like a bath! Turn it sideways and it will be in. Just in the nick of time I would add because the weight of this water in the bowl is starting to make both sets of my balls to bulge. That is, my eyeballs and my . . .!'

'That'll do, thank you,' Jayne stopped him, her smile like a breath of spring to the flagging John.

Thirty seconds later, the large oblong bowl was laid across the two front bench-seats. These were supporting both ends of the bowl whilst the centre of the bowl was supported by a small table and several books appropriately placed in the centre aisle of the caravan.'

'That takes the pressure off us now,' sighed John with relief.

'What do we do next, John?' asked Jayne as she changed her sopping clothes.

John looked at his watch. 'It's only 10.30 in the morning. There's plenty of time to sort the problem out. I'll go to the office and ask if there is a Castillo dealer nearby. If there is then I'm sure that he will come out to us and help us. Don't worry, Jayne, we will get it sorted.'

John's enquiries at the campsite-office revealed that there was indeed a Castillo caravan-dealer only eight miles away. With hope in his heart, and armed with the telephone number of the dealer, John returned to join Jayne in the caravan.

'Our problem is solved,' assured John as he waited patiently on the end of the telephone for the caravan-dealer to answer. 'No dealer is going to fail to help us in a situation as bad as this.' The dealer answered.

'Thank God you are there,' a very relieved John sighed into the mobile-telephone.

'What can I do for you, sir?' came the pleasant and cheerful Cornish accent.

John outlined the important points of their dilemma in double-time, stressing that the caravan was under warranty. Finally, John ended with, 'so if you can come out to us . . .' That's as far as he got before he was abruptly stopped in mid-flow.

'Sorry, sir, it's not our policy to make site calls.'

'But we're only eight miles down the road,' stammered John.

'That's as may be, sir, but our policy remains that we don't make site calls.' Any warmth that may have been in the voice previously was now gone, to be replaced by a very much take-it-or-leave-it tone. 'You'll have to bring the caravan in to us, sir, and what is more, sir, the caravan must be empty.'

John became aware of the familiar feeling of helplessness sweeping over him. 'But we have nowhere to put our gear. What can we do with our gear?' John pleaded. The silence that extended over the telephone plainly reflected the that's-your-problem-not-ours attitude of the dealer.

'Anyway, sir, did you buy the caravan from us?' the dealer questioned after the long pause.

'No,' replied John. 'I bought the caravan in South Wales.'

'Well frankly, sir, it is their responsibility to repair your caravan whilst under warranty. In any event, we couldn't possibly touch your caravan for another two weeks, so why don't you take your caravan back to the dealer in South Wales who sold it to you?'

'Take it back some three hundred miles with a pouring leak in the roof, is that what you suggest?' John said desperately, the disappointment showing in his voice.

'It would seem so,' the dealer replied flatly.

A Gaze into Holidaze

'You don't want to do this work, do you?' John asked sharply.

'I never said that, sir,' came the quick and smug reply.

John's annoyance started to show when he realised that he was being well and truly dumped by the dealer. 'Look, mate, we are in desperate trouble here. Are you going to help us or not?'

'It would appear that we cannot, sir. Good day.' The line went dead.

John looked at Jayne who was almost in tears. 'He won't help us, will he, John?'

John looked dismally at the slowly filling bowl. Then, feigning a brightness which he did not feel, returned to Jayne. 'Come on, sweetheart. He can't help, or should I say won't help, but there will be other Castillo-dealers who will help us. Trust me, we will sort it.'

Four hours later, and some five Castillo-dealers throughout the West Country later, John sat back on the bench-seat next to the bowl in total despair. He blankly looked across at Jayne. 'We're knackered, Jayne. Although some dealers pretend to be more helpful than others, their replies are virtually the same. All of them suggest that we take the caravan back to South Wales because, or so they claim, it is the Welsh dealer's responsibility to sort out the leak. When challenged about the three hundred mile towing of a leaky caravan, they all stress their sympathy and claim that they cannot touch the caravan for a month because they have too much work on!'

'Do you believe them?'

'No,' stated John flatly. 'I don't believe them. I think that they can't be bothered with a leak and that's about the size of it. One dealer in Devon did offer to look at it straight away to diagnose the fault.'

'Are you going to tow the caravan there?' asked Jayne.

'No,' replied John. 'They'll have a look at it and then order the spares. In the fortnight that they might have to wait for the spares to be delivered from the manufacturer, we'll still have to wait it out in a leaky caravan. Not a solution. So much for the splendid three-year warranty, eh Jayne?'

'Come on, John, cheer up.' Jayne got up. 'What about a nice cup of tea, eh?'

'That's your solution to everything, isn't it?' John joined Jayne in the small kitchen and, standing behind her, put his arms around her and kissed her on the neck.

Jayne turned in John's arms. 'What about going back to Wales? Have you rung Percy?'

'I swore I would not go back to that idiot company for even a tent peg,' John sighed in disgust. 'But I did ring him and pointed out our predicament.'

'And?' Jayne asked quietly.

'And I got the same response. Yes, he accepted the responsibility for the repair but, no, he could not see us right away even though he agreed it was an emergency. In fact, he quoted two weeks time which is a bit better than the others, I suppose.'

A Gaze into Holidaze

'Why don't you ring Mr Biggs at the manufacturers in Bristol and see if he can help. He seemed ever such a nice man.'

Although it was now 4 p.m. John rang Mr Biggs at Castillo Caravans in Bristol and explained the problem in detail for the sixth time that day. Mr Biggs listened carefully, interrupting John occasionally to ask a pertinent question. Finally, John finished his story stressing the point that the dealers had been generally most unhelpful.

Mr Biggs did not hesitate in his reply. 'To be honest with you, John, in the world of caravans, getting warranty work carried out by dealers, other than the dealer who sold you the caravan, can be difficult. It is not that some dealers do not want to do the work, although admittedly some don't, it is that they genuinely do have a high work commitment of their own.' He paused, as if expecting a challenge from John at this point. Receiving none he continued. 'Anyway, this is detracting from your problem. If you bring your caravan to our base in Bristol, we will repair the leak immediately.'

'That still means towing the caravan some two hundred miles with a leak in the roof. The upholstery and carpet will be ruined.'

'Yes, I wish I could send someone to you, John, but that is not our policy,' stated Mr Biggs. 'Anyway, don't worry about water damage because it's only water and we will make any damage good. Furthermore, we will make a financial donation to yourself for fuel, time and the inconvenience caused to you. Is that reasonable to you and your wife?'

John did not hesitate. 'We will be with you by 8 a.m. tomorrow morning, Mr Biggs, because we will travel through the night as necessary. Thank you, Mr Biggs, for your help.'

'Not at all, John. Goodbye.' The line went dead.

'Would you believe the rain has stopped,' said Jayne quietly.

John, deep in thought, appeared not to have heard her. 'You know I think the rain has stopped,' he said, suddenly jumping up. 'I'm going to borrow a ladder from the site-office and I'm going up on the roof to see the leak for myself. I've got a gut feeling that I can solve the problem temporarily. If the leak is only at the skylight then why not put some plastic sheeting over the damn thing and further seal it with that wide camping-tape that you can buy.'

And that's what they did. John borrowed a stepladder from the campsite-office and clambered up to study the outer-construction of the skylight, with Jayne supportingly holding the base of the stepladder. After a very brief inspection, John wobbled back down the shaking ladder, the legs of which had dug into the soft, now muddy ground from the previous rain.

'I think I can sufficiently solve this problem to last for the remaining couple of weeks of the holiday. Come on, Jayne, all we need is a square metre or so of plastic sheeting and some good quality wide tape.' John looked at his watch. 'It's 5 p.m. now. I'll ring Mr Biggs and tell him what I'm going to do and that if it doesn't work we'll take the van to him for the day after tomorrow. It if does work then we'll call in and get Clarence fixed in two weeks' time on the way home from the holiday.'

After ringing Mr Biggs, who was in full agreement with John's plan, they rushed into Truro and were just in time to catch a builders-merchant store before it closed. No problem with the purchase other than, although John only needed perhaps two square-metres of the plastic sheet and probably about six metres of tape, he was forced to buy a four hundred square metres of plastic sheet and two full rolls of tape.

'I've got enough plastic to completely cover fifty caravans,' laughed John as they drove back to the campsite.

'And about ten miles of tape,' Jayne joined in the joke. 'Never mind, better to be sure than sorry and it will always come in handy if we have further leaks.'

'Don't you dare joke about it, Jayne, and let's not tempt Providence,' John continued. 'I don't want to even think about another leak.'

Back at the caravan, John quickly cut out a suitable piece of the plastic sheeting and, armed with a roll of tape and scissors, once again scrambled up the stepladder. Jayne dutifully hung on to the severely wobbling legs of the stepladder as they dug ever more deeply into the soft mud.

'Hold it steady, Jayne,' pleaded John who precariously stood on the very top step of the unstable platform. 'I've just got to stretch a bit to tape the final strip and bob's-your-uncle!'

Jayne hung on grimly as she looked up at the black, evening sky. 'I think it's going to rain again, John. Have you just about finished?'

'Eureka!' exclaimed John in triumph. 'All finished.' With that he pushed himself upright from his leaning position by using the top of the caravan as a lever. Unfortunately, John's movement was too severe. The outside legs dug deeper into the mud and the sudden movement of centre of gravity caused the ladder to lean dangerously outwards.

Jayne moved quickly to prevent both ladder and John from falling. In so doing her foot slipped in the slippery goo, causing her to topple backwards to sit flat on her backside in the mud. Regrettably, she forgot to let go of the already unstable ladder. Result – both ladder and John fell to earth with a clatter of ladder and a great splash of John, all this accompanied with yet another heavenly downpour of monsoon-like rain.

Jayne, in the next half-hour and with an extremely wet and soggy bum, drove the mud-soaked John to the local Casualty Department. After three hours of waiting, which is normal on these occasions, a wait regularly punctuated with John's grizzles and groans, John was released with another sprained wrist.

'Same bloody wrist as the one I hurt in France

with those bloody dogs,' groaned John on the very wet return trip to the caravan.

'Never mind, you'll be okay in about a week to ten days so the doctor said,' returned Jayne dryly. 'Try to see the funny-side of it because it could have been a broken wrist!'

'I'm not in the mood for the funny-side to anything at this point in time. Anyway, what time is it Jayne?'

'Eleven p.m.,' Jayne answered. 'Hope the leak is okay in all this rain because with you falling and rushing to hospital I forgot to put the bowl in position.'

'Oh shit! The place could be flooded out by now. I just can't believe it. A brand-new caravan with a leaky roof covered in bloody plastic and tape to stop the water coming in. I bet it's in a hell of a mess.'

But it wasn't. The repair to the skylight was excellent and there was not the remotest sign of a water leak to be seen.

'Well done, John!' Jayne complimented. 'My hero has won the day. Not a drip in sight – well, not a drip of water anyway.'

'Very funny, ha-bloody-ha!' was all that John could think of saying.

'Well, I've got a treat for you after all you've done, John,' smiled Jayne mischievously. 'It's late enough and dark enough so follow me my little mud-covered gnome.' Grabbing two dressing-gowns and towels, she disappeared into the rain-swept night, but not before she had a quick rummage through an overhead locker.

Yes, the hot double-bath was like heaven to both of them as they lay, up to their necks in bubbles, listening to the rain as it drummed romantically on the roof above them. The only other body-parts of our happy travellers that were exposed above the slightly hissing foam as the millions of bubbles gently burst, were their right hands. Each of these hands held large glasses of red wine. Oh yes! Also exposed was the left arm of John – but this was only to keep the bandage dry!!!

****

The extra bit – a d-awning experience ...
The following month of July found John and Jayne as happy as bunnies on a farm-type campsite – a certified campsite as it's known in the trade – just outside Torquay in Devon. Clarence's leaks had been repaired as planned and as a bonus, John had cleaned and waxed him before leaving home in an attempt to get rid of all the evidence of the dreadful weather of the previous month. The evidence, in the form of numerous long, black-streaks, ran down the sides, front and back of the caravan staining the cellulose cruelly.

Now Clarence stood gleaming in the bright sunlight at the very end of a grassy field which was formed into a U-shaped valley which ran downwards to the sea. The caravan was at the very

A Gaze into Holidaze

bottom of the 'U' and at the end of the valley overlooking the blue, tranquil sea which gently caressed the rocks a hundred feet or so below.

John and Jayne had just arrived on-site and had already unpacked all of their general gear on to the grass. The sun at ten o'clock in the morning was already hot.

'This is more like it,' declared John, as he returned to the caravan, pulling the full aqua-roll, a cleverly-designed round water-container which could be pulled along the ground with ease.

'Yes,' smiled Jayne. 'The weather seems to have changed now and it's about time too.' She stretched herself lazily and looked around at their beautiful location at the base of the valley. 'It's lovely here, John, but it's quite a long way for you to go to the drinking-water taps, don't you think?'

'No problem,' replied John. 'I need the extra exercise and it will keep me active and fit.'

'Don't you think that we are a bit far down the slope of the valley, John?' Jayne pointed. 'See all the other caravans seem to have stayed more or less at the top of the valley.'

'That's their problem. We've got the best place on this site right here.' John looked out to sea and swept his arm around to stress his point. 'Just look at that view and what more could anyone want? And we don't have to share it with anyone if they wish to park their caravans at the top of the hill.'

Just then the mobile-phone rang. Frowning at the annoying disturbance to their peace and privacy,

John answered it as Jayne went inside the caravan.

'Hello, John. This is Derek, your caravan mentor,' said the cheerful voice from Wales. 'How are you getting on with everything?'

'Well, I suppose I've got to say fine, Derek, but it certainly hasn't all been beer and skittles since we bought the caravan – what with the disgusting weather and the few problems that we've had with Clarence.'

'Who is Clarence?' questioned Derek.

'Oh, sorry Derek, mate,' laughed John. 'Of course you didn't know that we've called the caravan Clarence, did you?'

'Children will be children,' returned Derek in mock sarcasm. 'Anyway, what problems have you had with – er, Clarence?'

John proceeded to tell him at length and, seeing the funny side of the events that had taken place, they both laughed at the end of the saga.

'I can see the funny-side of things now,' John joked. 'But I can assure you that there was the odd time when I got just a wee bit annoyed at life in a caravan.'

'I bet you did!' Derek's raucous laughter became distorted over the telephone. 'Tell me, John, have you put the awning up yet?'

'No, Derek, we haven't,' replied John. 'To tell you the truth we are not sure that we really need it.'

'Oh!' exclaimed Derek, his humour still coming through in spite of the crackling telephone. 'So you've only done the easy part of caravanning then? Come on, John, you've got to put your awning up to give all the other caravanners some entertainment. When I'm on a site and see a new caravanner putting up his awning for the first time, I normally sell tickets to the other caravanners to watch.' Derek, enjoying his own joke, deafened John with his loud laughter.

'Very funny,' replied John. 'Very funny indeed, Derek.'

'No,' continued Derek, his laughter almost completed. 'Seriously, John, you should put it up 'cos it provides a large, extra room for you and Jayne. Think of all that space for storage, eh?'

'I suppose so,' muttered John in reply. 'I've got an awning so I would be silly not to use it, I guess.'

'That's the ticket, John. Seriously, it's easy to put up and you'll find that as soon as you take the awning out of the bag there'll be loads of your fellow campers and caravanners only too pleased to help you. In fact, there'll be too many helpers and they can be a bit of a pain in the rump.'

'I'll give it a whirl,' John said confidently into the telephone. 'It will be easy I'm sure. Don't forget, Derek, Jayne and I are not novices because we have put so many tents up in the past it's not true – should be a piece of old doddle.'

'Of course,' said Derek. 'I'd forgotten about that. Anyway, the instructions are in the bag with the awning, and all you have to do is follow them and all will be well.' Derek's metallic laughter sounded once again. 'Well, better go now. Good luck, John, and regards to Jayne.' The phone went dead.

'Who was that?' questioned Jayne as she emerged from inside Clarence.

'Derek just making sure that everything was fine and dandy with us. He's a good friend is Derek.' Jayne nodded her agreement as John paused. 'He thinks we should put the awning up because it gives us extra space.'

'I think I'd agree with that. At the moment we are putting a lot of gear under the caravan which means it could get damp or stolen, or both. It would be better kept inside the awning. Also, if the weather turns nasty we can put our table and chairs inside the awning to eat. It would be rather nice sitting in the awning if it rained. You know, all cosy like.'

'Right,' said John positively. 'Straight after breakfast we'll put it up. I shouldn't think it will take us more than half-an-hour because, as I told Derek, we are not novices to the game, are we? We've put up our tents hundreds of times.'

So, breakfast eaten, dishes washed and put away, John and Jayne carried the two bags containing the awning, steel poles and canvas cover, from the car to the side of the caravan.

'Bloody-hell, these poles are heavy,' grumbled John as they placed the huge canvas bag containing the poles on the ground.

'Well, Percy offered you the choice of steel poles or carbon-fibre poles, or whatever he called them, and you insisted on the steel ones because you said they were stronger.'

'That could have been my first mistake,' John said quietly. 'I never dreamed they were going to be as heavy as this. How many of the buggers are in here, a thousand?'

Well, there weren't a thousand as the weight of the bag suggested, there were just thirty or so.

'Good grief, there's thirty bloody poles here,' claimed John when the contents of the bag lay on the grass. 'Thank God there are instructions with them.'

Jayne looked gloomily at the array of bits and pieces that lay on the ground before them. 'Gosh, there are lots of pieces, John. I don't recognise what half of them are going to do. It's not like putting up a tent is it?' She picked up a small transparent plastic bag which contained three small, plastic brackets and six self-tapping screws. 'What do you think these are for?'

John picked up the instructions and glanced quickly through them until he identified the parts that Jayne held out to him. 'Bloody hell! It says here that you must get those brackets into position by screwing into the side of the caravan. Sod that for a game of soldiers, that'll give us another leak with our kind of luck.'

'Well, what else can you do?' whispered Jayne.

'I don't know to be honest,' John declared. 'But one thing that I do know is I'm not tapping screws into the side of our caravan and that's a fact.' He looked around and pointed up the hill. 'I'm going up to one of those caravans at the top of the valley and see what they've done when they put up their awnings.'

Up the hill John went to return thirty minutes later with a knowing, confident expression on his face.

'Did you find out, John?' Jayne was encouraged by John's beaming smile.

'Yup!' stated John smugly. 'They said that there was no way that they would screw into the sides of their caravans either. The plastic brackets are for holding the poles but they didn't use theirs. They have bought some plastic holders that simply clip on to the bead that runs around the inside of the canvas awning. The poles then snugly fit into these holders and nothing damages the side of the caravan.'

'Great,' said Jayne cheerfully. 'Have we got these plastic holders?'

'No,' replied John. 'Unfortunately, we didn't know that we would need them. Yet another thing that good-old Gold Tooth forgot to mention to us.'

'Then what do we do without them?' interrupted Jayne.

'Well, about twenty-five miles away there's a caravan and camping shop near Newton Abbot and they sell them. We can be there and back in about an hour-and-a-half. Fancy it?'

John forgot about the holiday traffic. It was three hours later that they returned to the caravan,

A Gaze into Holidaze

but nevertheless were suitably armed with four plastic holders, one as a spare in case they lost one of them at some time or other. The time was now 3 p.m. and they hadn't eaten since breakfast.

'We'll eat when we've got this bloody awning up,' John stated emphatically. 'It will only take a half-hour and then we can settle down to a meal. Come on, sweetheart, keep the old pecker up. Let's count the bits and pieces to make sure that they're all there.'

They counted and they were.

'Right,' said John authoritatively. 'Step one says to thread the bead of the canvas roof through the slot running around the entire edge of the caravan.' John looked at Clarence and, sure enough, there was a slot of about ten or eleven metres long running along the roof and down the ends of the caravan. 'There it is. I'll pull the bead through and you sort of push-feed it towards me.'

They started the process of pulling and pushing. What John did not take into account was the sheer weight of the full-size canvas awning that they had obtained from Gold Tooth. Both John and Jayne were perspiring freely after a half-an-hour of this very strenuous exercise in the evening sun. Of the ten metres that was necessary to complete the threading of the bead, in this time they had accomplished only one side of the caravan – about three metres. What was even worse was the fact that the more bead that John and Jayne threaded, the harder the job became.

'We'll never finish at this rate,' Jayne said breathlessly.

'You're dead right,' agreed John. 'There's got to be an easier way than this because I can't believe that other people would go through this bother every time they put their awning up.'

'Well, why don't you go and ask someone up there?' Jayne nodded towards the caravans at the top of the hill.

'If I do that, the threading of the bead that we've already done will be useless because the moment we let the awning go, gravity will do its damnedest and the bead will fall back from whence it came to the ground.'

'Well, we can't go on like this because we are getting nowhere.'

So, John went up the hill and the bead did as John predicted – it fell to the ground under its own weight. Result or accomplishment for a half-hour's threading – sweet nothing!

Another half-an-hour passed-by before John ran down the hill, this time armed with an aerosol-can of thin oil. Once again, John's morale had been raised.

'Got some great tips from up there,' he panted enthusiastically as he joined Jayne at the caravan.

'Did they offer to help as Derek suggested they would?' said the starving Jayne.

'No,' replied John. 'But we don't need their help, darling, because they've given me all the gen. It seems that everybody gets trouble with the 'bead

A Gaze into Holidaze

rail', as they call it, the first time. All that's needed is a good squirt of this right round the rail.' He proceeded to squirt a generous supply of oil right round the ten metres of caravan-rail. 'Now Jayne, let's do it again. I'll pull the bead, you push as before.'

This time, in spite of the weight of the canvas, the bead slid effortlessly around the entire length of the bead-rail. The complete threading barely took five minutes.

'There you are,' shouted John gleefully. 'Easy-peasy! Once you know the tricks of the trade – bob's-your-uncle. Now for the poles.' He walked to the pile of poles lying on the ground. 'The bloke up there said that these would be easy to fit because they would either be (a) joined together with small springs as they do with the frames of modern frame-tents – well, we can see that this isn't so because they are not joined at all – or (b) they will be colour-coded to enable you to know what joins on to what.' John looked down at the thirty poles again. 'Well, that doesn't appear to be the case. Or (c), the poles will have identification numbers either stamped into them or stuck onto them.' This time he picked up several poles and inspected them carefully.

'Oh shit, bugger, bugger, damn!' John shrieked in response to his inspections. 'There's no bloody numbers on them at all.'

John made a grab for the 'Instructions for Erection.' He studied them in earnest for a full minute.

'Bollocks!' he screamed. 'It's got a sketch of all the poles fitted together in numerical order.' He turned to Jayne, face glowing red in anger. The remainder of his conversation was hissed through clenched teeth. 'It says here to fit pole 13 to pole 14, for example, and then they fit into socket 15. How the fuck can you do that unless you know which of these bastard poles is 13 and which is 14. These instructions were written by bloody idiots!'

Jayne remained quiet through John's outburst. When he had finished, his blood at boiling point, she put her arms around him. 'Would you like a nice cup of tea, John? It will make you feel a lot better.'

So, for the next half-an-hour they drank tea and ate sandwiches and biscuits until John seemed more rational, his temper subdued.

'I don't think I want the awning up now, John,' Jayne risked quietly.

'Jayne, sweetheart,' John replied, equally as quiet. 'That awning is going up even if I'm at it all bloody night.'

'Please don't swear, John.'

'Sorry, pet, but the manufacturers of that awning would make the proverbial saint swear. I promise I won't lose my temper again. It's simply not fair to you.'

'So, where do we go from here, John?'

'Well, there is a list of poles,' John said calmly. 'On the list, the numbers of the poles, in accordance with the sketch in the instructions, are clearly stated and it gives the length of each pole accordingly. The only thing that's lacking is, there is no identification-number on the poles themselves.'

'Are they so very different in length, John? I mean are they all of different lengths?'

'I'm afraid so,' replied John with a sigh. 'Or most of them anyway.'

'So you'll have to measure each one of them?'

'Yes, darling, yes. Once I know their length I can identify them to a number. Then I can refer to the picture and we are well away.'

'Do you have a tape measure for that?' asked Jayne.

'Guess what, precious?' John paused and shook his head. 'No! I thought that we had brought everything we could want, but Sod's Law says you always need the things you haven't brought!'

'Well, where are you going to get one?'

'See you soon,' replied John wearily. Up he got and started slowly climbing the hill yet again. It was now 5.30 p.m.

On his return, John and Jayne laboriously set about measuring the lengths of each pole. Although a tedious task because some of the pole-lengths differed by only a few millimetres in some cases, they soon accomplished their mission of identification. Once this was done, the awning finally went up quite easily, even if perhaps slowly. The entire enterprise of erecting the awning, including their journey into Newton Abbot to buy the pole-holders, took seven hours.

Exhausted, they showered, changed their clothes and went into Torquay for a first class Indian curry.

'That was fabulous,' said John as he leaned back in the comfortable chair of the restaurant as he listened to the delicate strains of the Indian sitar and savoured a large brandy.

'Yes, it certainly was a wonderful meal,' replied Jayne. 'The awning certainly seems a long way away now, doesn't it?'

'What awning?' came John's reply accompanied with a playful wink.

First thing the next morning, John went into the nearby village of Stoke Gabriel and purchased a pot of black paint, some fine brushes, and a half-dozen rolls of sticky-tape of different colours. By the time he got back to the caravan, Jayne already had bacon, eggs and mushrooms frying tantalisingly in the frying pan.

'Gosh, I'm certainly ready for that,' John said hungrily as he sniffed the mouth-watering aromas that wafted through the air inside the awning.

'I expect you are,' replied Jayne. 'You've been ages, where have you been?'

'Into town for these.' He held up a carrier bag.

'What's that for?'

'You'll see,' replied John. 'You'll see.'

By 11 a.m. all thirty poles were not only numbered boldly in black paint but they were all colour-coded with the brightly-coloured sticky-tapes.

A Gaze into Holidaze

'I'm certainly not going through that nonsense again,' John stated categorically. 'The erection of that awning proved to be a proverbial pain in the arse.'

And, generally speaking, over the remaining weeks of the holiday the awning did prove to be a pain in the buttocks. Yes, it was true that there was extra space to store things but the fact that you had the extra room tended to make you buy things that you would never have bought if you didn't have the extra space. Result – clutter!

Also, when the winds got up, which invariably they did in the night, all the awning did was creak and groan, a noise which was greatly amplified by the caravan. The most unpleasant sound merely got transmitted along the roof-poles of the awning and through the thin skin of the caravan, the inside of which, acted as an amplifier and loudspeaker. John and Jayne's sleep was greatly disturbed. In fact, whenever the winds got up during the night, they hardly got any sleep at all. 'Bloody thing is going to take off,' was John's usual comment at about 3 a.m. every time it happened. In fact, it never did happen to John and Jayne, but it certainly happened to some of the owners of the caravans at the top of the hill.

Furthermore, to keep the grass inside the awning in good condition, and at considerable expense, John and Jayne purchased a breathable groundsheet which gave a 'carpeted finish' to the inside of the awning. Indeed it was very pretty until it rained heavily whereby the water would run under, and be held by, the groundsheet only to become a soggy mess underfoot. This mess refused to dry out for days and was not a pleasant experience to say the least!

'What do you think about the awning, John?' asked Jayne towards the end of the holidays.

'Not much, to be honest,' replied John. 'On top of all the faults of the awning, I think it makes the caravan dark inside. Also, if it's warm enough to eat in the awning then, with a decent sweater on, it's warm enough to eat outside. If it's too cold for that we would eat in the caravan anyway.'

'Agreed,' said Jayne. 'I can't think of many advantages. Even when you pass the awnings that other people have set up on their caravans, they never seem to use them.' She turned to John. 'So?'

'So, we'll flog it,' said John without hesitation.

As a matter of interest, six months later, they did just that.

However, the time came when their holiday in Devon came to an end.

'What time shall we leave tomorrow?' Jayne asked on their last day.

'We'll leave early in the morning,' replied John. 'I'd say we'll get up at about dawn, which is say 5 a.m., and be on our way by six.'

'Gosh, that's early, John.'

'Yes I know, love, but that way we will miss all of the morning traffic that builds up around Torquay and Paignton and, don't forget, we've got a long way to get home.'

'Won't we disturb other caravans at that time of the morning?'

'No, I don't think so,' said John, confidently shaking his head. 'We'll pack everything up tonight and I'll even hook-up the car tonight. We won't bother with breakfast in the morning because we'll stop somewhere on the way back, say around Exeter. How does that sound?'

'Well, as long as we don't disturb anyone I don't mind,' answered Jayne.

True to their plans, at the crack of 6 a.m. on the following clear but crisp morning, John raised the caravan legs, threw the leg-brace into the back of the Volvo and gingerly pulled away to start climbing the hill of the valley.

'There you are, sweetheart,' John beamed triumphantly. 'Nothing to it, we're like a couple of professionals now. Pulling caravans – piece of old doddle. And, we were as quiet as mice so as not to disturb the rest of the site.'

Perhaps he had spoken a trifle too soon. By now they had travelled about halfway along the steep upward slope that was the base of the valley. What John had not taken into account in his planning was firstly, the weight of the caravan whilst going steeply uphill, and secondly, the early morning dew.

Yes, the ground was so saturated with dew that it seemed as if it had been raining quite heavily during the night. It hadn't. Whatever the reason, the coefficient of friction between rubber and grass was greatly reduced and the inevitable happened –

terrific free-spinning of the driving wheels. John lost full traction in a haze of burning rubber as the wheels spun, and spun, and spun.

'Shit, shit, shit!' was the best that John could offer at six o'clock in the morning.

'What's wrong, John?' was Jayne's humble response.

'Bloody wheels are spinning because of the morning dew. I can't go up, I can only go down.'

'Oh John, we're making so much noise with the engine racing like that. Can't you stop it? You'll wake everyone!'

John took his foot off the accelerator and thankfully the engine noise dropped to idling. 'I'll drop us back on the footbrake to the bottom once again. Then I'll run at it and we'll be fine.'

Well, they weren't. John slowly dropped the car and caravan backwards down the hill until they were back on the relatively flat part of the valley floor. Then, like a bat-out-of-hell, he raced again for the Everest-like brow of the hill. This time he didn't even get a third of the way up before the inevitable wheel-spin occurred again.

Three times John attempted the same manoeuvre only to be thwarted each time by the smell of burning rubber and the flying of mud. Poor Clarence looked really pathetic in his full country-camouflage of sticky mud and small tufts of turf and grass.

'Okay,' said John loudly to himself, realising that he was flogging-a-dead-horse in his attempts at climbing Table Mountain. At least that's what it felt like to John. 'I'll have to ride the clutch to prevent wheel-spin. As long as I take it steady we'll make it to the top.'

Well, they didn't. After a few attempts at riding the clutch it soon became obvious that the car's clutch plates could not withstand that kind of treatment.

'I'd better stop before I burn the clutch out,' gasped John, almost weeping in frustration. 'I shouldn't have attempted to put the car at the bottom of the valley. I can see now why the other caravanners parked up at the top of the hill. What an absolute prat I am!'

'Don't be so hard on yourself, John,' Jayne said quietly, placing a comforting hand on John's as he gripped the wheel like a vice in his anger. 'You didn't know that this was going to happen, did you?'

'No I didn't,' replied John, calming down as he reversed the train yet again back to the flat of the valley floor. Achieving this manoeuvre for the nth time, he switched off the engine and pushed his driving-seat back to relieve the stiffness in his long legs. Peace reigned.

'What time is it, love?' he asked quietly in defeat.

'Seven o'clock,' answered Jayne.

'God! We've been an hour trying to get up the hill. Some planning, eh? I deserve a kick in the arse for this, Jayne. I couldn't organise the proverbial piss-up in a brewery!' Then suddenly he smiled broadly. 'Derek told me to remember the golden rule of successful caravanning.'

'You never told me, John. What is it?' Jayne's frown illustrated her bewilderment, especially when she knew that John had willingly taken any advice that had been given to him regarding anything to do with the caravan.

'Derek said to always remember the six-'p'-rule.'

'The six-'p'-rule?' Jayne questioned. 'What on earth is that?'

'Planning and preparation prevents piss-poor performance!'

They both exploded with laugher and the laughter continued for minutes on end until their ribs were aching and the pain and tears forced them to stop. Finally, Jayne asked the inevitable question as she rubbed the streams of mirth from her eyes. 'What happens now then, John?'

'Well, to be honest, I think that we'll have to wait for the dew to dry out. It shouldn't take long and then I'll try again.'

But they didn't have to. Ant-like figures appeared from the caravans at the top of the hill and six of these figures worked their way down the steep slope towards them. Five minutes later John wound the window down as he recognised the man who had helped him with the awning problems. 'Good morning,' John greeted pleasantly. 'Hope we didn't disturb you.'

'Well, as a matter of fact, you did!' replied the man, none too cheerfully.

A Gaze into Holidaze

John looked around the group of men and could see from their faces that they also appeared to have suffered from an acute sense of humour failure.

'Sorry about that,' John said embarrassedly but still not losing his determination to smile. 'You see, I had to rev a bit to get up to the top of the hill.'

'Correction,' added Deadpan. 'To try to get up the hill is what I think you mean. It may have escaped your notice but you are still at the bottom of it. Your noisy efforts were in vain.' Deadpan turned his back on John, who remained quietly in his seat in the Volvo, completely at a loss for words.

'What are we going to do about this bloke?' Deadpan questioned his fellow miseries as they started to make tutting noises with their mouths.

'Well, I know what I would do with him,' said one of the group, a giant of a man who was dressed only in shorts and tee-shirt even though it was quite cold at that hour of the morning, sunrise or not!

'And what would that be, George?' asked Deadpan as he turned back to face John. John couldn't believe his eyes. The same friendly, helpful smile that John had known on the previous occasions when he had met this man, was firmly back in place.

'Help him up the hill, of course,' replied George. All of the group were laughing loudly by this time. 'What else?'

'You buggers,' shouted John, now realising that he had been well and truly and very profoundly teased.

'To be honest,' said the grinning now-not-so Deadpan. 'We felt guilty when we saw you going down the hill and felt that we should have stopped you. Unfortunately, you had gone too far and, in any event, you couldn't have turned around because the slope of the valley sides was far too dangerous.'

'Why didn't you tell me when I came up to see you about the awning?' John asked innocently.

'What, and spoil your holiday?' Chief Rescuer, alias Deadpan, said. 'All you would have done throughout your entire vacation is worry about getting back up the hill.'

'Well that's very thoughtful of you,' John agreed.

'Not thoughtful enough or we would have come to your aid before. The truth is you didn't disturb us at all this morning because we didn't hear a thing. We were only aware that you were having trouble when George here spotted you reversing back down the hill.'

'Yes, for about the hundredth time, I think!' John stated.

'As bad as that, eh? Well, not to worry, we'll soon have you on your way.' Chief Rescuer turned to George the Giant. 'George, can we use your 4x4 to pull the caravan up the hill? The car will be okay to drive up once the caravan's not behind it.'

'No problem,' grinned George.

And it wasn't. One hour later after profoundly

thanking all concerned, including Chief Rescuer's wife who insisted that John and Jayne had a full English breakfast before they left, the happy couple accompanied by a hose-cleaned Clarence, hurtled up the M5 homeward bound.

'There are two simple morals to this,' said John contentedly. 'One. Never park at the bottom of a valley if there is any danger that you can't get back up the hill. Two. Do without a sodding awning at all costs.'

'I agree,' replied Jayne, a twinkle in her eye. 'Just add that to the six-'p'-rule for caravanners, eh?'

****

The things you do for friends – and neighbours...

It was early May of the following year. John and Jayne were sitting quietly in the garden of their bungalow-home in West Wales, enjoying a pleasantly warm and sunny afternoon and planning their forthcoming caravan holiday to Switzerland.

'Let's take Clarence to Visp and Interlaken,' suggested John. 'We can set up those two locations as bases for touring the rest of the Bernese Oberland. Jayne, just think of all the fun we had there in the early days of the tent, do you remember?'

'I don't think that I will ever forget,' Jayne replied sarcastically.

'Oh, come on, Jayne,' John said indignantly. 'It wasn't as bad as all that.'

'Wasn't it!' Jayne continued her sarcasm. 'I seem to remember a severe lack of sleep and being sore for a month around the buttocks region.'

'Well, if you are quite honest, it wasn't really my fault, was it?' John said sheepishly. 'I admit that I did mis-time the journey down through France.' He paused. 'And I suppose that sleeping out in the open-air at that altitude was a bit silly.'

'A bit silly . . .!' Jayne exclaimed loudly but unfortunately was interrupted in her reply by the loud ringing of the telephone from inside the bungalow.

Saved literally by the bell, John dashed from the garden to avoid any further cuttingly playful remarks from Jayne. Although that Swiss camping-holiday did turn out fine in the end, John preferred to forget his disastrous planning efforts and still felt an absolute plonker even after all this time.

'Hello, 079 . . .' John panted into the receiver. 'John Barcrosse speaking.'

'Hello, John,' came the familiar voice of John's old school-chum, Mike.

'Hello, Mike, long time no see, eh? How is that good wife of yours? Are things in good old Gloucester okay?'

'Sue is fine and Gloucester never changes. Is Jayne okay?'

'Yes, she's fine. Actually, we were just planning our next caravan holiday when you rang.'

'Well, funnily enough, it's about the very point of holidays that I gave you a bell really.' Getting no reaction from John, Mike continued. 'Well not actually the caravan because as much as we'd like one, we can't afford one just now. No, I thought we'd pick your brains about Sue and me buying a tent. We know that you and Jayne have had years of fun out of your tents and so Sue and I have decided to take the plunge. You're the expert and we know nothing about tents so how about helping us in choosing one?'

'Be delighted, my old mate,' John replied proudly. 'Anything I can do for you would be my pleasure.'

'Well, there's a huge camping shop near us in Gloucester where they sell all sorts of tents. Ridge-tents, frame-tents, you name it, they've got the lot. Any chance that you and Jayne could pop over, say on Saturday, and give us the benefit of your experience?'

'Done,' said John enthusiastically. 'We'll be with you by two o'clock in the afternoon. How does that sound?'

Three o'clock the following Saturday found John and Jayne, accompanied by Mike and Sue, in a huge showroom of erected tents of every description. There were small and large ridge-tents, medium to huge frame-tents, and a vast array of bubble-tents to suit all sorts of tenters from a single-person to large families.

After about an hour of wandering around the impressive showroom where John highlighted the good and bad points of each type of tent, they finally came across a Cabanon which was identical to the frame-tent that John and Jayne still owned.

'This is the one that I would recommend,' said John as the four of them bunched around the outside of the tent. 'This is exactly like ours and we've been all over Europe in it. It's spacious with bags of storage space and you can stand up straight in it. That's very important for someone of your height, Mike, when you spend weeks on end in it. Furthermore, feel the quality of the canvas, it's the best.'

Mike felt the canvas with his finger and thumb.

'In my opinion I would look no further,' John continued. 'This is definitely the tent for you and Sue. Do you like it Sue?'

Sue nodded enthusiastically. 'Seems great to me!'

Mike did not answer. After a moment he looked across the showroom to the vast selection of bubble-tents. 'What about those, John?'

'I wouldn't touch them with a barge-pole,' replied John without hesitation. 'You can't stretch out flat in most of them and neither can you stand up straight. If you want to be able to do these things you've got to buy a very large bubble-tent and I think it would be difficult to put up, especially in a high wind.'

'Have you ever had one of those, John?' Mike asked.

'No,' John replied flatly. 'I've never fancied one in the least. I've seen far too many people with their large bubble-tents having terrible trouble trying to put them up,' John paused before adding, with a laugh, 'I think you've got to have a First Class Honours Degree in Tent Erection for those things.'

'Point taken,' agreed Mike finally. 'I'll get one like yours.' He looked at Sue and saw her nod of approval before returning to John. 'What about the four of us going camping next weekend, John? I have never put a tent up before and perhaps you could show me the ropes. You could come in your caravan.'

John saw the look of concern and lack of confidence on Mike's face which instantly flashed John's memory back to his early camping experiences. 'Of course I will,' John said reassuringly. 'What's more Jayne and I will join you with our tent and all of our camping-gear. In that way you can have some idea what bits and pieces you will need for your future camping without wasting money on things that you will never use.'

'But what about the comfort of your caravan?' said Sue, embarrassed by John's and Jayne's offer.

'No problem.' It was Jayne who replied to Sue's query. 'We're off in the caravan to Switzerland in the summer so we are not missing-out in any way. What's more, it would be great to get back under canvas again.'

The relief on Mike's and Sue's faces was plain to see. Having checked that the Cabanon was in stock, the two couples parted, having agreed that Mike and Sue would buy the tent during the following week. The following Friday morning they would meet at a Services on the M4 and travel down to Pembrokeshire together. Here they would spend two nights on John's and Jayne's favourite campsite, which should be sufficient time for John to introduce Mike to the joys of camping.

Everything went according to plan and Mike and Sue, after travelling all the way from Gloucester, arrived at the selected Services exactly on the agreed time of 9 a.m.

'We'll have a cup of tea before we go on,' said John. 'You've already come a fair old way and the two of you must be absolutely parched.'

John returned with a tray of teas and settled himself at the table. 'Everything go alright with the tent purchase?' John asked as he sipped his tea.

Mike glanced at Sue who immediately turned her head away to look out of the window with a look that John could only interpret as embarrassment. 'Well yes, we got a tent, John,' Mike whispered sheepishly.

'Come on, Mike, let's have it,' John said flatly, sensing the awkward silence between Mike and Sue. 'What's wrong?'

Mike blushed and averted John's eyes. 'I've got a tent, John, but it's not the one that you recommended.'

'Go on,' said John cautiously. 'Couldn't you get the Cabanon?'

'Well . . . er . . . yes,' came Mike's weak reply. 'But

A Gaze into Holidaze

when I went to get it I chatted to a salesman. He offered me a fantastic deal on a new range of nylon-tents that they had on special offer.'

'Nylon is not as good as canvas,' declared John coldly.

'But they dry quicker when they get wet,' Mike rushed in. 'The salesman told me that.'

'True,' agreed John, nodding slowly. 'What else did the salesman say, Mike?'

'He said that this tent is the latest design in a new conception of tents and it's only two-thirds of the price of the Cabanon.'

'Don't tell me,' John said, the truth starting to dawn on him. 'You've bought a . . .' John paused for effect, '. . . bubble-tent.' Mike nodded.

'You bloody fool, Mike.' John declared profoundly to the ceiling, hands shaking in the air in exasperation.

'I told him that,' Sue butted in. 'I begged him to take it back when he got it home. I told him that you would be annoyed, John, and frankly I don't blame you.'

'It's not a question of me being annoyed,' John stated flatly. 'You've got to camp in it and you've got to put it up. I've never put a bubble-tent up in my life and therefore I'm as green as you are when it comes to erecting the damned thing!'

The four sat in silence for several minutes until Jayne spoke up. 'Come on, bubble-tent or not, we are going to have a great weekend of camping in Pembrokeshire. Let's get going!'

JOHN BEVERLEY

During the two-hour journey as the two couples travelled in their separate cars to the campsite, John said very little other than to repeatedly mumble to himself, 'bloody fool,' and 'plonker!' He could not believe that Mike could have been so stupid as to totally ignore his advice. After all, it had been Mike who had asked for help in the first place.

Finally Jayne spoke up. 'You're not a happy bunny over this, are you, John?'

'No, I'm not," hissed John. 'We went all that way to Gloucester last Saturday to help the silly bugger and what did he buy – a soddin' bubble-tent. You can't educate folk, can you?'

'Look, John,' said Jayne calmly. 'It's no good going on about it, is it? There's no doubt that poor Mike was conned by the salesman so we should feel sorry for him.'

'Sorry for him!' John shouted, glancing at Jayne with a look of disbelief.

'Yes, sorry for him. You know that Mike would have been putty in the salesman's hands. And, not having much money, Mike was probably trying to save a bob or two.'

'Well, I hope that he's happy having saved a bob or two,' shrugged John impatiently. 'I'll tell you this for nothing, Jayne. He can put the sodding thing up himself because I refuse to help him.'

'Don't be so childish,' Jayne replied.

'I'm not being childish.'

'All right, selfish then.'

A Gaze into Holidaze

'I'm not selfish either,' John pouted. 'He bought it, he can put it up and that's final.'

But it wasn't. On site, two hours later, John and Jayne proceeded to erect their old faithful frame-tent. Thirty minutes later they were fully settled-in and sitting down inside their tent to a nice cup of tea.

'I'll take Mike and Sue a cuppa,' declared Jayne as she finished pouring. Two minutes later she was back. 'Poor Mike, he hasn't even got the tent out of the bag yet. He's sitting on a boulder reading the instructions and he's completely and utterly lost. John, please go and help him.'

'No,' was John's curt, single-worded reply.

'Well, it isn't often that I swear, John, but I think you're bloody mean and bloody spiteful. He's your friend and I think that you are bloody-well behaving like a spoiled brat. There now, I've said it!'

John looked up, mouth agape with surprise. Jayne never swore no matter how annoyed or frustrated she got. 'I've never heard you say naughty words like that Jayne,' he said, his pouting happily replaced by a smile.'

' You'd make the good Lord himself swear,' muttered Jayne. 'Now get off your arse . . . er . . . I mean backside, and give Mike a hand.'

John did as he was bid, much to the relief of Mike who looked absolutely dazed with the technicalities of the instructions. 'Thanks John,' he muttered. 'I'm very sorry, mate, and I know that I've boobed.'

JOHN BEVERLEY

John looked down at the pile of tent and support-stays as he tipped them from the tent-bag onto the ground. He glanced at the poorly made, cheap, nylon covering that he spread across the grass. 'I reckon you could be right, mate,' he said to no-one in particular. 'Never mind, Mike, let's give it a whirl, eh? Come on, we'll have it up in no time.'

But regrettably, that wasn't to be, but not because it was particularly difficult to figure-out the assembly of the tent, the instructions were quite clear really. It was the fact that the loops which had been put in the tent-cover to thread-up the support-stays were so badly stitched that at least a dozen of them snapped off leaving the tent, which by then should have been taut, badly sagging in both the middle and sides. This disaster was further compounded by the fact that the corner-patches for holding the ends of the support-stays and which then would form the bubble-shape of the tent, were hanging uselessly where only a half of the stitching had been completed during manufacture.

Finally, after a ridiculous assembly-time, the tent was up.

'It's rubbish, isn't it, John?' Mike stated this as fact rather than a question.

'It's not too good,' John replied quietly as they stood surveying the sagging bubble tent. John felt terribly sorry for his friend.

'I've been had, haven't I?' Mike said softly.

'No, you bloody-well haven't,' shouted John, suddenly taking charge of the situation. 'How much did you pay for this tent, Mike?'

'Three hundred and fifty pounds.'

'Okay, you were done, Mike, but I'm going to get you your money back. What time is it?' John looked at his watch. 'Midday! Right, that's it! We can take this down and be in Gloucester by five o'clock before that camping-shop closes. Come on, let's do it!'

And so off they went. After leaving the girls in the Cabanon with a bottle or two of wine, John and Mike raced back to Gloucester in record time to find the camping-shop still well and truly open.

'Leave this to me,' whispered John to Mike, fully aware of Mike's inability to take the bull-by-the-horns in situations such as this. Arriving at the counter, John, with a face like thunder, demanded to see the manager. The shop-assistant immediately sensed the mood of gloom that reflected in John's face for without further delay the manager appeared, as if by magic.

'Yes, sir, is there anything I can do for you?'

'Too true there is something you can do for me,' John began. 'A few hours ago I attempted to put up one of your bubble-tents in Pembrokeshire. It was so disgusting in its manufacture that I have brought it back to you.' John heaved the laden tent-bag onto the counter.

'Yes, I recognise the make, sir,' stated the manager. 'This is one of the latest stock that we've had in on a new and sensational design of tent.'

JOHN BEVERLEY

'Bullshit!' exclaimed John, his eyes unblinking as he looked at the manager. 'It may be sensational to you but it's rubbish to us punters. Half of the bloody stitching is missing which results in a tent that sags like the Hanging Gardens of Babylon. If you were in it in the rain you would be so wet that I reckon you'd feel like Jonah in the belly of the whale. Come off it, mate, it's c – r – a – p, crap!'

'Well we haven't had any trouble with them before,' declared the manager half-heartedly. 'No-one up to now has complained.'

'Don't give me the usual patter, Mr Manager,' John growled. 'You have sold faulty goods and I want my money back in accordance with my rights as a purchaser.'

The manager, realising that his bluff had not worked, instantly caved-in. 'Do you have your receipt,' he blundered. Mike produced it in a flash. 'One moment, sir, and I'll get your money.'

John and Mike waited patiently until the manager returned a few minutes later. 'There you are, sir, three hundred and fifty pounds. I'm sorry you were inconvenienced in this way but the company always honours its obligations to their customers.'

'Well, I think that you are going to have to obligate a bit more,' said John dryly.

'W . . . w . . . what d . . . do you m . . . m . . . mean, sir?' stuttered Mr Manager.

'Dead simple,' said John confidently, really starting to enjoy himself in the situation. 'My friend and I have driven about five hours from Pembrokeshire, West Wales, to your establishment. It will

A Gaze into Holidaze

also take us at least that time to get back. That's ten hours of travelling, ten hours out of our lives. Plus two hours that we have wasted putting up and taking down the monstrosity that you sell as a tent, makes it approximately twelve wasted hours of our lives. Do you get my drift?'

Mr Manager nodded, a glazed look on his face. Slowly he looked around at the gathering group of late shoppers who had been attracted by John's loud complaining, his face changing to give the usual vivid flushes of embarrassment.

'So,' continued John. 'Because there are two of us involved in this frightful cock-up you can multiply the twelve wasted hours by two to give twenty-four wasted hours of our lives. Well, I don't know about you Mr . . . er . . . Mr . . .,' John fumbled for Mr Manager's name.

'Er . . . Jarvis. Burt Jarvis,' Mr Manager bumbled clumsily.

'May I call you Burt?' John asked with authority.

Burt nodded, anxious to please. 'Certainly, sir.'

'Well Burt, I don't know about you but I certainly don't work for less than ten pounds an hour. Therefore, I reckon you owe us two hundred and forty pounds plus fuel for getting us here and back to West Wales.' John paused and coldly looked Burt right in the eye with not the least hint of a smile. 'Let's make it a nice round figure of three-hundred pounds, shall we?'

The six or so people who had gathered around them grunted their approval.

Burt Jarvis's flabber was gasted. 'I can't give you three-hundred pounds. I just don't have the authority to do that.'

'But you do agree in principle, don't you, Burt?'

Burt nervously looked around at the faces that blankly stared back at him. Slowly he nodded shyly in agreement.

'Good,' said John with satisfaction. 'What can you do for us then, Burt?'

And that is how Mike and Sue obtained their brand-new Cabanon frame-tent, identical in every way to the one that John and Jayne owned.

'Thanks, John,' said Mike, humble as they drove back to West Wales. 'I've been such a prat it isn't true.'

'Forget it, Mike. We all make mistakes but please – please, next time listen to good advice. Don't be like me because I learned the hard way by making mistake after mistake. Anyway, you now have a great tent and have saved yourself about two-hundred quid in the bargain.'

'Yes, thanks to you,' Mike said gratefully. 'You have changed a disaster into a triumph.'

'Just call me Superman,' laughed John.

They arrived back at the campsite after midnight to find Jayne and Sue as happy as larks after their partaking of the wine. Twenty minutes later the new tent was up and everyone bedded down comfortably for the night. For John and Mike it had been a very busy day. For Jayne and Sue it had been a very merry one!!

A Gaze into Holidaze

The following morning, all four tenters were up quite early and full of the joys of spring with not a hangover in sight. It was a beautifully crisp and clear morning which held the promise of a forthcoming warm and sunny day.

Jayne cooked breakfast of bacon and eggs whilst Mike showed Sue the wonders of their new frametent. Sue was thrilled to bits, especially when she heard that the new tent had cost them no more than the dreadful bubble-tent that they had been conned into buying. It was the start of a great day!

'What would you like to do today, folks?' asked John as he completed the washing-up of the breakfast dishes. 'Do you want to go for a walk or do you want to laze about the campsite?' He looked around to find the usual number of tents on the campsite for the month of May. Namely, theirs, a small bubble-tent and a slightly larger ridge-tent. There was no sign of the occupants of the other two tents.

'I'd like a walk,' replied Mike eagerly, his reply echoed by the willing nods of the girls.

'Right,' said John. 'Then we'll walk from St David's along the coastal-path to the lovely and picturesque village of Solva. It's about four miles, which, with the walk back from Solva will be around eight or nine miles. It's going to be a cracking day so all we'll need is a warm sweater and away we'll go.'

The walk along the Pembrokeshire coastal-path to Solva was magnificent. The track led along the top of the cliffs, occasionally dropping into little craggy coves, only to climb back up to the spring-flower-clad tops of the cliffs once again. Throughout the walk, the sound of the thunderous crashing of the blue-black sea as it smashed against the rocks at the base of the cliffs, mingled with the screaming of the seabirds as they hovered in the wind before diving deeply towards the troubled surface of the sea. The scenery was fantastically breathtaking, presenting an ever-changing kaleidoscope of colour, noise and spectacle.

The only part of the ramble which refused to be breathtaking, was the weather. In the two hours that it took to complete the walk, the weather had changed dramatically from friendly sunshine and corresponding warmth to the icy-chill of a heavy downpour. Both couples virtually ran the last mile of the walk to arrive breathlessly at a small, country-inn on the outskirts of the village.

'Typically Welsh weather,' panted John as they all removed their sweaters and shook them in front of the brightly-lit log-fire that blazed at them from an old, timbered fireplace.

'You can say that again,' agreed Mike, joining Jayne and Sue at a wooden-table beside the fire. 'At least the landlord had the good sense to light the fire. Obviously he knows the trials and tribulations of the Welsh weather in May.' They all laughed, not really caring about the downpour outside.

'What are you going to have?' asked John as he looked around the small, olde-worlde but very

A Gaze into Holidaze

attractive lounge of the pub. They had the place to themselves apart from another couple who sat at the other side of the room.

Taking their orders, John crossed to the small oak-covered bar, rang a tiny, brass bell and waited for service. Finally, after a few minutes, a small bald-headed, bearded man in a polo-necked sweater greeted him.

'Nasty day, sir,' smiled the barman. 'What can I get you?'

'Certainly is,' replied John and placed his order for drinks. 'Tell me. We've been caught with our pants down I'm afraid walking from St David's without any wet-gear. There's no chance of walking back in all of this rain because it certainly doesn't look as if it's going to let up.'

'I agree,' nodded Barman as he pulled on the pump. 'According to the weatherman on TV, this nasty rain is in for the day.'

'So, what time is the next bus for St David's?'

The man looked at his watch. 'Not for another two hours I'm afraid – if then. They tell me that the bus-crews are all off with flu, you see, and the buses now are a bit like the National Lottery for you and me.'

'The National Lottery?' puzzled John.

'Yes,' smiled Barman in good humour. 'It never comes.' With that, he burst into a deep-throated belly-laugh. 'You've got to see the funny-side of life, sir, haven't you?'

'Very funny,' John replied, not really seeing the

funny-side of the barman's little joke. John took the tray of drinks over to the others at the fireside. Sitting down, he explained to them the problem of the lack of transportation back to St David's.

'Don't worry about it, John,' Mike said with a chuckle, his cheeks starting to glow with the heat from the huge fireplace. 'At least we are marooned in the right place. A roaring fire and an unlimited supply of ale. What more could a man desire?'

They all laughed and continued to laugh for the next two hours. Well, laugh and drink fine Welsh-beer that is! Eventually, John crossed to the window and saw that there was no let-up in the rain.

'I'll see if I can get a taxi,' John said as he returned to the table.

'There's no need for that.' The voice came from the young-woman of the couple that John had seen when they had first entered the pub. 'We're going to St David's and we've rented an MPV so there's plenty of room to give you a lift.'

'Well, that's very kind of you,' said John. 'You see we've been caught in the rain and . . .'

'Yes, we heard.' This time the voice came from the male of the couple. 'We're just about to leave so, if you're ready . . .?'

'Yes, we are certainly ready and, once again, thank you.'

So, the two couples piled into a large MPV to accompany their saviours-of-the-day to St David's. During the return journey of no more than ten

A Gaze into Holidaze

minutes of idle but pleasant conversation, a number of interesting facts were learned about their hosts. The girl, who was in her early twenties, tanned and very attractive, was called Tania whilst her boyfriend, also in his early twenties, a tall pale-faced man with a shaved head, was called Rudy. They were both South African and on holiday touring throughout the UK. As luck would have it they were staying on the same campsite as John, Jayne, Mike and Sue – in fact, theirs was the small bubble-tent that John had spotted earlier that morning.

'To show our hospitality and eternal gratitude, you must come and have a bottle of wine with us,' said Jayne as Rudy dropped all of them off outside their tents.

'I don't think we should,' said Tania. 'We haven't had lunch and we've got some lamb-chops that we are going to have for our tea.' She paused and smiled warmly. 'Anyway, we've already sampled some of your beer in the pub and we are not used to drinking in the afternoons.'

'Nonsense,' shouted John, well into the party spirit. He opened the car door for Tania to get out. 'Come on, Tania, you can eat later. It's party-time now.'

And party they did. John's wine, the wine John always took with them by the caseful wherever they went, was enjoyed by all and soon the tent throbbed with laughter and joking. The rain did not stop but neither did the flow of wine. One could have argued that it was as wet inside the tent as it was outside.

After about an hour or so, still well into his cups, John spotted the return of the only other tenters on the site. Without hesitation, he dashed through the rain to invite the new couple to the party.

'Too true, blue,' came the unhesitating reply in a very slow Australian drawl. 'Just let me grab some tinnies and we'll be right with you.'

The rain went on and the party went on until it was now around 6 p.m. and, with the overcast sky, dusk was rapidly approaching. Having toasted queens, kings, presidents, prime-ministers, princesses, princes, Uncle Tom Cobblys-and-all, many times over, accompanied with much singing of hymns, national anthems and semi-dirty songs, the cosmopolitan party was gradually coming to its drunken conclusion. It became painfully obvious that all participants had consumed considerable quantities of alcohol on empty stomachs because no-one had had lunch and no-one seemed to be interested in dinner.

Rudy and Mike were sitting in the corner of the tent dreamily listening to the drunken Australian, whose name turned out to be Peter but was naturally and unanimously allotted Digger, struggling to play John's guitar as he fumbled something about a jolly swagman or jolly shwagman or such like. Jayne and Sue were sipping whisky, which had appeared from nowhere, and were giggling like two overgrown schoolgirls. John was standing, none too steadily, at the door-flap of the tent with Tania who was without doubt more drunk than anyone else.

'Donsh shee mush rain in Shoush Africa,' Tania mused, although drunk, her guttural accent becoming more pronounced. 'I liksh sher rain, I'sh donsh likesh sher shun mush.'

'We don't get mush, I mean much sun here,' said John, fighting hard to sound sober. 'I've alwaysh wanted shoo go . . .'

'I'msh going insh sher rain for sha walk shoo shober up,' slurred Tania. With that, she promptly stripped down to her very brief bra and even briefer panties and fell out of the door to land flat out on her face and stomach in the grass. 'Oopsh,' she giggled. Then, getting up with a loud, 'wheee!' at the top of her voice, she proceeded to staggeringly run around the perimeter of the field in the icy rain. Regularly every twenty yards or so she would fall down, only to miraculously find her equilibrium once more and shakily regain her feet. Twenty yards later – splosh! – she was down again on the rain-saturated grass, sometimes on her stomach, sometimes on her very muddy backside.

Although having great difficulty in focusing through the swirling fog in front of his eyes, John couldn't believe what Tania had done. Like a man in a dream, John watched the three circuits that Tania had made of the field. He chuckled to himself every time she fell down and actually cheered every time he saw the bikini-clad, mud-sodden figure manage to staggeringly regain her feet.

Finally, still chuckling to himself, but still not fully understanding what was going on, he saw Tania fall for the two-hundredth time at the far side of the field. This time she remained flat on her face and spread-eagled in the mud, the rain merrily bouncing off her buttocks.

'Rudy, better come here, me old mate,' John said casually, still trying to get the better of his eyes which refused to focus for more than a few seconds at a time.

'Why, washer masher,' came Rudy's reply as he poured himself another drink.

'Tania hash . . . er, has fallen down,' John struggled.

'Where ish she?' laughed Rudy. 'Don't worry Shohn, she'sh alwaysh doing shat.'

'But she's out in the field in the rain,' argued John. 'What's more she'sh got no closhes on, usher than her bra and panshee.'

'Aw! She'sh alwaysh doing shat at home. Shleave sher be. She'shll come in shoon.' With that, Rudy passed-out and fell to the floor.

'Mike, give me a hand,' shouted John turning to his friend. Unfortunately Mike proved to be a prone figure lying quietly at the side of the tent fast asleep.

By now Jayne and Sue joined John at the door. They looked at the distant, nearly-naked figure as it lay in the muddy-grass a hundred yards away. Then they looked at each other and . . . laughed, and laughed, and laughed.

A Gaze into Holidaze

That was all that John needed to get him into gear. 'The bloody fool will catch pneumonia,' he shouted as he raced across the field, splashing through the numerous pools of water that covered the ground.

Reaching the seemingly-dead figure, he went down on his knees and turned Tania over. She made a quiet squelching sound as the mud released her soundly-sleeping body. Even though the rain splattered heavily on the fixed smile of her face, Tania did not know anything about what was going on. She was not remotely aware, and cared even less, that her bikini-underwear was now like tiny see-through pieces of nothing.

John lifted the sleeping girl and slung her over his shoulder in a fireman's lift fashion. In this configuration, after falling himself three times, he finally reached the tent to be greeted by the loud applause of the two giggling girls.

'Come on, Jayne, I need your help.' John was by now totally sober. 'You and Sue take her in Sue's tent. Get her warm and get her into bed with something hot. The three of you had better sleep there tonight. Come on, I'll give you a hand.'

Again they lifted the dead-weight of Tania, who sluggishly opened her eyes, half-smiled and promptly and very profoundly proceeded to vomit. Fortunately, because they were holding Tania near the door, John only had to quickly turn the young woman's head to save the inside of the tent when the pourings of the young woman's stomach shot from her mouth and through the open door in a beautiful arc, to finally make a neat, conically-shaped pile on the grass outside.

And that was the end of the party. The Australians literally crawled back to their tent while Jayne, Sue and Tania slept in Mike's and Sue's new tent. Rudy was left to find his own way back to his bubble-tent at the far side of the field, and Mike slept in John's tent in exactly the same position in which he had collapsed earlier on in the party.

Just before noon the following morning, after the rain had finally stopped, Jayne was cooking breakfast for John, Mike and Sue. Tania had returned to her own bubble-tent to join Rudy at 7 a.m. that morning. 'Looking absolutely green,' was Sue's only comment about the poor woman's condition.

'God, I'm not sure that I'm alive,' groaned a grossly hung-over Mike. 'Are all of your camping parties like last night, John?'

'No, not all of them,' smiled John wickedly. 'Just most of them!'

A half-an-hour later there was a knock on the flap-door of the tent which was closed to keep out the painful, unwelcome light of the very-bright morning. John unzipped the flap and opened the door wide. There stood a greenly-pale Tania, her features ghoulishly drawn.

'I've come to apologise for last night,' she said sheepishly, face to the ground, unable to meet anyone's eyes.

A Gaze into Holidaze

'You've nothing to apologise for,' Jayne said quietly. 'We all had a good time but perhaps we had a little too much to drink.'

'You see. I don't drink at home. It's just that I enjoyed your company so much, I just went a little overboard.'

'Say no more about it,' said John, a gleam in his eye. 'Tell me, Tania, what do your eyes look like from the inside, 'cos they look terrible from the outside!' They all laughed, except for Tania who blushed to her very roots. John spotted this and immediately put his arm around her shoulder to comfort the young woman. 'I was only teasing, pet. Come on, forget last night ever happened. We have, haven't we, Mike?'

Mike groaned. 'Almost, almost!'

'Have you seen my purse?' Tania asked gloomily. 'I think I've lost it. I had it in the pub yesterday but I haven't seen it since and all my credit cards are in it.'

A rigorous search by the five hung-over tenters revealed the lost purse hiding under John's guitar. It was agreed that Rudy must have put it there when attempting to play 'Once a Jolly Swagman.'

'How is Rudy?' asked Jayne.

'Still asleep I'm afraid,' replied Tania. 'You see, at home Rudy's family are all Quakers so he also is not used to parties.'

There was silence while the four other people in the tent went on a guilt-trip to the moon and back. Jayne tried to ease the situation. 'Did you finally manage to eat your lamb-chops, Tania?'

'No, I'm afraid not. When I went to get them from the car this morning they had gone off. The smell was overpowering and I think it will remain in the car for many months to come. I hope the rental people will not charge us to valet the car when they smell it.'

'Air freshener may help,' volunteered John in a vague and useless attempt to help ease the burden of guilt that he felt. He was the one that got the wine flowing in the party and he knew it.

However, all's well that ends well. The following day was time to pack-up and return to homes many thousands of miles apart. Goodbyes were said to the Australians and South Africans and all were pleased that the repulsive odour of dead animals had totally disappeared from Tania's and Rudy's MPV.

'Did you enjoy camping over the weekend?' John asked Jayne as they drove homeward-bound along the M4.

'Yes, I did,' replied Jayne without hesitation. 'It was great to be back in the tent once again, but . . .'

'Yes, here comes the buts,' John declared with a frown.

'. . . I want my holiday with Clarence in Switzerland,' Jayne finished smugly.

'Roll on July,' agreed John with a shout. 'Look out Switzerland, here we come!'

****

A Gaze into Holidaze

Mustangs and a burst on the old guitar . . .
So the following July found John, Jayne and Clarence down in deepest Switzerland. Or, to be more precise, on a splendid little campsite in Visp, a small town not more than twenty miles or so from the wondrous, copybook mountain of the Matterhorn.

The weather was fantastic, being clear, sunny and very warm at around 30 degrees Celsius. Accordingly, John and Jayne had hired a couple of bicycles from the very railway-station in which they had slept during their adventure of a few years previously. It was certainly good to be back in the picturesquely-stunning countryside that they knew so well.

On one particular day, John and Jayne rode aimlessly along the base of a deep tree-lined valley following one of the many startlingly-blue but thundering rivers that ran throughout the region. To accompany their travels the multitude and variety of colourful Alpine flowers that proudly bloomed along the side of the narrow cycle-path, was a sight to behold.

After they had ridden perhaps ten miles or so they were attracted by a loud noise that suddenly burst from behind some trees not more than a half-mile ahead.

'What on earth can that be?' said Jayne, frowning at the sudden intrusion to the wonderful peace of their cycle ride.

'That's an aero-engine if ever I've heard one, and

a pretty powerful one at that,' John replied. 'Come on, Jayne, let's go and have a butcher's. It seems to be just around the corner of those trees.'

Two minutes later, as they rounded the trees, they were confronted by a small airfield which was buzzing with people, as they milled around a dozen or more WW2 fighter aircraft. It was one of these aircraft that had just noisily started up and attracted their attention.

'This is fantastic,' yelled John in an attempt to be heard over the roar of the huge radial engine, his eyes shining with childlike delight. 'Look at all these fighters, it's amazing. There's a Spitfire and Hurricane, no two Hurricanes.' John pointed. 'Over there, there's a pile of American P51 Mustangs and . . .' He broke off as, with a roar of throttle, the fighter that had started up, spun away from the crowd and taxied towards the far end of the grass field. John was bursting with excitement. 'That one about to take off is an American Wildcat like the one that John Wayne flew in *Flying Leathernecks*. Do you remember that film Jayne?'

Jayne smiled knowingly as she slowly nodded her head. How could she forget having sat patiently through *Flying Leathernecks* for about fifty times over the last few years? Yes, her John was a big John Wayne fan from way back, and Westerns and war movies were his bread and butter.

'I suppose you want to go in and see your little aeroplanes,' Jayne volunteered teasingly. 'I expect you want to go and touch one. They might even let

A Gaze into Holidaze

you sit in the cockpit of one of them, John. Wouldn't that be nice for you?'

'Do you think they will?' John rushed back, his enthusiasm bubbling through as he dismounted his bike. 'I'll go and find out what it's all about shall I, Jayne?'

Without waiting for a reply, he left Jayne still straddling her bicycle at the gate of the airfield and dashed inside soon to be engaged in conversation with what looked like, judging by the yellow armband that he wore, an official of the meeting.

Minutes later and still clutching his bike, John ran back to the bewildered Jayne. 'It's absolutely fabulous,' panted John, barely able to get his words out fast enough in his excitement. 'These aircraft are all privately owned by their pilots and, once a year, they meet here for a flying display.' John pointed to where the taxiing Wildcat had finally stopped and turned into the wind. 'They even have a runway of sorts over there . . .' John broke off at the sudden roar of the engine as the pilot opened his throttle to the full, which told the crowd that the Wildcat was commencing its take-off run.

'Come on, Jayne, it's only ten francs each to go in.'

It was a truly splendid afternoon where John, Jayne and the enormous crowd, were treated to a fantastic display of aerobatics and formation flying, carried out by extremely skilled pilots. These pilots had assembled for the occasion from all over Europe and the expertise, enthusiasm and dedication of these men and one woman was reflected not only in their flying, but in the vintage condition and cleanliness of their aircraft. Each aeroplane positively gleamed, whether it was a shiny aluminium P51 Mustang or a magnificently camouflaged De Havilland Mosquito, it did not matter. They were in prime and much-cared-for condition brought about by many hours of TLC – tender loving care!

After the display, John went to each aircraft in turn and passed the time of day with its pilot. John could not help but admire such men, and the one woman. Although John expected him to be an American, the pilot of the P51 Mustang was actually a Frenchman, currently serving with the French air force and flying Mirage jet-fighters. 'Would you like to sit in the cockpit of my Mustang?' The Frenchman asked in impeccable English.

'Oh, I'd love to,' replied John who, quicker than a flash and needing no second invitation, was up on the wing and into the pilot's seat faster than you could say Spitfire.

Jayne laughed inwardly at her man-cum-boy. He actually sat in the cockpit of that Mustang for the best part of an hour, his dreamy eyes suggesting that his mind and brain were somewhere above the clouds and thousands of feet above this planet Earth.

However, back to earth John had to come because at three o'clock on the still beautiful afternoon, the show came to an end. Reluctantly he climbed down

A Gaze into Holidaze

from the cockpit and hastily shook the Frenchman's hand in farewell. Not satisfied with that and with Jayne, as ever, at his heels, he went around every pilot and aeroplane once again to show them his appreciation and to say his goodbyes. Jayne reluctantly but finally had to tear John away or he would have stayed for the rest of the day.

'Gosh, I enjoyed that,' said John happily as they rode their hired bikes back to Visp railway-station. 'Imagine what it must be like to fly like that.'

'As free as a bird I would have thought,' replied Jayne, happy that John had fulfilled, albeit very briefly, his love of aeroplanes. 'What a piece of luck that we happened to cycle past that airfield on the very day of the display? What's the chance of that happening, eh?'

John nodded his agreement. 'We were lucky indeed.'

For the remainder of the journey, whilst they were handing-in their bikes at the railway-station at Visp, during the walk back to the campsite, whilst Jayne prepared a meal, during the eating of the meal, during the washing-up after the meal, during their usual supping-of-red-wine-by-candle-light as darkness embraced them while they sat outside the caravan on the warm and barmy night, John did not stop talking about the wonders of the aircraft, the flying display and the pilots that he had met.

Finally, Jayne had had enough. So, not wanting to offend John in any way, she quietly stood up and crossed to the caravan, disappearing inside to finally emerge carrying John's guitar.

John stopped in mid-'did-you-see-that?' sentence. 'I reckon you're trying to tell me something,' he said as he reached out to take the guitar from Jayne. 'You've had enough of my blabbering on about those aeroplanes, haven't you?'

'Well, yes, I suppose I have really,' replied Jayne. 'You've got to be honest, John, you have rabbited-on a bit about that flying display, haven't you?'

'Yes, point taken.'

'Well, let's make the most of this fabulous evening. Let's drink a couple of glasses of this lovely red wine and sing a few songs, shall we?'

'Done,' agreed John. As he spoke he simultaneously strummed a chord of 'C' and plunged into the melody line of John Denver's *West Virginia* to be immediately joined by the harmonising Jayne.

They had done this kind of singing for years where John played the guitar and sang the melody of the song in his strong baritone voice while Jayne very sweetly blended with her beautiful soprano tones. They weren't fabulous but they were good and on many occasions their laments could be heard over the campsites of Europe, often drawing fellow-campers to join them for a friendly sing-along.

It would appear that this was no exception because after they had been singing for about a quarter of an hour, Jayne noticed a man, in his early twenties, standing on the road which ran next to the campsite. He was leaning on the camp perimeter-fence and clapped his hands gently to the rhythms that John conjured up with his guitar. The man even applauded as John and Jayne finished each and every song.

'How long has he been there?' asked John as they finished yet another number to the appreciative clapping of the man on the other side of the fence.

'I don't know,' replied Jayne, smiling and nodding her head at the man. 'He seems to be enjoying our singing though.'

'No, it's my guitar playing that he's enjoying,' John added mischievously as he put his guitar down. Then, turning to the man, who was virtually a black silhouette against the glow of a background street-lamp, John shouted. 'Would you like to join us for a glass of wine?'

The man jabbered something back in a language that John certainly did not recognise. John looked at Jayne questioningly only to receive a shrug back from her to register her lack of understanding. John again looked at the man and, applying the universal gesture of invitation for a drink, moved his empty hand in a tipping manner to his open mouth. 'Come on in and have a drink with us, mate.'

Again the man replied in a language completely alien to John.

'Do you know what he said?' John asked Jayne.

'No, not a word of it to be honest,' replied Jayne.

'Well, I can't speak any language other than English and I'm not much good at that. You can speak quite a bit of German, Jayne. Go and ask him in German if he would like to join us for a drinkie-poo.' By now the red wine already consumed was slightly getting through to John.

'I don't think that my German is up to that but I'll give it a go,' Jayne volunteered.

Jayne joined the man at the fence and conversed with him for a couple of minutes before he suddenly and excitedly shouted, 'Salute!' and walked off into the darkness towards the nearby Visp. Jayne returned to the table, sat down and sipped from her glass.

'What did he say?' asked John.

'Well, to be frank, I don't really know for sure. The language he was speaking certainly wasn't German but seemed to be a sort of Slavic-type of lingo. I don't know, I've never heard it before. I tried to get him to speak in German and he may have tried, but in any event, we didn't get far.'

'Did you get any of it at all, the German bit I mean?' John enquired sarcastically. 'Or are you keeping the mystery to yourself?'

'Well, I think he said that he would like to have a drink but first he would go and get his five brothers from Visp.'

John burst out laughing. 'I thought you said you could speak German,' he said, absolutely cracking up. 'Five brothers from Visp, don't be daft. Who on earth would have five brothers living in Visp. Glad

A Gaze into Holidaze

I don't have to rely on you as our interpreter for directions, we would end up in Katmandu instead of Switzerland.'

'Well I did my best, John, and that's that.' Jayne was not amused.

And neither was John when, thirty minutes later, the man returned with five of his brothers, all fine specimens of men in their early to late twenties. Humbly dressed in baggy trousers and loose-fitting shirts that John could only describe as Turkish, they sported three guitars together with six dazzlingly white-toothed smiles in heavily tanned faces.

After hearty handshakes and much kissing and hugging, they sat cross-legged on the ground around the camping-table that John and Jayne were using but just within the range of candlelight that gave a pleasant glow to their dark faces. Attempts were made at introductions but it was plain to both John and Jayne that they could not even pronounce the names of their unexpected guests let alone remember them.

Immediately, John went inside the caravan for glasses and wine. 'We shall call you numbers one to six from left to right,' John offered good naturedly on his return to the group. 'Right numbers one to six, who wants a glass of wine?'

John thought that he had said something improper because as one person, they all shrugged in distaste at his suggestion. Lots of noisy jabbering once more in that mystic language did not help

John's understanding one little bit until he finally gave up and sat back down dejectedly at the table. 'Bloody-hell, Jayne, this is going to be just dandy. Six bloody blokes and we can't speak a word of conversation to any of 'em! What the blazes are we going to do?'

John need not have worried. As soon as he had finished speaking, the guitars of the group broke into a lovely, almost Latin-American-cum-gypsy intoxicating rhythm. After a few bars, all six men started singing harmoniously along with the music, their voices ranging from the deepest of bass-profundos, through the finest of baritones to the pitches of the highest tenors. All were cleverly interwoven to form the delightful strains of a lively ballad of unknown origin.

At the end John and Jayne applauded loudly with genuine and much deserved appreciation. The song had been fantastic, and exquisitely sung.

Number-six, the man whom they had originally met at the fence, gestured with his guitar in such a manner as to indicate that it was now John and Jayne's turn to sing a song. Not to be outdone, and to fly the British flag through and through, John and Jayne did as they were bid and met the request with another John Denver classic. At the finish, this was greeted with more heartily loud clapping and appreciative cheering by numbers one to six.

This went on for the next two hours with music from John and Jayne's repertoire of John Denver,

A Gaze into Holidaze

The Beatles, Simon and Garfunkel, being alternatively interlaced with numbers one to six's beautiful, traditional ballad and folk-singing, accompanied by the most fantastic gypsy-guitar playing imaginable.

Every time John offered the group a drink he was forced to accept the same not-too-polite shrugs of disapproval. These boys were not interested in booze by any stretch of the imagination.

Finally, the wonderful and magical night had to come to an end. Numbers one to six got up to leave and kisses-on-both-cheeks and friendly handshakes were exchanged.

'Before you go I have a question for you,' John said to number-three, one of the brothers who seemed to understand a little more of the attempted conversation of the night. 'Can you explain to me why neither you nor your brothers have joined Jayne and me in a small glass of red wine throughout the entire evening?'

By way of reply, probably because number-three did not have the ability to give a verbal reply, number-three suddenly back-flipped away from John and proceeded to cartwheel, handspring and somersault around the table in a ten-metre diameter circle. This was like a signal to the remaining brothers who, with much hand-slapping, hooting and laughing, proceeded to join in the antics of number-three, all six brothers finally ending in a three-two-one pyramid which finally collapsed with each participant culminating in a forward roll.

The answer to the puzzle was simple. The six brothers were part of a Romanian circus trupe which was performing in Visp for the next five days.

The following morning when John and Jayne got up, there, on the table outside the caravan, were two complimentary tickets for the Romanian Circus. They went the following night and experienced the wonders of the finest circus that they had ever seen in their lives. They were even invited backstage after the show to meet numbers one to six, their fellow performers and who else – the animals. A good time wasn't had by all – a most fantastic time was had by all!!

****

A poor little waif ...

After Visp, John, Jayne and Clarence crossed over the stunning mountain ranges of the Bernese Oberland to finally camp alongside Lake Thun at Interlaken. The weather had not changed throughout the holiday and, other than the odd thunderstorm which took place in the night, it remained clear, sunny and very hot.

On this particular day, John and Jayne had completed a wonderful climb about twenty miles from Interlaken. The ascent took them from the valley floor to the plateau of the Kleine Scheidegg which lay at about six thousand feet and just below the sheer face of the famous, or infamous perhaps, Eiger mountain.

A Gaze into Holidaze

John stood on the exact spot where Clint Eastwood stood when he made the *Eiger Sanction* movie. Obviously, Jayne was forced to take John's photograph with the Eiger in the background. This made John's day enough for him to adopt Clint's swagger as he walked around for the next few hours. Jayne's only comment – 'A pity you haven't got Clint's money and, yes, you need another five inches in height.'

By teatime, back on the campsite at Interlaken and Jayne having had her daily fix by feeding the ducks on the lake, our heroes were lying outside the caravan on their sun-loungers soaking up a few rays. They were both completely and utterly exhausted.

'Cor! My feet aren't half throbbing,' said John, wiggling his bare toes. 'Thank God we had decent walking-boots, eh, Jayne?'

Jayne sat cross-legged on her lounger, gently massaging her own feet. 'Yes, John, I wouldn't have wanted to make that climb without them, my feet would never have stood up to it. Still, it was so beautifully cool up there and the scenery so breathtaking it was well worth a couple of sore feet. Any blisters, John?'

'No, not one. I bet this chap has though. By the look of him he's got blisters on his blisters.'

Jayne looked up and followed John's gaze. There, limping towards them was a short man in his late fifties. He was very fat and wore a khaki, severely sweat-stained shirt that was loosely tucked into khaki shorts. These shorts were far too big for him, being extremely baggy and coming well below his knees. Almost meeting the shorts were thick woollen walking-socks, the feet of which disappeared into huge, military-style boots that had at one time been highly polished. Now, regrettably, they were badly scratched and scuffed. On his head, tipped slightly forward over the chubby, bespectacled face, was a broad-brimmed bush-hat. It was debatable whether the hat was tilted forward to protect the sweltering, sweat-covered face from the scorching sun or from the flies, which were enjoying their constant attack on the moist eyes that stared out blankly and were just visible from the shade of the broad-brim of the hat. Or was the hat tilted forward to allow for the huge rucksack that the man had on his back? A rucksack that reached from the top of his head – and in so doing, crushed the back of the hat's brim – to the middle of the more than generous buttocks that wobbled gently as the man walked slowly past John and Jayne.

'That man is absolutely cream-crackered,' said John as the man struggled to remove the heavy burden of his rucksack before allowing it to fall heavily to the ground of his intended pitch, about twenty yards or so away from where John and Jayne sat.

'The poor man,' whispered Jayne, more to herself than to John.

'He's a bit old for this back-packing lark I would have thought,' muttered John. 'He's the best part of sixty if he's a day and with all the extra weight he's carrying, the last thing he needs is a rucksack that's almost as big as he is.'

The man, after sitting on the ground for a minute or two in the shade of a tree, got up and started to unpack his gear.

'Go and help him, John. Go and help him before he falls down. No, better still, go and insist that he comes over and has a nice cup of tea before he does anything.'

John was gone like a shot. This man needed help badly.

'Hello, mate,' John smiled as he held out his hand. 'Can you speak English?'

'Too true, sport,' the man answered as he took John's offered hand.

'Is that an Australian accent I hear?' John asked, shaking the man's flabby hand gently.

'No, mate, I'm from Auckland, New Zealand.'

'Well, you're certainly a long way from home,' came John's friendly reply. 'My name's John and over there is my wife, Jayne.' John pointed.

'Hello, John, my name is Perry,' said the man as he waved cordially to Jayne who immediately returned the compliment. 'You blokes English?'

'Well, we're British or, to be more precise, Welsh,' replied John. 'Look, mate, if you don't mind me saying so, you look a bit shattered. Have you come very far?'

'No, not really,' Perry drawled. 'I broke camp this morning on the other side of the lake and travelled by steamer over here to Interlaken. I've only walked over the bridge from the steamer-port to here but it's so hot, I feel a bit crook.'

'Come on then, mate,' John offered. 'Come and have a nice cup of tea and a bite to eat with us.' John saw Perry hesitate, obviously not wanting to intrude on their privacy. 'It's no good, Perry, you've got to come. Jayne told me to tell you that if you hesitated then I was to tell you that the invitation wasn't a request, it was an order. As you know, Perry, you cannot disobey an order, can you?'

The two men laughed and crossed the short distance to where Jayne had already set the table under yet another tree and made tea and sandwiches.

Perry took Jayne's hand. 'My name is Perry, Jayne. Thankyou for your kind invitation to tea.'

'Not at all, Perry,' replied Jayne, her smile warm and friendly. 'You are more than welcome. Now please, sit down and enjoy your tea.'

They all sat down and enjoyed not only the early evening, but the night and several bottles of wine as well. Perry, during a short break after tea when he insisted on unpacking and putting up his tent himself before showering, was more than pleased to accept Jayne's invitation and joined the couple for dinner.

Apparently Perry, who was fifty-eight, had been an architect in New Zealand and married to his wife, Jenny. They had been devoted to each other and in spite of considerable efforts to produce little Perrys and Jennys, none had been forthcoming.

A Gaze into Holidaze

Unfortunately, four years previously, Jenny had died of cancer leaving Perry devastated. So devastated in fact that Perry had given up his architectural business together with his home, and had gone to live as a semi-recluse on his private yacht in the South Island of New Zealand.

Time went by and, during the last year, Perry had met an independent lady-friend and they had become very close. Now Perry had always wanted to backpack around Europe but because of work commitments had never got around to doing it. Getting older, Perry had realised that if he didn't do it soon he would never be able to do it. His lady-friend had had no desire whatsoever to do it, so, with his lady friend's blessing, he had set-off for an intended three-month trip.

All went well and Perry had successfully toured, using the rail-card system, around Poland, Austria and Italy. That is, all had gone well, until he had telephoned his lady-friend a week earlier from Italy, to find that the telephone was answered by Perry's best friend. The so-called best friend had claimed that he had called in on Perry's lady-friend by chance just to make sure that everything was fine and Perry's lady-friend was okay.

'So that's great,' said John, having listened with sad understanding to Perry's story. 'It's good to have a mate like that.'

Perry shook his head. 'I don't trust him. I cannot believe that this is coincidence and that my friend "just called in by chance" as he put it.'

JOHN BEVERLEY

John and Jayne spent the next fifteen minutes trying to reassure the obviously under-confident Perry that all was well back home in New Zealand. Perry being so far away from the problem, was obviously very concerned about the whole situation. Eventually, after several more glasses of wine and lots of coaxing, Perry gave in and agreed that his friend in New Zealand was probably only acting with his best interests at heart.

The one night led into a week of nights where Perry always came over to John and Jayne for a cup of tea at teatime or a nightcap if it was later than that. He never stayed more than a half-an-hour and made certain that he did not overstay his welcome. After pleasant conversation and a little fun and teasing, he would always leave on a bright and cheery note. Perry was a really nice man in every way.

Finally, after a week or so, the time came for Perry to move on. 'Thanks to you both for your kind hospitality,' he said after kissing Jayne on both cheeks and shaking John's hand.

'It's been great meeting you, Perry,' said John. 'Are you sure that you can walk with that rucksack of yours? It's nearly as big as you are, mate.'

Perry, standing there in his oversized shorts and huge boots, the back of his wide-brimmed hat crushed against the tall rucksack on his back, looked a sad and slightly pathetic figure. He smiled. 'Well, I've only got to carry it for another two weeks in France and then I'm going home. If you're

A Gaze into Holidaze

ever in New Zealand, both of you, you are always welcome to stay with me on my yacht.'

'Same to you, mate. If you are in the UK at any time I would be disappointed if you didn't look us up,' said John. 'You've been a good friend and we've enjoyed your company. When you get back to New Zealand, give your lady-friend a kiss from me.'

'I will.' Perry's reply was cheerful and his chubby face glowed with warmth as he turned away and trudged down the long path to the steamer-port.

'A really nice man,' said Jayne as Perry's back disappeared around a bend in the path. 'A really, really nice man.'

Two months later at 8.30 p.m on a wet and miserable October night, John lay on the settee in the lounge of the bungalow in West Wales. He smilingly listened to Jayne, a very accomplished classical pianist, struggling desperately to master the art of boogie-woogie on the piano. Things were not going too well in spite of several music-books on the subject that Jayne had bought a few weeks previously. Lots of practice on Jayne's part had not exactly borne the fruit of her labours.

'You're not going to play boogie-woogie as long as you've got a hole in your nose,' teased John, as yet another boogie-run from Jayne went disastrously wrong.

'Oh, thanks for your encouragement, John,' Jayne said impatiently as she slammed the music-book shut and got up from the piano to slump onto the settee next to John. 'I'll master it, you'll see.'

'No chance,' laughed John. 'You're a classical pianist not a . . .' The telephone rang, halting John in mid-sentence. He got up, crossed the room, lifted the receiver and spoke, annoyed at the interruption.

'Is that you, John?' The voice was a metallic tone sounding very far away. 'This is Perry.'

'Perry? Perry who?' answered John. 'I don't know a Perry.' John caught Jayne's arm waving for attention and saw her mouth silently exaggerate the word 'Switzerland'.

'You know,' the metallic voice continued. 'Perry from Switzerland.'

'Good God, Perry!' shouted John loudly – after all, his voice had to travel a long way to New Zealand.

'Don't shout, John,' Perry said. 'It's distorting over the telephone and I can't hear.'

'Sorry, Perry,' John almost whispered. 'How are things in New Zealand? A bit warmer than over here I bet?'

'I don't know, mate. I'm not in New Zealand.'

'Where are you then, Perry?'

'I'm in South Wales, sport.'

'What are you doing in Australia then, Perry?' John puzzled. 'I thought you were going home to New Zealand from Switzerland?'

'No, John, I'm not in New South Wales,' the metallic voice persisted. 'I'm in your South Wales – er, Swansea railway-station in fact. Do you think that you could pick me up?'

A Gaze into Holidaze

Forty-five minutes later, John and Jayne were hugging and kissing the still shorts-clad but now raincoat-covered and heavily-rucksacked Perry, like a long lost friend. Long – no, short in fact. Lost – most unlikely. Friend – most certainly, yes.

'Well, I told you in Switzerland, John, that if you ever invite a Kiwi to stay with you, you had better mean it because he certainly does,' Perry said, his face red with profound and genuine happiness.

'Perry, you are welcome to stay as long as you like,' Jayne said, her face glowing with warmth.

'Well, a week would be great, if it's alright with you?'

'Consider it done,' chuckled John. 'Come on, let me have your old faithful.' John helped Perry off with his rucksack and hoisted it on to his back before putting it in the boot of the Volvo. 'Bit chilly here in Blighty for shorts, old chum.'

'You can say that again,' agreed Perry. 'No matter, I've got some trousers in my rucksack.'

On the way to the bungalow, Perry explained that although he had intended to go back to New Zealand from France, France was so vast with plenty to see and Spain and Portugal were so close to France, that he would have been a fool not to have visited them. Then after that it would have been a shame for him not to have visited the UK.

'How's your lady-friend, Perry?' enquired John. 'Doesn't she mind you being away for so long?'

'Oh, she's alright,' replied Perry. 'When I left, I told her that I could be away for six months or more. I invited her to come with me but she wasn't too keen. She's not much of an adventurer you know?'

'Have you kept in touch?' Jayne asked.

'Oh, too true,' Perry drawled. 'I ring her once a week and she says she's fine. No, before you ask, there's been no further sign of my best friend.'

'Good!' said John, genuinely pleased.

Perry enjoyed staying with John and Jayne. After the first day he hired a small car and was only too pleased to revel in the beautiful countryside of Wales, North, West, Mid and South. It was on the fourth day that Perry discovered that Jayne played the piano and her love of music.

'Do you like traditional jazz?' Perry asked Jayne. 'I love traditional jazz.'

'Well, in that case there's a pub on the harbour at Bristol which plays trad-jazz every night,' replied Jayne. 'Would you like to go?'

During the two-hour drive to Bristol from Carmarthenshire, Jayne chatted to the now-trousered Perry all the way. He soon learned that although Jayne could play classical and popular music, she could not master boogie-woogie in spite of her efforts. Perry did not comment on this.

When they were seated in front of the stage in the buzzing jazz-pub and while John was getting a round of drinks at the bar, Perry excused himself and went to talk to the manager at the side of the stage. A few minutes later he returned to join John and Jayne at the table.

A Gaze into Holidaze

'Where have you been?' asked John innocently.

'Oh, I just wanted to see what time the jazz starts,' replied Perry. 'This is a nice pub, isn't it?'

'It's been going for years,' replied John. 'Jayne and I used to use it a lot. It's great here and if you like trad-jazz you'll be a very happy bunny. Cheers!' John raised his pint of ale.

Within minutes, the manager stepped up onto the stage and switched on the mike. 'Good evening ladies and gentlemen. Welcome to the Happy Frigate once again for a great evening of traditional jazz. However, before we start, we'll allow the boys of the band to have an extra pint by my introducing a fellow jazz-man from New Zealand. Ladies and gentlemen, put your hands together for our guest from down-under, Perry Knowles.'

The greeting was tremendous as Perry left the table, climbed onto the stage and seated himself at the piano. John and Jayne gaped, mouths open wide in astonishment as Perry turned to the audience and spoke, his Kiwi accent far more acute over the microphone. 'Thankyou, ladies and gentlemen, for your kind and warm welcome. I would like to dedicate this small musical presentation to a member of our audience tonight.' Turning to look at Jayne, he smiled and continued. 'This is for a lovely lady who is here tonight – Jayne.'

For the next ten minutes or so, John, and particularly Jayne, were enthralled with the finest rendering of boogie-woogie played on the piano that they had ever heard in their lives. Perry's performance was fluent, absolutely brilliant and musically flawless. At the end, the applause was deafening, to which Perry whispered a modest thank-you, gave a slight bow and returned to his seat at the table.

'That was wonderful,' shouted Jayne over the noise of the deafening applause. 'Give me a kiss.' She leaned over and gave the blushing Perry a big smacker on the lips.

'Well done,' said John, proudly patting Perry on the shoulder for all he was worth.

The evening and the jazz were excellent and all three of them had a marvellous time. This was rounded off with Perry's first fish-and-chips, a meal that he thoroughly enjoyed and scoffed as fast as he could.

As the car pulled into the drive of the bungalow Perry said, 'I've had a truly wonderful night. In fact, I can't remember when I have been so happy. Thank-you both for being such wonderful friends to an old timer like me.'

'The feeling's mutual,' said Jayne, her hand on Perry's arm. 'You are always welcome here in Carmarthenshire and so is your lady-friend if you like. What is her name, you have never said?'

'Anne,' replied Perry.

'Have you rung Anne this week?' Jayne enquired politely. Perry shook his head. 'Then why don't you do it now? Use our telephone.'

'Well, that's very kind of you,' Perry said. Then he consulted his watch. 'It's midnight now which

A Gaze into Holidaze

means it's midday back home in New Zealand and Anne will be at work. If you don't mind, I'll get up at 4 a.m. and ring Anne, she should be home by then.'

'No problem,' said John as he yawned. 'I'm ready for the sack'

They all were. They bade each other goodnight and went to bed, Perry setting his alarm-clock for 3.30 a.m. for his early morning call to Kiwi-land.

The next morning at about 8.30 a.m., Jayne gently woke John, tears running down her cheeks.

'What's the matter, darling?' John asked as he rubbed the sleep from his eyes.

Jayne could not answer, her choked emotions stopping her from uttering a sound. Instead, she took John's hand and led him from their bedroom to the hall where the telephone stood on a small table. 'He's gone,' was all she could sobbingly manage.

Beside the telephone was a small pile of coins. John instinctively knew in his mind that this pile of coins would be the exact cost, to the nearest penny, of the night-call to New Zealand. The pile of coins held down a slip of paper.

John looked at Jayne as he moved the coins and unfolded the piece of paper. They they both knew in their hearts that it was a message from Perry.

My Dear Friends, Jayne and John,

This is not much of a way to thank two genuinely wonderful human beings who have been so kind to me over the last four days.

JOHN BEVERLEY

Without warning, you shared your home with an almost perfect stranger, a stranger that you had only met once before and then only briefly in a foreign land.

In the last few days I have never felt such warmth, friendship and companionship since my lovely wife passed away four years ago. I really feel as if there is a firm and caring bond between us, which, unfortunately, I have to damage in the way I feel that I am forced to leave you.

This morning, I rang my lady friend, Anne, as planned. What I did not tell you was how much I cared for her and that I hoped that one day we might become man and wife. The telephone was answered by my so-called best friend, who did not hesitate to put Anne on the phone. She told me in no uncertain terms that she and my friend were now living together and, as such, she did not wish to see or hear from me again.

I feel, Jayne and John, that I am no longer good company and you certainly don't deserve to have my long face around you after the joy and laughter that we have shared.

Thank you once again for everything.

Your ever-loving friend,
Perry.

P.S. I would have taught you how to play boogie-woogie, Jayne, if this hadn't happened. Please forgive me. Perry.

A Gaze into Holidaze

John and Jayne rushed to Swansea railway-station but there was no sign of the plumply-dapper Perry. They tried the bus-station and even drove to Cardiff Airport but there was still no sign of Perry.

Fortunately, they did receive a Christmas card from him the following December which put their minds at ease by at least knowing that he was alive and hopefully well. There was a note on the card saying that he was intending to move to Australia and that when he was settled there he would get in touch.

He never did.

****

In Holland it is better, I think...

The following summer found our travelling quartet, John, Jayne, Clarence and Volv the Volvo, down in the South of France at the picturesque little place of Lantosque, about twenty miles or so north of Nice.

As usual it had been a long and tiring drive down through France from Dover. However, when they arrived at the lovely little campsite, set on the side of a hill in a shaded forest, the effort of travelling some six-hundred miles was well worth it.

'We're out of food and bits and pieces,' declared Jayne as John manoeuvred Clarence between a bell-type tent with a Dutch car outside it, and a caravan with a GB sticker on its backend.

'No problem,' John replied happily, fully satisfied with his expert parking of the caravan. 'There's a supermarket just down the road a few kilometres back so we'll just unload the back of the Volvo to make room for some provisions and off we'll go.'

Between them they unloaded various small items like blankets, bags of clothes and John's guitar, and piled them at the door of the caravan.

'Right, let's go,' said John, climbing in behind the wheel.

'Are you leaving the stuff there, John?' Jayne questioned. 'Why don't we put it in the caravan for safety's sake?'

'There's no need,' replied John, a little snappily after the long drive which showed Jayne that John was getting tired. 'The stuff is as safe as houses there, no-one's going to steal it.'

'And what if it rains?'

John laughed. 'Don't be daft, woman. Just look at the sky.' He looked upwards and made a sweeping gesture with his arm. 'There's not a cloud in the sky and it's bright sunshine. Anyway, we'll be back in a jiffy and then we can settle-in for our stay. Trust me, sweetheart, everything will be fine.'

It was quite true. The sky was clear and blue and the sunshine was hot and delightful. It even stayed like that until they were leaving the supermarket when, with a great boom of thunder and a bright flash of lightning, the heavens opened and gave forth a colossal torrent of rain.

'Bollocks!' muttered John to himself as they stood

A Gaze into Holidaze

in the doorway of the supermarket. He could feel Jayne's icy stare pierce the tee-shirt on his back.

'Trust you,' Jayne said quite casually. 'I should have known better. You do realise that our clothes, blankets and your guitar are out in all of this, don't you, John?'

John nodded sheepishly. 'Well it didn't look like rain when we left the campsite, did it? Anyway, it's too late to do anything about it now so don't worry about it.'

'I'm not worried about it. The clothes and blankets I can dry, your guitar is another matter. Will a soggy-wood guitar play okay or will it sort of sag a bit when you lift it? You know, a bit like wet cardboard.' Jayne's tone was unusually sarcastic.

John said nothing during the short drive back to the campsite. He was very annoyed with himself for his stupidity, knowing full well that to place the blankets, bags and guitar inside the caravan would have taken but a few minutes. Now he would most likely have to buy a new guitar because Jayne had been right, the guitar would definitely be ruined having been left outside in the flood of rain, a flood of rain that had now stopped completely to be replaced by clear skies and hot sunshine. 'Sod it,' John thought to himself. 'I'm definitely getting worse as I get older.'

As they drew up alongside the caravan they were surprised to find a very short, fat, middle-aged man coming out of the Dutch tent to meet them. He couldn't have been much over five-feet tall but seemed to be that dimension in any and every direction. He was like a smiling balloon that gently waddled towards them. Behind him was a tall, dark and rather elegant looking woman of about the same age.

'Good evening,' said the smiling Dutchman as John got out of the car, his English bearing little or no accent. 'My name is Lars and this is my wife, Rena.'

John took the offered hand. 'Hello! I am John and this is my wife, Jayne.'

'I hope you don't mind,' Lars continued. 'We saw your things outside when it started to rain and your friends did not seem to think of taking them inside so we thought that we would do it for you. Your bags and guitar are safe and dry inside our tent.'

'Our friends?' John asked with a puzzled expression.

'Yes, the British people in the next caravan. Are they not with you?'

John shook his head. 'Are you saying that the Brits in the caravan next to us saw our gear out in the rain and did nothing about it?'

'I am afraid so,' Lars nodded.

'Well, that's bloody typical that is.' John said sarcastically, his voice deliberately loud enough to carry to the British caravan a few metres away. 'I really must thank them for their kind efforts when I see them.'

'But instead we really must thank you,' Jayne

interrupted tactfully. 'It was very considerate of you and I don't know what we would have done if you hadn't acted so quickly.'

'The pleasure was ours.' It was Rena who replied in a deep, husky voice. Like Lars, her English was perfect. 'Please, we have coffee. Do come and have some before you settle yourself on your pitch.'

Inside the large bell-type tent it was spacious and cool and yet still cosy. John and Jayne sat around a small folding-table and drank the most delicious coffee that they had ever tasted.

'This coffee is pure nectar of the gods,' Jayne complimented Rena. 'What brand is it?'

'It is nothing special,' replied Rena. 'It is ordinary ground-coffee but what makes it taste so nice is this.' She reached into a small cupboard and came out with a unique percolator-type container. 'All you have to do is put a few spoons of ground-coffee in here and water in here. When the water boils it finds its way through the coffee and into the base of the container, you wait a few minutes and then pour. It is very simple.'

'We must get one of these, John,' Jayne said. 'Where did you get it, Rena?'

'Oh, we got this one in Holland but you can get them here in the supermarkets. They are very cheap to buy.'

And so, the following day, John and Jayne bought themselves the simple coffee percolator. However, they decided not to use it until they had finished the jar of instant-coffee that they had brought with them. Accordingly, the new coffee-percolator was put away inside the caravan and, as often happens, completely forgotten.

Things went quite well for a day or two during which time John had the satisfaction of advising their British neighbours that he thought that their lack of consideration, regarding leaving their articles out in the rain on their arrival, was totally unacceptable behaviour. The neighbours had since retaliated in the usual way by totally ignoring John and Jayne.

Not so the Dutch, who were starting to be a little overfriendly. Each night after dinner Lars and Rena insisted that John and Jayne joined them for a few drinks. It was very pleasant at first but after a couple of nights of conversation, particularly with Lars, John was beginning to tire of it and Jayne sensed John's looming irritability.

'What's the matter with you, John?' Jayne asked as they returned to Clarence after the second night with Lars and Rena.

'I think Rena is great,' declared John positively. 'However, Lars is getting on my proverbial tits!'

'I can see that,' Jayne replied.

'Everything I talk to him about I get the standard reply of – "in Holland it is better, I think." He does nothing but pump us about the British way of life. I tell him about our NHS, he says, "in Holland it is better, I think," and rabbits on about the Dutch health-system. I tell him about our industry, I get, "in Holland it is better, I think." I talk to him

A Gaze into Holidaze

about our education and I get, "in Holland it is better, I think." He's a bloody bore and he's starting to get right up my nose. If I said that in the UK we all have a pain the arse he would say, "in Holland it is a better pain in the even better arse, I think." Yes, Jayne, he definitely gets on my tits!'

'Well don't get angry with him, John. Remember they did take our stuff in out of the rain.'

'I know,' John nodded. 'I don't want to insult or offend him but he's getting through to me. If he thinks Holland is so bloody great why does he leave it to come on holiday? If it comes to that, why does half of the population of Holland leave Holland in the summer months if it's so great? Anyway, how are you getting on with Rena?'

'Oh, Rena is okay but perhaps a bit on the mumsie side. She lives her life through her children of which she has two, one boy of twenty and one girl of eighteen. She hasn't said much about the boy but she never stops talking about the girl.' Jayne suddenly chuckled loudly.

'What's that for?' John asked.

'Well, this is what she told me tonight. Apparently Rena and her daughter are very close, or to use Rena's words, they are like sisters rather than mother and daughter. So close in fact that when the daughter stays out all night with one of her many so-called boyfriends, Rena says that the daughter rings her first thing the following morning and says, "Mama! Last night I stayed with a new boyfriend and he made wonderful love to me all night long." Rena says that she replies with, "Oh, child, this is wonderful for you. Thank-you for ringing your Mama."'

John's mouth hung open as his flabber was once again well and truly gasted. 'What did you say, Jayne?'

'I said, "My, you are close, aren't you?" I couldn't think of anything else to say.'

They both roared with laughter.

'Now that's what I call an understanding Mum,' said John, wiping the tears from his eyes.

In spite of John and Jayne trying to keep their distance from Lars and Rena over the next few nights, the situation did not improve. No matter what subject was broached by John, and no matter how light that subject, the opening gambit from Lars was always the same, 'in Holland it is better, I think.' This to be followed by a detailed and long-winded explanation of how that particular subject was dealt with in Holland. John could take no more.

'We are off in the morning,' John told Lars as they sat in the Dutchman's tent after yet another long and boring night.

'I thought that you were staying for another two weeks,' replied Lars. 'I am disappointed to hear this because I have so much enjoyed our interesting discussions in the evenings over a glass of wine.'

'So have we,' John lied. 'But it is now time to move on.'

'Where are you going?' Lars enquired.

A Gaze into Holidaze

'Oh, a little campsite that we know in the Loire Valley at Saumur.' Jayne replied, smiling across the candlelit table at mumsie Rena.

'Do you know Saumur?' asked John, dreading that the answer from Lars might be 'yes.'

'No,' replied Lars. 'I have never been to the Loire Valley.'

John sighed in relief. Thank God for that! Then his usual mischievousness took over. 'Saumur is really quite lovely but there, in Holland it is better, I think.'

Jayne placed her hand in front of her mouth to stifle her sudden bout of coughing.

It took John and Jayne thirty-six hours before they arrived at their old campsite at Saumur. They parked the caravan right beside the wonderful river Loire and next to the foot-path that followed the river for many miles. The afternoon sun was gorgeous, as they relaxed on their sun-loungers and gazed dreamily across the wide, lazy expanse of water.

'A long trip, Jayne, but worth every mile of it just to get away from Laborious Lars and Mumsie Rena,' said John happily. 'Any chance of a cup of coffee for a very tired driver and dragger of caravans?'

'Slight problem,' replied Jayne. 'We've run out of coffee.'

'No problem at all, my love. We'll pop into Saumur and get some. What's more, we'll pick up a bottle of brandy at the same time and have our coffee with brandy. How does that sound?'

'Fabulous,' answered Jayne. 'Tell you what. We'll buy some proper ground-coffee and use our brand-new and unused percolator. You remember, it made fantastic coffee when we had it with Laborious Lars and Mumsie Rena?'

'Do you know what type of ground-coffee to get?' asked John.

'There is only one type,' replied Jayne.

But there wasn't. On arrival at the huge supermarket there were literally hundreds of different types of ground-coffee all stacked in their pretty little packages on the shelves. In spite of seeking advice from the non-English-speaking locals in the supermarket, John and Jayne were left to their own selection devices. Knowing nothing about coffee whatsoever, they finally selected a brand of ground-coffee that would be delicious, or so the less-than-helpful shop-assistant told them in her very-broken this-is-the-best-that-I-can-do English, which sounded Chinese, brogue. The brandy selection proved no difficulty whatsoever.

Excitedly and really desperately looking forward to the anticipated coffee, John and Jayne hurtled back to the campsite. With saliva on the lips and water soon on the boil, John hastily opened the packet of the longed-for ground-coffee to find – coffee beans!

'Bloody hell!' bellowed John. 'We can't use these little black bastards, can we?'

Jayne was as disappointed as John and her heart sank. She too was desperate for a drink. 'I know what I'll do, I'll grind the beans myself,' she smiled, trying to sound convincing to John.

'How are you going to do that?' John asked, his frustration prominent and his patience failing. 'Stick each bean up your . . .!'

'John, how dare you!' Jayne screamed her interruption. 'Don't you dare carry on any further.' Seeing that John had given up, she calmly continued. 'I'll grind them a few at a time with my garlic press.'

'You must be joking,' John chuckled in frustration. 'You'll be there forever and a day using a stupid garlic press. It'll be like painting the Forth Bridge with an artist's brush.'

John was right, Jayne was wrong. After fifteen painful minutes of crushing the beans, five at a time, in the small garlic press, Jayne had successfully managed to produce about a tablespoonful of a mangled, gritty, pith-like substance which was most unlikely to produce the desired aromatic and delicious liquid that was so desperately required.

'Sod it!' claimed John as he poked the black mush dubiously. 'That's it! I'm going back to the supermarket before it closes or we'll never have any bloody coffee. Trust me, I'll get the right one this time.'

And he did. Nearly an hour later after tearing to and from Saumur, John returned and parked the car outside Clarence. With a triumphantly smug look on his face he faced Jayne. 'Got it! It's right this time because I was lucky enough to find a Brit at the coffee-aisle who knew all about the different types of coffee. Let's put the kettle on, lass.'

The brew was completed and poured into two large mugs. Accompanying these mugs were two brandy glasses adequately filled with a generous portion of the amber liquid. Sprawled on their loungers and looking into a most magnificent sunset as the sun plunged into the river to cause the light to gently fade, our determined couple reached for their much-deserved coffees and brandies.

'Cheers darling,' whispered Jayne, love in her eyes.

John brought the warm mug to his lips in expectant ecstasy when . . .

'Good evening, John and Jayne. We thought that we would never find you. Can we have some of your coffee please? Yes?'

Yes. Laborious Lars and Mumsie Rena had followed them over six-hundred miles from Nice to Saumur. They had actually visited six campsites around Saumur before finally finding the one that held John and Jayne and their never-to-be-drunk coffee!

Fortunately, after only three more days and four more boring 'in Holland it is better, I think,' nights, Lars and Rena left for the remainder of their trip back to Holland.

'Never mind, precious,' said John as he waved to Lars and Rena in not-so-fond farewell. 'We've still got a week of our holiday left and we'll make the most of it. Trust me!'

****

A Gaze into Holidaze

Nice wine ...

After the departure of Lars and Rena, the holiday settled into a glorious routine allowing John and Jayne to enjoy the countryside of the Loire. A countryside that they both knew and loved so much. The weather remained sparkling and enabled the couple to once again hire bicycles and spend lazy hot afternoons cycling the beautiful country lanes of the area. It was wonderful.

One particular day, John and Jayne drove into Saumur to spend a relaxing morning wandering around the castle and generally sampling the culture of the area.

'Let's sample a little more culture,' said John after a splendid boat ride along the Loire river. 'Let's pop up to the supermarket and get some of those coloured sparkling-wines that we saw last time. We can then take them back to the campsite and then it's feet up for a wine-tasting session. What do you think?'

'Sounds like a good idea to me,' replied Jayne with enthusiasm. 'I've been dying to try those wines. They look so inviting sitting there on the shelves and we haven't had a relaxing drink for ages.'

'Not for two days anyway,' John smirked mischievously.

So that's what they did. A quick visit to the supermarket provided the pair with two-dozen bottles of sparkling-wine at a very reasonable cost. They had selected just about every colour of sparkling-wine that was available on the shelves of the supermarket and the variety proved to be both considerable and exciting.

Back at the campsite, Jayne got the glasses while John laid out the colourful array of bottles in a long row along the table.

'Which bit of culture shall we sample first?' laughed John as Jayne joined him on the sun-loungers. 'The sun is hot and it's time for us to party.'

'What time is it anyway?'

John looked at his wristwatch. 'Two forty-five.'

'Do you think it's a bit early for drinkie-poos, John?' Jayne half-heartedly questioned, knowing full well that when John was in a partying mood, time had no bearing whatsoever on the situation. 'The sun is still well above the yardarm, you know?'

John grinned wickedly. 'Well imagine you are in a submarine, sweetheart, then there is no sun or yardarm to worry about. Come on, which one do you want to try first?'

Jayne surveyed the line of sparkling-wine bottles. There was red wine, pink wine, green wine, light-blue wine, dark-blue wine, peachy wine, almost yellow wine. She was like a child in a sweetshop and just didn't know where to begin.

'Try the light-blue one,' came a cultured male voice from the footpath just in front of them.

'Yes, the light-blue one's an absolute darling.' This time the voice was female and the accent very *okay-ya*.

A Gaze into Holidaze

John and Jayne looked up at the two evening-strollers now standing in front of them. They were both in their mid-forties and extremely well dressed. The man was tall and elegantly slim whilst the woman was very blonde and matched the man's slimness and elegance. The beige trouser-suit that she wore was expensive and effectively enhanced her perfect figure.

'We had it last night and it was absolutely ace,' the female Okay-Ya continued. Then, with a wicked smile showing perfect, white teeth in her deeply tanned face, 'Er – the light-blue wine I mean, of course.'

The man chuckled which was enough to start John and Jayne laughing too.

'Are you staying near here?' John asked cheerfully, wondering where their hotel could be. To John's knowledge there was only the very small village at the entrance to the site and he was not aware of any hotel there.

'We are staying there,' replied the man, pointing with his finger to a touring caravan about five caravans and forty yards away.

'Oh, on the site,' said John pleasantly although being somewhat surprised. 'You look very well dressed for staying on a campsite. Scruff-order is usually the order of the day as far as we are concerned.'

'Well, one must always look one's best, doesn't one?' Okay-Ya butted in, her tone condescending. 'One's presentation should always be of paramount importance, don't you agree, er . . .?'

'John,' John finished Okay-Ya's question. 'I am John and this is my wife, Jayne.'

'Delighted to meet you, old boy.' The accent remained cultured as the man held out his hand. 'I am Charles and this is my wife, Helena.'

The couples shook hands.

'We are just about to sample some local culture in the form of very pretty sparkling-wines,' John offered. 'Would you care to join us?'

'Well, it is a bit early for us, old bean. So if you don't mind, I think we will decline.'

'Oh, Charles, don't be such a bore,' said Helena, fluttering her long, and very false, eyelashes. 'We would be delighted to join you for a drink.' Turning to Charles she said, matter-of-factly, 'Charles, do run along and fetch our special chairs and be a darling and bring our crystal wine glasses, will you?'

As John got off the lounger to provide Helena with a seat, Charles shuffled off as any good dog would. Helena looked down at the offered lounger, drew in her lips with distaste, but did not sit down.

Staring at John and Jayne's cheap wineglasses and with her face in a grimace that suggested that there was a nasty smell around, Helena continued. 'I think that wine tastes so much better in fine, crystal glasses of quality, don't you, darlings?'

'I suppose so,' replied Jayne. 'But when you're camping you sometimes have to make do, don't you?'

'Oh no, dahling!' Helena very heavily stressed the 'dah'. 'One must keep one's standards up at all times, musn't one?'

A Gaze into Holidaze

By now, Charles had returned carrying two lightweight but very expensive, comfortable folding-chairs. He unfolded them and held the back of one as an invitation for Helena to sit down. Helena glided around the table and took her place as only the Queen could have done. Charles then placed two beautifully-elegant crystal wineglasses on the camping-table and sat between Helena and John who, by now, had regained his place on his lounger.

'Will you pour, John?' Jayne asked meekly. 'We'll have the blue one that Helena recommended.'

'Superb choice, dahling,' Helena voiced her confidence overpowering. 'Some of these cheap sparkling-wines are really delicious, aren't they? Of course, they are not like proper champagne but one must make allowances, mustn't one?'

'Cheers!' said John once the wine had been poured.

'Chin, chin, dahlings,' came the, once again, overstressed 'dah' from Helena.

They sipped the wine and it was delicious. In fact, in no more than ten minutes the bottle of wine was empty.

'What a lovely wine,' said Jayne as she finished her glass. 'What makes the blue colour, John?'

'I'm not really sure to be honest,' John said, shaking his head.

'A-c-t-u-a-l-l-y,' Helena drew out the word as she once again fluttered her false eyelashes. 'The colour comes from a special ingredient made from a berry very similar to our dewberry. It is rather splendid, isn't it?'

And so the conversation went on, mainly supplied by the ever-so-okay-ya Helena. Charles, although a pleasant chap, was allowed to say very little. In fact, whenever he attempted to make any sort of point of discussion, he was promptly halted with the public-school, clipped-accent which said something like, 'Oh, don't be so silly Charles, dahling. How could you possibly know about something like that?' In the end, Charles was totally subdued and was literally afraid to open his mouth.

The same could be said of John and Jayne but not for the same reason. They wanted to debate quite freely but simply couldn't get a word in. Helena was certainly full of her very own importance. When education was discussed, Helena's input was simply, 'Well, one must go to the very best of private schools if one remotely hopes for success.' When health was discussed then Helena's input was, 'Of course, one should only be attended by private physicians.' For Helena's and Charles's world, money was essential and there was little doubt that they had plenty of it.

Jayne looked at John as the evening progressed and, after Helena had once again dominated some aspect of conversation or other, Jayne could tell that John was getting a little uptight about the situation. He definitely was not a happy bunny!

The evening went on, and in no time at all there were six empty bottles lying on the grass. John and Jayne, although a little tipsy, did not have a problem. Charles and Helena however, were a different matter.

A Gaze into Holidaze

'What do you do for a living, John?' asked Charles, completely out of the blue after one of his long periods of silence.

'I'm a manager in an engineering company,' replied John.

'Oh, howsh awful,' Helena butted in. "orrible dirty fingernails and things.'

Hello! Did John detect a slight change of accent here? Accompanied with a drunken slur of words, the clipped 'okay-ya' accent was being diluted by a strain of good old Yorkshire.

'What's your line, Charles?' enquired John as he poured more wine into Helena's glass.

'I'm a lecturer at a university in the north of England,' Charles replied slowly. 'I lecture students in . . .'

'Shex,' Helena interrupted, drinking down the freshly poured wine in one swallow. John hastily refilled her glass.

'I beg your pardon?' Charles turned to Helena, anger in his eyes.

'You teach 'em shex,' Helena slurred. 'I knowsh all aboush yoush shagging in the collegsh, lad. Aye, itsh 'appen I do!'

John looked at Jayne and they both smirked. It was incredible how Helena had changed at the drop of a hat. She was now broad-brushed, dyed-in-the-wool Yorkshire.

'Nice wine, isn't it?' John said innocently as he lit a candle to illuminate the table in the fading daylight.

'Thank God for the college, that's what I say. It's the only place I can get sex.' Charles's voice was raised in anger. 'I certainly don't get any at home from the likes of an old bag like you.'

'Who'sh you callin' sha bag?' squeaked Helena.

'What do you do, Helena?' asked Jayne, trying desperately to change the subject.

'She's a decrepit teacher of drama at the local College of Further Education,' Charles readily volunteered, his eyes blazing. 'She's never been to university or anywhere else for that matter. She has no qualifications and she's even conned her way into teaching drama.'

'Eh, lad, butsh yoush a nasty bugger when roushed. If yoush hadn't shagged me whensh I wash in the comprehenshive shchool I would have gone to univershity liksh yoo. Itsh yoo who made me pregnant!'

'Aye!' Charles's accent was also starting to slip, his temper vile. 'I married you because I thought I had made you pregnant and it was the decent thing to do. Afterwards, I found out that you had been banging every able-bodied lad in the comp. It could have been anybody's kid, you were sleeping with them three-in-a-bed!'

'Itsh not true,' Helena whimpered, her tears starting to make her heavy mascara run down her face. She rubbed her eyes with the back of her hand which resulted in one of the false eyelashes sliding onto her cheek making her look like a one-eyed parrot. Furthermore, red wine had now covered the front of her once-elegant trouser-suit.

A Gaze into Holidaze

'Yes, it is,' shouted Charles, his native Huddersfield now dominant in the now not-so-cultured voice. 'In the sixties you were one of the flower people, or should I say a flower-shagging machine. After you, an entire army would lie down exhausted because they certainly wouldn't have the energy to fight a war. Did you ever have an entire army, Helena?'

'More wine, Charles?' Jayne invited sheepishly. John was thoroughly enjoying himself.

'Well atsh leasht they had ballsh. Not shlike yoush, numb-nuts.' Helena was as drunk as a skunk.

'What did you call me?' screamed Charles.

'Numb-shnuts!'

'How dare you, you sexless freak. You're nothing but a slut!' Charles could no longer control himself, his face redly contorted in temper.

'Oh, go andsh play wish yourshelf,' said Helena, swaying in her chair. 'But yoush need a shtiffie to do shat, don'sh you, and you havensh gosh one of shosh.' With that her head fell to the table with a thud. Helena was well and truly out like a light.

Charles stared at the pathetic, wine-covered and unconscious form that lay half-on the table. He then looked slowly around at John and Jayne as if asking for help. Suddenly, he jumped up from his chair, turned and stomped off into the darkness of the campsite in the direction of his caravan.

The silence that prevailed after the monstrous shouting of Charles and Helena was almost overpowering, broken only by the gentle snoring of

Helena and the accompanying soft, swishing flow of the river. It was now past ten o'clock and Jayne nervously looked around at the darkened caravans and tents that surrounded them. 'Do you think anyone heard them arguing?' Jayne whispered quietly, afraid of disturbing the newly-descended peace.

'Must be deaf if they didn't,' replied John, slowly taking a long sip of wine.

'You shouldn't have done it, John,' Jayne admonished half-heartedly.

'Done what?' declared John. 'What did I do? I only invited them to have a drink – or did you do it? I can't remember.' Jayne didn't answer. 'Anyway, they didn't have to drink as much as they did and it's not our fault that they have their marital problems, is it?'

'No, I suppose not,' Jayne agreed reluctantly.

'Mind,' John grinned wickedly. 'I bet Helena's been a hell of a girl in her time, what with three-in-a-bed and all of that.'

'Cut it out, John, and have a bit of empathy and sympathy.'

'Don't understand big words like empathy,' teased John. 'After all, I'm just a dirty-finger-nailed engineer remember? Ask Helena, she'll tell you.'

Jayne was determined to be serious. 'I wonder what happened to the child?'

'What child?' asked John, finishing his glass of wine.

'You know, the one that Helena said was Charles's.'

A Gaze into Holidaze

'It died at birth and I couldn't have anymore.' The statement came from the collapsed heap half-on and half-off the table.

'Oh, I am sorry,' whispered Jayne as she placed her hand on Helena's shoulder.

Helena stirred and with a tremendous effort, sat up. She looked terrible with her blonde-grey hair dishevelled over an alabaster-coloured, wrinkled and tired face. The drawn face still had black streaks of mascara which reluctantly supported her estranged eyelash that rested halfway down her cheek. Gently, she removed the offending false-eyelash together with the one that had held its position. Helena looked very, very old.

'It was all my fault. Yes, I trapped Charles into marriage. I had had many, many lovers but they meant nothing to me. It was the way of the sixties and everybody was doing it.' Helena sniffed back the tears as she fought her way back to sobriety. Her accent was now broad-Yorkshire and there was no more pretence at the clipped accent of the public school.

'Are you alright now?' asked Jayne, a frown of sympathy on her face, a certain moistness in her eyes.

'I'm as right as I'll ever be, I suppose. I love Charles dearly but I'm afraid that after the death of our daughter, Emily, he was never able to forgive me. I think that he believes that the child was his but I am not really sure because he refuses to talk about it.'

Jayne placed her hand on Helena's but said nothing.

'We are both in our early sixties now and we are too old to change.' Helena paused and looked out over the river. 'As ye sow so shall ye reap,' she whispered, resignation in her voice.

John was shocked at her admittance of their age. Charles and Helena certainly did not look their years when first they had met but now, with the deep sadness in Helena's eyes, he could well believe it. Without make-up Helena looked as if she had earned every one of those sixty-odd years.

'I had better be going,' Helena said quietly as she stood up. 'Believe it or not, Charles will be very worried about me if I don't go back now.'

'I'll walk you home,' said John instantly, taking her arm to steady her. Although sounding sober, Helena's swaying suggested that she certainly was not.

'Thankyou, John.' Helena smiled and turned to Jayne who stood and kissed Helena on the cheek. 'Thankyou for a lovely party and I am very sorry that Charles and I spoiled your very kind hospitality.'

'Not at all,' said Jayne politely. 'I've enjoyed your company.'

John supported Helena back to their caravan where Charles waited on the doorstep. Charles put his arm around his wife before offering John his hand. Without a word being spoken, John shook Charles's hand and turned back to his caravan and Jayne.

A Gaze into Holidaze

'I don't half love you,' John said as he took Jayne in his arms.

'I love you too,' replied Jayne, nestling into John's shoulder. 'Let's value what we both have, shall we? Let's value each other?'

At seven o'clock the following morning John was up and showered, fully intending to make sure that Charles and Helena were alright. When he arrived at their pitch they had gone, leaving no trace that they had ever been there.

****

The Vikings . . .

The month of July of the following year found John and Jayne, accompanied by Clarence and Volv, down in Southern Spain at a seaside resort called Calpe, just north of Benidorm.

The area was quite beautiful in a rugged sort of way, with high mountain peaks within easy driving distance of the coastal plain of Calpe, Moraira and Benissa.

The couple had been on a reasonable campsite in Calpe for about a week and had settled-in quite well. The campsite was a bit on the primitive side but was, more or less, what John and Jayne had expected. They both knew before they ventured on their southern journey that, generally speaking, the further south that you travelled in Spain, the worse the campsites got. The Spanish crammed caravans and tents into their sites until guy-ropes were overlapping. Pretty dreadful really but if you wanted to be in southern Spain, then you simply had to put up with it – together with the ridiculous prices that they charged for a pitch.

Anyway, John and Jayne had a glorious week of swimming in the Mediterranean and walking the rugged, mountain peaks. The contrast between the hot, sandy beaches of the coastal plain and the clear, crisp air of the high mountains was quite stunning, as were the spectacular views from such places as the mountain village of Guadalest.

A splendid habit that John and Jayne had developed over the years, was their enjoyment of the *'menu del dia'* or menu of the day, which was served in most restaurants at an amazing price of about 900 pesetas, or around £4. For this you generally had a four-course meal accompanied with bread, olives, water and a bottle of wine. Fantastic value!

It was whilst consuming one of these meals in a little Spanish restaurant well up in the mountains, that John and Jayne met Sven and Heidi, a middle-aged couple from Denmark.

Heidi was a petite, dark and attractive lady of good figure, who was inclined to be a bit on the reserved side in spite of a constant and beaming smile. Sven, on the other hand, was a six-feet, barrel-of-lard character that weighed twenty-stone if he weighed an ounce. Sven was also very, very blonde and very, very hairy. He had long shaggy hair to his shoulders that matched the long, flowing beard and moustache that covered most of his face. Similarly it matched the blonde, now greying, mat of hair that sprouted from his chest to protrude several inches above the vee of his open-necked shirt. Looking out through all of this hair were piercingly blue eyes, which sparkled constantly and wickedly.

'I am a Viking,' he boasted proudly during a conversation, his voice deep and booming, his English perfect. 'You remember we used to invade Great Britain to plunder and rape.' This was followed by a deep belly-laugh that seemed to start in his sturdy mountain-boots. 'Perhaps we are of the same bloodline, John. Perhaps my great, great, great grandfather raped your great, great, great grandmother.' Again Sven roared with laughter so that all the other lunchtime diners turned to stare at him.

'Who knows?' John replied, a little annoyed but still unable to stop himself from joining in Sven's infectious humour. You just couldn't help liking this giant of a man.

After pleasant conversation for almost two hours, most of which ended in raucous laughter between the two couples, it was time for John and Jayne to leave.

'Nice to have met you,' said Jayne, standing to leave.

'We must meet again,' replied Heidi, her English also perfect. Delicately she kissed Jayne on both cheeks in the customary way.

'What are you doing tomorrow night?' boomed

Sven to John. 'There is a Danish restaurant on the Square in Calpe. Do you know where it is?'

'Yes,' replied John. 'I know the Square but not the restaurant.'

'You cannot miss it once you are in the Square. Let us meet up for a meal at 7.30 p.m tomorrow night. What do you say?'

John read approval in Jayne's eyes and nodded. 'Great,' he said. 'See you both at 7.30 p.m then.' John kissed Heidi lightly in the fashion of the Continent and turned to shake hands with Sven who had now stood and rounded the table. 'Look forward to seeing you tomorrow night, Sven.'

'Me too,' boomed Sven, his voice resonant over the noise of the busy restaurant. 'You are a good fellow, John.' With that, Sven took John in a great bear-hug clamping John's arms to his sides, and effortlessly lifted him high in the air like a limp doll. The entire restaurant stopped talking and turned to stare at the helpless and hapless John as he struggled for breath, boots dangling two feet off the marbled floor as he was crushed in the embrace of the hairy giant. You could have cut the atmosphere with a knife. To top it all, as Sven gently lowered John to his feet, he gave John a big, slobbering kiss right full on the mouth before releasing him.

John jumped back as quick as a pistol shot. 'What the bloody hell?' he shouted, attempting to shut out the thought of that hairy, soggy, wine-tasting kiss from his shocked brain by wiping the

A Gaze into Holidaze

back of his hand across his mouth. He then balled up both hands in tight fists. 'Are you some kind of nut or something or do you just want a punch on the nose?'

Sven could see John's anger. 'Please, John, I am very sorry.' His palm-fronted hands were held up in a gesture of appeasement. 'I did not mean to offend you. Please believe me.'

'Offend me!' John hissed through clenched teeth. 'I am not that way inclined so keep your kisses to yourself or, Viking or not, you'll get a punch up the bracket!'

The crowd was thoroughly enjoying the spectacle.

'Please, John,' Heidi whispered, rushing in between John and Sven. 'Sven meant no harm. It is customary in our country for two men to kiss on the mouth on greeting and when saying goodbye. It shows true friendship between the two.'

Jayne joined Heidi between the two men to ensure separation. John still remained red-facedly boiling in temper, whilst Sven, hands still outstretched in appeasement, retained a look of utter bewilderment on his face.

'That's enough, John,' said Jayne coldly. 'Look around the place. Everyone is staring at you. Now settle down and stop making a fool of yourself.'

'Me make a fool of myself,' said John, calming down a little. 'I was the one who got himself kissed by a bloke. What am I supposed to do? Kiss him back and think of England – or Wales?'

'John! Sven has already apologised and Heidi

has explained that it's their custom in Denmark,' said Jayne firmly. 'Now let that be an end to it and let's leave.' Jayne turned to Heidi and smiled as she placed her hand on Sven's shoulder. 'It's all over now, Sven, and John is very sorry for the way he reacted. We will see you both at 7.30 p.m in your Danish restaurant tomorrow night.'

Sven held out his hand to John, pleading in the blue eyes that peered out from the mass of blonde hair. 'I am very sorry, John,' he whispered.

'So am I,' John said, taking the offered hand. 'Let's forget it and meet up tomorrow night,' John grinned. 'But no more kisses, eh?'

They met the following night and had a great evening with Sven and Heidi. They enjoyed the delicacies of Danish cooking washed down with red wine and, although not the most wonderful combination, far too much traditional Danish lager.

In fact, they also met the following night, this time in a small Spanish restaurant on the promenade at Calpe and not far from Sven's and Heidi's hotel.

'It is a very great shame that our holiday has come to an end,' Heidi explained to Jayne. 'Tomorrow morning we must leave for Copenhagen. I have had such a lovely time and it has been wonderful meeting you and John.'

'Yes, it has been great,' replied Jayne. 'We still have a couple of weeks left yet so we still have time to top-up our suntans and wander the mountains. Never mind, Heidi, let's make the most of your last night.'

A Gaze into Holidaze

Heidi held up her glass of red wine and toasted. 'My friends, join Sven and me in a toast to good friendship.' They stood and clinked glasses.

'To lasting friendships,' said Sven, his teeth gleaming whitely through his beard as he smiled.

'Lasting friendship,' the remaining three echoed.

'But without blokes kissing each other,' John added good naturedly but mischievously, still holding up his glass.

'Without kisses,' echoed Sven, his deep belly-laugh once again booming around the small restaurant.

The night went on and on, laughter never being very far away from the humorous stories and experiences that were related by both parties. Sven and Heidi had never had a holiday in anything but hotels and were fascinated by the stories of fun and drama that John and Jayne related to them about their camping and caravanning experiences.

'I would love to try a caravan,' said Sven rather drunkenly because the wine had been flowing somewhat freely all through and after the meal. 'All that sun and wide, open spaces seem very attractive to me. What do you think, Heidi?'

Heidi was also well into her cups, but instead of slurring her words, spoke very slowly and precisely as if trying to master the art of English pronunciation for the very first time. An effort she did not need because her command of the English language was excellent. The giveaway as to her alcoholic level was her dark eyes which looked around with perhaps not quite the focus that they should have had. After all, it was Sven and Heidi's last night!

'I think that you have more sun when you go in a caravan,' Heidi said, each word dragged out.

'I don't think you need any more sun, Heidi,' John said, draining his glass for the umpteenth time throughout the night. 'You are going home with a lovely suntan. Have you been panic-tanning on the beach today?'

'Yes, I have,' Heidi replied. 'I have got white lines where my bikini has been. Would you like to see?'

Without waiting for a reply and using both hands, she innocently lifted her loose-fitting blouse to her neck to reveal a darkly-bronzed torso and two very large but very white, bra-less breasts. 'There,' she said, looking down at her feminine charms. 'I should have gone topless but there was no other woman on the beach doing it.'

John's eyes, and those of every other male in the restaurant, stuck out like organ-stops. Sven belly-laughed and Jayne blushed.

Heidi lowered her blouse back to its proper place much to the disappointment of John and his fellow diners, judging from the saddened looks on their faces. Then Heidi suddenly stood up and pulled her loose fitting skirt up above her waist to reveal her very tanned and very shapely, long legs, the thighs of which disappeared into the briefest of white panties. 'See, my legs are also brown, are they not?'

Once again, John's eyes nearly popped out of his

A Gaze into Holidaze

head to join the popped-out eyes of all the other men in the room. John sat with his mouth wide open until Jayne jabbed him discreetly in the ribs. Clearing his throat he pointed at a white linen patch that was attached to Heidi's left thigh. 'What's that then, Heidi? Have you cut yourself on the beach or something?'

Heidi looked at the patch through blurred but still-innocent eyes. 'No, that's my patch for my HRT. I'm not allowed to take it off to sunbathe.'

'What's HRT?' asked John, as innocent in mind as Heidi was holding up her skirt.

'Hormone replacement therapy,' Sven volunteered with a loud laugh on behalf of Heidi, who somehow in the last few minutes seemed to have lost control of her actions. Sven studied Heidi's leg-show. 'She's got lovely legs, hasn't she? Alas, she is getting older now.'

'Best put your skirt down now, Heidi,' Jayne said softly as she gently tugged at the other woman's skirt. 'Yes, you have got a lovely tan but I think it's best if you sit down.'

As if Jayne's words were a club that had hit Heidi over the head, Heidi sat down on her backside in her chair with an almighty thump. This was accompanied with an even louder thump as she slumped forward and hit her head on the table in front of her. Heidi remained in this position, well and truly out of her box and out like a light.

Sven roared with laughter. 'She always gets a little drunk on the last night of our holidays.'

JOHN BEVERLEY

'Sven, I think you had better take her home,' said Jayne. 'She has an aircraft to catch in the morning and she is going to feel terrible if she doesn't get some sleep.'

'Quite so, quite so,' Sven said vacantly, grinning from ear to ear.

'How will you get her back to the hotel? Is it very far?' Jayne asked.

'No more than a hundred metres from here,' answered Sven. 'I will help her walk, but not before I visit the toilet, yes?'

John and Jayne watched Sven get up carefully from the table, turn towards the toilet, lose his balance to regain it by leaning heavily on the unconscious Heidi's back, to then stagger down the aisle between the tables, knocking into each one as he passed. 'Excuse me please, excuse me please,' followed his progress until he was out of sight.

'He's never going to get Heidi back to the hotel,' Jayne stated firmly. 'Can you carry her, John? It's only a hundred metres according to Sven?'

'Yes,' said John flatly.

'Right. You go and pay the bill and take care of Heidi. I'll look after Sven when he comes back from the toilet. We'll leave together because Sven is the only one that knows the way back to the hotel.'

And they did. With Heidi over John's shoulder in a fireman's lift and Sven's bulky figure staggering along the pavement with his arms linked with Jayne's for support, they looked a ridiculous sight.

'All we want to do now is bump into the police,' volunteered John, breathless with his exertions.

A Gaze into Holidaze

But they didn't. Five hundred yards later, the quartet staggered up the stairs of the hotel to the top floor. John was cream-crackered and Jayne not much better after supporting Sven's often dead-weight to stop him falling over in the street.

'Bollocks! I'm absolutely cream-crackered,' declared John as he gained access to Heidi's and Sven's room and literally flung Heidi's sleeping body onto the bed. 'Some hundred yards that was and there were no lifts in the damned hotel!'

'You can say that again,' agreed Jayne as she helped Sven into a chair. 'Now, will you be alright, Sven? Will you make your flight okay?'

'Yes, we will be fine and thank-you. I have booked an early-morning call.' He staggered to his feet and kissed Jayne on both cheeks. 'Come and see us in Copenhagen soon.'

'We will,' replied Jayne.

'Goodbye, Sven,' said John, holding out his hand. 'You've been good company and a good mate.'

Sven stood and swayed. Then, taking hold of John's hand firmly and suddenly pulling him against his huge frame, he kissed John right on the mouth. 'There,' he said with that booming voice, 'I've done it again!'

John's face dropped in all seriousness for a few seconds before it broke into a huge ear-to-ear grin. 'You know a man could get used to that!'

They left the hotel and in spite of the invitation to Copenhagen, never saw Sven and Heidi again.

****

JOHN BEVERLEY

The laugh's on me . . .

During the last week of the holiday in Calpe, John and Jayne met yet another Dutchman and his wife whilst dining up in the mountains near Guadalest. The Dutchman was called Jan and his wife was called Gerda, both of whom proved to be excellent company during the lunch that they took on a wonderful terrace overlooking elevated and spectacular views through the high, mountain peaks to the sea, some twenty miles or so away.

John once again learned that most, if not all, of the Dutch nation seemed to love to laugh and joke at the drop of a hat. And, of course, their English was superb, as was their German, Flemish and French, which made conversation very easy as far as John and Jayne were concerned.

'How come you Dutch speak so many languages so fluently?' John asked over the *menu del dia*. 'Most Brits can just about manage one – English. Even English is debatable when you hear some Brits speaking.'

'I don't know really,' Jan replied. 'Perhaps it is the influence of British television because we get all of your programmes in Holland and when we watch them your language rubs off very easily.'

'And we are a small country surrounded by larger ones,' declared Gerda, taking a sip of the inevitable red wine with her meal. 'We are almost forced to learn their languages in our everyday lives. Great Britain is an island and almost isolated from the rest of Europe. Therefore, you don't have

A Gaze into Holidaze

the need to learn as many languages as we in Holland. You will find that Belgians are the same in their knowledge of other languages.'

'Yes, that is quite possible,' Jayne said, smiling as she remembered Igor and Martine from the years before.

'Can you speak Spanish?' John asked Jan.

'Only a little from taking holidays in Spain over a number of years,' replied Jan.

'Well, I've been coming here for quite a few years also,' stated John, gently shaking his head. 'I love Spain and the Spanish but I don't seem to be able to pick up any of the language short of please and thankyou. Jayne is better than me at it but I cannot pick up the lingo at all. It's much too fast for me.'

'Well,' smiled Jan. 'As long as you can toast them with a drink by saying . . .' Jan rattled off a mouthful of Spanish which meant absolutely nothing to John, or Jayne for that matter.

'Is that a toast to them?' asked John.

'It most certainly is,' Jan nodded. 'If you say that in a Spanish bar or restaurant, you will be bought drinks all night.'

'Well, I don't want to be bought drinks all night,' John said. 'However, I would like to show politeness to the Spanish particularly the ones who have made us most welcome in their country. Will you spare the time to teach me that expression, Jan?'

'Of course I will,' agreed Jan. 'It is very easy.'

Well, for John it wasn't so easy and it took him

almost a half-an-hour to manage to say and remember what sounded like, 'salute el forsal el canute.' (*Author's note – For the Spanish speakers, I am sure that there is no such phrase or sentence but to John that is exactly what it sounded like.*)

Soon it was time for Jan and Gerda to leave so they stood, shook hands and exchanged polite kisses.

'Very nice to have met you, John,' said Jan, an ear-to-ear grin on his face. 'Don't forget the little Spanish phrase that I taught you, will you?'

'Salute el forsal el canute,' said John proudly as he shook Jan's hand. 'I won't forget it now.'

'That's it,' grinned Jan. 'That's close enough anyway. The next time you are in a bar full of Spaniards you tell them that phrase and you will be fine. Bon voyage.'

That very evening, John insisted to Jayne that they went to their local Spanish bar and restaurant so that John could try out his newly-learned phrase.

On arriving at the very crowded bar, surrounded by Spanish people, both male and female, whom John and Jayne had got to know during their stay in Calpe, John ordered some wine. Turning to the crowd he raised his glass and, with a big boyish grin on his face, said with his best Spanish accent as loudly, proudly and clearly as he could manage, 'Salute el forsal el canute.'

The bar fell deathly-silent in an instant as if the friendly, burbling noise of enjoyment had been quashed by the flick of a switch. The silence lingered second by second for what seemed to John to be an eternity. Slowly, the grin disappeared from his face to be replaced by the deep flush of acute embarrassment. He lowered his glass to the bar and looked at Jayne whose blush was even deeper than John's.

John's eyes returned to the people around the room. Slowly, his gaze moved from left to right desperately searching the eyes in the faces in front of him. Some of the women present giggled, whether from nervousness or embarrassment, John could not tell. Most of the men avoided John's eyes with a polite smile, others held John's eyes with an arrogant glare of defiance. Some men stared back coldly with a glower of anger on their faces.

'Señor, if you please.'

John jumped as if he had been slapped at the sound of the quiet voice. Seconds earlier he had fully expected to have been slapped, or worse, judging by the expressions of almost hatred on some of the male faces in the bar. John looked down at a small, very Spanish-looking man who came just about up to his chest.

'Señor, I am Juan, the owner of this bar.'

'Pleased to meet you, Juan,' offered John weakly, glad of a friendly face and voice to break the unending, grave-like silence. However, when John studied the man's face in more depth he couldn't help but see that it was anything but friendly.

'Señor, I must ask you to leave. You have caused

much embarrassment to the ladies who are here tonight.'

'What have I done?' asked John meekly in his innocence, wishing that the ground would open and swallow him up. Anything to relieve the dreadfully-silent atmosphere of that room, a room that only a minute before had been bubbling with gaiety.

'Señor, if you come with me.' The tone was sharp. 'I will explain to you what you have done.' The little man stepped to one side and held his arm out towards the exit-door.

Jayne could not get through the door fast enough and John was not far behind. It was not just the hot air of the evening outside that made John freely perspire as he turned to face Juan. Some of his confidence had now returned which was probably because they were out of that bar and on their own. Furthermore, his previous meekness was rapidly being replaced with anger.

'Right, mate! What is all the fuss about? What have I done to upset that lot in there?'

' Señor, it is not what you did, it is what you said,' replied Juan.

'I gave them all a toast in friendship,' John said defiantly.

'No, Señor, you did not.' Juan paused. 'Although your Spanish was not good what you said was . . .' this time the pause was much longer before Juan continued very slowly, stressing and emphasising each word, ' . . . you toasted the juices of your loins.'

Jayne's mouth gaped. John's mouth gaped. They

were utterly stunned and were incapable of anything more.

'Señor, Señora, buenos noches.' Juan turned and was gone.

John and Jayne never did go back to that bar and restaurant and from then on were very, very wary of Dutch advice.

****

The laugh's on me, again . . .
'John, how do you fancy taking Volv and Clarence to Yugoslavia?'

It was a dreary and very cold January day in West Wales. In spite of the crisp six-inches of white snow that covered the surrounding countryside around the bungalow, the thick layer of dark, almost-black cloud that oppressively dominated the sky, ensured that the outlook from the bungalow windows remained depressing and forbidding.

John thought deeply before answering. 'I would really like to go. Everyone that I have met who's ever been there on a package-deal holiday speaks very highly of the place. Apparently it's very beautiful.'

'I've heard the same,' Jayne nodded.

'The way I see it, there are three points not in favour of the trip,' said John. 'One. It's a hell of a long way to go. Even though we have a month, it will probably take ten days or so to get there and return home. That leaves a little over a fortnight in Yugoslavia.'

'Well, that's okay,' said Jayne.

'Two,' John continued. 'I haven't worked out the mileage or anything but it has to be a round trip of around three-thousand miles. Volv is getting a little old now, sweetheart, and I'm not too confident that he'll make it.'

'Of course Volv will make it,' Jayne said, overcoming the reasonable objections that John had raised. 'You haven't had a moment's trouble with Volv, John.'

'Three, and it's a big three.' John looked at Jayne to make sure that she was about to take this final point in. 'There is a lot of political unrest in Yugoslavia at the moment and there have been suggestions that civil war could break out.'

'When?' asked Jayne.

'Who knows?' John stated flatly. 'Knowing our luck probably just after we arrive there.'

'Well, if we don't go next July then there may not be Yugoslavia to go to after that.'

John looked out through the window at the darkened sky. 'You're right, Jayne.' His dark eyes twinkled mischievously as he turned back to his wife. 'We'll go on one condition.'

Jayne got up to make some tea. 'What's that?' she said warily.

'We'll buy some tin helmets to wear throughout the holiday. So there!' With that John slapped her backside as she walked past him towards the kitchen.

The drive to Yugoslavia was very, very long and

A Gaze into Holidaze

the five days that it took them to reach Dubrovnik seemed endless. Even though they did not rush their journey and it was motorway and autobahn most of the way to make driving relatively easy, it was still incredibly tiring. They made good time during the daytime through France and southern Germany, stopping at regular intervals until nighttime when they rested over until the following morning. Even Austria wasn't too bad although the motorways of Austria were quite busy. It was after crossing the border from Austria into Yugoslavia that the pace was slowed. In comparison to the other European countries through which they had driven, the road network of Yugoslavia was primitive, to say the least. However, the coast-road that stretched south east from Rijeka to Dubrovnik was magnificent with its strikingly-clear, blue, sparkling seas of the Gulf of Venice to the west, and its dark-green pine-clad towering mountains rising steeply inland to the east. All this, held in a hot sun out of a cloudless sky, made the scenic value stunning.

'Fantastic scenery, John,' Jayne said, shaking off her travel weariness.

'It certainly is,' John sighed. 'I can't imagine that such a wonderful country could remotely contemplate going to war, can you?'

They spent their first night on a large, very busy campsite on the outskirts of Split. Here they were told that all camping in Yugoslavia was done on these huge, state-run sites and that camping outside of these sites was prohibited by law.

'A bit disappointing, eh Jayne?' John said to Jayne. 'We don't really like these big sites, do we?'

Even more disappointing was the price of food on the site which apparently had shot up by some thousand percent in the last few weeks.

'How can the locals afford this?' asked Jayne as she perused the nearly bare shelves of the camp-shop.

'I don't believe they can,' replied John. 'This is a very poor country and £2.50 for a can of beans is ridiculous by any standards. Come on, Jayne. We are not paying these prices. I'll bet you that they will be much cheaper in town, you'll see.'

But they weren't. The small shops in town were almost destitute of food. What small amount of food there was, was mainly in tins which were equally as expensive as at the campsite. Fresh food was also in poor supply and the bit that was available was barely decent enough for human consumption.

In one shop, an old woman dressed entirely in black was counting out what seemed like the last of her money from an old, worn, leather purse. Although John and Jayne could not understand the language, it was obvious that the old lady did not have sufficient funds to make the purchase of a rather decrepit looking cabbage-like vegetable that lay on the counter. The old woman was almost in tears as the shopkeeper put the vegetable back on the rack and shrugged at her.

'How much do you want for that?' John interrupted, putting his hand gently on the old woman's shoulder to stop her as she turned empty-handed to leave the shop. The man muttered something that John could not understand.

'I am sorry, mate, but I don't understand you,' said John, still restraining the old lady from leaving the shop.

The sallow-faced shopkeeper wrote a figure on a piece of paper and turned the paper so that John could read it.

'Bloody hell!' John exclaimed. 'The equivalent of nearly two quid for a soddin' cabbage!'

'Buy it, John,' said Jayne quietly. 'I cannot see an old lady like this go without a meal for the sake of two pounds.'

John did not hesitate. The cabbage was bought and given to the little old lady. Her withered and troubled face creased even more as her face lit up in a broad, toothless grin. She gripped John's arm and squeezed it tightly before she hobbled painfully from the shop.

'Welcome to Yugoslavia, eh?' said John as they walked back to the campsite, arms laden with groceries for which they had paid an exorbitant price.

'Never mind, John. We can afford it this once. Come on, we'll make the most of it and enjoy ourselves no matter what.'

The evening on the surprisingly empty campsite was spent with John and Jayne playing backgammon and listening to the interesting laments and chords of the 'Birdie Song'. The song from the distant clubhouse went on and on, and on and on, and on and on. As soon as the birdie track ended it was hastily replaced by yet another track of – the Birdie Song!

'Is this all they bloody-well have?' John complained. 'We might as well be in soddin' Butlins as be here. And the noise is ridiculous.' It was quite true. Although the clubhouse was perhaps three hundred yards away, it was still ridiculously noisy.

After about another hour of 'Da da da-da-da-da-da-, da da da-da-da-da-da, etc. etc.' John shook his head and stood up. 'Come on, pet. If you can't beat 'em, let's join 'em. Put on your dancing-shoes, girl, we're a-going a-jiving.'

Three hundred yards further on they entered the vibratingly-booming clubhouse. There was not a soul there. Not even a disc jockey. The only greeting they had for the hundredth time that night was from – you've guessed it – the Birdie Song!

At eleven o'clock precisely that night, with John and Jayne sleeplessly tucked up in bed, the Birdie was finally shot, or it went back to its nest, to allow peace to prevail. 'Welcome to Yugoslavia,' John whispered sarcastically into Jayne's ear as they finally snuggled into each others arms for the night. 'Don't worry, sweetheart. I'll find us a better campsite for tomorrow night.'

And John nearly succeeded. On leaving Split for their final destination of Dubrovnik, within thirty miles of Split John found a great little campsite just off the main road. Highly pleased, they left

A Gaze into Holidaze

Volv and Clarence in the parking area outside the main-gate of the site and walked into the adjacent reception building.

On entering, John and Jayne were greeted by two receptionists, one young male and one young female. Both wore huge dazzling smiles on their tanned faces which was just as well, because that was all that they wore. They were completely in the nude and as naked as the day that they were born.

John looked at Jayne and smilingly lifted his eyebrows in mischievous hope. Without a word, her face absolutely deadpan, Jayne shook her head slowly from side to side.

And that was that!

Back in the car they were on their way in two minutes flat. 'Well, I thought that the young chap was well hung, didn't you, Jayne?' John ventured.

Jayne burst out laughing. 'I was too embarrassed to look,' she said. 'But I saw you gawking at the pretty young lady as if you had never seen a naked woman before.'

'Not at all,' John lied. 'She could have been fully-clothed for all the notice I took of her.'

'I really don't like these naturists,' declared Jayne. 'I don't mind it if that's what they want to do but keep me out of it. It's definitely not for me.' She turned to John as they cruised along the coast-road to Dubrovnik. 'Did you know that that was a nudist campsite, John?'

'No, not at all,' John said, not too convincingly as he lied through his teeth.

'Say, honest,' Jayne said, looking him straight in the eye.

'Well, to be truthful,' struggled John as he searched for the right words. 'I thought that it might have been, judging from the enclosed fence around the site. Apparently there is quite a lot of nudism in Yugoslavia.'

'Well you'd better not deliberately expose me to it,' Jayne replied firmly, and she meant it.

And John did not deliberately expose Jayne to nudism for the remainder of the holiday. John fully understood how Jayne felt about the matter long before they had decided to go to Yugoslavia. Jayne did not even go topless on the beach in the UK when there was no-one but himself within miles of them. That's the sort of woman that Jayne was and John readily accepted that fact. Well, almost readily anyway, because secretly John would have loved to give a nudist-type holiday a go.

But accidents happen.

The following afternoon, John and Jayne arrived on another large campsite just outside Dubrovnik. A campsite, which on face value, was very similar to their previous campsite at Split. Yes, even the Birdie Song greeted them. However, sited right next to the wonderfully-blue sea made all the difference. It was beautiful.

'God, you can't get away from that tune, can you?' muttered John as they bedded Clarence down for their expected stay. 'It'll drive me bonkers eventually.'

A Gaze into Holidaze

Again, the campsite was very quiet regarding the number of people there. There were many touring and static caravans around the site but most of them were empty and deserted. A stroll around the camp-shop revealed the same story as Split, little stock at tremendously high prices.

Later in the day, after they had fully settled-in and had a snack, they drove into the fortress town of Dubrovnik. It was an old and historic town with picturesquely quaint buildings which were painted in pastel shades and dotted around a magnificently handsome harbour. This harbour contained an array of boats of all shapes and sizes and of all ages. It was a wonderful place which basked in the endless rays of a hot sun that caused severe heat-shimmering on the blue horizon of the clear, warm sea.

'This will be fabulous,' said Jayne as she shielded her eyes from the sun. 'I can put up with any problems of the campsite as long as we can enjoy this.'

They wandered the streets and shops of Dubrovnik and found the inhabitants, although perhaps a little on the surly side to each other, generally helpful and pleasant to them in spite of the language difficulties. In the evening they enjoyed a dinner in a harbour fish-restaurant whose tables were set outside in the warm, balmy air on a wooden platform which was literally suspended over the lapping water below.

'You can see the fish underneath us,' said John excitedly as he leaned over the low balustrade of the platform and gazed into the depths below.

'I've had a lovely first day in Dubrovnik, darling,' cooed Jayne as she gazed in awe at a blood-red, full moon that climbed out of the dark horizon of the sea. 'Look at the moon, John. It's magic.'

They sat there, hand in hand, for the next couple of hours enjoying the swishing-peace of the lapping waves below them as they gently teased the harbour walls. John and Jayne had come a long way but it had been worth every mile of their journey. They both looked forward lazily, but excitedly, to the adventures of the morrow.

The morrow found them lying dreamily on the rocks of a tiny cove not far from the campsite. Although the sun was very hot there were very few people in the cove to enjoy it. In fact, John and Jayne had only eight couples around them, of which half the women were topless whilst the other half were attired, as Jayne was, in their bikinis. Surprisingly, because the temperature was well up into the maximum heat of the day, only one man was swimming in the sea. Everyone else seemed content to just lie on towels and airbeds and lazily soak up the sun.

'Think I'll go in for a dip,' said John after a while. 'Fancy it, Jayne? It's so hot I've got to get in the sea.'

'Okay,' Jayne replied, taking John's offered hand and scrambling to her feet.'

They looked out to sea and saw that the man who had previously been swimming had returned to the rocks and was waist-deep in water, clumsily wading towards the shore. For a short time he remained in what John and Jayne assumed was still waist-deep sea, allowing the incoming waves to playfully splash over his shoulders. Then he stood up, not more than twenty feet in front of John and Jayne, and turning his back on any onlookers, placed his right foot high on a large rock. Shielding his eyes in an almost classical pose, he stared out to sea like a sun-bronzed demigod. John's assumption that the sea had been waist-deep was totally wrong. The sea had been only knee-deep as the sight of the bearded and naked Adonis with his foot on the rock, readily proved.

Jayne's jaw dropped and her eyes bulged in embarrassment. Slowly her mouth worked but no sound came from it.

'Cute little arse and lovely danglies,' volunteered John, not quite knowing what else to say.

Jayne spun around towards the shore in an attempt to avoid the smiling face of the bearded man who had now decided to face them. Again, Jayne's eyes popped from her head and she could not believe what she was looking at. With a tiny squeak, which was all the speech she could manage, she pointed at the couples who moments before had been lying harmlessly in the sun around them.

John turned shorewards. 'B-b-blimey,' he stuttered before beaming with a smile. He could not believe his luck.

As if the man putting his foot on the rock had been some kind of secret signal, every one of the eight couples stripped-off naked, until John and Jayne were the only human beings in the cove who were wearing a stitch.

With a further gasp, or was it a terrified shriek, Jayne jumped forward, gathered up all of her belongings in two seconds flat and ran up the rocky path that led out of the cove as fast as her legs would carry her.

John did the same, but without a shriek. Slowly, like wading through treacle, John unhurriedly, carefully and laboriously folded his clothes. He then picked them up and looked deliberately and admiringly around each of the ladies in turn. Then, with a cheeky smile and a hearty rendering of 'I'm forever blowing bubbles', he blew kisses at the girls, much to the annoyance of their male companions, before wandering up the path after Jayne.

'What do you think of that exhibition?' asked the annoyed Jayne as John joined her on the clifftop above the cove.

'Bloody disgusting,' lied John loudly as he put his arm around his wife. 'Absolutely bloody disgusting.'

Their remaining time in Dubrovnik was delightful although uneventful, as was their drive up the coast to a place called Porec in the north of Yugoslavia. Once again they were camped on another huge, government-run campsite and yet again it was relatively quiet. This time it was quiet regarding both people and noise.

It had been a long day, so John and Jayne decided

A Gaze into Holidaze

to have a meal with a bottle of wine before hitting the land of nod with an early night. By eight-thirty, the night warm and peaceful, they were fast asleep.

By nine-o'clock John was climbing the walls of the caravan to the tune of 'Da da da-da-da-da-da, Da da da-da-da-da-da, ...'

'That fucking Birdie Song gets on my tits,' he yelled. 'If I catch the bastard who wrote it I'll string him up by his balls!'

Jayne soothed and placated John for the next two hours until 11 p.m when, as John had repeatedly requested in a somewhat verbose manner throughout the two hours of the singing, 'the birdie had pissed-off to bed.'

A couple of days later found John and Jayne, in spite of the nightly Birdie Song, totally rested and having a great time in the harbour-town of Porec. Like Dubrovnik, it was old and quaint but much smaller, with its clusters of narrow streets that all seemed to terminate at the harbour.

'It's like Cornwall in the sun,' John offered as he and Jayne wandered through the cobbled streets.

'Similar,' replied Jayne. 'Similar and yet, I don't know, entirely different. Certainly the houses are painted more brightly than in Cornwall.'

'I fancy the people are much friendlier here than in Dubrovnik,' John said. 'Certainly there are more of them. It's far busier here with a more holiday-like atmosphere somehow.'

Jayne agreed. By now it was nearly lunchtime and the couple was right on the quayside of the harbour. As they ambled among the moored boats they eventually came to an old, brightly coloured galleon-type vessel with very white sails.

'You want a trip on a pirate galleon?' The question was put in broken English by a short, fat, dark and swarthy man dressed as a pirate. His broad smile revealed a host of yellow-stained teeth that allowed the odd gap to show through.

'How much?' asked John.

The man spoke very slowly in his broken English, but explained that the cost per head would be equivalent to ten-pounds sterling if John paid in Yugoslavian currency, but five-pounds per head if John paid directly in English money. The trip would take four hours, during which time the galleon would stop at an island off the coast where lunch would be served in a restaurant. What was more, after lunch the galleon would call in a cove off the mainland where those who wanted to could dive and swim off the ship.

'Hang on, mate,' John questioned. 'How far does a galleon sail in four hours? Not far on a lovely day like this with not a breath of wind to be seen.'

The man laughed. 'No, Englishman . . .'

'Welshman,' John interrupted good humouredly.

'What is Welshman?' Pirate asked innocently.

'Never mind,' John answered, realising that the joke had been lost on Pirate and John certainly didn't feel like giving a geography lesson at that moment.

Pirate continued. 'This galleon 'as engines to drive 'er. Sails are for show. She go in ten minutes.'

A Gaze into Holidaze

'Fancy it, pet?' John asked, turning to Jayne.

'I do,' replied Jayne without hesitation. 'I think that it will be great fun and we've got our bathing costumes with us. It will be better than going to the so-called beach as we intended.'

John turned to Pirate. 'What about wine, mate? You haven't mentioned wine. Do you supply any?'

Pirate flashed his yellow teeth. 'Ja! You drink wine for free all day.'

So that was the clincher. John paid in sterling and off they went, true to Pirate's word, ten minutes later on a very, very hot afternoon. The atmosphere on the galleon was quite lively between the hundred or so people who were aboard. There were French, Austrian, German, Dutch, Italian and of course, British, all babbling away loudly in their native tongue. Everyone was having a cracking time especially when the crew brought around literally tumblers-full of a rich, sweet, red wine.

Again, true to Pirate's word, the powerful engines that had been fitted to the ship soon drove her rapidly through the water until they were miles out to sea in no time at all. Also true to Pirate's word was the endless topping-up of the tumblers with the same rather splendid red wine. The topping-up was done from large, glass-jugs which in turn were topped up from absolutely enormous glass-jars which could barely be lifted by the crewmen who were doing their best to keep the wine flowing freely. To lift them they had to bend themselves at the knees in order to wrap their arms completely around the diameter of the jar. Then, straightening their legs and keeping their backs straight, they managed to lift the jar from the deck and pour some wine from the jar's narrow neck into the many waiting jugs. Quite a feat!

The pirate galleon, together with its now singing passengers, eventually stopped at the promised island, and disembarked the noisy and hungry horde to partake in lunch at a lovely, vine-covered restaurant not far from the shore. Although not great, the food proved to be adequate and the yet more wine, very palatable.

After bidding the little island a noisy and boisterous farewell, the pirate galleon headed back through the tremendously-blue Adriatic Sea towards the awaited cove on the mainland. Once again the wine flowed and the singing started. Each nation sometimes competed against, and sometimes harmonised with, their fellow Europeans. It was a great atmosphere.

After hearing John sing a solo of the Welsh tune 'Sospan Fach' to the crowd, Jayne realised that John was well and truly in his cups. This feeling was enhanced as they arrived just off the mainland, by John sighting a nude-male windsurfer who stood proudly on his board with legs spread wide apart for balance as he skilfully manoeuvred his craft over the waves.

'Bit cold on the old dangly bits, mate,' yelled John. 'Bet the old man's a bit shrivelled up never to be un-shrivelled again.'

A Gaze into Holidaze

The rest of the passengers roared with laughter. It was amazing how the humour travelled in spite of language. This was further proved, much to the embarrassment of Jayne, when a nude-male in his sixties hurtled past the galleon on a jet-ski. He was going very fast and passed the galleon with only a few yards to spare.

'That's it, mate,' hollered John after the departing jet-ski. 'Arse up and head down. A very wrinkled arse though.' Needing no encouragement the crowd on the ship roared.

The man on the jet ski obviously enjoyed the attention that he was getting, because his red, sun-burned body could be seen steering the craft in a fast circle to bring him and his machine back to a position where he could do a fast pass of the galleon once again. Now, however, the sea for some reason had become rougher so that when the naked man passed the galleon, this time the man and machine bounced wildly across the tops of the waves.

This was John's cue. Holding his testicles over his shorts with both hands, John joined the man's rhythmic bouncing with, 'Oouch! oh! ouch! oh! Give me a life on the ocean waves, a life on the ocean waves!' The crowd doubled up at John's holding of his matrimonial machinery and his sea-faring ditty.

John now had steam-up and was well and truly in a party mood. 'Challenge to all nations,' he shouted as he leapt to where the huge glass-jars were standing, perhaps half-full of red wine. Slowly, he bent and placed his arms firmly around the massive middle of the round jar and, straightening his legs, he lifted the jar to his chest where he successfully tilted it to allow him to take a long and steady swig of wine. Carefully, he replaced the jar back on the deck. The crowd applauded unceasingly. 'Any challengers?' John laughed as he went back to Jayne who was wiping the tears of laughter from her eyes.

'Thought you'd get a hernia,' she chuckled as she watched the other men from the crowd take up the challenge.

The swim in the cove was most welcome to John and Jayne for different reasons. Jayne to cool her perspiringly hot body, John to attempt to sober-up in the cool, fresh water of the Adriatic. Both partners were satisfied with the outcome although John's results were not quite perfect because he was still a little tipsy when they docked back at Porec an hour or so later.

'That was great fun, wasn't it, Jayne?' John said as they disembarked from the galleon, offering many goodbyes to the numerous fellow passengers who wanted to pat him on the back.

'Yes it was,' agreed Jayne, proud to see John's popularity in the limelight. 'What I'd like now to round off a perfect afternoon, is a chocolate ice-cream.'

'Blimey,' said John, putting an arm around Jayne's waist as they walked along the quay towards the small town. 'I bet they cost an arm-and-a-leg here. Remember the cabbage? What's an ice-cream going to cost?'

They wandered lazily through the town of Porec looking into the quaintly decorated shop-windows as they passed. It was 5.30 p.m and the shops and streets were quite busy with the evening trade. John still felt a wee bit drunk from the afternoon's fun and capers.

As they strolled, John looked ahead and saw two men, one at each side of the narrow cobbled-street, throwing something to each other. One man threw this small white blob whilst the second man caught the blob in what appeared to be a dish of some sort. By the time John and Jayne had arrived on the scene, a group of perhaps eight people had stopped to watch the two men.

'You like ice-cream for you and your wife?' one of the men, a darkly handsome man, asked a man in the front of the group of spectators. Again the English was almost perfect.

'Yes, please,' answered the man who was obviously English.

'You wonder how I know you English, eh?' smiled Handsome. 'It because you have a bulge in your pocket, eh? It is your money-bulge or is it bulge for your wife? All Englishmen have big bulge, yes?' A few people laughed but most, including the Englishman, did not think the remarks at all funny.

'You watch this, sir,' Handsome went on. 'You never see anything like this before.'

With that, he scooped some ice-cream from a nearby tub and literally flung it from his scoop, a distance of some twenty feet, to be caught in an ice-cream dish by his partner, a tall and weedy man. Both men were extremely smartly dressed in black trousers, long-sleeved white shirts with black bow ties and black waistcoats.

Similarly, Weedy scooped some ice-cream from his nearby tub and flung it in a high curve to be caught by Handsome, but this time in a dish which he held behind his back. The crowd, which had now grown to at least twenty people, applauded loudly.

This went on for about ten minutes with blobs of ice-cream hurtling through the air at all angles, to be cleverly caught, again at all angles, by the contorting duo. It really was a spectacular performance which John and Jayne had not seen before or, for that matter, since.

Finally, both dishes were full with ice-cream in a sort of small knickerbockerglory type of way. The two men approached the Englishman who had agreed to have the ice-creams at the start of the performance.

'You have pounds sterling, sir?' Handsome asked, with a sickly smile. The man nodded. 'Then that will be twenty-pounds, sir.'

The Englishman, who was well into his fifties, hesitated. 'That's a bit expensive, isn't it?'

The smile disappeared from Handsome's face, his voice became intimidating. 'You mean that you are not going to pay?'

A Gaze into Holidaze

'No, no. I didn't mean that,' mumbled the Englishman as he extracted twenty-pounds from his wallet. Handsome snatched the note from the Englishman's hand before the man and his wife hastened away up the cobbled street, obviously embarrassed.

The fixed and sickly smile returned to Handsome's face. He looked around the now large crowd and caught John's eye. 'Would you like ice-cream, sir?'

'Not at those bloody prices, I don't,' answered John, the glow of alcohol still warm in his blood. 'You can stuff your ice-cream, mate, where the monkey stuffs his nuts.'

'John, we don't want any trouble, do we?' Jayne whispered from the corner of her mouth. 'Remember we are in a foreign country and the police may not be so friendly.'

'There'll be no trouble, will there, sport?' John said flatly, noting the nodding heads of the crowd around him. 'Your ice-cream is far too expensive for my blood and that's all there is to it.'

Sensing that he and Weedy were losing the attention of the crowd, Handsome spoke up, his smile still just as sickly. 'Fair enough, sir. What if I make you an ice-cream, free of charge? Would that be okay with you? What do you say?'

'Let's get this clear,' John said, looking for the catch. 'You will make me an ice-cream and I will not have to pay for it. That is, you make it, I eat it and then I walk away?'

'Absolutely, sir.'

'Done,' said John, a grin on his face as he looked around the crowd.

The two men placed themselves twenty-five feet apart. This time, Weedy stood at the ice-cream tubs, there were several of them placed on his table, whilst Handsome stood at another table which had a small screen in the middle of it that hid the ice-cream dish in which the ice-cream would be built.

'We begin,' shouted Handsome.

For another quarter-of-an-hour, through a variety of banter and chatter from the duo, scoops of ice-cream flew in both straight lines at considerable speed and slow curving arcs through the air. These were all cleverly caught by Handsome, this time in another scoop, only to be placed in the hidden dish behind the screen in front of him. Weedy did the throwing, Handsome did the catching and building of the ice-cream.

Finally, after the miraculously clever exchange between the two men, Handsome yelled to John. 'Do you like banana and strawberry ice-cream?'

John nodded.

Through the air from Weedy arced two scoops of yellow ice-cream to be skilfully caught in Handsome's scoop only to disappear into the dish behind the screen. This was followed by a high trajectory blob of strawberry ice-cream, which again was caught in Handsome's scoop before disappearing behind the screen. The crowd applauded wildly as it appreciated the fantastically skilful show of ice-cream throwing.

A Gaze into Holidaze

'And now, ladies and gentlemen,' Handsome announced to the crowd. 'I will honour my promise to this Englishman.'

'Welshman,' declared John flatly.

'I will present this wonderful ice-cream, free of charge, to this . . . er, Welshman.'

At this, Handsome removed the screen and held up the newly created ice-cream in presentation to the crowd generally, and John in particular.

There on the dish was a gigantic, upright, perfectly-white ice-cream penis, complete with a strawberry-tasting glans and huge banana-tasting testicles. It was magnificent but John was not amused.

John crossed the cobbled street and took the ice-cream penis from Handsome. The crowd was dead silent as both men stared back at each other, eyes unblinkingly locked, both faces unsmiling.

Jayne swallowed hard and nearly jumped out of her skin when she saw John lurch slightly and suddenly in an attacking feint in Handsome's direction. Handsome jumped back a few feet in alarm when he thought that John was about to strike him.

'Thanks a lot, mate,' said John cheekily. 'I've never seen one nearly as big as this one.' Then, in the blink of an eye, John moved forward to cover the few feet of ground and stepped on Handsome's toe. As Handsome's mouth instantly opened in the normal reaction of, 'Ouch,' John thrust the strawberry end of the ice-cream penis into it. 'Always liked to share my things with good friends,' John said coolly as Handsome gurgled.

Handsome was dumbstruck. With ice-cream all over his face he turned to Weedy. 'We go now,' he spluttered. Literally running from the street he disappeared into a nearby ice-cream parlour, Weedy close behind him.

The crowd cheered and once again John was endlessly slapped on the back. 'Thank you,' said John as he and Jayne walked away up the street sharing what was left of the ice-cream penis.

'I'm so proud of you,' Jayne whispered as soon as they were out of hearing. 'I was afraid that you would thump him, God knows he deserved it. Charging those poor people twenty-pounds for those ice-creams was terrible.'

'Couldn't agree more,' replied John. 'Regarding my thumping that fool, let's just say that I used my brain rather than my brawn. Anyway, he was bigger than me.'

They both laughed.

That was their last day in Yugoslavia. Within months of John and Jayne leaving, Dubrovnik was heavily bombed and Yugoslavia entered a bitter and bloody civil war.

****

CHAPTER FOUR

DIVERSIONARY TACTICS

The following year saw big changes in both the professional and social lives of John and Jayne in that they both got lecturing jobs at some local Colleges of Further Education in South and West Wales. So it was goodbye to engineering management for John and goodbye to sales management for Jayne.

Although they had led successful industrial lives and careers, they both felt that they were getting older and the pressures associated with any form of industrial management at the time were not worth the little extra financial rewards. It was time for a change.

Of course, although John and Jayne both looked forward to their teaching and lecturing careers, there was another underlying factor that they had both considered very carefully before they gave up their industrial positions. Lecturing provided them with fourteen weeks of annual paid holidays, eight weeks of which had to be taken in July and August.

This was a real deciding factor for the two of them. From that time onwards, not only could they stay away with Volv and Clarence for eight weeks at a time in the summer, but other types of holidays could be explored. These could be either in the eight weeks of summer holidays or in the other weeks or fortnights of holidays at such times as half terms, Christmas or Easter. Yes, lecturing looked very satisfactory to John and Jayne.

****

Andorra, the magic box . . .
So, on the very first day of their very first July/August holidays that they both received from their respective colleges, John and Jayne found themselves well en route to Palafrugell, perhaps their favourite spot on the Costa Brava, if not their favourite spot in Spain.

'I love this part of Spain,' sighed Jayne as they crossed the French-Spanish border just west of Perpignon. 'And to think that we can stay on our favourite campsite for nearly eight weeks is fantastic.'

'I agree,' said John. 'Although now that we have more time, I think that we should explore the heart of Spain. You know, places like Madrid, Seville and Granada, just to mention a few. They say that inland of the Atlantic cost of Spain is fantastic and we could . . .'

'Hold your horses,' Jayne said, putting up her hand, demanding a halt to John's travel fantasies. 'Although I agree, we should and we will see more of Spain now that we have our eight weeks in which to do it. However, I don't agree that we should do it

A Gaze into Holidaze

this year. This is our first really long holiday and I think that we should relax a bit and explore the immediate area around our campsite at Palafrugell.'

And that's exactly what they did. After walking long distances of local coastline and wallowing in the sea and sun for two weeks, John and Jayne felt totally relaxed and at peace with the world. Their first year at college had been extremely demanding and now they both needed to unwind and let the world go by.

'Do you fancy this, John?' Jayne asked John at the campsite pool one day, just after returning from a long and hot shopping-trip into Palafrugell. 'I saw it in the travel agent's place in Palafrugell and I thought that it was a fantastic offer.'

John looked at the leaflet that Jayne handed to him. 'Mmm! Andorra. I've always fancied going there. It's a small independent state in the heart of the Pyrenean mountains. Apparently, it's quite a beautiful town.' John smiled wickedly. 'Oh yes, I almost forgot. I've heard that it's the cheapest place to buy booze in the entire region, if not the whole of Europe. They almost give it away, so I'm told.'

'Trust you to think of that,' Jayne admonished lightly. 'No, seriously, if you read on you will see that we can get bed and breakfast in a three-star hotel in the heart of Andorra for the equivalent of twenty pounds.'

'Well, that's not so cheap really,' said John. 'You can get bed and breakfast in the UK for just a bit more than that.'

'Not in a three-star hotel you won't,' insisted Jayne. 'And it's twenty pounds for the two of us and not twenty pounds each.'

'Good God!' John exclaimed. 'That is cheap.' He thought aloud for a few moments. 'It means that we don't have to drag Clarence over the high parts of the Pyrenees and we can buy a few bottles of quality booze whilst we are there. No, correction, we can empty Volv and buy lots of quality booze whilst we are there.' He looked up at Jayne. 'Jayne, sweetheart, book us up for a long weekend, Friday-night to Monday-night inclusive.'

The following Friday morning they were on their way and the drive up the narrow, winding roads as they drove higher and higher up into the mountains was breathtaking.

'Cor! It's just like the Alps, isn't it?' whispered Jayne as they reached the ultimate mountain-peak before descending steadily for their final run along the fertile valley that led to Andorra.

'You feel like God himself when you're up here,' John said as he breathed deeply, enjoying the cool, fresh, mountain air. He looked around at the still snow-clad peaks as they glistened and shimmered in the warmth of an unchallenged sun. 'It certainly makes you feel alive, doesn't it, Jayne?'

Two hours later they entered the large town of Andorra, a town which was unexpectedly nestled at the bottom of a valley surrounded on all sides by towering mountains.

'It's a bit disappointing, isn't it?' whispered Jayne as they drove through the centre of the town.

A Gaze into Holidaze

The sky was dark and a steady drizzle had started, forcing John to smudge the windscreen as he used his wipers. John looked around at the old, gloomy buildings. 'It's a bit like Newport docks in the winter without the docks really. Mind, this bloody weather doesn't help.'

By four o'clock in the afternoon they found their hotel, Los Montanas, with little difficulty. Much to their delight, there, secured to the wall of the hotel and as clear as daylight was the three-star sign. And, John noted, it really was right in the heart of the town which meant that they could walk the mountains in the day and enjoy a bit of lively nightlife when they got back.

During booking-in they soon found yet again that language was going to be a major problem. The receptionist, a pretty young girl of about seventeen who looked as miserable as sin, rambled on in a language that John and Jayne assumed as Andorran. They couldn't understand a word of it and even Jayne's limited German did not help one little bit. Finally, the necessary forms of registration were successfully completed.

'What time is breakfast in the morning?' John asked pleasantly as the receptionist handed him the key. The girl looked puzzled. 'You know, breakfast?' This time, John shouted loudly and held a mock plate with one hand and pretended to shovel food into his mouth with the other. Again the girl looked puzzled.

Jayne stepped in. 'Que hora es desayuno en la mañana?' she said in her best Spanish.

The girl smiled and babbled away for a minute or so in a language that was anything but Spanish.

'Did you get that, Jayne?' John asked when the girl had finished speaking.

'I got some of it, I think,' Jayne replied. 'I think she said that breakfast is at 7 a.m until 7.30 a.m and is taken in the café next-door.'

'Good enough,' John acknowledged. 'A bit early in the morning, but no problem. It just means that we can be on the mountains that much earlier. Come on, Jayne, let's go up to our room.'

Just as they were leaving the small reception-area, a door opened from behind the reception-desk and the girl was joined by a tall, swarthy man in his early thirties. His broad smile was infectious as he spoke, but his English proved to be terrible.

'Meester and Meeses, how yoo say, Barcrosse. Weelcom au hotel Los Montanas. Ay am Maanigerr.'

John and Jayne understood very little more after that other than they appeared to be the only guests staying at the hotel. Excusing themselves politely they, armed with their suitcases, made for the stairs that led to the first-floor upon which their room, number thirteen, was apparently situated.

This was the beginning of the first unusual experience. The floor of the small reception-area was carpeted in the deepest of brown colours to be almost black. Similarly, the stairs leading to the first-floor was covered with the same dark-brown carpet. No problem. However, when they opened

A Gaze into Holidaze

the fire-door which gave access to the corridor that led to their room they found, because there was not a single window in the corridor, that there was no natural light available whatsoever other than from the fire-door that John held open. Furthermore, the floor of the seemingly long corridor was also covered with the same dark-brown, shag-pile carpet and, to the amazement of John and Jayne, so too were the walls and ceilings of the corridor.

'God, it's as dark as a bloody coal-pit in here,' John declared in surprise. 'Have you ever seen shag-pile carpet on walls and ceilings before, Jayne?'

'Never,' sighed Jayne despondently, disappointment in her voice. 'It must be for insulation against the cold in the winter.'

'Insulation against the cold!' exclaimed John. 'Haven't they heard of central heating? Anyway, it's summer now, not winter.' Then, sensing that Jayne was a bit down, he attempted to lift her mood. 'Should have brought my Dad's miner's lamp, that would have been the answer. Come on, Jayne, there must be a light-switch here somewhere. Ah! Here it is just by the fire-door.'

Allowing the fire-door to close behind him, John switched on the light to reveal a long, dimly-lit corridor. At the far end of the corridor they could just make out the number 13 on the door of their room. Even the paintwork on the doors of the rooms was painted in the same depressing dark-brown colour.

'The owner must have a fetish for dark-brown and low-wattage light-bulbs,' grinned John in the dim light supplied by the single overhead unshaded light-bulb. Jayne didn't answer. 'Come on, Jayne,' John continued happily. 'Let's get the luggage into our room.'

The two of them advanced slowly down the long corridor, each struggling with a suitcase. They got about halfway to their room when, 'click', they were plunged into total and absolute darkness. They could see nothing.

'Bloody hell!' shouted John in frustration. 'I can't see my hand in front of my face. Where are you, Jayne?'

'Well, it's certain that I haven't gone far. I'm as blind as you are.' Jayne sounded nervous.

'Okay, let's not panic,' said John reassuringly. 'You stay put exactly where you are and I'll go back to the fire-door and switch on the light. I'll leave my suitcase here so don't move or you'll fall over it.'

John shuffled back down the corridor, hands feeling the walls for direction. He shuddered in the dark at the unpleasant feel of the shag-pile carpet on the walls. Finally, he saw the faintest of glow which signalled the presence of the light-switch, reached out and pressed it.

'And let there be light,' he grinned as once again the corridor glowed dimly.

Smartly, he advanced back down the corridor towards the waiting Jayne. He had only gone a few paces when, 'click', inky-black darkness returned. John hearing Jayne suck in her breath in fright, decided to take another couple of steps so that he could touch her shoulder to reassuringly show her that he was there and everything would be alright – CRASH!

'What's that, John?' Jayne almost screamed, blatant fear in her voice.

'It's okay, love,' said John sheepishly, his voice muffled by the shag-pile carpet of the floor. 'I tripped arse-over-tit over my suitcase.'

'We're never going to get into our room at this rate if you keep lying down on the job,' Jayne voiced nervously, trying hard to see the funny side of the event.

'Very funny,' answered John as he spat out bits of carpet and carefully struggled to his feet. 'Look, the light-switch is obviously on a timer, which is so short that you cannot walk the length of the corridor in one go. I'll go back to the light-switch and stay there. I'll then be able to keep switching it on when the light goes out to allow you to reach our room at the end of the corridor.'

'What about your suitcase?'

'Well, if you take your suitcase to the door of our room first, you can then come back for mine and I'll keep switching the lights on as required. Simple!'

'Yes, simple and crafty,' Jayne giggled, her confidence now returning. 'Don't strain yourself, darling, will you?'

'What do you mean?'

'Well, I'll do all the humping while you'll attempt to overtax yourself with all the switching.'

'You can do the switching if you like,' John said hastily, staring hopelessly through the blackness in the direction of Jayne's voice.

'No, John, you can do it. I'm only teasing so off you go.' Then, as an extra teasing sarcasm Jayne added, 'Mind you don't fall now, won't you?'

'Ha! ha! bloody ha!' John retorted, as he turned once again towards the fire-door. 'You know, it's so bloody dark in here I've become completely disorientated. At least we know how a mole feels, don't we?'

The plan worked. Soon John, Jayne and two suitcases stood outside room-number 13 albeit in inky-blackness when the light clicked out for the umpteenth time.

'Open the door then, Jayne,' John ordered.

'I can't because you've got the key,' Jayne replied.

'Oh yes, so I have,' John answered. 'It's here in my pocket. I'll have the door open in a jiffy.' There were long seconds of silence as John searched his pockets for the key. 'Shit, shit, shit,' he finally bellowed through the darkness.

'What's the matter now?' Jayne sighed.

'The key must have fallen out of my pocket when I fell,' John replied. 'I don't know how I didn't see it on the floor when I had the bloody light on but I didn't. I'll have to crawl along the floor and feel for it.' Off John went on all fours.

Ten minutes of John's swearing which sliced through the darkness like a knife, brought an, 'I've found it, Jayne.' Two further minutes of puffing

A Gaze into Holidaze

and blowing found John back at the door of number 13. A further five minutes of obscenities from John and heavy breathing from Jayne because they couldn't find the keyhole and then couldn't get the key in the lock once they had found it, eventually allowed the couple to enter their home-from-home for the next four days. It was now 6 p.m and it had taken over a half-an-hour to get from reception to inside their room.

This time, easily finding the light-switch, the room was soon illuminated brightly – a little too brightly.

'It's like a floodlit football-pitch in here. That light must be the same wattage as a bloody searchlight,' laughed John as he glanced around the bedroom. 'I don't believe it, Jayne. Look!'

Jayne looked slowly around the tiniest room that she had ever seen. The walls allowed a gap of about eighteen inches all around the double-bed with a little more space on one side to allow the door of the room to open and a small wardrobe to be placed. The floor and walls were covered with – you've guessed it – the same dark-brown, shag-pile carpet. Even the door to what appeared to be the bathroom was covered with the same carpet.

Jayne laughed. Either that or cry, she thought. 'Well, at least it's got a window,' she said, crossing to a small window set into the carpeted walls. 'You can shut the light off now because it's still daylight and I bet the view of the mountains will be . . .' She broke off. Facing her, and not more than ten feet away, was the brick wall of the next building.

'Eh, Jayne, look at me.' John's laughing voice boomed from the partially-open door of the bathroom. Jayne turned from the window to find John's knees sticking through from the bathroom into the bedroom. Closer inspection found John sitting on the toilet at a very peculiar and precarious angle. As he balanced his backside on the bowl whilst struggling to hold the door, which opened outwards into the bedroom, partially closed against his left knee, he laughed until the tears were running down his face.

'What on earth are you doing?' Jayne said, chuckling loudly at John's predicament.

'I am shitting at an angle in azimuth of forty-five degrees.' Their laughter boomed through the tiny room. 'This is not a bathroom, it's a bloody cupboard.' John giggled as he got off the toilet-bowl. 'Look at it, Jayne. How on earth could they get a sink, shower and toilet-bowl in a room four feet square? You can't even close the door when you are on the throne. Our bathroom in Clarence is much bigger than this.'

An hour later, not allowing themselves to be daunted by events, they fumbled their way through the 'Tunnel of Love', which was the nickname that John and Jayne had given to the dark corridor that led to the deserted reception-area, to burst out of the hotel in search of the joys of the night life of Andorra.

They wandered the streets of downtown Andorra for about four hours in the drizzle. During this time they bought a torch to tackle the 'Tunnel of

A Gaze into Holidaze

Love' on their return to the hotel, and sampled several bars which were dreadful and almost deserted. Finally, they ended-up in a small, shabby, pizza-restaurant which was equally as deserted as the bars.

'This place looks as bad as the rest of the town so let's hope the pizza is better,' John muttered as a shabbily-dressed waitress struggled with the language barrier as she took their order. 'You'd have more fun in Blackpool after it has closed at the end of the season.'

'What do we now, John?' Jayne asked timidly. 'It's nearly eleven o'clock and there is no point in walking the streets anymore.'

'Back to the hotel, Jayne. Andorra is disappointing I agree, but not to worry, we will certainly enjoy exploring the surrounding mountains tomorrow. They look fabulous.'

Back at Las Montanas they passed through the still-deserted reception-area and with the help of their newly purchased torch, easily won the battle of the 'Tunnel of Love'. Gaining entry to their room, John switched on the light together with the television which literally hung by its cables from the ceiling. Jayne washed, undressed and got into bed.

'Anything worth watching, John?'

'No, not really, pet. It's all in French or Spanish.'

'Never mind, I'm tired anyway. It's been a long drive through the mountains and to find the hotel rubbish when we got here is, well . . .'

'Part of life's rich tapestry,' John interrupted as he switched-off the television. He then undressed and switched-off the light to find that the room was immediately plunged into the same inky-blackness as the 'Tunnel of Love'.

'Now, when you get into bed be very careful, John. There's a very sharp edge on the shelf above the . . .'

There was a very loud bang which made the room itself shudder.

'Oh, shit and bollocks!' John screamed, jumping out of bed to switch-on the light. There he was, completely in the nude, jumping up and down and hugging what was obviously a very painful head. 'I've fractured my bloody skull, that's what I've done,' he shouted as he took a punch at the offendingly-sharp shelf-corner that ran across the whole width of the bed a few inches above the pillows. The bed shuddered as his fist made contact with the shelf-edge. 'Ow!' shouted John even louder than before, as he winced with the pain that shot up his arm. 'I've broken my bloody finger now,' he screamed, dancing even higher with the pain but not knowing whether to hold his hand or his head.

Jayne tried to stifle her laughter but it did not work. She just exploded and rolled around in the bed unable to stop.

'Thanks, Jayne,' John winced. 'Thanks a lot.'

'Well, I did warn you, didn't I? Come here, Cry Baby, let's have a look at it.' She looked at John's head and then at his hand. 'There, there, you'll

A Gaze into Holidaze

live. There are no bones broken although you might have a bruise on your hand tomorrow to match the lump you've already got on your head.'

An hour later, after bathing John's hand and head in cold water, they finally went to sleep.

At 7.30 a.m the following morning John and Jayne passed through the still deserted reception-area on their way to breakfast which was to be in the small café around the corner from the hotel. The only thing that had changed in Reception since they had passed through it the night before was that someone had erected a steel-mesh barrier which rose from the top of the counter to leave a gap of about a foot or so between the top of the barrier and the ceiling.

'Still no-one about,' Jayne said as they walked through.

'Yes, it's not good enough,' said John firmly. 'We are up for breakfast at this God-forsaken hour while they laze about in bed. And, what is more, I want to see the manager about changing our room.'

A few minutes later, John and Jayne were seated at a table in the deserted café next-door to the hotel. They waited for twenty minutes without any service whatsoever before John stormed across the room to the unshaven, scruffy little man who lounged behind the counter, smoking and reading a newspaper. He did not look up from his newspaper as John spoke.

'Breakfast, mate. We have come from the hotel next-door for breakfast.' The man, still not looking up just shrugged his shoulders and carried on reading his paper, allowing ash to fall onto his shabby sweater from the cigarette that dangled from the corner of his mouth.

Three times John posed the question of breakfast to Scruffy. Three times he received similar shrugs of the shoulders and three times a very positive and most definite, 'No'.

John was livid. 'Come on, Jayne. We're going back to the hotel to get that bloody manager.'

On their return to the hotel, Reception was still barriered, deserted and as quiet as the grave.

'Where's that soddin' manager?' hissed John through clenched teeth. 'It's eight o'clock now and he's still not here.'

Jayne was peering through the open mesh of the steel barrier at the notices that were pinned to a small notice-board attached to the wall behind the counter. 'There's a number to ring for emergencies on the wall over there by the telephone. I can't read it from here though.'

'Even if you could read it we haven't got a phone,' muttered John, despair showing in his voice as he carefully surveyed the steel barrier. 'I could climb over that easily,' he concluded. 'I could climb up the steel-mesh and squeeze over the top to drop onto the counter. Easy peasy! I'm going to ring that bastard and sort this hotel out.'

'No, John, you'll get into trouble. If you are caught they will think that you are robbing the place and you'll end up in prison.'

A Gaze into Holidaze

'Be a damn-sight better than this bloody hotel,' John snarled. 'And the food and surroundings would be better.'

'Calm down, John. Let's wait for another half-an-hour and see what happens. Surely the manager will be here by then.'

Jayne waited patiently while John waited like a caged animal, endlessly pacing aggressively up and down the small reception-area.

At exactly 8.30 a.m John stopped dead in his tracks. 'I'm going over,' he said, his tanned face expressionless, his lips drawn in temper. It took him only fifteen seconds flat before he jumped from the counter-top to the floor on the other side of the barrier. 'Right, Jayne,' he said masterfully. 'The printing is too small for me to see these numbers. Can you pass me my reading-glasses please?'

'I haven't got your glasses,' Jayne replied.

'Yes, you have. I told you to put them in your handbag when we left the caravan just in case I lost them.'

'No you didn't,' insisted Jayne. 'You told me that you wouldn't need them on this trip so I left them on the table in the caravan.'

'Oh, bollocks with a capital B!' John sighed in frustration. 'Okay! I'll be right back over because I'm wasting my time here.' Fifteen seconds later he was back at Jayne's side.

'What are we going to do now, John?' Jayne enquired innocently.

'We are not going to do anything, my love – you

are! Over you go. You don't need glasses so you ring the emergency number and sort it out.'

'I can't get over there.'

'Yes, you can because it's easy. I'll even give you a hand.' With that John effortlessly lifted Jayne and sat her on the counter. 'There, you're already halfway there.'

Slowly, Jayne dragged herself up until she stood on the counter and started the climb over the barrier, encouraged by John's hand which was placed firmly on her backside. 'Go on, Jayne, you can do it.'

A few minutes later Jayne was halfway up and at the stage where she would have to throw her leg over to lie along the top of the barrier, wedged between the barrier and ceiling.

'What do I do now?' she squawked, the barrier shaking precariously.

'Cock your leg over the top and lie along the top,' John said supportively.

Jayne did as she was bid and, seconds later, was lying totally wedged between the ceiling and the top-bar of the barrier, one bare leg dangling over each side of the barrier for balance, shorts stretched taut over the buttocks. 'I'm stuck, John,' she squeaked.

At that precise moment the front door opened and in walked a tall, well-dressed man in a business suit. 'What the hell is going on here?' His tone was very sharp in spite of the soft Cornish accent.

'Good morning,' Jayne managed quietly with a

smile from her elevated location. What else could she say?

'And who the hell are you?' John said, his tone matching the Cornishman's.

'I am the owner of this hotel,' Cornish replied. 'An owner who is damned annoyed and about to call the police.'

'Please don't call the police!' It was Jayne who had spoken, her voice frightened and pleading. She hadn't moved a muscle and was still lying like a circus act, pinned between ceiling and barrier.

John, leaving Jayne in her uncomfortable and precarious position hastily explained to the owner the events leading up to their attempted break-in. He concluded with, '. . . so you see, we weren't trying to steal anything. We are guests here in the hotel and all we wanted to do is telephone someone so that we can have some breakfast.'

The harshness disappeared from the Cornishman's face and he started to laugh. 'My name is Clive,' he said as he held out his hand. 'You had better help your wife down before she does herself a mischief.'

Minutes later they all sat around a table in the dining-room of the hotel, enjoying the pot of hot coffee that lay on the table before them. Continental breakfast was to follow.

'I certainly need this,' John commented as he drank the perfect, steaming liquid.

'I expect you do after what you've just been through,' Clive stated. 'You must have met René, my manager, last night. He is pretty useless to be honest with you and, of course, he can't speak any English other than to tell you he is the manager. What room are you in?'

'Number 13,' Jayne offered.

'Good God!' said Clive. 'You shouldn't be in there. Nobody should be in there if it comes to that because it is only fit for a storeroom. Like the rest of the hotel it needs refurbishing badly. I've only been here a month and I intend to do the place over before next season.'

'You mean you don't like dark-brown carpet on floors, walls and ceilings?' John joked.

'Not even remotely,' chuckled Clive before continuing. 'I don't know how the cock-up over breakfast arrangements occurred because we always serve breakfast here in the dining-room at between 8 a.m and 9 a.m.'

'Let's just put it down to language difficulties and let it go at that,' John said. 'I'll take you up on your offer of a change of rooms though, Clive, if I may?'

Clive smiled. 'Most certainly, yes. You can have the best room in the house.'

And they did. Clive gave them a huge and comfortable suite of lounge, bedroom and bathroom right on the top-floor and in the front of the hotel overlooking the mountains. John and Jayne were over the moon.

Unfortunately, the atmosphere of the town of Andorra did not change much during the rest of John and Jayne's stay. However, the weather

A Gaze into Holidaze

brightened up considerably allowing the couple to explore, on a daily basis, the panoramic scenery of the wonderful peaks that surround Andorra. Most nights they arrived from the mountains so tired after walking all day, that all they wanted to do was eat a simple meal in the good restaurant that they had found near the hotel, before retiring to bed at a reasonable hour.

The long weekend passed quickly and successfully and in what seemed like no time at all, they were saying their goodbyes to Clive.

'Good luck with the hotel, mate,' said John as he shook Clive's hand before getting into the Volvo.

'Thanks, John. I hope we'll see you again because if you come back to Andorra you won't recognise the old Las Montanas.'

'We'll be back,' Jayne lied. She liked Clive and knew that the hotel would be a good choice for the future. She also liked the mountains of Andorra but that is where her liking stopped. There was no way that she intended returning to the town of Andorra.

They left Las Montanas and headed back down the main road of Andorra, the way that they had come when they had arrived four days earlier.

'It wasn't so bad really, was it, John?' Jayne asked as she snuggled into the comfortable seats of the Volvo.

'Not for the price we paid it wasn't,' John replied. 'It will be even better when we get some cheap booze.'

JOHN BEVERLEY

Five minutes later, and just before the Spanish border, they found just what John was looking for. Just off the main road was a large, modern supermarket that sold just about everything, especially vast quantities of wines and spirits.

'Just what the doctor ordered, eh, Jayne?' John said grinning from ear-to-ear as he pulled up in the large, crowded car-park of the enormous building. 'If the prices are as good as I've heard they are then we'll have a good stock-up here 'cos it's even cheaper than Spain.'

'You and your cheap booze, John, makes me chuckle,' Jayne teased happily as they locked the car and walked towards the main entrance. 'Anyway, even if it is cheap don't forget you have to take it through customs at the border.'

'I've already thought of that,' said John smugly. 'I understand that it's the spirits that are really cheap here. Now I don't know how much you are allowed to take through at customs but it will certainly be at least a case each. Even if we have to pay their equivalent to VAT at customs, you know their IV something or other . . .'

'IVA,' Jayne helped. 'It's sixteen percent.'

'That's it, their IVA. Even if we have to pay that at sixteen percent we should still be cheaper than Spain if the booze here is as cheap as I think it will be, or should I say, hope it will be.'

It was even cheaper. John could not believe his eyes when he saw the prices per case of all the spirits that he could have dreamed of. He was just like the proverbial child in a sweetshop.

A Gaze into Holidaze

'Cor,' he said, his eyes shining brightly with excitement as he punched numbers into his pocket-calculator and pressed the 'equals' button. 'All the famously-branded spirits work out at about £2.50 a litre. I just can't believe it. Come on, Jayne, let's grab a trolley each.'

'A trolley each. Aren't you going over the top a bit, John?'

'No, Jayne, trust me. This is far cheaper than I'd hoped for and, as I told you, even if we pay IVA on every bottle, and the customs duty can't be more than sixteen percent, it only increases the amount to . . .' He paused as he punched more numbers into his calculator, '. . . there you are, it increases the amount to about £2.90 per bottle. Jayne, that's £2.90 a litre which would cost you all of £15 a litre in the UK and even £10 in Spain. Mate, we've just got to do it.'

Shortly afterwards, John and Jayne each had a trolley containing seven cases of various branded spirits. Whisky, gin, brandy, vodka, they were all there making a total of fourteen cases between them containing some eighty-four litre bottles.

'Cor,' said John, his eyes gleaming with satisfaction as they waited their turn at the checkout. 'All of this for around £250 with duty paid. Jayne, we've got enough spirits here to last us for the next ten years or more.'

'You're a happy bunny, John, aren't you?' Jayne smiled contentedly as John paid for the spirits with a signature against his cheque-card.

'You can say that again, precious.'

'How will you manage with the customs at Dover when we get back? Do you think it will be alright with all of these bottles of spirit?'

'No problem, Jayne. As long as the booze is for your own consumption you can take what you like in. They aren't bothered about a few bottles of spirits. It's valuables like diamonds, gold and, of course, drugs that they care about. Trust me, sweetheart, there'll be no problem either going into the UK or here at the border. I'll bet you that here they will wave us straight through and we'll not even stop.'

Ten minutes later, John and Jayne, Volv's boot packed to the brim with fourteen cases of spirits, arrived at the border-control. They were immediately flagged by a massive border-policeman into a space between a row of cars. All of the cars in the row had their boots open where policemen were peering inside, while a queue of other cars were obviously waiting for the same treatment.

'Oh, John,' Jayne whispered nervously. 'They seem to be checking every car.'

'No problem, Jayne. We are not smugglers so don't worry.'

As John spoke, the huge policeman who had directed them to the vacant customs-bay, opened John's door. With a grunt in English of the single word, 'Out!' he stepped to one side.

John got from behind the wheel and looked up at the uniformed giant who stood a good six-inches taller than himself. 'Can I help you?' was all that John could think of saying.

A Gaze into Holidaze

The giant stooped and looked around the rear seats of the car. He then strode around the front of the Volvo to where Jayne sat. 'You, out now!' Giant snapped, his bass voice rumbling from deep within his body. Jayne was out of the car like a shot. Giant, after a quick glance around where Jayne had been sitting, appeared satisfied.

John gave a silent sigh of relief.

Giant then looked over the top of the car at John before bounding back around the car to where John stood. 'You, open trunk, now!' he commanded.

John, astutely sensing the mood of the moment, had the boot open in a matter of seconds. 'It's only our luggage and a few bottles of spirits, constable. You know how it is. We are on holiday and . . .'

'No,' boomed Giant, pointing at the cases of spirits. 'One each only.'

'W-w-what do you m-m-mean?' stammered John, for a moment shocked. Then he regained his confidence. 'You mean that we are only allowed one case each. Oh, that's okay, we will gladly pay duty on the others.'

'No!' boomed Giant again. 'One bottle only.'

John froze. 'But that's ridiculous. We cross many borders in our . . .' That's as far as John got before Giant grabbed his arm and turned him to look at a large, grey building about a hundred yards away.

'You carry boxes there and explain to my sergeant. Go now!'

'You mean you want me to carry fourteen cases of spirits to that far-away building in all of this heat.'

'Go now!' repeated Giant, pulling himself up to his full height and resting his hand lightly on the butt of the Beretta that was strapped to his waist.

John needed no further bidding. He reached into the back of Volv and extracted a case of whisky. 'Jayne, put another case on the top, sweetheart, will you?' he said sheepishly. Loaded with the two cases, he turned and looked up at Giant. 'Are you going to help me, constable?'

Giant glowered down at John but said nothing.

'Then I'll take that as a no,' John hissed as he struggled with the two cases across the tarmac towards the distantly grey building, Giant walking empty-handed beside him.

'I'll help you,' Jayne volunteered, running alongside the now heavily-perspiring John.

'No thanks,' replied John as his perspiration dripped onto the top of the cases. 'God, it's hot! No, Jayne, you stay with the car in case somebody nicks the rest of the booze. I'll manage, precious, don't worry. I'll not let these bastards grind me down.'

Twenty minutes later, a saturated-with-sweat John, a very worried Jayne and a seen-it-all-before-so-I-couldn't-care-less Giant stood in a queue waiting to see the duty customs-control officer. This man was even bigger than Giant and, with his shaved head, looked twice as menacing. Patiently, he was dealing with a very small but noisy Spaniard who, it appeared to John and Jayne because they could only understand a little of the Spaniard's fury and articulate gesticulating, had been

A Gaze into Holidaze

caught with a few thousand more cigarettes in his car than he should have had.

After a further fifteen minutes of the one-sided Spaniard's conversation, Shaved-Head stood up from his seat behind the counter and towered over the Spaniard. Shaved-Head's face was deadpan but his eyes were cold and vicious. Spaniard shut up as if switched-off as he listened to Shaved-Head's single sentence in Spanish, a sentence that Jayne was able to translate in her head. 'We have confiscated your cigarettes. Now shut up and go or we will arrest you.' The Spaniard shot out of the door as if fired from a cannon, his little legs a mere blur to the eyes of the onlookers.

Shaved-Head grinned broadly at the hastily departing man. He then sat down, the grin disappearing instantly to be replaced by the same deadpan expression, the eyes bored. 'Next,' he boomed in English. John and Jayne shuffled to the low counter. Even sitting down, Shaved-Head was nearly as tall as John.

'There has been a mistake and . . .' John started but broke off as Shaved-Head held up his hand.

Shaved-Head then looked at Giant who immediately started speaking to report the events of the fourteen cases of spirits, which now lay in a neat stack at the back of the large room in which they all stood. John and Jayne understood not a word. The report finally completed, Giant stood smartly to attention and saluted Shaved-Head before taking his place once again behind John and Jayne.

John Beverley

Shaved-Head looked up at John, arrogance in his expression. In almost perfect English he said: 'You have exceeded the spirit allowance of one bottle per person for crossing the border from Andorra into Spain. You have three choices. One, you may pay the duty on all except two of the bottles and pass freely into Spain. Two, you can take only two bottles into Spain and leave the rest in Andorra as confiscated goods. Three, you may keep all of the bottles but remain in Andorra because we cannot allow you to cross the border into Spain without paying duty on the contraband.'

'How much is the duty per bottle?' asked John.

Shaved-Head consulted a thick book that lay on his side of the counter. 'Ten English pounds per bottle.'

'Ten quid a bottle,' shouted John. 'That's ridiculous. You are charging duty at four times what the bottle cost in the supermarket. Absolutely crazy!'

'That may be so,' Shaved-Head said. 'Nevertheless, that is the duty that must be paid. Therefore, Englishman . . .'

'Welshman,' John corrected defiantly.

'Therefore, sir,' Shaved-Head stressed the 'sir'. 'You owe the government of Andorra exactly eight hundred and twenty pounds. You may pay by cheque if you wish.'

'Wait a minute,' said John, suddenly a wicked grin on his face. He walked quickly to the back of the room and returned carrying a case of gin. He gave a sly wink to Shaved-Head. 'Perhaps we could

A Gaze into Holidaze

be sensible about this and you could kindly accept a small gift of friendship between you and me.'

Shaved-Head said nothing. He just sat back in his chair and, with his face still expressionless, looked John straight in the eye.

John smiled again before once again walking smartly to the cases at the back of the room. This time he returned to the counter with a case of whisky.

Jayne could not believe what John was trying to do. Surely his intent could not go unnoticed by Giant who stood behind and glared at the entire proceedings.

John smiled once again and pushed both cases of spirits across the counter towards Shaved-Head. 'How silly of me,' said John quietly. 'Of course, your wife would like a present too.'

Shaved-Head leapt to his feet. 'Are you trying to bribe an officer of the law?' he bellowed, his fists clenched in fury. 'If so I can have you arrested.'

'My husband didn't mean that,' Jayne intervened hurriedly, trying to take the heat out of the situation. 'It is only his way of being friendly.' Then, immediately changing her tone she tried another tack, innocence in her voice. 'Is there a limit to the number of crossings of the border that travellers can make in a day?'

Shaved-Head relaxed a bit. 'No, madam, there is not.'

'May I speak with my husband in private, sergeant?' Jayne asked. Shaved-Head nodded approval and sat down, his face still expressionless.

Jayne led John to the back of the room and they stood by the forlorn looking cases of spirits. 'John, why don't we go back and forth over the border taking two bottles at a time?' Jayne whispered. 'We are not breaking the law by doing this and in forty trips all the spirits will be in Spain?'

John thought for a moment. 'It's a good idea, Jayne, but there would be a major problem as I see it because we would need an extra pair of hands to do what you suggest. You over in Spain receiving the bottles and making sure that nobody nicks them, someone doing the same job on this side and me driving the forty trips across the border. Well thought out, sweetheart, but not practical because we are one pair of hands short.'

'Well, its more practical than you being arrested for bribing a customs official.'

'All right, all right,' John replied quietly. 'I know I read the wrong signals there with Shaved-Head. I thought that he would have jumped at twelve free litres of spirits.'

'You can say that again,' Jayne sneered. 'You read the wrong signals alright. What about asking Clive to be the third person to help?'

'No, Jayne, I don't want to do that. This is our problem not his. Anyway, pet, there is no way that I am going to pay the duty of eight hundred and twenty quid and that's that.'

'What will you do then?' Jayne asked. 'Let customs confiscate the eighty-two bottles?'

'No way,' John answered sharply. 'Let them have

a great party at our expense, no way.' Then he spoke more softly. 'We've lost the game, pet. As far as I'm concerned we'll take the whole lot back to the supermarket where we bought them and stand outside the door and give a bottle to everyone that comes out. We can wish them Merry Christmas as we do it if you like.'

Jayne kissed John lightly on the cheek. 'It's not Christmas,' she said.

'Who cares,' smiled John. 'Come on, that's all we can do.'

John told Shaved-Head that he would not pay the duty but would give the bottles away to the local people. Shaved-Head merely shrugged his indifference.

It took John and Jayne three quarters-of-an-hour to return to the supermarket. Namely, thirty-minutes to carry the fourteen cases from the customs-office back to the car, still unaided by Giant, and fifteen minutes to drive back to the store.

Just as they were pulling into the car park once again, Jayne had a sudden brainwave.

'John, I've still got the receipt for the cases of spirits. Why don't I try and get a credit-note for the amount that we've spent on booze and then we can work out the money on other things?'

John laughed good-humouredly. 'Jayne, sweetheart, you've got more chance of flying than getting a credit-note. You haven't got a clue of the language and they certainly can't speak English.'

'Let me try,' insisted Jayne. 'We've got everything to gain and nothing to lose. Don't start giving the bottles away yet.' With that she jumped out of the car and ran into the supermarket.

Fifteen-minutes later she returned to the car grinning like a Cheshire cat as she pulled a flat trolley behind her. 'Told you I could do it,' she laughed as John gave her a big squeeze. All we have to do is take the cases back to the department where we bought them and bob's-your-uncle, they'll give us a credit-note.'

And they did. A credit-note was issued with the minimum of fuss.

The final laugh came when they had to work out the £250 or so that they had spent. They had cooking-pots coming out of their ears, a two-feet diameter cheese that would feed a family of six for a month, about ten tons of chocolate, and numerous presents for all the family.

Finally, they left the supermarket for the border with Volv fully loaded. However, this time they had only two bottles of spirits in the car.

'Let the bastards pull us up now,' said John arrogantly.

'Yes, we are okay now,' answered Jayne.

On reaching the border for the second time that day, the policeman on duty, a different one from Giant, just waved them through with total lack of interest.

****

A Gaze into Holidaze

Of floating things . . .

When John and Jayne had been lecturing for about two years, they had a stroke of luck in that they were able, by devious means and the swapping of lectures with fellow lecturers, to take a three-week break in the autumn of the year.

So, without hesitation they, with a just-serviced Volv and Clarence, found themselves on a splendid campsite just outside Falmouth in Cornwall.

They had been there for only a few days when the forecast told them that the south-west of the United Kingdom was in for continuous rain, rain and more rain.

'Well, that's going to cramp our style,' John declared as he switched-off the bad news from the television. 'Here we are in glorious Cornwall in the autumn and it looks as if we are going to be literally bogged-down in the confines of Clarence.'

'We could always go for a walk in the rain,' Jayne suggested.

'Go for a walk in the mud, you mean?' John replied looking out at the torrential rain. 'What's more, like the plonker that I am, I've forgotten to bring our wet-gear.'

'Well, we'll just have to go out and buy some in Falmouth, won't we?' Jayne said stubbornly. 'The rain has never bothered us before, has it?'

'Didn't really want to spend a lot of money on wet-gear,' John grumbled.

'Oh, stop whingeing,' said Jayne sharply. 'We pay what we have to because we certainly can't do anything without wet-gear and that's that!'

They didn't have to pay much at all as it turned out. In Falmouth they found a bargain-store that sold just about everything including plastic wet-gear at £3.50 a set.

'Do you think it's any good?' Jayne asked as she eyed the green, hooded-coat and matching trousers. 'It looks a bit thin to me.'

'It'll be fine, Jayne, trust me,' John assured her. 'I know it's a bit thin but it'll do for this break. Why spend more?'

Not far from the bargain-store was a travel agent with a very invitingly-deep doorway. This John and Jayne readily accepted when they were caught in a sudden downpour as they were racing back to the car.

After a few minutes of passing the time looking through the numerous adverts for sunny, autumn destinations abroad, John caught Jayne's arm and pointed to a brochure that was lying idly at the bottom of the window-display.

'Hey, Jayne, do you fancy that?'

'Narrowboating on the canals,' Jayne read. 'Yes, I've always wanted to do narrowboating but I've always considered it too expensive.'

'Listen to you,' John teased. 'You're the one that always says, "You pay what you have to pay."' Jayne laughed at John's high-pitched mimicking. John took her arm. 'Come on, let's check it out.'

At one o'clock on the following Monday afternoon, they arrived at a little place called Monkton Combe, a village just outside Bath. This was the

A Gaze into Holidaze

home of the forty-foot, two-berth narrowboat that they had hired for seven days, Monday to Sunday.

'We're a bit early, John. We are not supposed to have the boat until three o'clock.' Jayne stated as John parked the car.

'Don't worry, Jayne. I'll bet you that they'll let us go early at this time of year and we can chug along for about four or five hours before it gets dark. Trust me.'

And they could have done too if it hadn't been for the fact that the boat was undergoing an alternator change. However, after a couple of hours passing the time of day in the very snug and cosy country-pub in the village, they returned to the boatyard where the forty-footer was awaiting them.

'Cor!' said John excitedly. 'It's as big as a naval frigate, Jayne. That's what we'll call her – *Frig-It*. Get it Jayne? *Frig-It*?'

'Very funny, very funny.' Jayne was not amused. 'Never mind what you call the boat, can you handle it, that's the point?'

'Piece of old doddle,' John replied. 'Jayne, it's not exactly built for water-skiing, you know. It only chugs around at about three or four miles-an-hour.'

'What about the back steering stick? Can you handle that?'

'You mean the stern tiller, I think,' replied John smugly. 'Of course I can. All you have to do is point it the opposite way to the way you want the front to go. Easy peasy!'

After the quickest of handover-briefings from

the boatyard hired-hand, which covered everything from daily engine-maintenance, to the central-heating system, flushing the toilet, making the double-bed and tying up at night, they were on their way. It was 3.30 p.m and the rain had stopped, leaving the autumn sun trying to break through the thinning clouds overhead. They were accompanied for the first, very slow two-hundred yards by the hired-hand who then, with a friendly wave and a very loud shout of farewell to overcome the noise of the engines which were situated immediately below the wooden platform upon which they were all standing, leapt over the side onto the bank and was gone. John and Jayne, and the good ship *Frig-It*, were now well and truly, for better or for worse, on their own.

'Isn't this fantastic!' shouted Jayne, beaming like a Cheshire-cat as she sat on the stern-seat next to John. John, of course, stood proudly like Captain Ahab steering the narrowboat as it sped along the canal at its maximum of three knots.

'You handle the boat very well, John, considering you've never done it before,' Jayne complimented.

'It really is very easy, Jayne. Come and have a go. There's no other traffic about so you can't go wrong.' Jayne got to her feet and John handed over the tiller to her. 'Right, mate, gentle movements with the tiller. If you move the tiller to the right look, the bow moves to the left.' John demonstrated. 'And vice-versa.' He again showed Jayne the movement of the bow in the opposite direction.

A Gaze into Holidaze

After a few minutes of Jayne's steering, John was confident enough to sit down and let her get on with it. She was doing splendidly.

'Fancy a glass of wine, darling?' John enquired after Jayne had been steering for about half an hour.

'I'd love one,' Jayne replied as they passed under a low bridge to rejoin the avenue of trees that arched their yellow, brown and golden leafy-branches over the boat as it passed along the canal. All the time the sun, which now shone from a cloudless sky, flickered through the trees as they ambled along the still waterway.

'This is heaven,' Jayne continued dreamily as John disappeared into the lounge of the boat to get a bottle of wine.

He was just returning when there was a terrified scream from Jayne at the tiller. 'John, come quickly! Help me! Which way do I turn it? There's a boat coming towards us.'

John ran frantically from the lounge, past the toilet and shower, through the kitchen and bedroom, and leapt up the steps onto the tiller-platform. Here the frightened Jayne was holding on to the tiller like grim death.

'Which way do I turn it, John, which way?' Jayne screamed, panic in her eyes.

John gave a lightning glance forwards which revealed a boat a long way off coming towards them. It also revealed the bow of *Frig-It* hurtling, as much as it could hurtle, directly at the bank.

JOHN BEVERLEY

John snatched the tiller from Jayne's hand and pushed her savagely out of the way so that she sat down hard on her backside with a thud. With all of his weight behind his arm, he hauled the tiller over to the correct position and slammed the throttle into reverse in a desperate attempt to straighten and slow the boat. Too late! With a sighing and none-too-gentle thud, *Frig-It* buried her curving bow into the soft earth of the bank.

John put the throttle into neutral and then slammed it back into reverse. *Frig-It* refused to budge from the bank.

'What's happened, John?' Jayne asked ashamedly. 'Why isn't the boat moving?'

'I'm afraid we've run aground, Jayne. No matter. There's a pole on the roof of the boat so I can push us off from the bow. It'll be just like punting in Cambridge.'

Without another word, John jumped onto the cabin roof which ran almost the entire length of the boat, grabbed the pole and ran along the roof to the bow. Burying the end of the long pole into the mud, he pushed with all his strength. No good! The boat was well and truly fast.

'Do you want a hand, mate?' The male voice was friendly.

John turned to find that the boat that had been quite a long distance away from them when John first attempted to stop *Frig-It* from hitting the bank, was now only a few yards away. On the bow of the boat was a scruffy, bearded individual who had an almost twin of himself on the tiller in the stern.

'Thanks,' shouted John humbly. 'I've gone aground and I can't get her off.'

'No problem, mate,' came the reply. 'It happens with novices all the time.'

'How do you know we're novices?' John shouted as he caught a rope that was tossed to him from the other boat.

The man smiled, revealing many gaps in his set of yellow teeth as they appeared through the dense undergrowth of his shaggy beard. 'Could you be anything else? I'll tow you off.'

Five embarrassing minutes later, John and Jayne were on their way after sincerely thanking the two willing rescuers from the other boat with a ten-pound note.

'Come on, Jayne,' John said authoritatively after about a further ten-minutes of travel. 'Back you come to the tiller.'

'Oh, I don't want to, John. Not after the last time.'

'Well, you've got to,' John insisted firmly. 'If you don't, perhaps you won't drive again. It's a bit like a car after an accident, you must drive straight after the accident.'

Reluctantly, Jayne took the tiller once more and John made her drive for the next couple of hours, but made sure that she drank only coffee. Wine was certainly out of the question for the moment.

For the first time in his life, John moored a boat. He had taken over the tiller from Jayne and when they came to a straight part of the canal which was way out in the country and remote from any form of human life, John eased the narrowboat alongside the bank of the canal. This part of the canal had long planks of wood running lengthwise along the canal-bank for perhaps fifty metres in an effort to create moorings for narrowboats.

'Oh, these planks are very handy,' John said as he neutralised the throttle. 'Much better than mooring against a rough and muddy bank.' With that, armed with the mooring line which was permanently attached to the centre of the boat, he stepped the short distance from the boat to the top of the wooden plank.

As his Wellington-booted foot touched the top of the green and mildewed plank, John's foot shot out from under him.

'Oops!' he laughed, easily recovering his balance. 'Jayne, you'd better watch out for that.'

'Look out for what, darling?'

'I just slipped on this slimy plank. It's very slippery especially when wearing Wellies like we are. Please be careful.'

'I will,' replied Jayne as John hammered a long, sleek spike into the ground. 'Shall I help you to moor *Frig-It*?'

'Well, you can come and watch if you like,' John replied as he fastened the mooring rope to the steel spike. 'You never know when you'll have to tie-up the boat. Switch the engine off and come over here on the bank. Watch you don't slip on that plank.'

A Gaze into Holidaze

For the next few minutes, John hammered in two more spikes and showed Jayne how to moor the boat by fixing a double-hitch knot around the bow and stern spikes. 'There,' he said, satisfied with his efforts. '*Frig-It* isn't going anywhere tonight. Note, Jayne, how simple it is to tie that double-hitch knot, and you must tie-up with a double-hitch. If you use a single-hitch then the rope could become unfastened and the boat could drift away.'

Darkness fell quickly and the surrounding countryside around the boat became as dark as pitch. This was made worse by the sky which had once again clouded over with a promise of heavy rain to come.

In the narrowboat however, John and Jayne were as happy as pigs in the you-know-what. Jayne had cooked a lovely meal of bangers and mash on the gas-cooker, followed with tinned peaches and cream for sweet. All of this simple but fine meal was washed down with lots of red wine which proved to be a trifle over-sweet.

'Because you came back and steered at the tiller after your little lack of concentration this evening, I thought you deserved a little brandy.' John smiled as he poured a couple of nightcaps. 'This should make us sleep like logs.'

And it did. Other than hearing a few piercing and disturbing owl-hoots throughout the night, they slept like deaf folk. At about 6.30 a.m the following morning, they were awakened by the loud drumming of the rain as it bounced off the roof of the cabin above them.

'This is lovely and cosy, John,' Jayne sighed as she snuggled up to her husband. 'It's so peaceful here, isn't it?'

'Yes, darling. It's very peaceful and quiet. However, at seven o'clock it must be up and at 'em as they say.' He listened to the drumming of the rain. 'Well at least if gives us a chance to try our new wet-gear today, Jayne. At seven I'll get showered and things and then go and do my engine checks.'

By eight o'clock, after a hearty bacon-and-egg sandwich, they donned their new wet-gear and climbed to the tiller-flat. John effortlessly started the big diesel-engine, untied the boat and off they went into the torrential rain.

The canal wound through the beautiful Somerset countryside which, in spite of the heavy and constant rain, proved to be a wonderful ever-changing kaleidoscope of autumn colour. It was fantastically beautiful and presumably, because of the time of year, they seemed to have the beauty all to themselves because there was hardly another boat travelling on the canals in any direction.

Yes, there were many, many moored narrow-boats along the canal. Some were deserted and forlornly waiting for next summer. Some were very much lived-in with smoke from their wood-burning stoves coming out of chimney pots, smoke which clung to the abundance of bric-a-brac and assorted items that congregated on the long roofs of the vessels.

'I didn't realise that so many people lived per-

A Gaze into Holidaze

manently on the canals,' said Jayne, amazed at the array of plants, wood for burning, junk-for-a-rainy-day and families of bicycles, that were piled high on the roof of a moored seventy-foot narrowboat as *Frig-It* slowly eased past it.

'A lot of them are called water-gypsies,' John replied as he carefully steered *Frig-It* through a particularly narrow passage between two lines of boats that were moored directly opposite each other in the canal. 'Blimey, they don't give you much room sometimes, do they?'

Turning the next sharp, tree-overhung bend in the canal, John, Jayne and *Frig-It* were confronted with their first lock which seemed to tower hugely and menacingly above them. John expertly pulled into the 'reserved for lock-users only' mooring platform, a mooring platform that was provided for narrowboats at every lock along the canal.

Jayne looked up in awe at the tall, black, wooden-gates that were immediately in front of them. Closed they held back millions of gallons of murky canal-water. 'Why do they have locks, John?'

Taking the twenty-feet long midship mooring-line, the rope permanently attached to the centre of the narrowboat so that the centre of the boat could be tied-up first during the mooring operation, John stepped ashore. 'It's the only way a boat can travel up-hill and down-hill, Jayne. It will become more obvious to you when we go up to the lock and I show you how it works.'

Jayne studied John as he secured the midship

line. 'Why do they have that middle rope so long, John? It's a bit long to tie-up, isn't it? There's loads of rope left over.'

'Well, the length is quite cleverly worked out really,' John replied. 'It's long enough from where it's attached to the centre of the boat, for the steersman to get hold of the end while still standing on the tiller-flat before he gets off the boat to tie-up. However, the rope is not long enough to reach and get tangled around the propeller should it be dropped accidentally overboard. The fact that you've got a lot of line left over when you've tied-up doesn't matter at all.'

John finished securing the bow and stern lines and then shouted to Jayne. 'Come on, Jayne, out you get and be careful of that slippery plank that I showed you last night. All moorings have them.'

Jayne carefully stepped from the tiller-platform and onto the small jetty. 'Do you know how to operate a lock, John?'

'Well, to be honest, no,' John replied. 'I know the principle of the thing and I know that you release water from, or put water into the lock, by using this piece of kit.'

'What is it, John? Looks like some sort of spanner.'

'They call it a paddle-key. I'll show you how to use it soon, Jayne, because I am hoping that you can operate the locks while I drive the boat in and out of them.'

'Okay,' nodded Jayne. 'It suits me fine because I

certainly don't want to drive the boat on my own through those narrow lock-gates. I don't think I could steer well enough for that.'

John soon figured out the simple workings of the lock and then patiently explained the principle of lock operation to Jayne. Jayne nodded her understanding and watched John as he ensured that the up-stream lock-gates were closed and their paddles down, before opening the down-stream paddles to release the water from inside the lock. She watched, fascinated as the level of the water inside the lock dropped rapidly some twelve feet or so in a few minutes, causing the water outside the lock and in the canal below the gates, to roar with violent turbulence as the huge volume of water was released.

Once the water-level in the lock was the same as the canal water-level, John leaned on the very heavy lock-gate and it slowly and steadily opened. Soon he had the opposite gate opened and the mouth of the lock gaped invitingly.

'Do you think you can close the gates and lower the paddles on them after I drive in?' John asked.

'No problem,' declared Jayne confidently. 'Once you're in the lock all I have to do then is open the paddles on the up-stream gates and up you come, right?'

'Right,' said John with a grin. 'But it's raining heavily and everything will be slippery. Please be careful.'

Soon, John and *Frig-It* were safely in the bottom of the lock and the down-stream gates were closed with paddles successfully and easily lowered by Jayne. Eagerly she ran through the muddy grass to the up-stream gates and fitted the paddle-key to the appropriate paddle.

With determination she tried to turn the long handle of the key. It would not budge. She put all of her weight behind the handle and strained and strained at it until her Wellington-clad feet slid backwards in the mud. Still the same result, the paddles would not budge and did not rise the remotest fraction of an inch.

Gingerly, with paddle-key in hand, Jayne walked to the edge of the lock and looked down at John some ten feet below her. 'I can't open the paddles,' she said. 'I don't think I'm strong enough.'

'I was afraid of that,' John shouted up with a laugh. 'It's not your fault. It's always a bit difficult to raise the paddles that have water-pressure acting on them and I'm not surprised that it's too much for a little girl like you. So much for women's lib, eh? Hang on, pet, I'll be up in a jiffy.'

Jayne bit her lip in an effort not to react to John's sarcastic wit. She watched John slowly and very cautiously climb onto the boat's roof before carefully, one slippery and slimy rung at a time, ascend an iron ladder. A ladder which went from the black surface of the water at the bottom of the lock to the top of the vertical greenly-slimed walls. As she did so, she reached out her left hand, the hand that held the paddle-key, to lean on the metal safety-railing that stood at the very edge of the lock to prevent anyone from falling into the water below.

Now, the safety-railing was secured at its base by sturdy bolts which unfortunately, over the fullness of time, had worn the holes in the base itself. This allowed the top of the railings to move perhaps a distance of four inches. When Jayne felt this movement as she leaned on the railing she panicked that she would lose her balance and fall into the water below. Therefore, she did what anyone in the circumstances would have done. She opened her left hand to grab at the top bar of the railings for support. PLOP! Into the murky waters of the bottom of the lock the paddle-key fell, never to be seen again.

Jayne's eyes popped with horror, as did her mouth. Slowly, she looked at John who had just managed to haul himself over the top of the lock having completed his strenuous climb up the ladder. 'John,' Jayne choked, her voice little more than a sheepish gurgle.

'Yes, pet,' John answered, breathless from his climb.

'I've dropped the paddle-key in the lock.'

'Oh, balls!' John shouted. 'Shit, shit and double shit! How the hell did you do that?'

'Well, I . . .'

John wasn't listening. With a constant flow of blasphemous comments in which 'bloody woman, sod it and shit' seemed quite prevalent, John disappeared back down the slime-covered ladder.

Fortunately, there was another paddle-key in the storage-locker aboard *Frig-It* so all was not lost and John was able to raise the paddles on the upstream gates and successfully flood the lock. Unfortunately, John, because he was in a fit of temper went at the offending paddles like a bull-at-a-gate. In fact, such were his efforts and show of manly muscle-power that, with the noisy tearing sound of r-r-r-r-r-r-i-p, the jacket of his £3.50 wet-gear split from shoulder to buttocks. Meanwhile, by means of a similar ripping sound the seat of his wet-gear trousers split and gaped wide open sufficiently to show John's very skimpy underpants.

Jayne could not control her laughter in spite of John's blood-curdling scream. There was John, red in the face as he desperately turned the long handle of the paddle with both hands, hood up against the rain but with all of his sweater-covered back open to the ghastly elements. The only show of colour in the entire scene was John's bright red shreddies as they peeped from his split trousers.

'Nice underpants, John. Always thought that you looked sexy in red.'

John had to see the funny side of the events. Soon he was as doubled-up with laughter as Jayne. 'The only part of me that's not wet is my bloody head,' he roared. 'That's 'cos the only part of my wet gear that's serviceable is the bloody hood!'

Ten minutes later they were fully under control and chugging along through the rain as happy as pigs in muck, even though John was totally saturated with rain. Later that afternoon, they passed through a small town where they moored-up, bought a roll of wide plastic sticky-tape, and repaired John's wet gear. Upon completion of the repair John looked a bit strange with the light-grey of the tape against the dark-green of the wet-gear, but he didn't care. It kept him dry.

'Come on, Stripey,' teased Jayne as they set off once more. 'Any chance of a little kiss from my little pet zebra?'

'No chance,' grunted John, enjoying the teasing. 'Anyway, it's better to look silly and be sensible than look sensible and be silly. My old Dad told me that.'

The next four locks went as smoothly as silk with the pattern of operation now set. John operated the locks because he was physically stronger, and Jayne drove the boat through them because she had no choice. And their system worked very well particularly when Jayne's confidence and steering skills grew to such a level that she could enter and leave the lock with only one half of the lock-gates open. This actually halved the workload on John.

Soon, they reached their first swing-bridge, a bridge which carried a road or track over its span but was so low over the canal that a narrowboat could not pass underneath it. Reserved mooring facilities were also provided at this swing-bridge, so that after mooring *Frig-It,* John and Jayne went to investigate how it worked.

It was simple. You merely crossed the bridge to undo a padlock which locked the bridge into position. Then re-crossing the bridge it was relatively easy to push on the bridge structure thus causing it to swing away from the canal to allow the boat to pass through.

Jayne operated the bridge easily, so it was agreed that throughout the remaining five days of the trip John would operate the locks while Jayne would operate the swing-bridges.

'This plan will enable both of us to practice the driving and mooring of the boat,' John said. 'But don't forget Jayne, when you step off the boat to . . .'

'I know,' Jayne interrupted, mimicking John's deep voice. 'Watch you don't slip on the slimy plank.' She sighed. 'John, I'm not a child so don't keep nagging me.'

However, John had the last laugh of the day. When they came to the next swing-bridge, Jayne, when laboriously putting her weight against the structure of the bridge in her commendable efforts to open it, split the seat and leg of her wet-gear trousers.

'Very, very sexy,' sighed John as she flapped towards him panties and bare thigh on open display. 'Thank the good Lord for sticky-tape, eh? Do you fancy a little bit of hanky-panky when you take your trousers off to repair them? You know, Jayne, a bit of passion in the mud?'

'No, thank you.' There was no hesitation in Jayne's reply.

A Gaze into Holidaze

'Well, at least I know where I stand,' John laughed as he eased away from the mooring and into the centre of the canal.

Just as it was getting dark they moored at a very nice country-pub that was situated right alongside the canal. Here they rounded off the day with a splendid bar meal and a few pints of the local ale.

It was here that they met a middle-aged couple who apparently were moored a couple of hundred yards further along the canal. In conversation with the pair, John and Jayne found that they were going in the same direction along the canal but, where John and Jayne were turning *Frig-It* around at Devizes, the couple were going on for the next few weeks during which they hoped to reach the River Thames and eventually London.

John and Jayne thought that they were a nice enough couple but it was painfully obvious to them that the man was very much in charge and utterly dominant in the relationship, whereas the woman was very inoffensive and totally under the thumb of her husband.

'Allow me to introduce us,' the man said after a few minutes of conversation. 'This is my lady-wife, Tilley, as in lamp.' His laughter bellowed through the almost deserted public-house. 'I am Major Hugh Greenfield and I have just retired from the Army, what?'

'Pleased to meet you,' said John. 'This is . . .'

The man interrupted rudely. 'But you may call me Sir or Major.' Again the booming, loud laughter.

About an hour later and on their way back to *Frig-It* from the pub, Jayne asked what John thought of the couple.

'I though Tilley was nice but Colonel Blimp got on my tits a bit,' John replied frankly.

'My sentiments exactly,' whispered Jayne. 'That poor woman nearly jumped out of her skin every time he spoke to her.'

'He didn't speak to her,' John said. 'He ordered her and commanded her. That lady was a bag of nerves all night.'

'Not a bit of wonder the way he treated her,' Jayne said. 'I think he believes that he is still in the Army.'

'Nothing to do with us, Jayne. We'll not see them again.'

But John was wrong. The following sunny and clear morning, after about an hour's travel along the canal, John and Jayne came to their first lock. The down-stream gates were wide open and there, already inside the lock, was one of the longest narrowboats that John had ever seen. It must have been a seventy-footer if it was an inch. There, on the stern tiller-platform, were Tilley and Colonel Blimp.

'Thought you'd arrive soon, what?' Blimp bellowed as John jumped onto the mooring platform. 'What about operating the lock seeing as you're there, my old chum.'

'I bloody knew it,' hissed John out of the corner of his mouth. 'The lazy bastard is going to get an effortless lift up the lock while I do all the donkey work.'

'Oh, don't make a fuss, John. You're younger than he is so go and help him.'

John didn't have time to reply. 'Come on, Jayne, old girl,' boomed Blimp loudly. 'There's plenty of room for two boats alongside each other in here. You can have a lift with us.'

Jayne looked at John. 'What shall I do, John? I'm a bit nervous to go in the lock with the other boat. It looks very narrow to drive in there and park alongside him. Is there enough room for two boats at the same time inside the lock?'

'Jayne doesn't fancy it,' John shouted to Blimp. 'You go on ahead. I'll operate the lock for you and then I'll refill it for ourselves.'

'Nonsense!' blared Blimp. 'Come on now, Jayne, do as you're told. Chop! Chop!'

'The bastard! I'll give him bloody chop, chop.'

But John's annoyance was in vain. Jayne had already moved the boat out from the jetty and was chugging towards the narrow gap between Blimp's boat and the wall of the lock.

John watched worriedly, but his fears soon proved to be unfounded. He was so proud as Jayne, like a true professional, entered the narrow gap between Blimp's boat and the wall of the lock. Satisfied, he closed the down-stream lock-gates and lowered the paddles before opening the paddles of the up-stream gates. Slowly and side-by-side the two boats successfully rose to the top of the lock. Throughout the entire process, Blimp never ceased to bark orders at Tilley, orders that were totally unnecessary and orders that only succeeded in getting the poor woman in a terrible fluster.

'Nothing to it, old sport,' Blimp shouted as John pushed the heavy lock-gates open, to allow both boats to continue upstream. 'We'll carry on first to the next lock and you can follow us.'

'Are you going to help me at the next lock?' John demanded coldly. 'Or do I do all the work?'

'No, old sport, not at all,' Blimp replied as he steered his narrowboat out of the lock, leaving Jayne rocking in the wash. 'Tilley will help you at the next lock, won't you Tilley, old girl?'

When they arrived at the next lock, Blimp was idly drifting in mid-canal waiting for the gates to be opened. Tilley was on the top of the lock waiting for John who soon leapt off *Frig-It* and ran up the steps to join her. Because the level of the water in the lock was the same level as the down-stream water-level of the canal, the lower lock-gates opened easily. Tilley tried her best to help with the paddles and gates but frankly her efforts were almost useless. Kindly and as gently as he could so as not to embarrass the poor woman, John told her to keep out of the way.

Soon after John had opened and closed the appropriate paddles, both boats were in the lock and rising, yet again to Blimp's usual booming, meaningless and superfluous orders.

However, for some reason which John failed to

see, Blimp's boat kept drifting to the back of the lock to strike the lower-gates with a considerable thud. He would then drive the boat forward on her engines only to be immediately pushed back against the gates with the same sickening thud once he had selected a neutral gear. The lock was half-full when Blimp drove the boat right forward for his bow to touch the upper-gates thus leaving a big gap between his stern and the lower-gates.

'Tilley!' Blimp ordered, his voice loud and authoritative. 'Catch this stern-rope when I throw it up and secure me to a bollard. I want to stop this damned boat from drifting back.' Quickly he threw the rope upwards from the tiller-platform.

Well, it could have been the bad throw that snaked the rope upwards well astern of where Blimp intended. It could have been Tilley's keenness, or fearful nervousness in helping her husband. It could simply have been her plain awkwardness in helping her husband. In any event, she leaned over the lock too far and, with an ear-splitting shriek, plunged headfirst for about six feet before hitting the surface of the water in the lock with a gigantic splash.

'God!' yelled Blimp. 'She can't swim.' In a flash and without a moment's hesitation, he jumped over the stern of his boat and disappeared into the dark waters of the lock. Five seconds later he surfaced with the struggling Tilley. Slowly the big narrowboat of Blimp started to drift backwards towards the two figures in the water.

JOHN BEVERLEY

'Bloody hell!' shouted John in alarm. 'They'll get crushed against the lock-gates.' In almost the same time that it took to make the statement, John did three things. First, he ripped the lifebelt that was kept for such emergencies from its wooden holder on the top of the lock and slung it into the water where Blimp and Tilley struggled to keep afloat. Second, he jumped from the top of the lock onto the tiller-platform of Blimp's boat and slammed the throttle forward, forcing the idling engine to propel the boat away from the two struggling figures. Third, he leapt back onto the top of the lock and tied-up the bow of Blimp's boat to a bollard so that it could not under any circumstances move backwards.

Ten minutes later, both boats were safely moored outside the lock and the blanket-covered Blimp and Tilley were in their cabin. Accompanied by John and Jayne they were drinking gallons of hot toddy, a blend of whiskey, sugar and scalding hot water.

'Are you sure that you are alright?' Jayne asked Tilley who sat and sipped her drink, her face positively glowing.

'Yes, thank you, Jayne, I'm fine. It was a bit of a shock at the time but I'm okay now.'

'Bloody silly thing to do, what?' Blimp said jokingly.

'A bloody silly thing to do,' John said flatly. 'You frightened the brown stuff out of me. You could have been crushed or caught in the propeller – or simply drowned.'

A Gaze into Holidaze

Blimp held out his hand causing the blanket to slip open to reveal his huge stomach. 'Can't drown if you've got a permanent lifebelt round your middle like me. Anyway, thanks to you, old boy, me and the old girl didn't really come to any lasting harm.'

John took his hand and shook it warmly. 'Are you going on now?' he said sarcastically with a smile. 'If you are, I'll open all the locks for you to save you the work.'

Blimp's eyes twinkled mischievously. 'Point taken, old boy. Point taken.' He looked at Tilley. 'I don't suppose you feel up to moving today?' Tilley shook her head. 'I thought not.' He turned back to John. 'No, we'll stay here a couple of days to get our breath back before moving on. Better to be sure than sorry.'

'I couldn't agree more,' John replied.

John and Jayne said their goodbyes and left, leaving the middle-aged couple to recover in their own privacy and in their own time.

They chugged along the canal until dusk, enjoying the wonderful stillness and peace that the surrounding countryside brought them.

After they had moored for the night, yet again outside a charming country-inn, Jayne fed the ducks from the stern of the boat. Even a gathering of swans joined in the feast as they majestically arrived to bully the smaller ducks out of the way. Jayne was wise to their bully-swan tactics, and was careful to ensure that all of the river-visitors, ducks and swans alike, had a fair share of the available bread.

Our couple spent a very peaceful night until 7 a.m. sharp the following morning when there was a violent tapping on the bedroom-window that faced the canal.

'What's that?' whispered Jayne.

'I don't know,' replied John, still half-asleep. 'Rain I suppose.'

'It's not raining,' said Jayne urgently. 'I think someone wants to come in.'

'They can't come in from that side of the boat unless they can walk on water,' John snapped as he swung out of bed. 'In that case, I suppose it could be your mother because she claims to be able to do that, doesn't she?'

'Very funny, John, very funny.' Jayne paused as the loud tapping started again. 'There it is again, John. Something is wrong and somebody is trying to attract our attention.'

John pulled back the curtains of the bedroom in one bold sweep of his hands. Because of the deep aisle of the narrowboat, John's head was at a level about two-feet above the surface of the canal. It was this that allowed John to look straight into the black, staring eyes of two huge swans. As they saw him they moved their heads sharply forward and started pecking the window.

John's first reaction was to jump back in fright before it dawned on him what was happening. Laughing, he returned to the window and looked

A Gaze into Holidaze

past the huge heads of the two swans to see about fifty ducks bobbing up and down on the water. All parties were looking at John in earnest.

'You'd better get up, sweetheart. We have about fifty guests for breakfast.' He looked at the puzzled Jayne as she sat up in bed. 'Yes, darling, all of your mates have turned up and they want feeding.'

And fed they were, even before John was fed with his favourite bacon-and-egg sandwich washed down with a couple of steaming mugs of tea. As Jayne cooked the breakfast, John cast off and quite easily turned the narrowboat through one-hundred and eighty degrees in one of the wide turning-areas provided for that purpose at various locations on the canal. They were now heading back the way they had come.

'All good things come to an end,' said Jayne as she enjoyed the bright autumn sun that filtered through the overhanging trees as they slid along the canal.

'Not at all, Jayne,' John comforted. 'We've got a long way to go yet to get back to base and we've still got a couple of days left.'

'It's just that I'm having such a good time.'

'Me too, Jayne, me too,' John sighed. 'And it looks as if the weather is going to be kind to us for the remainder of the trip. Today is like a spring day and it's certainly great to get rid of the old stripey wet-gear. I felt like a bloody convict from Alcatraz in my wet-gear.'

The weather did hold for them, and they didn't

need to use their repaired wet-gear for the remainder of the adventure. All they needed were jeans, a heavy-woollen sweater and the inevitable Wellington boots to combat the muddy banks upon which they sometimes moored. The remainder of the trip went without incident other than perhaps one minor one and two not-so-minor ones.

The minor incident occurred when John was steering the narrowboat into the usual jetty adjacent to a lock. As he was pulling in he could see some young swans lurking in the water alongside the jetty. However, knowing that they would soon get out of the way, as swans and ducks always did when they saw a boat coming, he was not concerned.

Unfortunately, on this occasion they did not move. Before John even knew what was happening and certainly before he had a chance to do anything, two of the young swans were caught between the boat and the jetty. John frantically tried to steer the boat away from the swans whilst simultaneously ramming the throttle into reverse. However, the boat was going too slow to immediately respond to either tiller or engines, it merely slowed even more but still threatened to crush the two young swans who were by now screeching loudly at the threat of being turned into a pâté.

John scrambled along the narrow ledge which ran the length of the narrowboat until he stood directly over the two panicking birds. By now the birds were desperately flapping their wings in an effort to rise away from the hull that was trapping them against the jetty. The terrified squawking, accompanied by an occasional puff of shredded feathers, was a very disturbing event that would undoubtedly melt the heart of any normal animal-loving human being.

John rammed his Wellington-boot against the top of the jetty and with his back against the cabin, pushed back with all of his might. Slowly, very slowly, the heavy hull moved backwards away from the wooden jetty, releasing the trapped swans who immediately flapped away as fast as the combination of webbed-feet and wings would allow them.

'Thank God they are alright,' John sighed to himself as he scrambled back along the narrow ledge towards the tiller-flat.

Suddenly, like a bat-out-of-hell and with wings fully extended to gain maximum speed and aggression, came Mummy Swan. Sensing that her babies were in danger, she literally flew at John and attacked him with a combination of hissing and pecking with no holds barred.

John could do nothing to defend himself because he was grimly hanging-on with both hands to the support-rail on the roof of the boat. If he let go for a second he knew that he would fall into the canal and be trapped between the hull and jetty as the young swans had been. He was also very concerned about the possible pecking of his unprotected matrimonial equipment, but all he could do about this was to lean heavily against the side of the boat, keeping his pride and joy covered from the marauding and squawking fiend.

Through frantically flapping wings and a large head that held a sharp beak and black, angry eyes that was inches from his face, John gauged how far the boat was from the jetty. About a metre or more. That was close enough. He leapt from the narrow ledge of the boat and landed firmly on the jetty to run as fast as he could to the tiller-flat, hissing and viciously-pecking swan on his heels every hurried step of the way.

Gaining the tiller-flat, he charged down the steps into the kitchen, slamming and bolting the door behind him. Finally, he flopped onto a chair with a loud sigh.

'You seem flustered,' said Jayne, who had been in the toilet all of the time and with the cabin radio going, had heard nothing of the calamity outside.

John looked up. 'Just had a visit from one of your friends who told me, in her own way, that her children weren't ready for orange sauce at this particular time!'

John did not leave the protection of the cabin for at least another hour.

The first not-so-minor incident happened about two hours later when John, yet again, was coming-in very steadily to moor at yet another wooden jetty at yet another lock. It was just getting dusk and Jayne was busy in the kitchen as John made a perfect landing alongside the jetty. To tie-up midship, he cockily grabbed the twenty-foot midship line and even more cockily jumped from the tiller-flat onto the wood of the jetty. To be more precise, he landed with one foot on the slippery-slimy plank that he had warned Jayne about so often.

As soon as his weight went onto his Wellingtoned foot, it shot out from under him causing him to topple backwards and, by half-twisting his upper body, grab desperately at the only thing possible to stop him going into the canal – the very edge-combing of the tiller-flat. This downward momentum produced by the weight of his body caused the boat to move away from the jetty such that the other one of his Wellington-booted legs went into the canal right up to the top of his thigh, the boot rapidly filling with black canal-water.

So, there was John. In the blink of any eye, John had become a human, somewhat sagging, bridge between land and boat. He had the heel of one foot frenziedly searching for a grip on the slippery wooden jetty, the other foot dangling deep into the canal whilst his hands clung on so desperately to the edge-combing of the tiller-flat, that his fingers gouged small indents into the wood. All the time, because of the acute strain that John was forced to apply to his body in his attempt to drag the boat nearer to the jetty, John's eyeballs stood out like hat-pegs, the six-pack of his stomach muscles became more like a firkin, his buttocks and teeth were firmly clenched and his anus was puckered like a rosebud. – No chance! – The boat stubbornly remained in a state of equilibrium about five feet from the jetty.

'Jayne, help me,' John croaked with the massive effort of keeping his body about two feet above the surface of the canal. No answer.

'Jayne, for fuck's sake help me!' This time the shout was emotionally much louder because John knew that he could not hold on much longer. Already his entire body was shaking and convulsing under the strain.

'Why are you doing that?' Jayne asked casually as she looked down at John from the tiller-flat.

'About bloody time you showed yourself,' John wheezed. 'For Christ's sake, jump ashore and pull the boat in – now!'

The entire incident had only taken about a minute from John's slipping on the jetty to his embarrassed recovery. The effort had been more than considerable and so he remained doubled-up for a few minutes, holding his stomach painfully and fighting to get his breath back.

When John explained to Jayne what had happened, she burst out laughing and showed him little sympathy.

'Trust you to laugh,' John said as he painfully straightened-up and removed the water-filled Wellington boot.

'Well, John, you've got to admit something,' Jayne grinned wickedly. 'I've warned you about that plank often enough, haven't I?'

The last not-so-minor incident happened on the last day of the holiday. Because John and Jayne had made good time travelling back to Monkton Combe they actually had a day to spare.

A Gaze into Holidaze

'We'll pop up to Bath,' said John decisively. 'We can then spend the night there at a great little pub I know and move on to the flight of seven locks in the morning. We can then be back in plenty of time to give the boat back to the yard.'

And that's what they did. They had a great night in a very old and charming pub at Bathampton before going on to the seven or so locks at Bath.

They had descended about two locks in the flight when John made a decision. 'I think this is a waste of time that we don't really have.'

'Why?' asked Jayne who was at the tiller and had already enjoyed the driving through the two locks.

'Well, we've experienced about twenty-five locks and God knows how many swing-bridges up to now. Going down this flight is just a waste of time. We are at a turning-point in the canal so if we turn *Frig-It* around and go back up the two locks, we can be back in Monkton Combe in the early afternoon. This means that we can make an earlier start back to Cornwall and Clarence.'

Jayne readily agreed and in the next ten minutes swung *Frig-It* into a perfectly manoeuvred five-point turn to moor the boat at the base of the first of the two locks. They were now ready for the ascent.

No problem. The first lock went as smoothly as silk and Jayne chugged out the other side and went on a distance of about a hundred and fifty yards to moor at the base of the second and final lock. Patiently she waited for John.

While Jayne was doing this, John was busy doing his bits and pieces to the first lock. After he had closed the lock-gates and dropped the paddles, which was customary and courteous for other canal-users, John spotted an instruction on a notice-board at the side of the lock. The instruction was simple and asked all lock-users to empty the lock of water after use. Although an unusual request, John set about complying with the instructions without complaint. Although it would take another ten minutes or so to empty the lock, rules were rules as far as John was concerned. It was whilst undergoing this task that John heard Jayne's frantic yet angry scream which tore across the hundred and fifty yards of canal-bank.

'John, come and help me with this fucking boat, will you?'

John was shocked and could not believe his ears. He had never since he had known her, heard Jayne swear in any shape or form. Not a 'bloody', 'bugger' or 'shit' had passed her lips let alone 'fucking' in her description of the boat.

Quickly, he turned to look at Jayne and took in the problem at a glance. Jayne was bent over almost double on the very edge of the jetty with perhaps a foot of space left before she would be well and truly in the canal. In both hands she held the very last foot of the twenty-foot midship line which had allowed the boat to drift way out into the wide canal. In spite of Jayne's crouching as low as she possibly could in her attempt to hold the narrow-

A Gaze into Holidaze

boat, gradually *Frig-It* was pulling Jayne closer and closer to the edge of the jetty. Soon, either Jayne would have to let go of the rope or she would be in the canal, she had no other choice.

John left his chores at the first lock like a sprinter leaving his starting blocks. He ran and ran as fast as he could but knew in his mind that there was little chance of his reaching Jayne before the inevitable happened. He was within thirty yards when he heard another frantic shout from Jayne.

'Oh, John!' she screamed at the very top of her voice. 'The fucking boat is getting away!'

'Can I help?' came the gentle and cultured voice from behind Jayne.

Jayne looked over her shoulder as she struggled with the weight of the boat. There, with arms reaching out to help her, was a middle-aged priest.

'G-g-gosh,' stammered Jayne. 'I am sorry, vicar. I didn't see you standing there.'

'Not at all, my child,' the vicar replied as he grabbed and hauled back on the rope.

By now John had arrived and between the three of them soon had *Frig-It* safely moored.

'I truly am sorry, vicar,' said Jayne as she held out her hand to the man.

'Don't worry about it, my child,' the vicar said, laughing as he took Jayne's offered hand. 'Under the circumstances I would probably have said the same thing. Goodbye to you.' With that he doffed his hat and continued at a brisk walk down the canal-path.

John grinned at the departing figure. 'Bet he's never heard such language, Jayne. You ought to be ashamed of yourself.'

'I am,' replied Jayne. 'I don't know what came over me. I just panicked and the boat just made me so angry.'

'What happened?' John asked quietly as they sat in the stern of *Frig-It*.

Jayne looked at John and took a deep breath. 'Yesterday, if you remember, we saw a boatload of women going through the locks. Well I thought that if they can operate the things then so can I.'

John sighed deeply. 'Go on, Jayne.'

'Well, you were a long time at that first lock so I thought to save time and to help you, I would see if I could open the down-stream lock-gates for you. So I left the boat tied-up and started up the steps to the top of the lock. By chance I happened to glance around, I don't know why, and I could see the rope slipping around the bollard and the boat drifting out into the centre of the canal.'

'Didn't the double-hitch hold?' John asked.

Jayne looked at the floor of the tiller-platform and said nothing.

'You didn't tie a double-hitch knot, did you, Jayne?'

'I forgot,' Jayne whispered.

'Well, you certainly won't forget again, will you?' John laughed. 'You know between us we're a right couple of plonkers, aren't we?'

'You're a bigger plonker than I am,' replied Jayne. 'Am I forgiven?'

A Gaze into Holidaze

'Come 'ere,' John growled teasingly as he lifted Jayne to her feet and kissed her lovingly.

On the drive back to Falmouth, John and Jayne just talked and laughed about their seven-day adventure on the narrowboat.

'Did you enjoy it?' John asked.

'I loved every minute of it.'

'Would you like to do it again?'

Within a week they had booked up another seven-day trip with the same company for the following year. This time they planned to sail the hostile waters of the Welsh canals around Llangollen, in deepest North Wales.

****

And it's got its own pool . . .

This particular year found John and Jayne staying for two whole months at their favourite campsite in Palafrugell, on the Costa Brava.

'We have found our haven and our heaven, John,' Jayne said time and time again whenever they were there. There was no doubt about the fact that, circumstances permitting, one day they would live there permanently. The beauty and climate of the place was second to none and the people, Catalonians, were extremely friendly, welcoming and helpful.

In fact, the only snag that John and Jayne found with Catalonia was the language. The Catalonian language was as different from Castilian Spanish as Welsh was from English. This caused a number of problems to John and Jayne who were struggling to learn Spanish. Catalonian was a complete mystery to them.

With living in Spain in mind, John and Jayne decided that it would be a good experience for them to rent a villa somewhere in the region for two months the following year. This meant that during their current stay in Clarence, they would hunt around all the numerous letting-agencies in the area and find a suitable villa.

This they did during the first two-weeks of the holiday but so far had not found anything that they particularly fancied. Most villas were either too small, too big or simply too expensive. There were plenty of apartments for rent, but John considered that most of these would probably be far too noisy to meet their needs. Peace and quiet was everything.

After one particular visit to an estate-agent and having been shown several apartments, John and Jayne were a little despondent. 'God, Jayne, I reckon the walls in some of those places are so thin that you could hear a man having a pee, not to mention breaking wind,' John said. 'What we want is a nice villa tucked away in a remote spot by the sea, preferably with its own pool.'

Jayne agreed. 'It's finding one to meet our budget is the problem, John.'

'We'll find one, Jayne. You mark my words, sweetheart, we will find one.'

A Gaze into Holidaze

And find one they did. In the last week of their holiday they were walking the pine-covered coastal-road which went from Begur to a splendid little resort called Aigua Blava. Just as the road reached the top of the descent from the high hills to the sea, they came across a dirt track which was just about wide enough for a car and led down through the pine forest towards the sea. At the top of this track, hammered into the hard ground at the side of the road, was a hand-painted sign. It read, 'Villa, Aquilar.'

'If my Spanish is on form,' said John, a small gleam of excitement in his eye. 'I reckon that that says there is a villa to rent down that track.'

'Your Spanish is correct, John.'

'Right, let's go and check it out.'

The track wandered and twisted gently downwards for the first half-a-mile, passing between three or four huge and beautiful villas as it did so. Then, for the next quarter-of-a-mile it wound through the pines to steeply and finally descend into a dead-end which was literally cut into the face of the hill. There, at the side of the track, again cut into the very hillside was a very large but very old villa. There was a wide iron gate leading into the obvious parking area of the villa, and wired on to this locked gate was another hand-written sign similar to the one at the side of the road. The sign read, 'Aquilar', and gave a telephone number to ring.

'I think that's a French number,' said John. 'Shall we give it a ring, Jayne?'

Jayne turned and looked down at the sea crashing on the rocks a hundred feet below them. She then looked up at the villa as it snuggled into the surrounding pine forest. 'Oh, it's fantastic, John. Just look at that fabulous panoramic view of the sea. Yes, let's ring the number by all means but I think that we should have a look around the villa first.'

'Well the place looks deserted and it's all shuttered up,' said John. 'Why don't we hop over this silly little wall and have a look-see.'

'Do you think it will be alright?' Jayne asked nervously.

'Of course it will,' said John confidently as he pushed Jayne towards the low wall. 'Come on, up you get.'

From the paved parking-area they climbed a steep flight of steps which turned sharply to the right to lead to a huge, tiled terrace. In the middle of this terrace was a large swimming-pool, the water of which looked very blue and inviting in the morning heat.

'I'm going up to the villa,' John said. 'I'll knock on the door and if no-one answers I'm going in for a dip. It's too good an opportunity to miss.'

'We haven't brought our cossies with us so we can't go in,' Jayne said firmly. 'Anyway, it's not our pool so we shouldn't go in.'

'Jayne, we are a married couple, mate,' John smiled mischievously, a wicked gleam in his eye. 'We'll do a bit of skinny-dipping, eh, Jayne?'

A Gaze into Holidaze

'That's what you think,' Jayne replied sharply.

Two minutes later, after knocking heavily on the front door of the villa and receiving no answer, John had stripped off and plunged into the cool clear water of the pool.

'Cor, it's gorgeous, Jayne,' shouted John as he splashed away merrily. 'Come on, in you come.'

Jayne looked around the area below them before carefully studying the villa and the remote forests behind it.

'There's no-one around for miles,' John encouraged, floating on his back in the water.

'Alright, but turn your head.' Thirty seconds later, her clothes neatly stacked at the side of the pool, she was in.

'There you are, Jayne,' John laughed as he swam across towards the fully immersed Jayne. 'Skinny-dipping at last.'

'Not really, John. I've still got my bra and pants on.'

John roared with laughter and splashed water teasingly into Jayne's face. 'Spoilsport, that's what you are. A bloody spoilsport!'

An hour later they had toured the entire surrounding gardens of the villa. Set into five separate terraces which rose, one above the other, the garden was laid fully to blossoming shrubs and bushes. Because it was mid-August, the blossoms were at their peak and their flowers gave a wonderfully scented fragrance to the still, hot air that surrounded the villa.

The villa itself was set on the second terrace above the pool. This was the largest of the tiled terraces and formed a wide patio outside the now shuttered patio-doors of the villa.

'John, it's magnificent,' sighed Jayne as she stood on the terrace, John's arm around her waist, her head on his shoulder, looking out at the sea which was carpeted below them. 'I would feel like a millionaire if we had this place for two months next year.'

'What about Clarence?' John asked playfully.

'Oh, I'm sure that Clarence wouldn't mind us leaving him home for one year,' Jayne said affectionately. Suddenly she became more serious. 'Do you think that we would be safe here, John? We are about a mile off the Begur road and it is a bit remote.'

'No problem,' assured John. 'Anyway, we've got some neighbours a half-mile or so up the road. What more do you want?'

'I'd love it, John. Do you think we could afford to rent it?'

'I'll let you know in the morning,' replied John. 'I think we might be pleasantly surprised. Yes, it's a good location and it's got its own pool but it is old and we don't know what it's like inside.'

'I don't care what it's like inside, John, because in Spain you and I live outside most of the time. I want it.'

'I'll ring first thing in the morning, pet.'

John was on the public-telephone of the camp-

A Gaze into Holidaze

site for a long time while Jayne remained on their pitch cooking breakfast. By the time that John returned from the telephone, Jayne was sitting at the laid table outside the caravan.

'How did it go?' Jayne asked, unable to hide the excitement on either her face or in her voice as she studied John's facial expression.

'Well, to be honest, I'm not sure that it's what we want,' John said, his face expressionless. 'I got the owner who is French as we guessed and lives in Lyon. However, his English was good so there was no communication difficulty. He only uses the villa in the spring so it is vacant for us next July and August if we want it.'

'Great,' said Jayne, puzzled by John's lack of enthusiasm. 'Go on, John, tell me about it.'

'Well,' John began slowly, his face still lacking any emotion whatsoever. 'It has four bedrooms, a kitchen, three bathrooms, a lounge and a dining room.'

'Wonderful,' said Jayne, still unable to understand John's aloofness.

'Oh yes,' John continued, 'I almost forgot. The rent also includes a twenty-foot diesel-boat which is permanently moored in the harbour at Llafranc.'

'A boat,' Jayne shouted in glee. 'Who would have thought of a boat and you have your European Boat Licence, John. Fantastic!'

John still remained unemotional, an almost bored expression on his face. 'There is only one problem, Jayne.'

'What's that, John?'

'Because it's only used mainly in the spring the place is a little run down which means we would have to clean it.'

'No problem!' shouted Jayne.

'Let me finish, Jayne.' John's face was even more serious as he shook his head slowly from side to side.

The excitement rapidly faded from Jayne's eyes to be replaced with bitter disappointment. 'I know what you are going to say, John,' she said quietly. 'We can't afford it, can we?'

John's solemn face turned to Jayne and his sad eyes held hers for a long moment. Then, with a sudden shout of, 'Yippee!' he leapt to his feet, grabbed Jayne around the waist and lifted her high in the air. 'It was a snip of a price,' he shouted, his eyes now sparkling with fun and pride. 'I've done a great deal and booked it for July and August next year. What do you think of that?'

'And the boat is included?' Jayne asked, bubbling over with excitement.

'And the boat is included. We even have automatic permission to park the car in the harbour car-park, and you know how difficult it is to park in Llafranc. I'm over the moon, darling, are you?'

In reply Jayne put her arms around John's neck and kissed him long and passionately. Finally, John broke away to gather his breath. 'Cor, Jayne, I should book a villa more often!' he whispered hoarsely.

A Gaze into Holidaze

In the first week of July of the following year, John and Jayne flew from Cardiff to Girona airport and collected their hired Peugeot motorcar. An hour later, in the late afternoon, they turned off the Begur-Aigua Blava road and bumped down the dry, dusty track. As they descended the final steep hundred yards to the dead-end, they turned the last corner and there, breathtakingly in front of them, was the magnificent cove above which the villa nestled.

'It's just magic,' sighed Jayne as the scenic spectacle hit her like a punch in the stomach.

'Yes, it is,' John agreed. 'I thought the last ten months would never pass and finally here we are. Well worth waiting for, eh, Jayne?'

'Yes, darling. Well worth waiting for.'

The key to the villa was hidden exactly where the French owner had said it would be and they entered the villa without difficulty. Inside it was dark and smelled very musty.

'First thing to do is to open the gates of the drive for me to get the car in off the track. Then I'll get these shutters down.'

'I would have thought that the owner would have done that for us,' Jayne said. 'After all, he's known we were coming for the last ten months.'

'I suppose you're right,' John agreed. 'Never mind, it won't take a jiffy after I've brought the car in. Then we can open the doors and windows and let some light and air into the place.'

It took more than a jiffy for John to remove what

proved to be very heavy, metal, internal shutters. After what seemed to be hours, but was in fact only fifteen minutes, John learned the method of removal of the heavy frameworks. However, he also learned that the only place to store these frameworks was upstairs in one of the bedrooms. This was fine for the upstairs shutters because John only had to carry them from the various bedrooms. However, for the shutters in the lounge, kitchen and dining-room it meant that John would be forced to make several journeys up the stairs carrying the large, awkwardly heavy items.

'I'll help you,' offered Jayne.

'Pet, you always muck-in whenever you can. On this occasion it's far too much for you because these damned shutters are very heavy. Thanks anyway, love.'

By six o'clock, over an hour later, John was carrying the last shutter up the stairs. He was wearing only a pair of shorts by this time and the perspiration was dripping off him onto the tiled floor.

'Might as well unzip my fly, Jayne,' John joked as he struggled up the stairs carrying the large framework.

'What do you mean?' Jayne quizzed.

'Well, if I carry like a donkey, I might as well look like one.'

Five minutes later John was finished and ran down the stairs into the kitchen where Jayne was preparing a salad.

A Gaze into Holidaze

'Think I'll have a bath,' he said. 'I must be starting to pong a bit after all that humping and dumping.'

'Do you want the good news or the bad news first?' Jayne stated, lips drawn back.

'Give me the bad news first,' said John warily.

'First, we have no water, hot or otherwise. I went for a bath earlier and there is nothing coming out of the taps, so obviously the water needs to be turned-on. Second, we have no lights so the mains needs to be turned-on also. It will be dark in another hour or so and we will need the lights.'

'What's the good news?'

'The good news is that I haven't found anything else wrong, yet,' answered Jayne. 'Well, nothing other than the house-phone has been cut-off so we have no contact with the outside world.'

'I'll get the owner to reconnect it,' said John. 'In the meantime, we have our mobile phone. No problem.'

John found the main fuse-box easily and soon the lights worked normally. The water-mains were a different kettle-of-fish however. John searched the villa high and low but failed to find the stopcock anywhere.

'I'll have to give the owner a ring,' said John. 'We cannot manage without water. Why the hell didn't Marcel, that's the owner's name by the way, leave a list of where things are. What a prat! I'll try and get him on the mobile. It should be no problem because we have a good signal here.'

But they didn't have a good signal. 'It's because

we are way down the hill and the fact that the villa is cut into the actual hillside itself doesn't help,' said John as he came in from the terraces outside in his attempts to telephone the owner.

'What are you going to do, John?'

'I have no choice. I'll have to drive back the few miles to Begur and use a public-telephone. I shouldn't be more than half-an-hour. Will you be alright here on your own?'

'Of course I will,' replied Jayne.

Over an hour later John returned to find a very worried Jayne sitting on the terrace in the dark. 'I'm sorry, love, but the bloody phones wouldn't take coins and I had to hunt around for a phone-card. I expect you were frightened.'

'I'm okay,' answered Jayne bravely. 'It's you I was more worried about. Did you get sorted out about the water stopcock?'

'Yes. It's at the top of the bloody garden of all places. Never mind, I've got a torch in the car so I'll soon find it. Oh yes, and Marcel has agreed to have the telephone reconnected forthwith. That will be a blessing considering our lack of signal on the mobile.'

Because the top of the garden was a huge area, it took John another half-an-hour, accompanied with the most foul and profane Anglo-Saxon swearing – as he was well out of earshot of Jayne – before the offending stopcock was found. It took another quarter-of-an-hour for John to open the badly-corroded stopcock with the aid of a long-searched-for branch of a tree. It was now nine o'clock in the evening when John joined the ever-patient Jayne on the terrace outside the lounge.

'Well, we've got water now,' said John. 'Half-an-hour and we'll have hot water.'

'Do you know where the immersion heater switch is?'

'It's on,' replied John. 'Marcel told me where the switch was. Then a quick shower and we'll pop down to Aigua Blava for a meal and a bottle of wine. How does that sound?'

'Great,' answered Jayne. 'I've made a bed up for us while you were playing with the shutters. What about unpacking?'

'Leave it until the morning. Everything looks better in the daylight.'

And in the daylight everything did look better. Which was just as well because an inspection of the inside of the villa showed it to be very old and very worn. The walls were tired-looking and badly needed decorating, whereas the furniture was old, scratched, very French and ridiculously uncomfortable.

'Doesn't matter,' said John. 'As you said Jayne, we spend most of the time outside and we have that lovely view together with an even lovelier pool – and there's the boat. Tell you what, let's have breakfast, unpack and then go and see the boat. I know you said that today we'd relax around the pool after settling-in, but it's only ten miles or less to Llafranc. At least we can go and sit in the boat if nothing else.'

'Just sit in it?' queried Jayne, cautiously.

'Just sit in it,' agreed John. 'Honest. I know how tired you are because you didn't sleep much last night. So we'll just go and sit in the boat to get a feel for it. Then we'll come back and lie by the pool.'

'Promise, John?'

'Promise, and scout's honour,' John teased.

Half-an-hour later, after introducing themselves to the harbour-master and getting the keys to the boat, they stood at the allocated quayside-mooring looking down at the vessel below them.

'Oh, it's lovely,' said Jayne as John stepped over the side and on to the boat.

And it was. It was at least a twenty-feet long open-boat with a stern-tiller and a centrally mounted in-board diesel-engine. In the bow and stern were two masts which were rigged not with sail, but with a sail-like canvas for providing shade to the occupants when required at sea. All around the large tiller-platform were wooden seats and in the very bow was a raised locker in which the anchor, some life jackets and various ropes and nautical equipment was stored. The condition of the boat was excellent.

John helped Jayne into the stern of the boat where they both sat in the hot sun and held hands.

'Great, isn't it, Jayne?' said John, grinning like a schoolboy.

'Yes, it is,' answered Jayne. 'It's so calm here the boat is hardly rocking at all.'

'That's 'cos we're in the harbour.' John paused and then asked a question, innocently. 'Shall I just start her up, Jayne, just to see if she is in working order?'

Jayne said nothing and just smiled. As the engine coughed into life she thought, 'John must think I'm green. The next thing will be to ask for a little ride around the harbour.'

'It's very calm, Jayne. What do you say to a little trip around the harbour?' John asked matter-of-factly.

'Just in the harbour and nothing more,' Jayne insisted.

Quite professionally, John reversed the boat away from its mooring and chugged gently around the narrow passages of water between the dozens of moored boats of all shapes and sizes that bobbed up and down as they passed.

'Aw, come on, Jayne,' shouted John loudly above the noise of the engine. 'We might as well go just a little way out to sea.'

'It looks a bit choppy to me,' Jayne shouted back.

'Nonsense,' declared John. 'You are in very safe hands. Trust me!'

The sea wasn't very choppy at all when they rounded the harbour wall – it was downright rough. This caused the boat, which was very shallowly drafted, to ride quite ruggedly up and down what looked to be huge waves and troughs. Jayne said nothing as she sat quietly and nervously in the stern of the boat.

However, in no time at all she actually loved it especially when she saw how well John handled the boat. After about an hour of total wind-blowing, tossing around-all-shapes, pitching and rolling, they returned into the protection of the ruggedly-craggy high wall of the harbour.

'Did you enjoy that, Jayne?' John asked as he slowly and carefully guided the boat into its allocated mooring.

'It was wonderful,' replied Jayne as John jumped out of the boat to tie-up. 'Shall I help you to tie-up, John?'

'No need this time,' John said masterfully as he bent and tied a couple of double-hitches to secure the bow and stern lines. 'I'll teach you how to tie-up next time.' Jumping back aboard the boat he continued. 'I'll just shut the engine down now and bob's-your-uncle, we'll go back to the villa.'

He turned the ignition key and – nothing happened, the engine still continued to throb.

'Oh yes, silly me,' said John in a voice designed to impress Jayne on his uncanny knowledge of all things marine. 'Of course, this is a diesel. To stop the engine all you have to do is press this little button here.' He leaned over and pressed a short, black button that protruded out of the central panel just below the ignition switch. 'There,' he said confidently.

'Throb, throb, throb, throb,' said the engine.

'Shit! Shit! Shit! Shit!' said John. 'I can't switch the bloody engine off. Oh, bollocks!'

For the next quarter-of-an-hour, Jayne sat quietly and unobtrusively in the stern of the boat trying to

A Gaze into Holidaze

hide the blushing embarrassment that she felt as she saw the mocking half-smiles on the faces of the holidaymakers who passed along the quayside. Meanwhile, John, backside in the air most of the time, wrestled inside the engine-housing frantically pulling at any lever that showed itself in an attempt to stifle that constant throb, throb, throb of the engine.

Finally, he straightened and looked blankly across the harbour. 'Bloody, soddin', shittin' boat,' he said as he took a big kick at the side of the engine-housing which, in view of the fact that he was wearing just flip-flops, was not one of John's better ideas.

'Ow!' he yelled, more in frustration and disgust at his helplessness and stupidity than any pain that the kick had caused.

'Can I help?' asked Jayne calmly, trying to support her husband.

'Do you know how to throttle the living daylights out of this bastard engine?' John snarled. Jayne shook her head. 'Then you cannot,' he hissed. Then, realising that he had been undeservedly short with Jayne for a reason that wasn't remotely her fault, he apologised. 'Sorry, Jayne, that wasn't called for. It's just that I can't stop the little bugger and I don't know what to do. I don't know much about diesels and I've tried everything I can think of.'

'Won't it eventually run out of fuel?' Jayne asked innocently.

'Yes, but in about three bloody weeks at the rate this thing uses fuel,' replied John sarcastically.

'Shall I go and get help?' Jayne asked, a positive note in her voice. 'There must be somebody in the harbour who can help.'

'Yes, you better had,' John nodded sheepishly. 'I feel a right plonker and I suppose I should stay with the boat with this bloody engine running.'

Off Jayne went only to find that everyone in the harbour who should have known about boats, was at lunch or somewhere. There was no-one around who could possibly help. She rushed back to John to find him sitting despondently in the stern.

'Any luck?' asked John hopefully.

'Throb, throb, throb,' said the engine.

'No, John, everyone's at lunch. Even the old fishermen have disappeared.'

'Balls!' sighed John. 'Just my bloody luck.'

"Ere, can I help, mate?' The Cockney voice sounded close but John could only see a small lad of about ten years old standing on the quayside above the boat. He was thin and bare chested and wore over-sized shorts that came to well below his knees with the waist almost up to his nipples. He looked a comical sight.

'Was that you, son?' John asked him.

'Yeh!' came the reply. 'My Dad's got a boat like this one and 'e could never stop it when 'e first got it.' The boy jumped down uninvited into the boat. 'My Dad was told it's a common fault with this type of engine. 'E's 'ad it fixed proper now but what 'e used to do was this.'

A Gaze into Holidaze

The boy reached inside the engine and pulled off a red lead that was connected to something or other. The engine coughed, spluttered and ground to a halt after a couple more attempted but half-hearted throbs.

'Well done, mate,' John shouted with delight as he shook the boy's shoulder. 'I thought the damned engine was going to run forever. Thanks very much and thank your Dad for me, will you?'

The boy's face beamed with pride. 'That's okay,' he said. 'Glad I could 'elp.'

They shook hands and John slipped a ten-pound note into the boy's hand.

'Now, mister,' the boy said, looking down at the note in his open palm. 'I didn't do nuffink so I don't want this.'

'What's your name?' enquired John.

'George,' came the reply.

'Well, George, I'm John and that lady there is my wife, Jayne. Are you on holiday here, George?' The boy nodded. 'Well, that tenner should buy an ice-cream or two during your holiday. Take it with our pleasure 'cos you certainly earned it as far as I am concerned.'

'Okay, guv. Ta, I'm sure.' With that George, coyly blushing with gratitude, turned and ran along the quayside to disappear into the crowd of milling holidaymakers outside the harbour gates.

On their return to the villa, John was immediately on the telephone to Marcel to explain the fault in the boat's ignition system. Marcel apologised profusely and promised faithfully to contact the boat-contractor whom he used in Palafrugell, to get the fault rectified.

Within an hour of John's call, Marcel was back on the telephone. 'The fault will be fixed first thing in the morning, John, so please don't worry yourself any more. The engine will stop when you press the little black button below the ignition switch. You know the one?'

'I know the one,' John replied flatly.

Most of the next day John and Jayne relaxed by the swimming-pool lazing in the hot sun, which they had had since they saw it majestically rise out of the sea early that morning. The location of the villa was fantastic, providing absolute peace. In fact the only noise was that of the seagulls as they cried to each other, and the swish of the sea as it caressed the rocks a hundred feet below them.

After lunch they wandered down a steep and narrow path which twisted dangerously down the cliffs to a large craggy rock. This rock jutted out into the sea but curved around sufficiently to form a small, natural harbour about twenty-five yards wide.

'This is great,' said John as soon as he saw the expanse of calm water created by the rock. 'I've just got to fish this bit. You stay here and I'll get my fishing-gear.'

Ten minutes later, after a mad scramble up and down that dangerous cliff-path, John was back with Jayne armed with his rod and dangling a piece of cheese on the end of the line.

A Gaze into Holidaze

They had a very enjoyable hour of fishing, John dangling, Jayne watching. Unfortunately they caught absolutely nothing.

'I don't think fish like cheese,' said Jayne as John collapsed his telescopic fishing-rod.

'Of course they do,' John laughed. 'We do, don't we? Next time I'll put a piece of bread around the cheese because perhaps they would prefer a cheese-sandwich.'

On their return to the pool, Jayne sprawled out lazily on the sun-lounger while John dived into the pool and swam a few lengths.

'Ah, that's better,' John muttered as he climbed from the pool, water dripping from his very-tanned body. 'Fancy a gin-and-tonic, Jayne?'

'Love one,' Jayne replied.

'Right! I'll pop up to the villa and make one. Plenty of ice in the fridge I trust?'

'Should be,' Jayne answered. 'I put water in the ice-cube tray this morning and it should have frozen by now. However, the fridge is old and has seen better days so perhaps it hasn't had time to freeze the cubes yet.'

John bounded up the steps to the terrace above and still wet, walked bare-footed into the kitchen. Taking two glasses from the cupboard, he poured a generous amount of gin into each. Grabbing a lemon from the fruit bowl he quickly cut four thin slices and threw them into the waiting glasses.

'And now for the ice and tonic,' he said loudly and happily to the empty kitchen as he grabbed the handle of the fridge-door. There was a loud bang accompanied by a blue flash. This knocked John back against the table with such force that one of the glasses fell off the table and smashed to smithereens as it hit the tiled floor.

'Jesus Christ!' screamed John, instantly realising that because he had been standing in a small puddle of water made by his wet feet, his contact with the electrical appliance through its handle had electrocuted him in the form of a severe shock. He had been very, very lucky. He could have been killed.

At that point Jayne rushed in. 'What's happened, John? I heard you shout and then a glass smashing, I knew that something was wrong.'

'Keep back, Jayne,' John ordered sharply. 'The floor is wet and there is an electrical fault in the fridge making it live. Just wait right there for a minute and don't move.'

Very gingerly he reached into the kitchen-drawer and pulled out a pair of rubber gloves. He put them on his hands and without moving his feet even an inch, but with his right hand holding the back of a chair for extra support, he leaned his body towards the fridge as far as he could. Then, stretching his left arm to the full, making certain that he did not touch the fridge in any way, he took hold of the power-cable and pulled the fridge plug from the socket in the wall.

'There, it's safe now Jayne. You can come in.'

'Oh John,' she sobbed, crossing the short distance to take John in her arms to hold him to her. 'You could have been killed.'

'There, there,' John comforted her, smoothing her hair gently.

'I'll make you a nice cup of tea,' said Jayne. 'That'll calm you down.' Without another word, she released herself from John's arms and took the few bare-footed steps across the kitchen-floor to where the metal kettle stood on top of the electric-cooker. She reached for the kettle. 'Ow!' she shouted as she drew back her hand as if she had been scalded.

'What's the matter, Jayne?' John snapped.

'I just had an electric shock and it hurt,' Jayne replied, massaging her tingling arm.

'Shit!' shouted John. 'Again your feet are bare and must be wet from where you stood near me. And, it would appear that we now have a fucking faulty cooker!'

'Oh, please don't swear, John. That only makes it worse.'

'This bloody villa would make a saint swear!' John hissed as he crossed the kitchen in two strides and once again grabbed the cooker-cable and pulled the cooker-plug from the socket.

'It's safe now, Jayne,' snarled John, his temper getting the better of him. 'I'm no electrician but I don't think that this cooker should be plugged into a mere socket in the wall. It should have special wiring heavy enough to take the appropriate electrical current.'

Without another word he crossed the kitchen to the hall and picked up the telephone. 'Thank God we've got the house-phone back on line,' he muttered as he dialled the number. With lips drawn tightly back and teeth gritted he waited for the connection to be made.

'Marcel, is that you?' he eventually bellowed into the telephone. 'This is John . . . no, this is a bloody angry John . . . Why am I angry? Because you just nearly bloody-well killed me and my wife, that's why . . . How? By your soddin' ancient electrical equipment, that's how . . . .Yes, the fridge nearly killed me and the cooker nearly killed Jayne . . . Getting someone to call in the morning is not good enough, particularly when we cannot communicate with the sods . . . What do I want? I want you down here right now, that's what I want. The place is electrically dangerous and I hold you totally responsible . . . I know you live in Lyon, but hell, that's only about five hours drive away . . . So, it's night time. Drive through the bloody night, can't you? You've got things called headlights, haven't you? Well, let me put it this way, if you are not outside this villa with a decent electrician to check all of the internal wiring of this villa by eight o'clock tomorrow morning, I am going to call the police and the local council. Do I make myself absolutely clear?'

At eight o'clock the following morning a none-too-happy Marcel accompanied by a swarthy, grinning electrician knocked at the door of the villa.

'Good morning,' said John flatly. 'Thanks for coming with the electrician.' He glanced over the

A Gaze into Holidaze

shoulders of the two men at the choppy, grey sea and the black, stormy clouds. 'I see it has been raining heavily during the night so you must have had a miserable journey, Marcel.' John stared into the dark eyes of the Frenchman, his unblinking eyes causing the Frenchman to quickly look down at the floor in embarrassment. John went on. 'I would make you a splendid hot cup of coffee, Marcel, if the bloody cooker worked. My wife and I haven't had a hot meal or drink since breakfast yesterday.'

'I am so sorry, John,' Marcel grovelled. 'Let me instruct my electrician, Ramon, to carry out the electrical work that has to be done on the villa and then we can go outside and talk about the problem.'

'The bloody place is old and the wiring is old,' John said. 'The soddin' place needs complete rewiring. The only thing that seems to work here is the bloody pool and, give it a chance, we haven't been here long enough to allow it to break-down yet.'

'You won't have any trouble with the pool,' Marcel said with haste. 'It is serviced every two weeks and cleaned twice a week.'

John just snorted and went out through the patio-doors onto the terrace, leaving Marcel in the kitchen to instruct the electrician. Still angry about the failure of the electrics of the villa, John looked up at the stormy sky and leaned on the ornate iron railings that surrounded the terrace and patio area. He soon jumped up with a start as he felt a now-familiar sudden and hurtful tingling sensation that shot up his arm. 'God!' he whispered to himself. 'These bloody railings are live with electricity. Where the hell is that coming from?'

His search soon revealed what must have been the problem. At the edge of the patio area was an ornate metal light which was still switched-on from John and Jayne's activities of the night before. When John studied the electrics at the base of the lamp, he found that half of the plastic cover to the electrical control-box was completely missing. The obvious had then happened once the torrential rain of the previous night had poured onto the visibly-bare wires. John said nothing as Marcel joined him on the terrace.

'John, I can only apologise for what has happened but are you quite sure that you felt an electric shock last night in the kitchen?'

'Do you think I am stupid?' John snarled viciously. 'It's you who has rented out a seemingly dangerous villa. My wife is still in bed with shock and I think that I will have to get a doctor for her.' The last part was a bit of a lie really because Jayne was having a bit of a lie-in to overcome the effects of the champagne that they had drunk the night before.

'Come now, John, surely you are exaggerating,' Marcel said, plainly trying to calm the angry John down.

'Oh, yes,' John shouted. 'That's what you think,

is it? The place is falling apart so much that the wall holding up this very terrace is cracking.'

'What are you talking about?' Marcel questioned.

'The bloody wall holding up this terrace is cracked and weak,' John lied. 'You just lean over the railings and you will see it.'

Marcel hastily strode forward and placed both hands on the iron railings. There seemed to be a long buzzing sound. In this time Marcel physically shook from head to toe before he managed to tear himself from the railings. 'Holy Mary, Mother of God!' he gasped.

'Take my point?' John smirked as Marcel rubbed his hands painfully. 'Now I think you'll agree that regarding this villa you've neglected it and you've suffered severely from the BBB disease.'

Marcel looked up questioningly from his agonising hands. 'BBB? What is BBB disease?'

'Brains between buttocks!' John said flatly.

During the next fifteen minutes Marcel ate humble pie as if baked by his old mother. He gave John a rental reduction equivalent to two-weeks free accommodation and went immediately to Begur and Palafrugell to buy a brand-new fridge and electric cooker.

When Marcel returned back at the villa one hour later, he was followed by a van which when emptied revealed not only the new fridge and cooker, but a host of other electrical appliances. Namely, a chest-freezer, an electric-kettle, a toaster, two electric fan-heaters and a spin-drier. All were carried up the steps from the van to the kitchen by the driver and his assistant.

'There,' said Marcel as he joined John and the now fully-awake Jayne. 'I hope that this makes up for everything. Incidentally, the boat has also been repaired.'

John smiled for the first time. 'How long for the rewiring to be sorted out?'

'Ramon will be finished in two days if that is not too inconvenient to you?'

'Two days is fine,' John answered, the wicked gleam of old shining in his eyes. 'Fancy a coffee, Marcel?'

And that was the last they saw of Marcel. Ramon, the electrician, finished in two days as planned and from then on the electrics behaved perfectly for the remainder of the holidays.

Unfortunately, that wasn't the case with the plumbing. Two days later, on returning from Aigua Blava, John and Jayne were greeted as they walked into the hall of the villa by a torrential stream of smelly water with large lumpy-bits in it. This water flowed freely down the stairs to disappear under the door which led to an underground cellar.

'I hope that's not what I think it is,' said John none-too-casually as he ran up the stairs.

Jayne looked at the flow of water with distaste and wrinkled her nose at the disgusting smell. 'What is it, John?' she shouted, her voice resonating through the large hall.

'It's shit!' John said casually as he joined Jayne

back in the hall. 'The toilet on the top of the stairs is not just blocked it's overflowing because the ballcock in the cistern is broken off. Bloody Spanish plumbing pisses me off!'

'Oh, John, it's terrible,' said Jayne, recoiling at the stench.

John walked over to the flow of water and looked down into it. Then with a smile he turned to look at the serious-looking Jayne. 'I don't remember eating that, Jayne, do you?'

They both roared with laughter which echoed throughout the huge house.

Another quick telephone call to the ever-apologetic Marcel resulted in a plumber solving the problem a half-hour later. Furthermore, a host of cleaners arrived to re-clean the toilet, stairs, hall and cellar a few minutes after that.

'All's well that ends well,' laughed John, as he poured himself and Jayne a large brandy. They sat on the patio, looking out to sea at the huge fullmoon that had climbed slowly out of the ocean to bathe the panoramic view in its soft, sensual light.

Jayne raised her glass to John. 'Never a dull moment, eh, John?'

'Not with you around, darling, not with you around.'

For the next few days the weather continued to deteriorate and both the seas and the winds became very agitated. Rain was never very far away and the once-dusty track that led from the main coastal-road to the villa, became a muddy quagmire. The steep stretch of track had been virtually washed away to leave huge and deep potholes which caused the little Peugeot to catch its exhaust every time it attempted the hill.

It was during one of these downpours that John and Jayne were sitting in a very Spanish-type café in Begur when in walked that little rescuer, George. The people with him, John and Jayne assumed were his parents and grandparents.

'Hello, George,' greeted Jayne. 'What are you doing here?'

'Oh, I'm 'ere with me Mum and Dad and me Grandad and Grandma,' George replied cheekily.

'Nice to meet you,' John said to the adults. 'I'm the chap that George rescued when I couldn't stop the engine of my boat. George stopped it for me just like that.' John snapped his fingers.

'Yes,' said Dad, his accent more Devonshire than London. 'He told me all about it, and the tenner you gave him. It was very kind of you.'

'Not at all,' said John. 'Would you like to join us?'

George's parents and grandparents, who were actually staying in a caravan outside Begur, were very good company and a very pleasant afternoon was had by all, in spite of the torrential rain outside. As they were leaving, Jayne invited all of them over to the villa for a meal that night.

After discussion, it was agreed that it would be too late for little George to attend. However, because the grandparents readily volunteered to look after him, Dick and Dora, George's parents, would be

A Gaze into Holidaze

over the moon to come. John gave them instructions on how to find the villa and they agreed to meet at seven-thirty that night.

By 6 p.m. not only did the rain get much worse, but the winds became very high, causing the sea below the villa to be tremendously rough. In fact, when Dick and Dora arrived at precisely the agreed time of seven-thirty, the hearty meeting and greeting of the two couples when they met at the front door, was almost totally lost in the noise of the violent crashing of the waves against the rocks below.

'Cor, blimey!' exclaimed Dick in his Devonshire/London accent. 'What a night? It's not fit for a dog to be out on a night like this.'

'Dick didn't mean that the way it came out,' Dora said quickly, her accent heavily Cockney. 'We think that it's really lovely of you to ask us to your villa tonight. What Dick meant was that the weather is so awful for this time of year. You don't expect it in Spain, do you?'

'You certainly don't,' replied Jayne. 'You come to Spain for the sun because you can have any amount of this horrible weather at home.'

'No trouble finding the place then, Dick?' John asked politely.

'Not at all, John. Your directions were excellent and we followed them to the last letter.' Dick laughed. 'The only thing they didn't cover was where the knocker was on your front door.'

'Glad you made it okay,' John nodded. 'Well, it's wet and windy outside so let's get wet, but not windy inside, eh? What would the two of you like to drink?' Like John and Jayne, Dick's and Dora's preference was red wine so John poured four glasses and they settled in front of a huge open-fire that John had lit for the occasion.

Like in the afternoon, Dick and Dora proved to be excellent company. They had a lot in common with John and Jayne, particularly from the caravan-holidays point of view. Also, Dick was a mechanical engineer as John had been before he turned to lecturing, and Dora was a schoolteacher in a primary school.

Throughout dinner and the remainder of the night, all the four of them did was joke, laugh and drink lots of red wine. They discussed every subject under the sun including the untouchables of politics and religion, and although sometimes the conversation became a little heated, it was always lightened with an appropriate joke by either John or Dick.

'How's it going?' asked Jayne of John on one occasion when they were alone in the kitchen.

'Great,' John replied, eyes shining with the effects of the consumed alcohol. 'Dick's a great lad and he's a laugh a minute. How do you get along with Dora?'

'Fine,' Jayne answered. 'She's a really nice lady. From her accent you'd think that she was rough but she certainly is not. They are a lovely couple.'

'With a great lad called George,' John added.

The night went on and the jokes got funnier and

the men got drunker. Everyone was having a great time. Finally the conversation got round to hobbies.

'What do you think of fishing, John?' asked a slurring Dick.

'Done it,' replied an equally slurring John. 'Why don't we go and have a fish now? I've got two good sea-rods and . . . oh, I haven't got any bait.'

Jayne interrupted soberly. 'Come on you two, don't be so daft. It's eleven-thirty now and it's blowing a gale outside.'

'Fish better when it's rough,' Dick volunteered. 'Also fish better in the dark. Done any night fishing, John?'

'No!' John replied. 'Always wanted to though.'

'Come on then,' said Dick. 'What are we waiting for?'

'Now you behave yourself, Dick,' Dora chastised. 'You heard what Jayne said, it's too rough to go fishing.'

'And it's far too dangerous to go down that cliff-path to the lagoon,' Jayne insisted. 'One slip in the dark, and it is pitch dark out there with no lights, and you'll fall and break your necks.'

'Got a torch,' John slurred smugly.

'Right,' said Jayne, impatience coupled with anger in her voice. 'If you two walk through that door, Dora and I are going to bed.' Jayne turned to Dora and asked quickly, 'Will you stay the night, Dora?'

Dora nodded. 'I think that's a good idea. I don't think that Dick could drive up that track to the Begur road in this rain anyway.' Her expression became suddenly worried. 'Do you think it's really dangerous for the men to go down that cliff, Jayne?'

'Yes, I do,' Jayne replied. 'But how can you stop them?'

They both looked at the giggling men who were now dressed in cagoules and armed with the two sea-rods and a torch.

'Adiosh,' said John drunkenly. 'Keep my side of the bed warm.' Dick just giggled and followed John out into the driving rain, slamming the front-door behind him.

They were both halfway down that winding, slippery cliff-path before they realised two things. One, it was bloody dangerous and two, they didn't have any bait with which to fish.

'Shall we go back?' shouted Dick over the howling of the wind.

'Na!' replied John, full of intoxicated bravado. 'Who needs bait anyway? Tell you what, we'll fish and pretend the hook is a spinner.' Dick roared with laughter but the noise was torn immediately away from his mouth by the vicious wind.

It took them another quarter-of-an-hour to fumble across the last thirty yards of ruggedly sharp but very slippery rocks to reach the spot where the rocks curved to form the lagoon that John had previously discovered with Jayne.

'Bloody hell, it's rough out here,' declared a soakingly-wet Dick.

'Na!' answered an equally saturated John. 'Just a bit draughty, that's all. Come on, we'll get out to the end and fish in the lagoon. It's calmer in there.'

'You must be joking,' yelled Dick, getting more sober by the second. 'Look at the waves crashing over the end of the rocks, you'll never be able to stand up in that.'

'Yes I will,' insisted John, his pride not allowing him to back down.

'And there's a swell of at least ten feet in the lagoon,' argued Dick, who by now had completely lost his nerve. 'I'm staying here where I am. Sod the fishing.'

'Okay,' shouted John, his brains well situated somewhere between his buttocks. 'I'm going to the end. I'll bring you back a fish.'

But John never got as far as even pointing his rod at the sea. Within the next five yards of his determined, hands-and-knees crawl over the cruel rocks, a huge wave crashed against his prone body and hurled it against a jagged rock. On impact with the rock all the wind was knocked out of him. Simultaneously he was forced to release the fishing-rod from his grasp and the rod disappeared into the depths of the foaming lagoon. If it hadn't been for the huge rock, John would have been with his fishing-rod at the bottom of the sea, because he would have stood no chance in those boiling churning waters.

Dick wasn't so lucky. The next wave crashed into him to send him over backwards into the heaving waters of the lagoon. John watched fascinated as, with a terrifyingly long 'A-a-a-a-a-h-h-h-h,' which seemed to go on forever through Dick's slow-motion backward arc, Dick disappeared into the black, terrifying waters.

'Bloody hell!' John yelled, as he saw Dick's head break the foaming surface of the lagoon to be followed by his shoulders and arms as they thrashed about helplessly in an effort to keep afloat. One moment Dick was at the top of the swell and almost level with John, the next instant Dick was ten feet below John as the swell ebbed. This went on for about another ten panic-stricken waves until, suddenly and miraculously, the swell lifted Dick higher than previously and dumped him unceremoniously on his backside exactly on the spot where he had stood not sixty seconds previously.

Both men needed no further bidding. Like a couple of Olympic athletes with the acquired vision of night-owls, they not only reached the cliff-path in two seconds flat but scrambled up it, sometimes on all fours, to reach the front-door of the villa in a record time of about five minutes. Very impressive considering that the journey had taken them nearly half-an-hour going down, even with the light of the torch.

Jayne opened the front door and glowered at the two saturated, dripping figures. 'Gosh, that didn't take you very long, did it? You've only been gone about three-quarters-of-an-hour.'

The two men said nothing. They just stood there shivering and dripping, dripping and shivering.

'Catch anything?' Jayne went on flatly. 'Other than colds, obviously?' She studied them more carefully. 'Where are the two rods?'

A Gaze into Holidaze

'Gone,' replied John, his hand muffling his mouth.

'And your torch that my Mother gave you for Christmas?'

'Gone,' replied John, even more muffled.

'Well, you'd better come in and get some hot drinks inside you and some warm clothes on,' Jayne said as she stepped aside to allow the two men into the comfort of the fire-heated lounge.

'Good Lord!' exclaimed Dora when she saw Dick in front of the fire, steam slowly curling from his wet clothes. 'What happened to you, Dick?'

'I got swept into the sea by a big wave,' Dick answered meekly. 'This huge wave caught me and threw me backwards into the sea.'

'My God!' Dora shouted, her hands rushing to her mouth in horror.

The pale-faced Dick turned from the fire to face John and Jayne. 'You see, John, it could have been worse. In fact it could have been a lot worse.'

'Why Dick?' John asked, grinning in an effort to relieve the tension that showed on Dick's face. 'So you got a good dowsing in the briny, mate. So what?'

'I CAN'T SWIM!!'

Dick and Dora after a hearty breakfast, left the following morning. Dick by then appeared none the worse for his extraordinary fishing experience in the sea – well almost a fishing experience anyway – other than two hugely bruised and tender buttocks when the sea had dumped him back on the ragged rocks of dry land. Almost dry anyway!!

****

Throughout the entire two months of the holiday, John and Jayne had developed a waving acquaintanceship with a young Spanish couple who lived in the first villa at the top of the track. Or to be more precise, they had developed the waving relationship with the lady of that villa. Every time that John and Jayne passed the huge and very luxurious villa, a feat that they had to carry out whenever they went anywhere in the car, the woman would always give a friendly wave from the terrace, to which Jayne would wave in return. Accordingly, John would give a short hoot of acknowledgement on the horn of the Peugeot. On weekends when the man of the house was not at work, John and Jayne would receive a friendly wave from both of them.

Because the holiday was coming to a close, John suggested to Jayne that they invited the couple to dinner one evening.

'But I think that they are Spanish, John,' Jayne said.

'So?' questioned John.

'Well, what if they can't speak English? We can't speak much Spanish so how would we be able to communicate?'

'There you go with those negative waves,' teased John. 'Come on, Jayne, let's do it. It's time we broke away from the Brits and developed some Spanish relationships. Who knows, it might help us with our Spanish or lack of it?'

'What about dress for the evening?' Jayne asked.

A Gaze into Holidaze

'Scruff-order, of course,' John replied, his usual mischievous grin plucking at the corners of his mouth.

'How do you mean, scruff-order?'

'You know, Jayne, jockstrap and gaiters!'

'Oh, come on, John, be serious. You know that the Spanish when they are out to dinner, are always well dressed so we don't want to let them down.'

'Okay,' John agreed. 'I'll wear planters, you know, slacks, shirt and tie. You can wear a nice dress. How's that?'

John invited the couple, whose names turned out to be Juan and Anna, the very same day. Although Anna was not there when John drove up to the couple's villa, Juan readily accepted John's invitation in perfect English.

'Are you English?' asked John. 'I mean, we thought that you and your ... er ...'

'Wife,' Juan helped. 'Anna is my wife.'

'Well, my wife, Jayne, and I assumed that you were a Spanish couple.'

'We are Spanish,' Juan answered proudly. 'Or perhaps to be more precise, Catalonian.' John could now hear a faint foreign accent breaking through in Juan's speech. 'However, both Anna and I speak English also.'

'Wonderful,' John laughed. 'I'm afraid that both Jayne and I have very, very limited Spanish and absolutely no Catalonian whatsoever.'

'Hablais Espanol un pocito,' Juan said.

'Pardon?' replied John.

Juan laughed. 'When would you like us to come?'

'How about seven-thirty for eight next Saturday?' John suggested.

'Anna and I would be delighted,' Juan answered, offering John his hand.

Juan and Anna arrived dead on time on a warm and beautiful evening. They all sat out on the patio, where Jayne had laid the table for dinner, and drank aperitifs of sherry and vermouth. As Jayne had predicted, both Juan and Anna were elegantly dressed, Juan in a dark blazer and slacks, Anna in a very reserved but very Spanish blouse and flowing skirt.

'I brought this wine for you to try, John,' Juan said as he took out a bottle of red wine from a bag that he had carried when they first arrived. 'I hope you like it. It's the same wine that they drink at the Inauguration Ceremony of the various presidents of the United States of America.'

'Wow!' said John. 'That's fantastic. It's a pity to drink it really with all that history behind it.'

'Please don't concern yourself,' Juan said reassuringly as he went once again to the bag. 'It is not a very expensive wine and I have brought several for you so that perhaps you might like to take them home with you to England.'

'Wales actually,' said John. 'We are Welsh and we live in Wales.'

'Ees that so?' Anna joined the conversation. 'I theenk that Gales . . . I mean Wales, ees a beet like Catalan. Eet's people want to be independent and 'ave their own language and government.' Anna's English was excellent but heavily accented.

John looked long and longingly at the beautiful and slender young woman in her late twenties. What an absolute sweetie she was! Jayne noticed this and smiled.

'I think that you have mesmerised my husband,' Jayne teased. 'May I say how beautiful you look in that outfit, Anna?'

'Why, thank you so much,' Anna smiled, revealing her perfect, white teeth.

John snapped out of his trance and looked nervously at the handsome Juan who just sat there quietly, smiling knowingly.

The evening went splendidly and the conversation over dinner and afterwards was adult, intelligent and sensible. The open and frank discussions revealed that Juan had been educated at the Harvard Business School in the USA and he was now the managing director of a company in the nearby town of Palamos.

Anna, who was not working at that time, was about to finish her PhD in the history of art.

'What would you like to do with your PhD when you get it?' Jayne asked.

'I don't know at thees moment een time,' replied Anna. 'I have been offered a position een the Museum d'Art een Barcelona but I am not sure that I want thees. I would very much like to enter politics but I don't know how.'

On a brief break with John and Jayne mixing

gins-and-tonics in the kitchen, Jayne cuddled up to John and said, 'Anna is lovely, isn't she, John?'

'Yes,' John agreed, guessing what was coming. 'And I think very wealthy. Juan also must be wealthy being the managing director of his father's factory.'

'I think you could fall for her, couldn't you?' Jayne was determined that she was not going to be diverted from her course by John.

'Yes, Jayne,' replied John, putting a reassuring arm around Jayne's waist. 'I could fall for her if I hadn't already fallen for you. Come on, plonker, give me a kiss.' They kissed, hugged and returned to Juan and Anna on the terrace.

Eventually the conversation turned to travel. It became obvious that both Juan and Anna were well travelled and had been all over the world.

'I like to travel,' said John. 'I don't think you could call Jayne and me worldly, but we have been over most of Europe and we've been to the Maldives and the USA a few times.'

'I also like to travel,' declared Anna as she sipped her gin-and-tonic. 'But I don't like to fly.'

'Why not?' asked Jayne. 'It's very safe and very quick.'

'Si,' agreed Anna nodding her head so that her long hair bounced silkily on her slender shoulders. 'It ees very safe and I fly a lot een and out of Girona. 'owever there the weather ees often very bad.'

'Is it?' asked John. 'You surprise me.'

'Si,' Anna continued with a nod, her brow wrinkled in concentration as the more alcohol she

A Gaze into Holidaze

drank, although she had consumed very little, the more she had to concentrate on her English. 'Si, the weather ees often very bad, especially een the night. Eet ees probably due to the montanas . . . sorry, the mountains, around the aeropuerto . . . I mean airport. One night we were coming een to, how you say, land at Girona when the pilot came over the speaking system and 'e said, "Fuck! We must divert to Barcelona."'

John froze, his eyes widened and his mouth gaped. Slowly he turned to look at Jayne to find that her eyes and mouth were even wider. As she caught John's eye she quickly looked away in embarrassment. 'I was absolutely sure that this beautiful, delicate image was truly a lady,' he thought to himself. 'How wrong can a bloke be? What shocking language!!'

Juan had obviously noticed and felt the chill of the dazed, shocked expressions on John and Jayne's faces because he hastened to clarify what Anna had said.

'Yes, John, I was with Anna on that flight. We were returning to Girona from Brussels and the pilot, as we were landing, said, "Fuck!" And what is more we did divert to Barcelona that night.'

John thought deeply, unable to believe his ears. Both of his charming guests swearing disgustingly like this, he simply could not believe it. Then the truth suddenly dawned on him.

'Oh, you mean FOG,' stated John, a smile of understanding pulling at the corners of his mouth.

'That's right,' agreed Anna. 'Fuck, and the avion . . . I mean, aeroplane 'ad to be diverted to Barcelona. It was very inconvenient for us.'

Juan and Anna have now been friends of John and Jayne's for a very long time and they visit each other whenever they are in each other's countries. However, it was years later before John and Jayne had the courage to tell them of the 'fuck' confusion.

Juan and Anna just laughed and laughed and laughed.

****

It had been a good holiday in the villa and a lot of fun had been had by John and Jayne. Also, they had met and made some good and long-lasting friendships.

The pool had proved to be fantastic, even though every time the wind remotely got up it was filled with pine-needles from the surrounding trees. True, as Marcel had said it would be, the pool was cleaned twice a week. However, the Spanish poolcleaners got crafty. They soon realised that John, because he couldn't stand the mess of pine-needles and leaves in the pool for more than a couple of hours, cleaned the pool himself. Hence, when they arrived a couple of days later after the wind had ceased, they had huge grins on their faces as they found that their work had been done for them.

A Gaze into Holidaze

Also, the boat had been great fun. John and Jayne had got a tremendous kick out of fishing from it in the numerous tiny and very beautiful coves along the coast which could only be reached by sea. Yes, John had had to buy another rod to replace the one that was lying on the bottom of the lagoon.

During their flight home, John asked Jayne if she preferred the villa to their caravan holidays in Spain and elsewhere.

Her reply?

'Look out Clarence and Volv, here we come!'

CONCLUSION

SO WHAT, IF ANYTHING, CAN BE CONCLUDED?

Well, there is certainly the fact that all active holidays demand a learning curve which allows for mistakes to be made. Both John and Jayne made perhaps more than their fair share of mistakes but they found that there was, in all of the active holidays mentioned, always an abundance of help on hand and, more often than not, sound advice to be taken. John and Jayne can now, after about twenty-five years, claim to be experienced active holiday-takers and have even extended their active-holiday repertoire to abseiling, paragliding and micro-lite flying. And still they make silly mistakes. Isn't that what humans are like? For example, only a week before this book was written, John and Jayne were attempting to turn Clarence around in a tiny hard-standing on a very, very muddy farm in the wilds of Exmoor. Through extremely heavy rain that had severely lashed fields of non-existent drainage over the last few months, the field in question was like a soggy, custard pudding. Certainly a no-go for a front-wheel drive like John and Jayne's new car. Did this deter John? No chance! In fifteen seconds flat of clever manoeuvring, the car and the caravan were up to their axles in mud and were well and truly stuck. Being November, there wasn't a soul around until the farmer came to their rescue and towed them out. The mistake here was two-fold. One, John should never have attempted going on the quagmire of grass with a front-wheel drive car. Two, John forgot to raise the jockey-wheel whereby it acted like a plough and dug into the quagmire sufficiently for potatoes to be planted. Yes, humans make mistakes and a learning curve must certainly be envisaged and allowed for.

Then, there are people. People come in all shapes and sizes, from all sorts of social backgrounds which give rise to all sorts of characters, accents and behaviour. However, generally speaking, people are people and most are friendly, helpful and very often generous. All people, no matter how difficult they seem to be, like to laugh, and laughter is the name of the game when it comes to active holidays. John and Jayne have made many long-lasting friendships throughout their years of holiday adventures and still regularly travel to different parts of Europe, with occasional trips to faraway places, to meet the genuine friends many of whom are mentioned in this book.

Therefore, and in summing up, active holidays mean – fun, fun, fun, and even more fun. Hope you enjoyed the stories and remember – watch this space!!

THE END